I0523941

Thomas Starr King, Merrill G. Wheelock

The White Hills

Their legends, landscape, and poetry

About the Author

Taryn Daniels writes sweet romance on the picturesque shores of Nantucket Island.

Aside from tending to her fluffy fur babies and being a mom-taxi, Taryn can be found daydreaming about awkward situations and swoon-worthy moments to delight her readers.

Read more at https://Payhip.com/TheColabPress.

Thomas Starr King, Merrill G. Wheelock

The White Hills
Their legends, landscape, and poetry

ISBN/EAN: 9783337388676

Printed in Europe, USA, Canada, Australia, Japan

Cover: Foto ©Andreas Hilbeck / pixelio.de

More available books at **www.hansebooks.com**

THE WHITE HILLS;

THEIR LEGENDS, LANDSCAPE, AND POETRY

BY

THOMAS STARR KING

WITH SIXTY ILLUSTRATIONS
ENGRAVED BY ANDREW FROM DRAWINGS BY WHEELOCK

BOSTON:
WILLIAM F. GILL & COMPANY,
309 WASHINGTON ST., OPPOSITE OLD SOUTH CHURCH.
1876.

Entered according to Act of Congress, in the year 1859, by

CROSBY, NICHOLS, AND COMPANY,

In the Clerk's Office of the District Court of the District of Massachusetts.

RIVERSIDE, CAMBRIDGE:

STEREOTYPED AND PRINTED BY

H. O. HOUGHTON AND COMPANY.

To

EDWIN PERCY WHIPPLE,

THIS BOOK IS INSCRIBED WITH ADMIRATION AND GRATITUDE.

PREFACE.

THE object of this volume is to direct attention to the noble landscapes that lie along the routes by which the White Mountains are now approached by tourists,—many of which are still unknown to travellers; to help persons appreciate landscape more adequately; and to associate with the principal scenes poetic passages which illustrate, either the permanent character of the views, or some peculiar aspects in which the author of the book has seen them.

Where so many landscapes are described in detail, there cannot fail to be sameness and repetition. It would have been more to the author's mind to arrange the volume by subjects instead of by districts, and to treat the scenery under the heads of rivers, passes, ridges, peaks, &c. But it was found that such a distribution and treatment, although it might have given the book more artistic unity, would have made it less valuable on the whole, than to construct it as a guide to particular landscapes, and a stimulant to the enjoyment of them.

2

If the volume shall be found to have any value apart
from the illustrations, it will, no doubt, be chiefly due to
the poetic quotations that are interwoven with the text.
Great care has been used to make them pertinent to the
particular scenes with which they are brought into connection. The best poetry in which mountain scenery has
been reflected is not found in separate lyrics or descriptions, but is incidental to poems of larger mould and purpose. No collection has been made for mountain tourists
such as sea-side visitors may command in the admirable
" Thalatta," edited by Mr. Higginson. One cannot carry
a poetic library on a journey among the hills. And the
author believes that he has done a service to travellers,
and supplied a need that is often confessed, by interweaving with his own inadequate prose, passages from
Bryant, Emerson, Longfellow, Whittier, Lowell, and Percival, that interpret the scenery of our highlands, and by
culling fragments, often equally applicable, from Wordsworth, Scott, Tennyson, Goethe, Shelley, and Byron. The
aim has been so to introduce the poetic selections, that
instead of being mere additions and ornaments, they
shall continue and complete the description attempted,
or embody the predominant sentiment of the landscape.

The author acknowledges the important assistance in
many instances derived from Rev. Benjamin Willey's
" Incidents of White Mountain History ; " and all readers
will confess a large indebtedness to Professor Edward

Tuckerman, for the very valuable chapters he has communicated on the exploration and botany of the White Hills. It is to be regretted that the unexpected bulk of the volume has prevented the publication of a list of the plants of the mountain region, which was to have been printed as an appendix.

Boston, October 20, 1859.

TABLE OF CONTENTS.

LIST OF ILLUSTRATIONS.

LIST OF ILLUSTRATIONS.

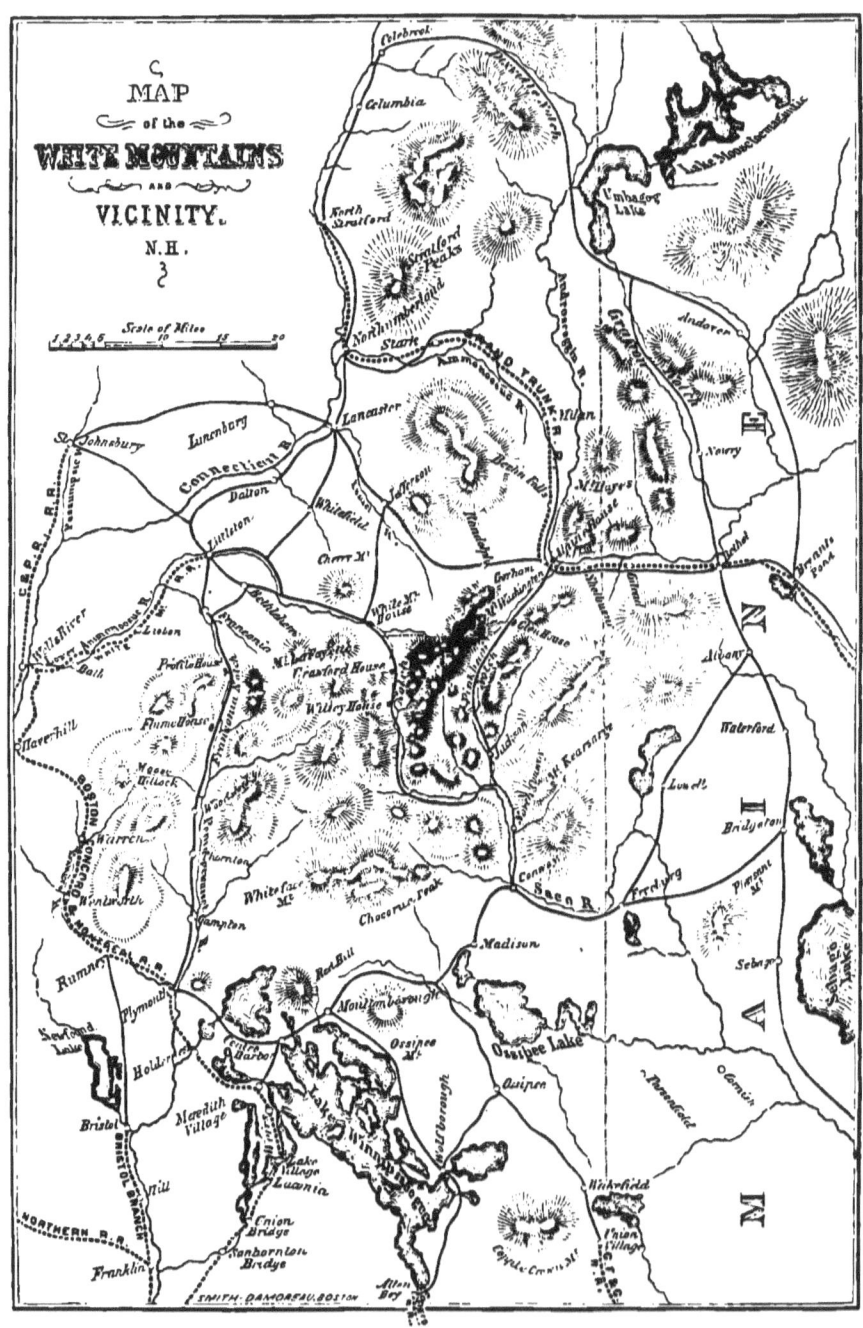

THE WHITE HILLS.

" *The best image which the world can give of Paradise, is in the shape of the meadows, orchards, and cornfields on the sides of a great Alp, with its purple rocks and eternal snows above ; this excellence not being in anywise a matter referable to feeling, or individual preferences, but demonstrable by calm enumeration of the number of lovely colors on the rocks, the varied grouping of the trees, and quantity of noble incidents in stream, crag, or cloud, presented to the eye at any given moment.*"

" *Of the grandeur or expression of the hills, I have not spoken ; how far they are great, or strong, or terrible, I do not for the moment consider, because vastness, and strength, and terror, are not to all minds subjects of desired contemplation. It may make no difference to some men whether a natural object be large or small, whether it be strong or feeble. But loveliness of color, perfectness of form, endlessness of change, wonderfulness of structure, are precious to all undiseased human minds ; and the superiority of the mountains in all these things to the lowland is, I repeat, as measurable as the richness of a painted window matched with a white one, or the wealth of a museum compared with that of a simply furnished chamber. They seem to have been built for the human race, as at once their schools and cathedrals ; full of treasures of illuminated manuscript for the scholar, kindly in simple lessons to the worker, quiet in pale cloisters for the thinker, glorious in holiness for the worshipper. And of these great cathedrals of the earth, with their gates of rock, pavements of cloud, choirs of stream and stone, altars of snow, and vaults of purple, traversed by the continual stars,—of these, as we have seen, it was written, nor long ago, by one of the best of the poor human race for whom they were built, wondering in himself for whom their Creator could have made them, and thinking to have entirely discerned the Divine intent in them—' They are inhabited by the Beasts.'* "

RUSKIN.

INTRODUCTORY CHAPTER.

THE FOUR VALLEYS.

Two groups of mountains are included under the general title of "The White Hills,"—one, the Mount Washington chain, or the White Mountains proper,—the other, the Franconia range, of which Mount Lafayette, a thousand feet lower than Mount Washington, is the highest summit. We commence by calling attention to this simple fact, because many persons, even now, in spite of the excellent guide-books, go into New Hampshire, with confused notions of the topography of the region which attracts them, and leave with no map in their mind's eye of what they have seen. We have even seen maps, that were regularly sold in the mountain hotels, which represented the Franconia range as a westerly continuation of the great White Mountain chain, and which placed Montreal a little south of Portland. Once a traveller who was just entering the hill country, and who seemed to be eager to find "The Notch," asked us if it was situated on the top of Mount Washington. And one guide-book, that, a very few years ago, was sold to travellers from New York and the South, described "The Profile" as only a short walk from the Willey House. They are about thirty miles apart. We advise all travellers, therefore, to study a good map of the mountain region, carefully, before starting, and to consult it so faithfully, between the prominent points of their journey, that the geography of the country which gives them pleasure and refreshment, may not be distorted and dislocated in their memory.

There are four avenues of approach to the two highest ranges of the New Hampshire mountains,—the valleys of the Saco, the Merrimac, the Androscoggin, and the tributaries of the Connecticut. Railroads connect with every one of these natural paths, except the Saco. And by each line of railroad one may reach some point among the highest hills, on the evening of the same day that he leaves Boston, or in about twenty-four hours from New York.

There is ample reward, as we shall hope to show, in any method of approach. Whichever path travellers may select, they

cannot err
In this delicious region.

We shall devote a few pages to a statement of these routes, the times they require, and the general character of the scenery to which they first introduce the traveller.

And in doing this, we are entirely independent of any preferences for railway or stage companies, and of any influence from the rival-ries of hotels. This book is devoted to the scenery of the mountain region. We intend to state fairly from what points the noblest views are to be gained, what are the characteristics of each district, and along what routes the richest beauty lies; with no thought in any case of the nearness to or distance from any hotel, or stage line, or railway station. It is assumed that the public houses are all good, and that the stage lines are equally worthy of patronage. And we take it for granted, also, that travellers are moved to spend their money and time, not primarily to study the gastronomy of Coös County in New Hampshire, or to criticize the comparative upholstery of the largest houses there; but to be introduced to the richest feasts of loveliness and grandeur that are spread by the Summer around the valleys, and to be refreshed by the draperies of verdure, shadow, cloud, and color, that are hung by the Creator around and above the hills.

THE ANDROSCOGGIN VALLEY.

The quickest access to the White Mountain range itself is gained by the valley of the Androscoggin. This noble river flows by the extreme easterly base of that range, where the forms are the most noble and imposing. Within a very few miles of the foot of Mount Washington, it receives the Peabody River, which issues from the narrow Pinkham Pass between Mount Carter and the White Mountains. This stream is supplied in part from the southeast slopes of the highest mountains of the chain, and is often swollen into a tremendous torrent by the storms, or the heavy and sudden showers that drench their sides. It is the Androscoggin which has engineered for the Grand Trunk Railway, that connects Portland and Montreal, the St. Lawrence with the Atlantic. That Company are indebted to it for service in their behalf that was patiently discharged centuries before Adam.

Leaving Boston in the morning by the Boston and Maine, or the

Eastern Railroad, for Portland, and thence at noon, by the Grand Trunk Railway, travellers reach the Alpine House in Gorham, N. H., by the cars at about five in the afternoon. They can then proceed by stage, seven or eight miles further, along the bank of the Peabody River, to the large hotel in "The Glen," a most charming opening, where the four highest elevations of the Mount Washington range are in full view from the piazza. If the weather has been dry, and the road is hard, this distance can be travelled in about an hour and a half. The road rises about eight hundred feet from the railroad in Gorham. In very muddy weather more than two hours are needed to reach "The Glen."

Some travellers have but a very few days for the whole tour of the mountain region, and desire, in that time, to see the points of interest that are the most striking, and that will produce the strongest sensation. These will hurry at once by stage to "The Glen," after their day's ride in the cars, that they may reach as quickly as possible the very base of Mount Washington. Their object will then be to make the ascent of it at once, and hurry around to "The Notch," which is thirty-six miles from "The Glen," requiring nine or ten hours by stage. Others, though they have more time at command, hasten from the cars to "The Glen," because they suppose that there is nothing worth staying to see in Gorham.

But in this they strangely mistake. The scenery is not very attractive from the front of the hotel, which was not wisely placed in the valley ; but no point in the mountains offers views to be gained by walks of a mile or two, and by drives of five or six miles, that are more noble and memorable. In the latter part of this volume we shall call attention in detail to the attractions with which this whole valley, including "The Glen," is encompassed. We will simply say here that, for river scenery in connection with impressive mountain forms, the immediate vicinity of Gorham surpasses all the other districts from which the highest peaks are visible. The Androscoggin sweeps through the village with a broader bed, and in larger volume, than the Connecticut shows at Lancaster or Littleton.

Only an hour's ride from the hotel carries one to the Berlin Falls, where the river pours its whole tide through a narrow rocky gateway. It descends a hundred feet in the course of a few hundred yards, and then shoots its rapids directly towards the swelling bulk of Mounts Madison and Adams that tower but a few miles distant, and form the northeastern wall of the Mount Washington chain. It is very seldom that the spectacle is afforded of a large river running *towards* the highest mountains of the region which it drains. And it is still more rare and rich a privilege to find such a view combined with a grand cataract, as in the case of the Androscoggin at Berlin.

Less than an hour's ride to a point below the hotel in Gorham, discloses another view of the river, where, broken by charming islands, and winding through cultivated meadows, it offers exquisite relief to Mount Washington and the two next highest mountains of the chain, which are installed in a magnificent group above the stream, but a few miles off. No one who sees this picture, at the fitting hour of the afternoon and through a favoring air, will be content with a single introduction to its complex and symmetrical beauty.

Such views are illustrations of the loss which tourists suffer, if they have taste for landscape, by not including a day or two in Gorham, for the sake of drives along the Androscoggin, in their plans of a visit to the eastern side of the great chain. The wildness and majesty of the scenery in " The Glen " we cannot be tempted to disparage. Certainly the impression which the hills make upon the senses here is singularly grand. The spot is a little plateau, rising from the banks of the Peabody stream, and guarded on the southeast by the steep, thin, heavily-wooded wall of Mount Carter, and on the northwest by the curving bulwarks of the great ridge, over which spring the rocky domes or spires of Washington, Clay, Jefferson, Adams, and Madison. The comparative impressiveness of the view cannot easily be overestimated.

But it is not landscape beauty that is given in " The Glen." To have that, there must be meadow, river, and greater distance from

4

the hills, so that they can be seen through large intervening depths
of air. Going close to a great mountain is like going close to a
powerfully painted picture ; you see only the roughnesses, the
blotches of paint, the coarsely contrasted hues, which at the proper
distance alone are grouped into grandeur and mellowed into beauty.

> 'Tis distance lends enchantment to the view,
> And robes the mountain in its azure hue.

Even the height of a great mountain is not usually appreciated by
looking up from its base. If it rose in one wall, and tapered regularly with a smooth surface, like a pyramid, or Bunker Hill monument, the expectations of many persons who rush to the foot of
Mount Washington, and suppose that they are to receive an overpowering ocular impression of a mile of vertical height, would be
satisfied. But a great mountain is protected by outworks and braced
by spurs ; its dome retreats modestly by plateaus ; and it is only at
a distance of some miles that the effect of foreshortening is corrected,
and it stands out in full royalty. And from such a point of view
alone, by the added effect of atmosphere and shadows, is its real
sublimity discerned. The majesty of a mountain is determined by
the outlines of its bulk ; its expression depends on the distance,
and the states of the air through which it is seen.

A visit to New Hampshire supplies the most resources to a traveller, and confers the most benefit on the mind and taste, when it
lifts him above mere appetite for wildness, ruggedness, and the feeling of mass and precipitous elevation, into a perception and love of
the refined grandeur, the chaste sublimity, the airy majesty overlaid
with tender and polished bloom, in which the landscape splendor of a
noble mountain lies. The White Mountain region is singularly rich
in the varieties of landscape charm which the hills assume. The
ridges are so well broken by cones and peaks, the slopes are so
diversified, and the valleys wind at such various angles, that a month
is insufficient to exhaust the treasures of ever changing beauty which

they hold. This is true even for the tourist who goes to study and enjoy Nature with his eye alone, and with no intention or capacity to use a pencil. Sometimes a distance of ten miles produces a change in the aspects of one ridge, as marked as if we had passed to a different zone. Certainly North Conway and Gorham, Bethlehem and Bartlett, Jefferson and Shelburne, Berlin and Jackson, could not at first be suspected of being set within about equal distance of the same chain of hills.

We should see, then, that by driving as quickly as possible to the very bases of the mountains, and by the general eagerness to get the coarser stimulant of their wildness, travellers lose the opportunity of seeing the deeper landscape loveliness which the mountains wear, and of cultivating the sense to which it is revealed. After the first visit, at any rate, this should be the chief purpose and aim.

And by living several weeks in any valley, and driving frequently over the principal roads, a person is able to learn, not only just where the best pictures are to be seen, but also what a great difference is made in the effect of a landscape by a very slight change of position on the road. A spy-glass is good for nothing, as a help to the sight, unless you get the exact focus. It is quite remarkable how this law of focus-points holds in studying the mountain region. Sometimes the beauty of scenes depends on the hour when you visit them, sometimes on the nicely calculated distance. We have stayed within a few miles of a mountain wall, upon which the forenoon spectacle in clear weather was worth riding every day to see. But in the afternoon, the westerly light made the forests look rusty ; roughened the slopes of the ridge ; reduced the height of the massive bastions, and chased away their dusky frown. Some hills need rain, or a thick air, to tone down the raggedness of their foreground, and reveal the beauty of their lines. Others show best under the noon-light ; others demand the sunset glow. A prominent charm of North Conway is, that it is one of the proper focal points for Mount Washington. Bethlehem Village is another. And the same distinction must be awarded to portions of the Androscoggin valley near Gorham, in relation to Mount Adams and Mount Madison.

4 *

Is it not one of the rich rewards of a long visit in any valley, to be able to drive directly to the seats which Nature has fixed along her picture-gallery, for studying leisurely, to the best advantage, her masterpieces of drawing, her most fascinating combinations of sublimity and loveliness, and the most mystic touches of her pencils of light, that edge the " mountain gloom " with " mountain glory ? " Travellers in New Hampshire do not think enough of the simple fact that every triumph of a human artist is only an illusion, producing a semblance of a real charm of air or foliage, of sunset cloud, or dewy grass, or mountain splendor, which Nature offers. If a man could own all the landscape canvas which the first painters of the world have colored, it would not be a tithe so rich an endowment, as if Providence should quicken his eye with keener sensibility to the hues of the west at evening, the grace of trees, and the pomp of piled or drifting clouds.

We have called attention to this law of focal distance in connection with the Androscoggin valley, and to the privilege which belongs to Gorham among other places near the White Hills that rightfully claim our interest, because it is less known, thus far, than any other point of so easy access. And let any traveller who stays in Gorham before going to " The Glen," and who is disposed to test this law in the most satisfactory and decisive way, drive in an open wagon from the Alpine House down the river towards Shelburne. He will find, on the return drive, that a perfectly finished picture is shown from a small hill, about four miles from the hotel, just at the turn of the road that leads to " The Lead-mine Bridge." Mount Madison sits on a plateau over the Androscoggin meadows. No intervening ridges hide his pyramid, or break the keen lines of his sides. He towers clear, symmetrical, and proud, against the vivid blue of the western sky. And as if the bright foreground of the meadows golden in the afternoon light, and the velvety softness of the vague blue shadows that dim the desolation of the mountain, and the hues that flame on the peaks of its lower ridges, and the vigor of its sweep upwards to a sharp crest, are not enough to perfect the artistic finish of the picture, a *frame* is gracefully carved out of two nearer hills, to seclude it from any neighboring roughness around the Peabody valley, and to narrow into the most shapely proportions the plateau from which it soars. It is not probable that the tourist

will find any other point in the region, where one of the White Mountains is singled out from the rest and drawn so firmly in isolated grandeur. And yet he will find that a quarter of a mile, either way, from the insignificant hill on which his wagon rests, spoils the charm of the picture by breaking the frame, or cutting away the base, or shutting out some portion of the meadow foreground, or extinguishing the flashes of the silvery river.

This view, during the long midsummer days, can be enjoyed after

tea, and before sunset, when the light is most propitious, on the same
day that the traveller leaves Boston. A drive of three quarters of
an hour from the Alpine House in Gorham, on the Shelburne road,
is the only exertion it costs. Or, the same time devoted to a wagon
ride towards Berlin, or towards Randolph, will bring out other mountains of the range, framed off in similar ways from the chain, in
majesty equally impressive ; though no other view, perhaps, combines
so many elements of a fascinating mountain-landscape.

THE SACO VALLEY.

By the Saco valley the tourist is led to the extreme *westerly* base
of the Mount Washington range, as by the Androscoggin valley he
reaches, at once, the extreme *easterly* declivities. The nearest point
to the Saco route accessible by railroad is the shore of Lake Winnipiscogee. The borders of this charming sheet of water may be
reached in about five hours. One can go by the Boston and Maine
railroad, connecting with the Cocheco railroad at Dover, which ends
at Alton Bay, or by the Boston, Concord, and Montreal road, which
has a station on the shore of the lake, at Weir's. By the Alton Bay
route, the steamer traverses the length of the lake thirty miles to
Centre Harbor ; from Weir's, the steamer's track is across the lake
diagonally to Centre Harbor, and is twelve miles. We shall devote
a separate chapter to the scenery of Lake Winnipiscogee, and of its
immediate neighborhood, and therefore will not detain the reader
here with any prelude about its attractions.

From Centre Harbor, the distance to the base of the White Mountain range at the Crawford House, which is situated just beyond the
further gateway of " The Notch," is sixty-two miles. It is travelled
wholly by stage. Until within a very few years, this was the only
route by which the heart of the hill-country in New Hampshire
could be reached. And we question if now, when the cars carry

visitors so much more speedily to villages much nearer the two great ranges, so much pleasure and profit are gained from the journey, as when the approach was gradually made along the line of the Sandwich range to the Saco at Conway ; and when every traveller went away with delightful recollections of the ride through Bartlett, up the narrowing and darkening valley, which gradually prepares the eye and mind for the desolation and the gloom of " The Notch," through which the Saco, as a mere rivulet, hurries towards the meadows below.

The journey from Centre Harbor to " The Notch " is naturally livided by Conway, where there is a large and excellent hotel. Leaving Boston in the morning, crossing Lake Winnipiseogee and stopping only to dine at Centre Harbor, Conway is the nearest point to the Mount Washington range that can be reached by regular stage the same night. This is still thirty-two miles from the Crawford House and " The Notch." If the roads are in tolerable condition, and the afternoon is not excessively hot, the passengers, who make thus their first excursion to the Hills, will not only be interested in the varied forms of the Sandwich range, but will have a glorious view, in the evening light, from the top of Eaton Hill, before entering Conway, of

> the mountains piled
> Heavily against the horizon of the north,
> Like summer thunder-clouds.

They might be mistaken for clouds, until one sees that their form is permanent, and that their edges, firmly drawn and not fleecy as cloud-shapes are, show a delicate gleam of thoroughly tempered steel against the evening sky. What refreshment for the fatigues of the journey, and what glorious promise for the morrow, in those cool, dark towers and domes that swell along the northwest, and on whose heights no tropic-breath is ever blown !

Conway is too generally considered now a mere resting-place for the night. Many persons, if they should fail to rise early enough for the morning stage to " The Notch," would hardly know what to do with a day thus left unemployed upon their hands. And yet, if they have any taste for landscape, they might take excursions by wagon from the hotel, that would make them grateful for the interruption of their journey. Let them drive, for instance, some nine miles to Chocorua Lake, in which the rugged, torn, lonely, and proud-peaked mountain reflects the ravage of its slopes and the vigor of its lines,—and, when a week is over, let them say if they would willingly drop this picture from the portfolio of their memory. Many of the most competent artists, who have made faithful studies during summer vacations in New Hampshire, award superiority to Chocorua for picturesqueness over any view that they have found of Mount Washington.

After this view is taken, (or instead of it. if there is time only for one,) let an excursion be made to Gould's Pond, about equally distant in another direction. Chocorua and the Mote Mountain will form many charming associations, during the winding drive, until Potter's Farm is reached. Here is a combination of lake and mountain scenery different from anything to be found between Centre Harbor and "The Notch." Fortunate will the tourist be, who can find any other view, along this whole favorite avenue to the mountains, that he can call more fascinating. The lake is a fine broad expanse of water, with many islands. The Rattlesnake range, one of the guardian walls of North Conway, stretches off to the right, overtopped by the feminine beauty of the slopes of Kiarsarge. To the left are "The Ledges" and the neighboring heights. A little below these, and on nearly the same line, rise the Mote and Chocorua, towering over intervening hills. And in the centre, the White Mountains, back of all, heave their bulk crowned by the dome of Mount Washington. Any grand landscape-view of the highest range, with a lake or a wide river prospect in the foreground, is so rare, that special attention should be called to each of them in any guidebook. Yet not one in a thousand of the summer visitors to New Hampshire has ever seen either of these views, so easily accessible from Conway. Not one in a thousand, probably, has ever heard of the scene which we last described. Nature cunningly hides the gems of her landscape a little away from the noisy and dusty paths, and imposes the condition of leisure, calmness of mind, and reverent seeking, before they shall be enjoyed.

From Conway to "The Notch" the distance is thirty-two miles, and is travelled by stage in half a day; so that from Boston to the Crawford House, at the foot of the White Mountain range, resting in Conway only, requires, by the Saco route, a day and a half. The whole ride up from the hotel in Conway, if the day is clear, is a continuous delight to one who has an outside seat on the stage. By the meadows of North Conway, and in full view of the White Mountain battlements that frown upon that village from the north; by the charming Kiarsarge, which, long after it is passed, draws the eye to look back upon it, still hungry for the exquisite droop of its folds, as of drapery falling from a ring ; through the Bartlett village, which is only a long winding lane among steep hills, cool with thick and dark

green verdure ; into, and soon out of, the little mountain basin over which the clumsy crest of Mount Crawford peers—a perpetual monument to the old patriarch of the district, who kept, for years, a small inn for travellers in this secluded bowl, and drove a team, four in hand, to the Crawford House, when he was over eighty ; and six miles further on, until two mountain lines shoot across each other, and, by a sudden turn of the road, open, and allow us to ride into the pass, where

> the abrupt mountain breaks,
> And seems with its accumulated crags
> To overhang the world;—

thus we are swept on, and find that no two miles of the ride are monotonous, and that each hour introduces us to scenery of fresh character and charm. After the Crawford House is reached through the upper gateway of "The Notch," where there is just room, under the decaying crags that face each other, for the little mill-stream of the Saco and the road; after Mount Willard has been ascended, and

Washington scaled, and the whole mountain visit is finished, we may remember our first sight of "The Notch," and the subsequent experience, in the language of Whittier :—

> We had checked our steeds
> Silent with wonder, where the mountain wall
> Is piled to heaven; and through the narrow rift
> Of the vast rocks, against whose rugged feet
> Beats the mad torrent with perpetual roar,
> Where noonday is as twilight, and the wind
> Comes burdened with the everlasting moan
> Of forests and of far-off waterfalls,
> We had looked upward where the summer sky
> Tasselled with clouds, light-woven by the sun,

Sprung its blue arch above the abutting crag,
O'er-roofing the vast portal of the land
Beyond the wall of mountains. We had passed
The high source of the Saco; and, bewildered
In the dwarf spruce-belts of the Crystal Hills,
Had heard above us, like a voice in the cloud,
The horn of Fabyan sounding; and atop
Of old Agiocchook had seen the mountains
Piled to the northward, shagged with wood, and thick
As meadow-molehills—the far sea of Casco
A white gleam on the horizon of the east;
Fair lakes, embosomed in the woods and hills:
Mooschillock's mountain range, and Kiarsarge
Lifting his Titan forehead to the sun.

All as true as it is vivid, except the "Titan forehead" of Kiarsarge.
No summit so little deserves that title. Queenly forehead would be
more appropriate.

But we have skipped North Conway, of which the graceful mountain just spoken of is only one of the gems, in our notice of the ride
from Centre Harbor to "The Notch." It is not because we have
overlooked it, but because we reserve a separate chapter for it, farther on. This village, five miles above Conway Centre, and twenty-
five miles from "The Notch," is not to be considered, or alluded to,
as one point on the route, to be merely driven through. It is a place
to stay in, where the mountains are to be studied, where the mind is
to rest as in a natural art-gallery, and in an atmosphere saturated
with beauty.

From the heart of Waumbek Methna, from the lake that never fails,
Falls the Saco in the green lap of Conway's intervales;
There, in wild and virgin freshness, its waters foam and flow,
As when Darby Field first saw them, two hundred years ago.

But, vexed in all its seaward course with bridges, dams, and mills,
How changed is Saco's stream, how lost its freedom of the hills,
Since travelled Jocelyn, factor Vines, and stately Champernoon
Heard on its banks the gray wolf's howl, the trumpet of the loon!

With smoking axle hot with speed, with steeds of fire and steam,
Wide-waked To-day leaves Yesterday behind him like a dream,
Still, from the hurrying train of Life, fly backward far and fast
The mile-stones of the fathers, the landmarks of the past

The steeds of fire and steam do not vex the air of North Conway even with any echoes as yet ; and it is not till it passes beyond the meadows which lie under "The Ledges" and "The Mote," that the Saco is "vexed" with "dams and mills." As to "bridges," the Bartlett farmers can testify that the Saco vexes *them*, in every time of freshet, more than it is troubled by their piers.

North Conway has been the favorite resort among the mountains for artists. And after the first of July, its hotels and private houses are often crowded with visitors who desire to spend several days at least, if not several weeks, in quiet enjoyment of mountain scenery. Why is it that so few persons make provision, in the programme of their tour for waiting two or three days in one spot, and for taking the short jaunts, in their own hired wagon, to the rarer and secluded landscapes in which the glories of the mountain districts are con-centrated? Such is the true way to get adequate and lasting impressions of the character of the hill country. People, in the majority of instances, reach Conway Centre the same day that they left Boston and caught their first view of Winnipiscogee. They hurry through North Conway to "The Notch," whether it rains or shines, the day after. They ascend Mount Washington the third day ; and, on the fourth, are driven to Franconia for an equally rapid glimpse of its treasures ; or, perhaps not waiting for that, push on to Littleton for the Connecticut valley cars. A large proportion of the summer travellers in New Hampshire bolt the scenery, as a man, driven by work, bolts his dinner at a restaurant. Sometimes, indeed, where railroads will allow, as on the eastern side, they will *gobble* some of the superb views between two trains, with as little consciousness of any flavor or artistic relish, as a turkey has in swal-lowing corn. One might as well be a railroad conductor for a week on an up-country train, so far as any effect on mind or sentiment is concerned, or any real acquaintance with Nature is gained, as to take to what we Yankees call "pleasurin'," in such style.

Where persons do not have a margin of a few days, they may lose the whole object of their journey. It sometimes happens that not more than a few perfect hours for sight-seeing are drawn out of the week. Day after day may turn up a blank. Perhaps there is rain; or vapors are heavily folded over the great ridges; or there is incessant sunshine, without any clouds to give relief to the eyes and expression to the hills; or a slaty and chilly sky spreads a mournful monotony over scenes that you want to see transfigured by the

> Mysteries of color daily laid,
> By the sun in light and shade.

And then a week may be given, in which, to those who can stay in a place like North Conway or Gorham, every day will be a prize. South wind, north wind, and west wind will come by turns, and do their best.

> It may blow north, it still is warm;
> Or south, it still is clear;
> Or east, it smells like a clover farm;
> Or west, no thunder fear.

Varying with each hour the favored visitors will have the full range of summer views, the anthology of a season's art, gathered into a portion of a single week. The mountains seem to overhaul their meteorological wardrobe. They will array themselves, by rapid turns, in their violets and purples and mode colors, their cloaks of azure and caps of gold, their laces and velvets, and their iris-scarfs.

One day it will be so clear, that, for the eye, space seems to have been half annihilated. Every sharp ridge lies in the sky like the curving blade of an adze, and the pinnacles tower sharp as spears. Then the few shadows that spot the slopes seem engraved upon them. Such is the day for *proof-impressions* of the roughness and raggedness, the cuts and scars, the ravines and spurs, the boundary lines of shrubbery and rock, that make up the surface of the mountains. In an air like this, from the top of Mount Washington, the vessels in Portland harbor will be distinctly descried by the glass.

Then will come a day sacred to great clouds. How majestically they will sail through the azure, perplexing the eye with their double

beauty,—the blazing fleece which moves and melts in the upper blue,
and the fantastic photograph's which they leave upon the hills below,
often draping a mountain like Madison or Kiarsarge in a leopard-skin
of spotted light and gloom !

> They rear their sunny copes
> Like heavenly Alps, with cities on their slopes,
> Built amid glaciers—bristling fierce with towers,
> Turrets, and battlements of warlike powers—
> Jagged with priestly pinnacles and spires—
> And crowned with domes, that glitter in the fires
> Of the slant sun, like smithied silver bright;—
> The capitals of Cloudland.

Or perhaps the south wind fills the air with dusty gold, and makes
each segment of a district that was prosaic enough a week before,
seem a sweet fraction of Italy. Possibly, it tries its hand at mists.
Then what mischief and frolic ! It brindles the mountain sides with
them. Or it stretches them across their length, as though it meant
to weave all the vapors which the air could supply, into a narrow and
interminable web of fog. Now, again, it twines the mists around
their necks ; then it smothers the peaks with them, and soon tears
them apart to let the grim heads look out ; and before long, in more
serious mood, it bids them stream up and off, like incense from mighty
altars. Sometimes, for half a day it will revel in a rollicking temper,
and will wind a ruff around the neck of solemn Chocorua ; or it will
adorn the crown of Kiarsarge with a trailing veil of vapory Mechlin ;
or it will compel the bald head of Adams, much to the improvement
of his phrenology, to sport a towering peruke, with a *queue* a few
miles long streaming upon the breeze. And then there will be sunsets and dawns, each of which would amply repay for the journey.

The difficulty is, that in rushing so fast as many of us do through
the mountains, the mountains do not have time to come to us. These
old settlers are tardy in forming intimate acquaintanceships. With
them " confidence is a plant of slow growth." Their externals they
give to the eye in a moment, on a clear day ; but their character,

their aspects of superior majesty, their fleeting loveliness of hue,—all
that makes them a refreshment, a force, a joy of the rest of our year,
they show only to the calmer eye, to the man who waits a day or
two in order to unthink his city habits, domesticate himself as their
guest, and bide their time. If we could learn, or be content, to use
a week at some central point of any valley, instead of hurrying
through all of them,—to spend the same money at one spot that is
usually spread over the lengthened journey,—to take the proper times
for driving quietly to the best positions,—we should see vastly more,
as any of the intelligent visitors in North Conway will assure us.
We should understand not only topography, but scenery. We
should not carry away jumbled recollections like dissolving views, but
clear pictures in memory. The mountains would come to us, which,
it is said, they refused to do for the author of the Koran.

THE PEMIGEWASSET VALLEY.

The Pemigewasset is the main source of the Merrimack. It opens
the natural avenue to the Franconia range, which is easily reached
from Boston in a day. By the Boston, Concord, and Montreal Railroad, taking trains which connect with that road either from the station of the Boston and Maine or the Boston and Lowell railways, the
traveller reaches Plymouth, N. H., which is about one hundred and
twenty miles from Boston, a little after noon. Having dined in Plymouth, he takes the stage for either of the two excellent public-houses
in the Franconia Notch—the Flume House, which is twenty-five
miles distant, or the Profile House, which is five miles further.
Either of these houses will be reached before sunset, and the tourist
will have the benefit of the afternoon light, while he

tracks

The winding Pemigewasset, overhung

By beechen shadows, whitening down its rocks

Or lazily gliding through its intervals,
From waving rye-fields sending up the gleam
Of sunlit waters.

The whole ride, if the day is pleasant, will afford various and perpetual delight. The valley, for most of the way, is broader than
that of the Saco above North Conway, and gives a larger number
of distinct pictures on the upward drive. The hills do not huddle
around the road ; the distances are more artistic ; and the lights and
shades have better chance to weave their more subtle witchery upon
the distant mountains that bar the vision,—upon the whale back of
Mooschillock, and the crags and spires that face each other in the
Franconia Notch.

The picture of the Pemigewasset, seen from a bend of the road in
the little village of Campton, will be one of the prominent pleasures
of the afternoon. How briskly it cuts its way in sweeping curves
through the luxuriant fields ! and with what pride it is watched for
miles of its wanderings by the Welch mountain completely filling the
background, from which its tide seems to be pouring, and upon whose
shoulders, perhaps, the clouds are busily dropping fantastic shawls of
shadow ! In this part of its course, the river is scarcely less free
than it was in the days which Whittier alludes to, in his noble apostrophe to the Merrimack :—

Oh, child of that white-crested mountain whose springs
Gush forth in the shade of the cliff eagle's wings,
Down whose slopes to the lowlands thy wild waters shine,
Leaping gray walls of rock, flashing through the dwarf pine.

From that cloud-curtained cradle so cold and so lone,
From the arms of that wintry-locked mother of stone,
By hills hung with forests, through vales wide and free.
Thy mountain-born brightness glanced down to the sea'

No bridge arched thy waters save that where the trees
Stretched their long arms above thee, and kissed in the breeze:
No sound save the lapse of the waves on thy shores,
The plunging of otters, the light dip of oars.

But the most striking views which the ride from Plymouth to **the**

G

Flume House affords, are to be found after passing the "Grafton House" in Thornton. The distant Notch does not show as yet the savageness of its teeth; but the arrangement of the principal Franconia mountains in *half-sexagon*—so that we get a strong impression

of their mass, and yet see their separate steely edges, gleaming with different lights, running down to the valley—is one of the rare pictures in New Hampshire. What a noble combination,—those keen contours of the Haystack pyramids, and the knotted muscles of Mount Lafayette, beyond! He hides his rough head, as far as possible, behind his neighbor, but pushes out that limb which looks like an arm from a statue of a struggling Hercules that some Titan Angelo might have hewn. A visitor with an eye for these strongest

lines of expression in the mountains has finely said : " As in Flax-
man's drawings of Homeric heroes and horses, one fine hair-stroke
reveals the whole beauty and force of that regal fancy, so these outlines of the hills, by the Divine Hand, wonderfully express the
immense vitality curbed, but not lost, which shot them up from central abysses." The downward roll of that spur of Lafayette strik-
ingly resembles the convolutions of the famous Trinity Cape, on the
Saguenay.

The Pemigewasset valley was early settled by Scotch emigrants.
Possibly they were attracted by some resemblance to the Highland
scenery of their old home. No mountain of Perthshire or Inverness
is so high as Lafayette ; and they could not have seen, in the
Trossachs, mountain-walls more sheer and threatening than " The
Notch " would have showed them, if they could have clambered into
it before the present road was made. In fact, a visitor familiar with
Scott's poetry, driving up to " The Notch " and into it for the first
time, about sunset, would recall this passage from " The Lady of
the Lake," and feel that it might have been written for Franconia :—

> The western waves of ebbing day
> Roll'd o'er the glen their level way;
> Each purple peak, each flinty spire,
> Was bathed in floods of living fire.
> But not a setting beam could glow
> Within the dark ravines below,
> Where twined the path, in shadow hid,
> Round many a rocky pyramid,
> Shooting abruptly from the dell
> Its thunder-splinter'd pinnacle;
> Round many an insulated mass,
> The native bulwarks of the pass,
> Huge as the tower which builders vain
> Presumptuous piled on Shinar's plain.
> The rocky summit, split and rent,
> Form'd turret, dome, or battlement,
> Or seem'd fantastically set
> With cupola or minaret,
> Wild crests as pagod ever decked,
> Or mosque of eastern architect

Nor were these earth-born castles bare
Nor lacked they many a banner fair;
For from their shiver'd brows display'd,
Fai o'er the unfathomable glade,
All twinkling with the dew-drops sheen   .
Tha brier-rose fell in streamers green
And creeping shrubs, of thousand dyes
Waved in the west-wind's summer sighs.

Of the resources of wildness and beauty within the five miles of the
Franconia pass—the Eagle Cliffs, the Profile, the Basin, the Flume,
the Cascades, and the ascent of Mount Lafayette, we are to treat, of
course, in another chapter. Now, we must briefly allude to the
approach to the mountains by

THE CONNECTICUT VALLEY.

The same train which is left at Plymouth by those who wish to go
directly by stage to the Flume House, will carry passengers some
seventy miles north of Plymouth, to Littleton. This village is on the
Lower Amonoosuc River, very near its junction with the Connecticut.
The cars that leave Boston in the morning reach Littleton about
five in the afternoon. From Littleton it is eleven miles to the Profile
House in the Franconia Notch, and twenty-two miles to the Crawford
House, near the White Mountain Notch. So that a traveller, on the
same day that he leaves Boston, can reach the great Franconia
range from the northwest, before the purple has faded from Lafayette, and the expression of the Profile has faded out in the twilight.
Or, later in the evening, about nine o'clock, he can be landed by stage
at the gateway of the Notch ; or can stop at the White Mountain
House, five miles nearer to Littleton than the Crawford House,
and thus save an hour's ride after dark. To reach Franconia the
same day, from Boston, one can choose between the Littleton route

with its eleven miles staging, or the Plymouth route, up the Pemigewasset, with the afternoon stage drive of twenty-five or thirty miles.
But if one desires to reach the White Mountain Notch on the
same day that he starts from Boston, the Littleton route is the only
one that will enable him to do it. By the Saco valley, it will be
remembered, a day and a half of continuous travel is required, with
sixty miles of stage riding.

The peculiarity of this approach to the mountains is that the
highest ranges are seen first of all. The ride from Littleton to Beth-
.ehem brings into full view the whole extent of the White Mountain
range, and also the grand outlines of Mount Lafayette and its neigh-

boring peaks. The stages reach Bethlehem at about the time in the afternoon when the light is most favorable, and begins to flush the Mount Washington range with the richest coloring. It is a great pity that Bethlehem is not one of the prominent stopping-places for travellers who seek the mountain region. No village commands so grand a panoramic view. The whole horizon is fretted with mountains. If the public houses here were more attractive or commodious, persons could be tempted to pass two or three days; and they would find themselves more and more fascinated with the views from the village of the solid pyramid of Lafayette, and of the steep slopes, crowned by the dome of Mount Washington, whose cascades feed the Connecticut.

Bethlehem is about as far from Mount Washington as North Conway is, and lies on the opposite side. The drives in the neighborhood, commanding as they do, within short distances, both the Franconia and the White Mountain Notches, and the meadows of the Connecticut, are very varied and delightful. The town lies, also, at the favorable landscape-distance from the hills. An enthusiastic villager used to speak to us with great contempt of the Notches in which people rushed to burrow like moles. and remarked, " I tell 'em, if they want to see *scenyury*, this is the place." Whether his taste for natural beauty was affected by the fact that he kept a small public house in Bethlehem, is a question we will not raise. That his opinion was correct is more clear.

The Connecticut valley is also reached from the *eastern* side, by the Grand Trunk Railway of Canada. This road crosses the Connecticut at Northumberland, some thirty miles above Gorham. From this point it is nine miles, by stage, to Lancaster, N. H.; which is one of the most charming villages the Connecticut can boast. By this route one can leave Boston in the morning, and reach Lancaster between eight and nine in the evening. This town, which is the county seat of Coös, has not been prominent as a place of resort for the lovers of mountain scenery; but we are sure that it is destined hereafter to attract a far larger proportion of visitors and guests. If the Grand Trunk Railway had passed through it, according to the first intention, it would doubtless have been the great rival of North Conway. A new, spacious, and excellent public house has now been finished in Lancaster, and it must hereafter take its place as one of the most attractive resorts, in the near neighborhood of the mountains.

The drives about Lancaster for interest and beauty cannot be surpassed. The river flows directly through the town, and its intervale has a never wearying charm.

> The tasselled maize, full grain or clover,
> Far o'er the level meadow grows,
> And through it, like a wayward rover,
> The noble river gently flows.
>
> Majestic elms, with trunks unshaken
> By all the storms an age can bring,
> Trail sprays whose rest the zephyrs waken,
> Yet lithesome with the juice of spring.

Grand combinations, too, of the river and its meadows with the Franconia range and the vast White Mountain wall, are to be had in short drives, beyond the river, upon the Lunenburg hills. There are several hills of moderate height around the town from which picturesque sections of the mountain surroundings are to be enjoyed. The Franconia Notch may be reached in four or five hours; and afternoon drives to various points within ten miles can be taken, where both the great ranges are included within the sweep of the eye. We would especially speak of the spectacle from Bray Hill, on the edge of Whitefield, around which Nature spreads, about five in the afternoon, as gorgeous a feast of color on the meadows and cultivated uplands, that lie within the wide circle of larger mountain guards, as New Hampshire can supply.

A ride of eight miles to the village of Jefferson, where the road from Gorham unites with the Cherry Mountain road to "The Notch," gives, as we shall show hereafter, the very grandest view of the White Mountain range, and of Mount Lafayette. also, which can be found. Here Mount Washington towers, in satisfactory majesty, above the whole curving line of the confederate summits.

Stern Sagamore! where are the tawny tribes
Who gave to thee a name, and roved supreme
Around thy foot? the travelling sun, each day
Returning from the prairies of the West,
Will tell thee he has seen their sepulchres
. Where the lank wolf the lonely desert roams;—
Thou hast survived them all, and to this day
Thou gazest upon argent streams, and lakes
Dreaming among the hills, and clustering elms,
That seem like columns of decaying fanes,
About whose mouldering shafts and capitals
The ivy clings most beautiful but sad;
And thou beholdest too the haunts of man—
His rural homes embowered 'mid waving groves,
His yellow harvests billowing in the breeze,
And the proud monuments that mark his skill,
For which he lauds himself unto the skies;—
But dost thou not contemplate by the side
Of these his works the solemn village spires,
Whose frequent curfews knoll from day to day
Reluctant generations to the grave?
Our very works are tombstones to our dust!
Achilles rears his mound and saith, "I lived!"
God utters forth a voice, and mountains rise
And whisper to eternity, "I am!"

What a pity that the hills could not have kept the names which the Indian tribes gave to them! The names which the highest peaks of the great range bear were given to them in 1820, by a party from Lancaster. How absurd the order is! Beginning at "The Notch," and passing around to Gorham, these are the titles of the summits which are all seen from the village just spoken of: Webster, Clinton, Pleasant, Franklin, Monroe, Washington, Clay, Jefferson, Adams, Madison. What a wretched jumble! These are what we have taken in exchange for such Indian words as Agiochook, which is the baptismal title of Mount Washington, and for words like Ammonoosuc, Moosehillock, Contoocook, Pennacook, Pentucket. Think, too, of the absurd association of names which the three mountains that rise over the Franconia Notch are insulted with—Mount Lafayette, Mount Pleasant, and Mount Liberty! How much better to have given the highest peaks of both ranges the names of some great tribes or chiefs, such as Saugus, Passaconaway, Uncanoonuc, Wonnalancet, Weetamoo, Bomazeen, Winnepurkit, Kancamagus,—words that chime with Saco, and Merrimack, and Sebago, and Connecticut, and Ossipee, and Androscoggin.

Even the general name, "White Mountains," is usually inapplicable during the season in which visitors see them. All unwooded summits of tolerable eminence are white in the winter; and in the summer, the mountains of the Washington range, seen at a distance in the ordinary daylight, are pale, dim green. The first title, "Crystal Hills," which the white explorers gave them, it would have been better to have retained. But how much richer is the Indian name "Waumbek!" The full title they applied to them was Waumbek-Methna, which signifies, it is said, "Mountains with snowy foreheads." Yet not a public house in all the mountain region bears the name of Waumbek, which is so musical, and which might be so profitably exchanged for Alpine House, or Glen House, or Profile House, or Tip-Top House. We are surprised, indeed, that the appellation "Kan Ran Vugarty," signifying the continued likeness of a gull, which it is said one Indian tribe applied to the range, has not been adopted by some landlord as a title to a hotel, or in some village as the name of a river, on account of its barbarity.

Would this be worse than to give the name "Israel's River" to the charming stream, fed from the rills of Washington and Jefferson, which flows through the Jefferson meadows, and empties into the Connecticut? The Indian name was Singrawac. Yet no trace of this charming name is left in Jefferson or Lancaster. Think of putting "Mount Monroe," or "Mount Clay," or "Mount Franklin," or "Peabody River," or "Berlin Falls," or "Israel's River," into poetry. The White Mountains have lost the privilege of being en-

7

shrined in such sonorous rhythm and such melody as Longfellow has given to the Indian names in his lines :—

> Down the rivers, o'er the prairies,
> Came the warriors of the nations,
> Came the Delawares and Mohawks,
> Came the Choctaws and Camanches,
> Came the Shoshonies and Blackfeet,
> Came the Pawnees and Omawhaws,
> • Came the Mandans and Dacotahs,
> Came the Hurons and Ojibways,
> All the warriors drawn together
> By the signal of the Peace-Pipe,
> To the mountains of the prairie,
> To the great red Pipe-stone quarry.

The eastern wilderness of Maine is more favored in this respect, of which Whittier has written in his poem of "The Lumbermen:"—

> Where the crystal Ambijejis
> Stretches broad and clear,
> And Millnoket's pine-black ridges
> Hide the browsing deer:
> Where, through lakes and wide morasses,
> Or through rocky walls,
> Swift and strong, Penobscot passes
> White with foamy falls;
>
> Where, through clouds, are glimpses given
> Of Katahdin's sides,—
> Rock and forest piled to heaven,
> Torn and ploughed by slides!
> Far below, the Indian trapping,
> In the sunshine warm;
> Far above, the snow-cloud wrapping
> Half the peak in storm.
>
> O'er us, to the southland heading,
> Screams the gray wild-goose;
> On the night air sounds the treading
> Of the brindled moose.
> Noiseless creeping, while we're sleeping,
> Frost his task-work plies;
> Soon, his icy bridges heaping,
> Shall our log-piles rise.

The lumbermen work, also, during the fall and winter, in the wilderness that slopes into Randolph and Jefferson. They pile the hemlocks and the hackmetacks by the stream, so that

> When, with sounds of smothered thunder,
> On some night of rain,
> Lake and river break asunder
> Winter's weakened chain,
> Down the wild March flood shall bear them ·
> To the saw-mill's wheel,
> Or where Steam, the slave, shall tear them
> With his teeth of steel.

But " Whipple's Grant," and " Hart's Location," and " Israel's River," and " Knot-Hole" road, are not so redolent of poetry as crystal Ambijejis and Katahdin and Millnoket. The lower portion of New Hampshire is more fortunate in this respect, as the following passage from Whittier's " Bridal of Pennacook" will convince our readers delightfully :—

> The trapper, that night on Turee's brook,
> And the weary fisher on Contoocook,
> Saw over the marshes and through the pine,
> And down on the river the dance-lights shine.
>
> For the Saugus Sachem had come to woo
> The Bashaba's daughter Weetamoo,
> And laid at her father's feet that night
> His softest furs and wampum white.
>
> From the Crystal Hills to the far Southeast
> The river Sagamores came to the feast;
> And chiefs whose homes the sea-winds shook,
> Sat down on the mats of Pennacook.
>
> They came from Sunapee's shore of rock,
> From the snowy sources of Snooganock,
> And from rough Coös whose thick woods **shake**
> Their pine-cones in Umbagog lake.
>
> From Ammonoosuck's mountain pass
> Wild as his home came Chepewass;
> And the Keenomps of the hills which **throw**
> Their shade on the Smile of Manito.

7 *

With pipes of peace and bows unstrung,
Glowing with paint came old and young,
In wampum and furs and feathers arrayed
To the dance and feast the Bashaba made.

Bird of the air and beast of the field,
All which the woods and waters yield,
On dishes of birch and hemlock piled,
Garnished and graced that banquet wild.

Steaks of the brown bear fat and large,
From the rocky slopes of the Kiarsarge;
Delicate trout from Babboosuck brook,
And salmon spear'd in the Contoocook;

Squirrels which fed where nuts fell thick
In the gravelly bed of the Otternic,
And small wild hens in reed-snares caught
From the banks of Soudagardee brought;

Pike and perch from the Suncook taken,
Nuts from the trees of the Black Hills shaken,
Cranberries picked in the Squamscot bog,
And grapes from the vines of Piscataquog.

But the Indian names and legends are shorn from the upper mountain region. They have not been caught for our literature. The valleys are almost as bare of them as the White Mountain cones are of verdure. What a pity it is that our great hills

Piled to the clouds,—our rivers overhung
By forests which have known no other change
For ages, than the budding and the fall
Of leaves—our valleys lovelier than those
Which the old poets sang of—should but figure
On the apocryphal chart of speculation
As pastures, wood-lots, mill-sites, with the privileges,
Rights and appurtenances, which make up
A Yankee Paradise—unsung, unknown
To beautiful tradition; even their names,
Whose melody yet lingers like the last
Vibration of the red man's requiem,
Exchanged for syllables significant
Of cotton mill and rail-car!

We can scarcely find a settler who can tell any story learned in childhood of Indian bravery, suffering, cruelty, or love. Looking up to the great range from the village of Jefferson, we must say with Hiawatha :—

> Lo! how all things fade and perish!
> From the memory of the old men
> Fade away the great traditions,
> The achievements of the warriors,
> The adventures of the hunters,
> All the wisdom of the Medas,
> All the craft of the Wabenos,
> All the marvellous dreams and visions,
> Of the Jossakeeds, the Prophets!

HISTORY OF THE EXPLORATION OF THE WHITE HILLS

" You ask," he said, " what guide
Me through trackless thickets led,
Through thick-stemmed woodlands rough and wide?
I found the water's bed.
The watercourses were my guide;
I travelled grateful by their side,
Or through their channel dry;
They led me through the thicket damp,
Through brake and fern, the beavers' camp
Through beds of granite cut my road,
And their resistless friendship showed;
The falling waters led me,
The foodful waters fed me,
And brought me to the lowest land,
Unerring to the ocean sand.
The moss upon the forest bark
Was polestar when the night was dark,
The purple berries in the wood
Supplied me necessary food;
For Nature ever faithful is
To such as trust her faithfulness."

Before proceeding to the chapters on the avenues to the highest
mountains, and the pictures which they supply, let us glance at the
most important visits which have been made to the loftiest range for
exploration and for the purposes of science.

The first mention of the White Mountains in print, occurs in John
Josselyn's New England's Rarities Discovered, printed in 1672, a
book now chiefly memorable as furnishing the earliest account of our
plants ; and this writer, in his Voyages, printed a year or two later,
gives us the best part of the mythology of our highest hills. The
story, as Josselyn tells it, is curious enough ; and its resemblance to
one of the most venerable of Caucasian traditions should seem to suggest some connection of the people which transmitted it, with the

common Asiatic home of the bearded races. "Ask them," says Josselyn, "whither they go when they dye, they will tell you pointing with their finger to Heaven beyond the white mountains, and do hint at *Noah's* Floud, as may be conceived by a story they have received from Father to Son, time out of mind, that a great while agon their Countrey was drowned, and all the People and other Creatures in it, only one *Powaw* and his *Webb* foreseeing the Floud fled to the white mountains carrying a hare along with them and so escaped ; after a while the *Powaw* sent the *Hare* away, who not returning emboldened thereby they descended, and lived many years after, and had many Children, from whom the Countrie was filled again with *Indians.*" *   The English name of our mountains, which had its origin, perhaps, while as yet they were only known to adventurous mariners, following the still silent coasts of New England, relates them to all other high mountains, from *Dhawala-Giri*, the White Mountain of the Himmalayah, to *Craig Eryri* or Snowdon of Wales ; but it is interesting to find them also, in this legend, in some sort of mythical connection with traditions and heights of the ancient continent, the first knowledge of which carries us back to the very beginnings of human history.

Josselyn spent fifteen months in New England, at his first visit, in 1638, and eight years at his second, in 1663 ; but there is no reason to suppose that he visited the mountains till the latter period,† which was twenty years after the journeys of which Winthrop's History has preserved a record. It is to Darby Field of Pascataquack that the credit is now generally assigned of being the first explorer of the White Mountains. Accompanied by two Indians, Winthrop tells us, Field climbed the highest summit in 1642. It appears from the account that " within 12 miles of the top was neither tree nor grass but low savins, which they went upon the top of sometimes, but a

---

* Josselyn's Voyages, p. 185. "The Indians gave them the name of *Agiocochook.*" Belknap, N. H. iii. p. 31. There are one or two other, so called, Indian names.

† Mr. Savage, in a note to Winthrop, correcting Belknap's misstatement, takes this view, which appears to have all the evidence in its favor.

continual ascent upon rocks, on a ridge between two valleys filled
with snow, out of which came two branches of Saco River, which met
at the foot of the hill where was an Indian town of some 200 people.
. . . . By the way, among the rocks, there were two ponds, one a
blackish water, and the other a reddish. The top of all was plain
about 60 feet square. On the north side was such a precipice, as
they could scarce discern to the bottom. They had neither cloud
nor wind on the top, and moderate heat."* This appears to have
been in June, and " about a month after he went again with five or
six in his company,"† and " the report he brought of shining stones,
&c., caused divers others to travel thither but they found nothing
worth their pains." ‡

Of these others are particularly mentioned Thomas Gorges, Esq.,
and Mr. Vines, two magistrates of the province of Sir Ferdinando
Gorges, who went " about the end " of August, of the same year.
" They went up Saco River in birch canoes . . . to Pegwaggett,
an Indian town. From the Indian town they went up hill (for the
most part) about 30 miles in woody lands, then they went about 7
or 8 miles upon shattered rocks, without tree or grass, very steep all
the way. At the top is a plain about 3 or 4 miles over, all shattered stones, and upon that is another rock or spire, about a mile in
height, and about an acre of ground at the top. At the top of the
plain arise four great rivers, each of them so much water, at the first
issue, as would drive a mill, Connecticut River from two heads, at the
N. W. and S. W., which join in one about 60 miles off, Saco River
on the S. E., Amascoggin which runs into Casco Bay at the N. E.,
and Kennebeck, at the N. by E. The mountain runs E. and W.
thirty miles, but the peak is above all the rest."§ There can be but
little doubt that Field, entering the valley, it is likely of Ellis River,
left it for the great southeastern ridge of Mount Washington, the
same which has since been called Boott's *Spur.* This was the " ridge

* Winthrop, N. E., by Savage, ii. p. 67.   † *Ibid.*   ‡ *Ibid.* p. 89.
§ *Ibid.* p. 89   Hubbard's account (Hist. N. E. p. 381) is made up from both of Winthrop's.

between two valleys filled with snow, out of which came two branches of Saco River," and it led him, as probably the other party also, to the broadest spread of that great plain, of which the southeastern grassy expanse, of some forty acres, has-long been known as Bigelow's Lawn, and the " top," to the north, where the two ponds are, furnished Gorges with a part, no doubt, of the sources of his rivers. The writer sought to trace this early way in 1843, leaving the road, in Jackson, at about four miles distance from the Elkins farm-house in Pinkham woods, and striking directly up Boott's *Spur* to the summit ; and was surprised, after struggling through the region of dwarf firs, and surmounting a considerable space of the bald region, with the first view of the peak of Mount Washington, as a pretty regular pyramid, in what appeared a plain (which is just the way it struck Gorges, and also Josselyn), that had ever occurred to him. Davis's bridle-path, opened in 1845, traverses the bald part of the same ridge, and afforded the same view, while it was in use. But the other early account, that of Josselyn, indicates possibly another way of ascent, as inviting, perhaps, to a new comer to the mountains, as it is difficult, and even dangerous. " Fourscore miles," says Josselyn " (upon a direct line) to the Northwest of *Scarborow*, a Ridge of Mountains run Northwest and Northeast an hundred leagues, known by the name of the *White Mountains*, upon which lieth Snow all the year, and is a Land-mark twenty miles off at Sea. It is rising ground from the Sea shore to these Hills, and they are inaccessible but by the Gullies which the dissolved Snow hath made ; in these Gullies grow *Saven* bushes, which being taken hold of are a good help to the climbing discoverer ; upon the top of the highest of these Mountains is a large Level or Plain of a days journey over, whereon nothing grows but Moss ; at the farther end of this Plain is another Hill called the *Sugar-loaf*, to outward appearance a rude heap of massic stones piled one upon another, and you may as you ascend step from one stone to another, as if you were going up a pair of stairs, but winding still about the Hill till you come to the top, which will require half a days time, and yet it is not above a

Mile, where there is also a Level of about an Acre of ground, with a
pond of clear water in the midst of it; which you may hear run
down, but how it ascends is a mystery. From this rocky Hill you
may see the whole Country round about; it is far above the lower
Clouds, and from hence we beheld a Vapour (like a great Pillar)
drawn up by the Sun Beams out of a great Lake or Pond into the
Air, where it was formed into a Cloud. The Country beyond these
Hills Northward is daunting terrible, being full of rocky Hills, as
thick as Mole-hills in a Meadow, and cloathed with infinite thick
Woods."* There are several points in which this narrative of Josselyn's surpasses both the others already given, and perhaps it might
have been expected to. We miss indeed an account of the author's
journey from the coast, and of the way in which the wilderness
struck him, but perhaps this is in some good part made up to us by
a passage of his Voyages, where, after describing "the countrie
within" as "rockie and mountainous, full of tall wood," he says,
"one stately mountain there is surmounting all the rest, about four
score mile from the sea," and then goes on as follows: "Between
the mountains are many ample rich and pregnant valleys as ever eye
beheld, beset on each side with variety of goodly trees, the grass
man-high unmowed, uneaten, and uselessly withering;" and "within
these valleys . . . spacious lakes or ponds well stored with fish and
beavers; the original of all the great rivers in the countrie,"† which,
add only the black flies, "so numerous up in the country that a man
cannot draw his breath but he will suck of them in,"‡ really gives a
rather striking sketch of what he must have seen and encountered.
In the Voyages, Josselyn corrects what he says of the snow's lying
the whole year upon the mountains, by excepting the month of August,§ and after remarking that "some suppose that the White
Mountains were first raised by earthquakes," he adds that "they
are hollow, *as may be guessed by the resounding of the rain upon the
level on the top*."‖ The pond on the top, in this account, may have

* Rarities of New England, p. 3.   † Josselyn's Voyages, p. 43.
‡ *Ibid.* p. 121.   § *Ibid.* p. 55.   ‖ *Ibid.* p. 58.

been due to extraordinary transient causes ; it is not mentioned by
the other visitors of the seventeenth century, and has not been heard
of since. There is nothing else to be noticed but what was suggested
at the beginning, that the author's remark about the mountains being
" inaccessible except by the gullies," seems to point to an ascent, in
this case, by one of the eastern gulfs or ravines.

We next hear of an ascent of the White Mountains by " a ranging
company," which " ascended the highest mountain, on the N. W.
part," so far, as appears, the first ascent on that side, April 29, 1725,
and found, as was to be expected, the snow deep, and the alpine
ponds frozen.* Another ranging party, which was " in the neighborhood of the White Mountains, on a warm day in the month of March,"
in the year 1746, had an interesting and the first recorded experience of a force, which has left innumerable proofs of its efficiency
all through the mountains. It seems that this party was " alarmed
with a repeated noise, which they supposed to be the firing of guns.
On further search, they found it to be caused by rocks, falling from
the south side of a steep mountain."†

The Western Pass of the mountains may have been known to the
Indians, but it was not turned to account by the English till after
1771, when two hunters, Timothy Nash and Benjamin Sawyer,—the
former said by Messrs. Farmer and Moore to have made the discovery, but the latter certainly admitted to a share in its benefits, and
himself not yet forgotten in the hills,—passed through it. A road was
soon after opened by the proprietors of lands in the upper Cohos, and
another, through the Eastern Pass, was commenced in 1774.‡ Settlers began now to make their way into the immediate neighborhood
of the mountains. The townships of Jefferson, Shelburne which
included Gorham, and Adams now Jackson, successively received
inhabitants from 1773 to 1779, and the wilderness, if as yet far
enough from blossoming, was opened, and to some extent tamed.

It was now that the first company of scientific inquirers approached
the White Hills. In July, 1784, the Rev. Manasseh Cutler of Ips

* Belknap, N. H. iii. p. 35.   † Ibid. p. 27.   ‡ Ibid. iii. p. 36.

wich, a zealous member of the American Academy of Arts and Sci-
ences, the Rev. Daniel Little of Kennebunk, also a member of the
Academy, and Colonel John Whipple of Dartmouth, afterwards
called Jefferson, the most prominent inhabitant of the Cohos country, visited the mountains, " with a view to make particular observations on the several phenomena that might occur. It happened unfor-
tunately that thick clouds covered the mountains almost the whole
time, so that some of the instruments, which, with much labor, they
had carried up, were rendered useless." Others were broken. They
made some unsatisfactory barometrical observations, from a compu-
tation of which, the elevation of the principal summit above the sea
was reckoned at ten thousand feet; but were disappointed in an
attempt at a geometrical admeasurement from the base.* It is likely
that the plants of the higher regions were observed, and Mr. Oakes
possessed fragments of such a collection made, either now or later, by
Dr. Cutler; but the latter did not notice them in his memoir on the
plants of New England published the next year in the transactions of
the Academy, nor is there any mention of them in the six small volumes of his botanical manuscripts which have come to my knowledge.
Belknap has preserved a single passage from a manuscript of Dr.
Cutler's, which, in the absence of anything else, has possibly interest
enough in this place to be quoted. " There is evidently the appearance of three zones—1, the woods—2, the bald mossy part—3, the
part above vegetation. The same appearance has been observed on
the Alps, and all other high mountains. I recollect no grass on the
plain. The spaces between the rocks in the second zone, and on the
plain, are filled with spruce and fir, which, perhaps, have been growing ever since the creation, and yet many of them have not attained
a greater height than three or four inches, but their spreading tops
are so thick and strong, as to support the weight of a man, without
yielding in the smallest degree The snows and winds keeping the
surface even with the general surface of the rocks. In many places,
on the sides, we could get glades of this growth, some rods in extent,

* Belknap, N. H. iii. p. 37.

when we could, by sitting down on our feet, slide the whole length. The tops of the growth of wood were so thick and firm, as to bear us currently, a considerable distance, before we arrived at the utmost boundaries, which were almost as well defined as the water on the shore of a pond. The tops of the wood had the appearance of having been shorn off, exhibiting a smooth surface, from their upper limits, to a great distance down the mountain." *

The way by which Cutler ascended the mountain is .indicated by the stream which bears his name in Belknap's and Bigelow's narratives, and was doubtless very much that taken and described by the last-mentioned explorer. " In less than half a mile, southward from this fountain " of Ellis River, at the height of land between the Saco and the Androscoggin, in Pinkham woods, " a large stream, which runs down the highest of the White Mountains, falls into Ellis River, and in about the same distance from this, another falls from the same mountain ; the former of these streams is Cutler's River, the latter New River." † Cutler's River was still known to the inhabitants of the solitary house in these woods, in 1840, when the writer followed its course, on his way to the upper region of the mountains ; and the name, he was then told, by persons long resident in the place, and acquainted with the later explorations of Bigelow and others, was given to it at Dr. Cutler's express desire.‡ It ought to be handed down. •

President Dwight passed through the Notch in 1797, and again in 1803, and has left in his Travels a description of the scenery which is still valuable for its particularity and appreciativeness, and an interesting account of the first settlers of Nash and Sawyer's, and Hart's Locations. It appears from this that Eleazar Rosebrook planted himself in the former tract, where he was succeeded many years after by the late well-known Ethan Allen Crawford, in 1788. Abel Crawford, who married Rosebrook's daughter, and whom very many remember as the worthy Patriarch of the mountains, began his

---

* Cutler MS. in Belknap, iii. p. 34.   † Belknap, N. H. iii. iii. p. 44.
‡ MS. notebook, 10th Aug. 1840.

clearing thirteen miles below Rosebrook's, in Hart's Location, a few years later ; and one Davies, at about the same time,* in the tract at the end of the Notch valley, afterwards occupied by Willey.† And this writer has also preserved a note of some importance on one of the great fires which have devastated the mountains of the Notch. " When we entered upon this farm," says he, speaking of Davies's, just mentioned, " in 1803, a fire which not long before had been kindled in its skirts, had spread over an extensive region of the mountains on the Northeast ; and consumed all the vegetation, and most of the soil, which was chiefly vegetable mould, in its progress. The whole tract, from the base to the summit, was alternately white and dappled ; while the melancholy remains of half-burnt trees, which hung here and there on the sides of the immense steeps, finished the picture of barrenness and death." ‡ Old Mr. Crawford used to speak (in 1845 or 6) of the great fire which reduced Mount Crawford to its present condition, as having occurred some thirty years before. The time may well arrive when careful records of these irreparable mischiefs, which destroy in their progress the very vital ity of our mountains, and leave nothing but crumbling rocks, the shelter of a strange and spurious vegetation,—nothing but the ruins of nature,—shall possess a mournful value.

In July, 1804, Dr. Cutler visited the mountains a second time, in company with Dr. W. D. Peck, afterwards Professor of Natural History at Cambridge. Barometrical observations obtained on this occasion, and computed by Mr. Bowditch, gave an elevation to the highest summit of 7055 feet above the sea.§ A collection of the alpine plants was made by Dr. Peck, and was afterwards seen by Mr. Pursh, whose citations, in his Flora of North America, printed in 1814, enable us to determine the earliest recognition of several of the most interesting species.

---

* Both were there at the time of Dr. Dwight's visit in 1797, and had come in since Rosebrook's clearing was begun. E. A. Crawford says it was " soon after " 1792, that his father commenced in Hart's Location. (Hist. of White Mountains, p. 19.)

† Dwight's Travels, ii. p. 143.

‡ Ibid. p. 152.

§ Mem. Amer. Acad. iii. p. 326.

In 1812 a general account of the White Mountains was published by Dr. Belknap, in the last volume of his history of New Hampshire. This was made up in part of communications from Dr. Cutler, but contains also interesting original information, which has been already referred to. There does not appear to be any reason to suppose that the historian himself penetrated the wild parts of the mountains, but the name of Mount Washington was first published in his work.

Up to this time no thorough survey of the Natural History of the Mountains had been carried out. We have seen the beginnings of an acquaintance with the plants. And Mr. Maclure, and George Gibbs, Esq., had each made more than one visit to different parts of the region, with a view to the examination of its geology and its minerals. But Dr. Bigelow's "Account of the White Mountains of New Hampshire," published in 1816, from explorations made during the same season, determined in great measure the phænogamous botany of our Alps, while it furnished also a statement of all that was known of their mineralogy and zoölogy. Dr. Francis Boott, Mr. Francis C. Gray, and the venerable Chief Justice Shaw, were members of this party, which accomplished, from barometrical observations, perhaps the most satisfactory determination of the height of Mount Washington that has been made ; assigning to it an altitude above the sea of 6225 feet. Dr. Boott returned to the mountains in the next month, (August,) and added a "considerable" number of species to the botanical collection. Dr. Bigelow entered the mountains be the Eastern Pass, and followed Cutler's River, making the passage of the dwarf firs by a way opened a few years before by direction of Col. Gibbs.* The knowledge of these journeys has now disappeared from the neighborhood, with the early inhabitants. But in 1840, all was still remembered, from Cutler's time, down, at the solitary house of D. Elkins, in the Pinkham woods ; and I found it easy, in the company of the late Harrison Crawford, an honest man, and one who knew thoroughly his native hills, to trace again the old way of ascent. In 1819, Abel Crawford opened the footway to

* Account, &c., in New Eng. Journal of Med. and Surg. Nov. 1816.

Mount Washington which follows the southwestern ridge from Mount Clinton ; and three years later Ethan Allen Crawford, who had suc ceeded to his grandfather Rosebrook's farm in Nash and Sawyer's Location, opened his new road along the course of the Ammonoosuck.* These two became now the common ways of ascending the mountains, and the wilderness of the Eastern Pass was rarely disturbed. Botanists were gainers by this change, at least those whose researches were carried on without camping out. The southwestern ridge and Mount Washington together afford a better view of the whole vegetation than is obtainable by the eastern paths ; and two points on this ridge,—the Lake of the Clouds, and especially the ravine called Oakes's Gulf, between Mount Washington and Mount Monroe, are peculiarly rich in rare plants ; the latter possessing indeed almost all the alpine plants of the mountains, and two (the Eyebright and the Rhinanthus) which are found nowhere else ; and Ethan Crawford's road by the Ammonoosuck, passed. as it struck up the peak of Mount Washington, close by the hanging gardens of the Great Gulf.

In 1820, Messrs. A. N. Brackett and J. W. Weeks of Lancaster, with Ethan Crawford as guide, ascended the southwestern ridge by the new path. from the head of the Notch, and explored the summits of the whole range as far as Mount Washington ; estimating the heights of the seven highest points by means of a spirit level, and giving the names to these points which they have since borne.† The interesting account of this visit may be found in the New Hampshire Historical Collections for 1823. The path over Mount Clinton had been advertised, and that following the Ammonoosuck had attracted still more attention from its appearing to promise facilities for a carriage road of some seven miles toward Mount Washington, and visit-

* E. A. Crawford's Hist. of the White Mountains, pp. 42, 49.
† Some doubt having been entertained within a few years, as to which is Mount Adams and which Mount Jefferson, and an error in the use of these names having even found its way into the first edition of Mr. Bond's map,—it was corrected in the second,—it seems proper to copy the definite language of Messrs. Brackett and Weeks, who gave the names. "Mount Adams is known by its sharp terminating peak, and being the second N. of Washington," and "Jefferson is situated between these two." And the writer heard Col. Brackett say that this was just as his party understood it.

ors, aiming mostly at the ascent of the summit, began more frequently to find their way to the inns of the west side. But the inner solitudes of the mountains were very seldom entered. Now and then a naturalist, or a lover of woods and hills, penetrated the forest, or climbed the dark steeps ; or an angler (not a man with a "fishpole" hooking trout, but a hearty admirer of nature and her clear brooks, who catches his dinner for his soul's health as well as his body's) followed the streams ; but rare enough it was that such hills and streams could tempt to more than a brief day's delay, with all their visible glories and balsamic airs.

Many alpine plants, and it is what adds manifestly to their interest, are confined to very small areas.* And the most promising botanical regions, in mountains of the height and general character, and in the degree of latitude of ours, are the secluded and difficult banks of alpine rivulets which descend the steep slopes of the hidden south-eastern ravines, and the little hanging gardens, sometimes all but inaccessible, which these runnels form, on favoring shelves of rock. Thus it was not to be expected that any single survey of the botany of the higher region of the mountains, however careful, should do more than give the general features of vegetation, with such part only of the special and exceptional ones as the good luck of the occasion might bring into view. A considerable number of peculiarly interesting species has been added to the flora of the White Mountains since Bigelow first delineated their botanical geography, and there is little doubt that more remain to be found.

Benjamin D. Greene, Esq., collected the plants of the southwestern ridge in 1823, and Mr. Henry Little, a student of medicine, explored this part of the mountains the same year. In 1825, William Oakes, Esq., and Dr. Charles Pickering, made, together, extensive researches, adding some species, new to the flora, of much interest ; and the former returned, and continued his investigations, the follow-

---

* " Les aires fort restreintes sont plus nombreuses que les aires très vastes. Il y a beaucoup d'espèces qui, par leur rareté, sont exposées à disparaître de la scène du monde." A. De Candolle Geogr. Bot. I. p. 588.

ing year. Dr. J. W. Robbins explored, with much care, the whole
range, in 1829 ; descending into and crossing the Great Gulf, and
traversing for the first time, at least so far as scientific interests were
concerned, all the eastern summits ;—and also made important additions to the flora of the mountains ; while before this, the practised
eye of Mr. Nuttall had detected several species, of such rarity, that
few have seen them since.

But the longest of these were short visits, too short for a loving
acquaintance with the mountains, or a satisfying experience of their
wealth of wholesome enjoyment. S. A. Bemis, Esq., was perhaps
the earliest to delay longer, and return oftener,—to make a home for
the time of the White Hills ; and certainly the sunny valley of Mount
Crawford, and its cheerful views, and the then sufficient neighboring
streams, might well attract an admirer of nature ; nor has the attraction yielded yet, after more than thirty years ; or the example failed
to win others to the same untiring pleasures.

The writer of these pages first visited the White Mountains in
1837. It was then a secluded district, the inns offering only the
homely cheer of country fare, and the paths to Mount Washington
rarely trodden by any who did not prize the very way, rough as it
might be, too much to wish for easier ones. But it was not long*
before the Crawfords turned foot-paths into bridle-paths, and in 1840,
a party,—it included Dr. Charles T. Jackson, then occupied in the
Geological Survey of New Hampshire, who delayed long enough at
the mountains to ascertain some altitudes,—reached Mount Washington on horseback by the way from the Notch. This introduced
all the changes that have followed, and the various appliances of
luxury which now meet the visitor to the White Hills.

NOTE.—From the Life of Dr. Belknap (N. Y. 1847, p. 102,) it appears that both he, and
Dr. Fisher of Beverly, were of the party which visited the mountains in 1784, though neither of them succeeded in reaching the summit. " Dr. Fisher," we are further told,
" was left behind at the Notch, to collect birds, and other animal and vegetable produc-
tions." There were seven persons in all in the party, which, we can well believe, was
the subject of much speculation," as it passed through Eaton and Conway.

LAKE WINNIPISEOGEE

"In those happy spots of nature where land and water, above and below, combine their charms, it is hard to tell whether the stony upland height, or the liquid deep beneath, most lures the sight. I believe it was Goethe who first said that lakes are the eyes of the landscapes; and if there be reason for such a figure, it is not strange such features in the countenance of the world should fix our regard. Certainly they add to that countenance the same sort of brightness and animation which the organs of vision give to the human face; and as our glance, perusing the living traits of a man, is never satisfied till it reaches his eye, so on the earth, we seek after water, and are not quite content till our attention, long vagrant, rests upon it."

SUMMER BY THE LAKE-SIDE

NOON.

WHITE clouds, whose shadows haunt the deep,
Light mists, whose soft embraces keep
The sunshine on the hills asleep!

O, isles of calm! — O, dark, still wood!
And stiller skies that overbrood
Your rest with deeper quietude!

O, shapes and hues, dim beckoning, through
Yon mountain gaps, my longing view
Beyond the purple and the blue,

To stiller sea and greener land,
And softer lights and airs more bland,
And skies — the hollow of God's hand!

Transfused through you, O mountain friends,
With mine your solemn spirit blends,
And life no more hath separate ends.

I read each misty mountain sign,
I know the voice of wave and pine,
And I am yours, and ye are mine.

Life's burdens fall, its discords cease,
I lapse into the glad release
Of Nature's own exceeding peace.

O, welcome calm of heart and mind.
As falls yon fir-tree's loosened rind
To leave a tenderer growth behind.

So fall the weary years away;
A child again, my head I lay
Upon the lap of this sweet day.

This western wind hath Lethean powers,
Yon noon-day cloud Nepenthe showers,
The lake is white with lotus-flowers!

LAKE WINNIPISEOGEE.

Does this word mean " The Smile of the Great Spirit," or " Pleasant Water in a High Place ? " There has been a dispute, we
believe, among the learned in Indian lore, as to the true rendering.
Whatever the word means, the lake itself signifies both. Topograph-
ically, under the surveyor's eye and the mill-owners' estimates, it is
pleasant water in a high place ; about thirty miles long, and varying
from one to seven miles in breadth ; with railroad stations on its
shores at Alton Bay and Weir's ; and a little more than a hundred
miles distant from Boston. To the poet whose exquisite verses we
have chosen as a prelude to this chapter, and to all who have an eye
anointed like his, it is the smile of the Great Spirit.

It is easy to give a general description of the character of the
shores of Winnipiseogee, to count its islands, and to enumerate the
mountain ranges and peaks, with their names and height, that surround it. But it is not so easy to convey any impression, by words,
of the peculiar loveliness that invests it, and which lifts it above the
rank of a prosaic reservoir in Belknap and Carrol counties in New
Hampshire, about five hundred feet above the sea, into an expression
of the Divine art renewed every summer by the Creator. There is
very little cultivation around the borders of Winnipiseogee. The
surroundings are scarcely less wild than they were, when, in 1652,
Captains Edward Johnson and Simon Willard carved their initials,
which are still visible, on the " Endicott Rock," near its outlet.

The straggling parties of Indians who pass by it now, on their way
to trade with the visitors at the Flume House in Franconia, see it
but little more civilized in expression than their forefathers did, whose
wigwams, before Massachusetts felt the white man's foot, spotted the
meadows of the Merrimac below.

> Where the old smoked in silence their pipes, and the young
> To the pike and the white perch their baited lines flung;
> Where the boy shaped his arrows, and where the shy maid
> Wove her many-hued baskets and bright wampum braid.

And yet it is not a sense of seclusion amid the forests, of being shut
in by untamed hills amid the heart of the wilderness, that Winnipiseogee inspires.   Indeed, the lake is not shut in by any abrupt
mountain walls.   Its islands and shores fringe the water with winding
lines and long, low, narrow capes of green.   But the mountains retreat
gradually back from them, with large spaces of cheerful light, or
vistas of more gently sloping land, between.   The whole impression
is not of wild, but of cheerful and symmetrical beauty.

Artists generally, we believe, find better studies on Lake George.
It may be that there is more of manageable picturesqueness in the
combination of its coves and cliffs ; but we think that, for larger proportioned landscape—to be enjoyed by the eye, if it cannot be easily
handled by the pencil or brush—Winnipiseogee is immeasurably
superior.   We cannot imagine a person tiring, through a whole summer, of its artistic and infinite variety.   While it could hardly be that
the eye, in the daily and familiar acquaintance of a whole season
with Lake George, would not feel the need of wider reaches in the
mountain views, richer combinations of the forest wildness with retreating slopes and cones bathed in " the tenderest purple of distance," and with glimpses, now and then, such as the New Hampshire
lake furnishes, of sovereign summits that heave upon the horizon their
vague, firm films.

Mr. Everett said, a few years since, in a speech, that Switzerland
has no lovelier view for the tourist than the lake we are speaking of
affords.   And Rev. Mr. Bartol, of Boston, in his charming volume,

" Pictures of Europe," tells us : " There may be lakes in Tyrol and Switzerland, which, in particular respects, exceed the charms of any in the Western world. But in that wedding of the land with the water, in which one is perpetually approaching and retreating from the other, and each transforms itself into a thousand figures for an endless dance of grace and beauty, till a countless multitude of shapes are arranged into perfect ease and freedom, of almost musical motion, nothing can be beheld to surpass, if to match, our Winnipiseogee." It is, of course, in moving over the lake, on a steamer or in a boat, that this " musical motion " of the shores is caught.

We will abide the judgment of any tourist as to the extravagance of this quotation, if he has an eye competent to look through the land to landscape, and becomes acquainted with the lake from the deck of a steamer, on an auspicious summer day. The sky is clear ; there are just clouds enough to relieve the soft blue and fleck the sentinel hills with shadow ; and over the wide panorama of distant mountains, a warm, dreamy haze settles, tinging them, as Emerson says the south wind, in May-days,

> Tints the human countenance
> With a color of romance.

Perhaps there is at first a faint breeze, just enough to fret the water, and roughen or mezzotint the reflections of the shores. But as we shoot out into the breadth of the lake, and take in the wide scene, there is no ripple on its bosom. The little islands float over liquid silver, and glide by each other silently, as in the movements of a dance, while our boat changes her heading. And all around, the mountains, swelling softly, or cutting the sky with jagged lines of steely blue, vie with the molten mirror at our feet for the privilege of holding the eye. The " sun-sparks " blaze thick as stars upon the glassy wrinkles of the water. Leaning over the side of the steamer, gazing at the exquisite curves of the water just outside the foamy splash of the wheels, watching the countless threads of silver that stream out from the shadow of the wheel-house, seeing the steady iris float with us to adorn our flying spray, and then looking up to the broken sides of the Ossipee mountains that are rooted in the lake, over which huge shadows loiter ; or back to the twin Belknap hills, that appeal to softer sensibilities with their verdured symmetry ; or,

further down, upon the charming succession of mounds that hem the shores near Wolfboro' ; or northward, where distant Chocorua lifts his bleached head, so tenderly touched now with gray and gold, to defy the hottest sunlight, as he has defied for ages the lightning and storm ;—does it not seem as though the passage of the Psalms is fulfilled before our eyes,—"Out of the perfection of beauty God hath shined ? "

The lines of the Sandwich Mountains, on the northwest, of which the lonely Chocorua, who seems to have pushed his fellows away from

him, is the most northerly summit, are the most striking features of
the borders of the lake. An American artist who had lived many
years in Italy, on a recent visit to this country, went to Winnipiscogee with the writer of these pages. He was greatly impressed and
charmed with the outlines of this range, which is seen at once from
the boat as she leaves Weir's landing. He had not supposed that
any water view in New England was bordered with such a mountain
frame. And before the steamer had shot out from the bay upon the
bosom of the lake, he had transferred to his sketch-book its long
combination of domes and heavy scrolls and solid walls, all leading
to a pyramid that supports a peak desolate and sheer.

The most striking picture, perhaps, to be seen on the lake, is a
view which is given of the Sandwich range in going from Weir's to
Centre Harbor, as the steamer shoots across a little bay, after passing Bear Island, about four miles from the latter village. The whole
chain is seen several miles away, as you look up the bay, between
Red Hill on the left, and the Ossipee mountains on the right. If
there is no wind, and if there are shadows enough from clouds to
spot the range, the beauty will seem weird and unsubstantial,—as
though it might fade away the next minute. The weight seems to
be taken out of the mountains. We might almost say

> They are but sailing foam-bells
> Along Thought's causing stream,
> And take their shape and sun-color
> From him that sends the dream.

Only they do not sail, they repose. The quiet of the water and the
sleep of the hills seem to have the quality of still ecstasy. It is only
inland water that can suggest and inspire such rest. The sea itself,
though it can be clear, is never calm, in the sense that a mountain
lake can be calm. The sea seems only to pause ; the mountain lake
to sleep and to dream.

But there is one view which, though far less lovely, is more exciting to one who has been a frequent visitor of the mountains. It is
where Mount Washington is visible from a portion of the steamer's

track, for some fifteen or twenty minutes. Passing by the westerly declivity of the Ossipee ridge, looking across a low slope of the Sandwich range and far back of them, a dazzling white spot perhaps—if it is very early in the summer—gleams on the northern horizon. Gradually it mounts and mounts, and then runs down again as suddenly, making us wonder, possibly, what it can be. A minute or two more, and the unmistakable majesty of Washington is revealed. *There* he rises, forty miles away, towering from a plateau built for his throne, dim green in the distance, except the dome that is crowned with winter, and the strange figures that are scrawled around his waist in snow.

Why should all the nearer splendors affect an old visitor of the hills less than that spectacle ? Why should Whiteface, which seems, at a careless glance, much higher by its nearness, or the haughty Chocorua, move less joyous emotions than that tinted etching on the northern sky ? Why will not a cloud thrice as lofty and distinct in its outline, suggest such power and waken such enthusiasm ? Is there a physical cause for it ? Is it that the volcanic power expended in upheaving one of the supreme summits,

> when with inward fires and pain
> It rose a bubble from the plain,

is permanently funded there, and is suggested to the mind whenever we see even the outlines in the distant air,—thus making it represent more vitality and force than any pile of thunderous vapor can ? Or is it explained by the law of association,—because we know, in looking at those faint forms, that their crests have no rivals in our northern latitude this side the Rocky Mountains,—that the pencilled shadows of their foreground are the deepest gorges which landslides have channelled and torrents have worn in New England,—and that from their crown a wider area is measured by the eye, than can be seen this side the Mississippi ?

How admirably and tenderly Mr. Ruskin has touched this point in a passage, which our readers will thank us that we quote for them,

10 *

from the third volume of "The Modern Painters:" "Examine the nature of your own emotion (if you feel it) at the sight of an Alp; and you find all the brightness of that emotion hanging, like dew on gossamer, on a curious web of subtle fancy and imperfect knowledge. First, you have a vague idea of its size, coupled with wonder at the work of the great Builder of its walls and foundations; then an appre, hension of its eternity, a pathetic sense of its perpetualness, and your own transientness, as of the grass upon its sides; then, and in this very sadness, a sense of strange companionship with past generations in seeing what they saw. They did not see the clouds that are float- ing over your head; nor the cottage wall on the other side of the field; nor the road by which you are travelling. But they saw *that*. The wall of granite in the heavens was the same to them as to you. They have ceased to look upon it; you will soon cease to look also, and the granite wall will be for others. Then, mingled with these more solemn imaginations, come the understandings of the gifts and glories of the Alps, the fancying forth of all the fountains that well from its rocky walls, and strong rivers that are born out of its ice, and of all the pleasant valleys that wind between its cliffs, and all the châlets that gleam among its clouds, and happy farmsteads couched upon its pastures; while together with the thoughts of these rise strange sympathies with all the unknown of human life and happiness, and death, signified by that narrow white flame of the everlasting snow, seen so far in the morning sky.

These images, and far more than these, lie at the root of the emo- tion which you feel at the sight of the Alp. You may not trace them in your heart, for there is a great deal more in your heart, of evil and good, than you ever can trace; but they stir you and quicken you for all that. Assuredly, so far as you feel more at be- holding the snowy mountain than any other object of the same sweet silvery gray, these are the kind of images which cause you to do so; and, observe, these are nothing more than a greater apprehension of the *facts* of the thing. We call the power 'Imagination,' because it imagines or conceives; but it is only noble imagination if it imagines or conceives *the truth*."

And from the hint of these last words, let us have a little talk with our readers concerning enthusiasm in seeing such scenery as the Lake furnishes in charming days. Sometimes, people go into New Hampshire with such apathetic eyes, that they have no relish for richness of landscape, or for mountain grandeur. There is no *smack* in their seeing. And there are others, who, if they are not disappointed in the outlines, the heights, and the colors that are shown to them, still think it vulgar to show enthusiasm. Any glee, or clapping of the hands, or hot superlative, is almost as heinous to them as a violation of the moral law. Just as some women think health vulgar, and cultivate languor, there are persons who repress real feeling, and assume the *blasé* mood as a matter of gentility or manners.

The foundation of this feeling it is not easy to understand. A visit to Lake Winnipiscogee, a journey to the mountains, if we have been hemmed within city walls, or chained to a prosaic landscape, most of the year, ought to be made a vacation season, a jubilee for the eye, which was formed for free range of the splendors which the Creator has scattered over space. The eye is the chief physical sign of the royalty of man on the globe. Our hands stretch but a few feet from our bodies ; hearing reaches comparatively but a little way ; but the sense of sight relates us consciously to the unbounded. The beast has no perception of the breadth and depth of space. His eye is a definite faculty, bound to bodily service, like a finger, a wing, or a claw. But think of the reaches of distance through which the eye of man is able to soar ; think of the delicate tintings it can distinguish and enjoy ; think of the sublime breadth and roofing it supplies to our apparently insignificant existence,—reaching as it does to the Pleiades and the Milky Way and the cloud-light in the belt of Orion !

To learn to see is one of the chief objects of education and life. First as infants we learn to push the world off from ourselves, and to disentangle ourselves as personalities from a mesh of sensations. Then we gain power to detect and measure distance ; then to perceive forms and colors ; and at last to relate objects quickly and properly to each ether by a sweep of the eye. And this process is crowned by the poetic perception of general beauty, in which our humanity flowers out, and by which we obtain possession of the world. " The charming landscape which I saw this morning is indubitably made up of some twenty or thirty farms. Miller owns this field, Locke that, and Manning the woodland beyond. But none of them owns the landscape. There is a property in the horizon which no man has but he whose eye can integrate all the parts, that is, the poet. This is the best part of these men's farms, yet to this their warranty-deeds give no title." The general beauty of the world is a perpetual revelation, and if we are impervious to its appeal and charm, a large district of our nature is curtained off from the Creator, " and wisdom at one entrance quite shut out."

As soon, therefore, as we become educated to see, and just in proportion to our skill in seeing, we get joy. The surprise to the senses in first looking upon a noble landscape, ought to show itself in childlike animation. The truly cultivated perception is chiefly conditioned by the recovery of the innocence of the eye. Forms and colors look as fresh to the truly trained intellect, as they do to the uncritical sense of the little child that chases its golden-winged butterfly without any competence to measure the horizon, or any feeling that it is pursuing its fluttering enticement unroofed in immensity. Mr. Ruskin tells us, in his work on the Elements of Drawing, that every highly accomplished artist has reduced himself, in dealing with the colors of a landscape, as nearly as possible to the condition of infantine sight. So that perpetual surprise and enthusiasm are signs of healthy and tutored taste.

And let us not forget that the charm which the person discerns who feels rapture amid such scenes as Winnipiseogee offers, is not illusive. It is founded on fact. The man who sees the most beauty in that landscape, deals with the facts as demonstrably as if he were engaged all day in dipping buckets of water from its treasury, or shovelling sand and felling birches on its shores. Agassiz finds marvel enough for a month's study, and for unbounded admiration, in a single grasshopper from a field on one of its islands. Jackson sees quarries of truth in the direction and dip of the mountain chains that border the Lake, where a common eye detects nothing but blank bareness of ledge, or a slope of ordinary forest at a certain angle. Mantell might unfold from a pebble stone at the foot of Ossipee the history of the globe for a hundred thousand years. And just as these men deal with facts more thoroughly than the purblind vision which overlooks these wonders, so the artistic eye deals more faithfully with facts, and with more facts, too, when it delights in the beautiful curves and windings and fringes of the lakes, islands, and shores, enjoys the shape into which the substance of Chocorua is sculptured, and finds the breezy or the sleeping water of the Lake, a fountain-head of joy for a tired mind and a wilted frame. A man that is insensible to beauty, is blind to facts. Goethe tells us that he once had a present of a basket of fruit, and was in such raptures at the sight of the loveliness of form and hue which it presented, that he could not persuade himself " to pluck off a single berry or to remove a single peach or fig." Were not the bloom and the symmetry as truly facts, as the weight and juices of the products which the basket held ? If half a dozen pictures could be seen in an Art gallery of New York or Boston, with perspective as accurate, with tints as tender, with hues as vivid and modest, with reflections as cunningly caught, with mountain-slopes as delicately pencilled, as the Lake exhibits in reality, fifty times in the summer weeks, what pride there would be in the artistic ability in the country, and what interest and joy in seeing such masterpieces from mortal hands ! A great many, no doubt, would be willing to spend profusely, to own one or two such pictures, colored on less than a dozen square feet of canvas, who do not estimate very highly the privilege of looking upon the real water-colors of the Creator, of which every triumph of a human artist is only an illusion.

Great eloquence we cannot get except from human genius. There is nothing in external nature that supplies its place. The music of a symphony by an orchestra is an achievement that cannot be dimmed

by a comparison with any melodies and harmonies of air and woods
and sea. Statuary may be perfect, and is not compensated by the
ordinary aspects of human life. Architecture is a creation of the
human intellect, adding to the stores of beauty in the world. But
pictorial landscape is exceptional among the arts in this, that it is an
inadequate transcript of what God is creating every day. A cultured
and reverent eye can have for nothing the originals, freshly laid on the
canvas of matter, in a beauty that cannot be adequately translated.

And then think what it cost to arrange a landscape which we can
see from the little steamer, as she rides from Weir's to Centre Har
bor! Think of the mad upheavals of boiling rock, to cool and harden
in the air ; think of the centuries of channelling by torrents and frost
to give their nervous edge to distant ridges and crests ; think what
patient opulence of creative power wrapped their sides with thickets,
that grow out of the mould of pre-adamite moss and fern, and spotted
their walls with weather stains in which the tempests of ten thousand
years ago took part. Consider, too, the exquisite balancing of widely
sundered forces, represented in the clouds that sail over that Sandwich chain and cool their cones with shadow, or in the mists that
sometimes creep up their slopes and twine around their brows, or in
the streams, those grandchildren of the ocean, that revel in their
ravines. Bear in mind what delicate skill is exhibited in the mixture of the air through whose translucent sea we catch their mottled
charm, and how the huge earth spins on its axis without noise or jar
to give the ever shifting hues that bathe them from golden dawn to
purple evening. And now, when we remember that all this is only
the commencement of an enumeration of the forces that combine in
producing a landscape, is a little visible exultation anything more
than an honest expression of the privilege a mortal is endowed with,
in being introduced to the Creator's art ?

Let us remember that pure delight in natural scenes themselves,
is the crown of all artistic power or appreciation. And when a man
loses enthusiasm,—when there is no surprise in the gush of evening
pomp out of the west,—when the miracle of beauty has become

commonplace,—when the world has become withered and soggy to his eye, so that, instead of finding its countenance " fresh as on creation's day," he looks at each lovely object and scene, and, like the travelling Englishman, oppressed with *ennui*, finds " nothing in it," —it is about time for him to be transplanted to some other planet. Why not to the moon? No Winnipiseogee is there. There are mountains enough, but they show no azure and no gold. There are pits enough, but there is no water in them; no clouds hover over them; no air and moisture diffuses and varies the light. It is a planet of bare facts, without the frescos and garniture of beauty, a mere skeleton globe, and so perhaps is the Botany Bay for spirits that have become torpid and *blasé*.

The points of rest on the borders of the lake are, as we have already stated, Centre Harbor and Wolfboro'. Steamers ply to and from these points, from the railroad stations at Alton Bay and Weir's, several times in the day. Thus, when the weather is pleasant, persons may pass the larger part of the day on the lake, and may take their meals on the boat if they choose. From Wolfboro' there are many pleasant drives in which the lake is brought into the landscape. Copple Crown mountain, not difficult of ascent, and about five miles from the hotel, furnishes one of the best general views of the lake, and shows, besides the hills in which it is set, some thirty other sheets of water, large and small, that enliven the outskirts of the great mountain district in New Hampshire and Maine.

The steamer stays over night at Wolfboro', and not unfrequently an excursion is made to see the lake by moonlight. What can be more charming than, at the close of one of the long days of June, to see the full moon rise over the lower end of the lake just before the sun goes down? When the evening is fair and the water still, the glimmer of its brassy disk, just clearing the narrow belt of haze behind the mountains, may be seen in the long mellow wake that seems to sound the depths of the roseate or pale blue water, while the day yet glows along the gray hill slopes, and is brightening the young

11

green of the tree-tops with touches of gold. Then when the sunlight is withdrawn, and the evening zephyrs have folded their wings, what delight to see the moon brighten, to notice how the mountains gradually flatten as the color is drained from them, to watch the islands with their marshalled rows of tall pines seem to stir as we pass them, as the light shimmers upon the water around their dark forms, and soon to see the lengthened image of the moon become a straight upright column of gold hanging in the sapphire deep!

Do not say, oh reader, that it is "all moonshine" if we assure you that there is a great difference, in moonlight. No place better for testing it than Wolfboro'. Science has analyzed the sun-rays, and has shown that the proportions of their elements vary in the four seasons, according to the changing necessities of vegetation. A spirit delicate enough for lunar photography, no doubt, could tell the month of the year by the quality of its moonlight, and be able also to individualize each evening of its dispensation, from the gentle radiance of what a child calls the baby moon to the ample flood of its maturity. Make half a dozen excursions on the lake at night, and see if, with different winds and temperatures, you find the moonlight twice alike. Notice how sometimes it is thin, bluish, and chilly, as if it had been skimmed in the upper ether before reaching our air. Sometimes you find it deathly white. Bogles and spectres seem to pervade it. It appears to be the ghost of sunshine, shed upon the earth from a dead world. Again you will find it pouring a weird hue and influence, suggesting fairies and frolicsome fays. It is the element then of Ariels and Peasblossoms, the woof of inexhaustible Midsummer Night's Dreams. Then as we pass the slope of one of the cultivated islands in the lake,

The velvet grass seems carpet meet
For the light fairies' lively feet;
Yon tufted knoll with daisies strewn
Might make proud Oberon a throne,
While, hidden in the thicket nigh,
Puck should brood o'er his frolic sly;
And where profuse the wood-vetch clings
Round ash and elm in verdant rings,

Its pale and azure-pencilled flower
Should canopy Titania's bower

But what a rare joy when, in some warm summer evening, we can sail on the lake while the moon is full in a double sense, and seems to pour out in larger liberality than usual from its fountains! Its beams do not rain in silver streams, but gush, as it were, from all the veins of the air. Every globule of the atmosphere exudes unctuous light. And its color is so charming—a delicate luminous cream! One can hardly help believing that Gunstock and Ossipee enjoy their anointing, after the withering heat of the day, with such cool and tender lustre. And how still the lake lies, to have its surface burnished by it into liquid acres of a faint golden splendor!

From Centre Harbor, at the upper end of the Lake, the drives are very attractive. The guide-books report them in detail. We have room to call attention only to the excursion which is most interesting, that is, to the summit of " Red Hill," which rises about five miles away, and stands about two thousand feet above the sea. Near the top of the mountain, where its ledges of sienite are exposed to the action of the air, they have a reddish hue. But it owes its name, we believe, to the fact that it is covered with the *uva ursa*, the leaves of which change to a brilliant red in autumn. The excursion is easily made in the afternoon, or between breakfast and dinner. Its unwooded peak is lifted to the height from which scenery looks most charming. And there is no point except this, along the regular mountain route, beneath which a large lake is spread. But here Winnipiseogee stretches from its very foot, and its whole length is seen as far as the softly swelling hills that bound it on the southeast. There is only one point from which the view of it is more attractive, —that is from the highest of the Belknap mountains, which stand, not at one end of the lake like Red Hill, but midway of its length. Mount Belknap is visited from Laconia, and very few have seen from its summit the lovely mirror in which its own feminine form, and its smaller sister hill, are repeated. But whoever misses the view from

Red Hill, loses the most fascinating and thoroughly enjoyable view, from a moderate mountain height, that can be gained from any eminence that lies near the tourist's path. The Mount Washington range is not visible, being barred from sight by the dark Sandwich

chain, which in the afternoon, untouched by the light, wears a savage frown that contrasts most effectively with the placid beauty of the Lake below. Here is the place to study its borders, to admire the fleet of islands that ride at anchor on its bosom—from little shallops to grand three-deckers—and to enjoy the exquisite lines by which its bays are enfolded, in which its coves retreat, and with which its low capes cut the azure water, and hang over it an emerald fringe. And if one can stay there late in the afternoon, as we have stayed, and see the shadows thrown out from the island and trees, and the hues that flush the Lake's surface as the sun declines, he will be prepared to enjoy more thoroughly the description of such an hour and such a view, with which Percival has enriched American literature.

Thou wert calm,
Even as an infant calm, that gentle evening;
And one could hardly dream thou'dst ever met
And wrestled with the storm. A breath of air,
Felt only in its coolness, from the west
Stole over thee, and stirred thy golden mirror
Into long waves, that only showed themselves
In ripples on thy shore,—far distant ripples,
Breaking the silence with their quiet kisses
And softly murmuring peace.

Far to the south
Thy slumbering waters floated, one long sheet
Of burnished gold,—between thy nearer shores
Softly embraced, and melting distantly
Into a yellow haze, embosomed low
'Mid shadowy hills and misty mountains, all
Covered with showery light, as with a veil
Of airy gauze. Beautiful were thy shores,
And manifold their outlines, here up-swelling
In bossy green,—there hung in slaty cliffs,
Black as if hewn from jet, and overtopped
With the dark cedar's tufts, or new-leaved birch,
Bright as the wave below. How glassy clear
The far expanse! Beneath it all the sky
Swelled downward, and its fleecy clouds were gay
With all their rainbow fringes, and the trees
And cliffs and grassy knolls were all repeated
Along the uncertain shores,—so clearly seen
Beneath the invisible transparency,
That land and water mingled, and the one
Seemed melting in the other. O, how soft
Yon mountain's heavenly blue, and all o'erlaid
With a pale tint of roses! Deep between
The ever-narrowing lake, just faintly marked
By its reflected light, and further on
Buried in vapory foam, as if a surf
Heaved on its utmost shore. How deep the silence!
Only the rustling boughs, the broken ripple,
The cricket and the tree-frog, with the tinkle

Of bells in fold and pasture, or a voice
Heard from a distant farm, or hollow bay
Of home-returning hound,—a virgin land
Just rescued from the wilderness, still showing
Wrecks of the giant forest.   .   .   .   .

.   .   .   .

I gazed upon them,
And on the unchanging lake, and felt awhile
Unutterable joy,—I loved my land
With more than filial love,—it was a joy
That only spake in tears.

But the beauty of the lake cannot be judged from a point so high as Red Hill. Its varied charms are not to be seen from one spot on its shore like Centre Harbor. They must be sought along all its intricate borders, among its three hundred or more islands, and in boats upon its own bosom. This is the way to find the most delightful single pictures. This is the way to study at leisure landscapes which the swift steamer allows you to see but a moment. This is the way to find delicious " bits," such as artists love for studies, of jutting rock, shaded beach, coy and curving nook, or limpid water prattling upon amethystine sand. At one point, perhaps, a group of graceful trees on one side, a grassy or tangled shore in front, and a rocky cape curving in from the other side, compose an effective foreground to a quiet bay with finely varied borders, and the double-peaked Belknap in the distance. Or what more charming than to sail slowly along and see the numerous islands and irregular shores change their positions and weave their singular combinations ? Now they range themselves on either hand, and hem a vista that extends to the blue base of Copple Crown. Now an island slides its gray or purple form across, and, like a rood-screen, divides the long watery aisle into nave and choir, followed by another and another, till the perspective is confused and the vista disappears. Then in the distance, islands and shores will marshal themselves in long straight lines, fronting you as regular as the phalanxes of an army ; and if the sun is low present the embattled effect the more forcibly, with their vertically shadowed sides and brightly lighted tops. Or

at another spot, through an opening among dark headlands, the summit of Chocorua is seen moving swiftly over lower ranges, and soon

the whole mountain sweeps into view, startling you with its ghost-
like pallor, and haggard crest.   On a morning when the fog is clearing, is the time to be tempted towards the middle of the lake, to see
the islands, whose green looks more exquisite then than in any other
atmosphere, stretch away in perspectives dreamy and illusive.   Two
or three miles of distance seem five times as long, when measured
through such genial, moist, and silvery air.   And now, if we will bend
westward, between curving shores that will grant us ample passage,
we shall be glad to find ourselves in the encircled bay near Weir's,
and can have leisure to enjoy in silence the gentle slopes of the Bel-
knaps, and the succession of mounds that heave away from them to
the southeast, while the fog is rolling up into clouds, and the sunshine
slipping down a broad cultivated field on one of the swelling cones,
burnishes it to emerald.   And towards evening we may glide down
the narrow inlet around which Centre Harbor is built, and follow the
shadows, while

> Slow up the slopes of Ossipee
> They chase the lessening light.

When they have dislodged it all, we can watch, as we return to the
village, the " Procession of the Pines," which rise on the southwestern ridge that hems the cove, and be tempted to fancy, as they
darken, while the saffron horizon is dying into ashy gray sky, that
each of those grotesque and weird forms holds the soul of some grim
old Sachem.

If the shores of the Lake were lined with summer-houses, how
might the charms of boating upon Winnipiseogee enrich our literature !   Our readers of course know what " The Autocrat of the
Breakfast Table " says of the privilege and pleasure of boating.
" Here you are afloat with a body a rod and a half long, with arms,
or wings, as you may choose to call them, stretching more than
twenty feet from tip to tip ; every volition of yours extending as
perfectly into them as if your spinal cord ran down the centre strip
of your boat, and the nerves of your arms tingled as far as the broad

blades of your oars. This, in sober earnest, is the nearest approach to flying that man has ever made, or perhaps ever will make. . . . . I dare not publicly name the rare joys, the infinite delights, that intoxicate me on some sweet June morning, when the river and bay are smooth as a sheet of beryl-green silk, and I run along ripping it up with my knife-edged shell of a boat, the rent closing after me like those wounds of angels which Milton tells of, but the seam still shining for many a long rood behind me."

Ah, if "The Autocrat" would visit Winnipiseogee for a season, and cleave its glossy azure with his canoe, and tell us how mountain peaks and lake rhyme themselves in his imagination,—or what fancies visit him when he pauses at some rare scene, and the silver has dripped from his resting oar-blades, and the wrinkled curves from his prow have smoothed into calm, and headland, mountain chain, emerald fringes of an island shore, and the snowy islands of the over-brooding blue are repeated beneath him in the sleeping silver! Would that the creeks and armlets of our inland bay, with all their settings, might be reflected thus in "The Atlantic!" Shall we never have our "lake-poets" to celebrate for us the surroundings of Winnipiseogee, as the Cumberland lakes have been interpreted by Wordsworth and his friends? Here is a passage in which Words-worth describes his rowing over Windermere with a companion :—

> Soon as the reedy marge
> Was cleared, I dipped, with arms accordant, oars
> Free from obstruction; and the boat advanced
> Through crystal water, smoothly as a hawk,
> That, disentangled from the shady boughs
> Of some thick wood, her place of covert, cleaves
> With correspondent wings the abyss of air.
> —" Observe," the Vicar said, " you rocky isle
> With birch-trees fringed; my hand shall guide the helm
> While thitherward we shape our course; or while
> We seek that other, on the western shore,
> Where the bare columns of those lofty firs,
> Supporting gracefully a massy dome
> Of sombre foliage, seem to imitate
> A Grecian temple rising from the Deep."
> " Turn where we may," said I, " we cannot err

In this delicious region." Cultured slopes,
Wild tracts of forest ground, and scattered groves,
And mountains bare, or clothed with ancient woods,
Surrounded us; and, as we held our way
Along the level of the glassy flood,
They ceased not to surround us; change of place,
Producing change of beauty ever new.
Ah! that such beauty, varying in the light
Of living nature, cannot be portrayed
By words, nor by the pencil's silent skill;
But is the property of him alone
Who hath beheld it, noted it with care,
And in his mind recorded it with love!

Why is it that the reflections in a still river or lake as we float over it, or wander by its shores, are so much more charming than the actual scenes? The shallowest still water, it has been happily said, is unfathomable. Wherever the trees and skies are reflected, there is more than Atlantic depth, and no danger of fancy running aground. Has the reader ever looked at a landscape by bending his head low, thus turning his eyes upside down, and noticed how much richer are the colors, how much sublimer the sky, how much more vast and impressive the revelation of space? So the landscape turned upside down in the mirror of a lake is unspeakably more bewitching. The mountains that point to the nadir are more fascinating than those that soar to the zenith. The vines and grasses that fringe the unsubstantial coasts below have a sweeter grace than those which can be plucked. Is it not Coleridge who compares with this the superior fascination we find in a character, or in a natural scene, when reported from the imagination of a great poet, than when we see the elements of it in the real world?

We shall not find this exquisite under world, this bottomless deep of ideal beauty, described with strokes more vivid and airy than in the following passage from Rev. Mr. Bartol's "Pictures of Europe," in which he portrays a lake of the Tyrol which no map has ever reported. "Into the pellucid water glides our little boat. As I gazed, I felt almost unsafe, suspended at some dizzy height; for it was as if only the thinnest, finest layer of gossamer fabric were stretched there for a horizontal veil or floor, and on both sides, the unfathomable abyss. On smoothly darts our secure vessel. I look over her side into the infinite chasm. What keeps her from falling down? On what mysterious support does she ride between these rival skies? How, through this hollow sphere, holds she her level way? Is she a fairy bark, and are we spirits transported now towards some sphere of the blessed? From this mood I was diverted a little, and my mind saved from losing itself in pure ecstasy, by observing the huge forms of the inverted hills, running downward as far as upward, in their erectness, they climbed. What refinement of pleasure was there in remarking the minuteness, as well as vastness of the copy! Ah! no copyist of the old masters can render his original upon the canvas as faithfully in every line and hue, or with expression so perfect and speaking, as it pleases God here to translate his own works in the engravings of this marvellous page. He, too, writes his name in water; and, if it fades with the ruffling wind, it fades but to return again with spell more sweetly binding than if it had not vanished at all. How we admired the submarine curving lines, the diverse shades,—each angle flashing back the light, each vapor-shrouded point jutting from the mighty mass,—the shreds of woolly cloud floating underneath, and the winds blowing gently round the spectral mountain's brow as truly as about the other mountain on high! How the double glory divided our regard, till we drew towards the shore from which we were to roll on wheels again by a road hedged in on one side by verdant woods, and on the other by amber streams, that, with their clear, delicious color, told us whence the lake derived its crystal character to make it like 'one entire and perfect chrysolite!'"

But it is time that we should say something of the charms of color which a long visit by the lake shore will reveal. Many persons suppose that they have seen Winnipiscogee in passing over it in the steamer on their way to Conway and "The Notch." Seen the lake! Which lake? There are a thousand. It is a chameleon.

It is not a steady sapphire set in green, but an opal. Under no twc skies or winds is it the same. It is gray, it is blue, it is olive, it is azure, it is purple, at the will of the breezes, the clouds, the hours. Sail over it on some afternoon when the sky is leaden with northeast mists, and you can see the simple beauty of form in which its shores and guards are sculptured. This is the permanent lake which prosaic geology has filled and feeds. And this was placed there to dis- play the riches of color in which the infiniteness of the Creator's art is revealed to us more than in the scale of space.

We have said that the lake is an opal. If persons with artistic delight in color should keep a journal of what would be shown to them during a few weeks, they would be surprised at the octaves that are touched in the course of a short season, and at the suddenness of their transitions. People should learn to notice the changes and combination and range of colors, not merely for the joy that is given at the moment through definite perception, but also for the education of taste in the appreciation and enjoyment of art. How can a per- son, that has not observed minutely and faithfully the hues and har- monies of a landscape at different times of day, and under widely different conditions of air and cloud and light, intelligently compre- hend and judge the products and the genius of the masters of land- scape, as displayed in our art rooms ? The effect of White Mountain journeys should be seen in our homes, in a purer delight in art, and an intelligent patronage of it. And it is only close observance of the ever changing expressions which flit over the face of Nature, that en- lightens taste, and makes it competent for this. It has been well said that a connoisseur who has scampered over all Europe, and who most likely cannot tell the shape of the leaf of an elm, will be voluble of criticism on every painted landscape from Dresden to Madrid, and pretend to decide whether they are like Nature or not. And thus many a person may pronounce upon the tone of a picture, that it is not natural, who has no conception of the scale and freaks of color which a fortnight reveals among the mountains and by Winnipiseogee.

If the lake were to be painted as it may sometimes be seen in the forenoon of a day when clouds are flying over the sun, the water should be dyed the intensest blue, with a single horizontal line of white towards the farthest shore. But if the painter is to report it as it appears a few moments after, when the sun emerges from the clouds, he must make a picture in which there is no deep blue, nor any definite color, but one broad field of glittering and tremulous brightness. Another picture would show the azure surface deepened to indigo, and its usually dark islands rising out light upon the darkness around them.   Under a drapery of drowsy clouds, when the shores cut harshly the gray water that is ruffled by the lazy wind, the canvas can glow with no splendors, but will suggest chiefly the throbbing sound of the wavelets that crumble upon the clean beaches

In tender curving lines of creamy spray.

A view taken in smoky weather will show the lake with its delicate web of cross ripples as a beautiful lace pattern, miles in extent, tinted pale blue, cream white, and rosy gray.   Or as the charming Proteus appears on some clear, calm evening, the artist that copies it must stripe the canvas with different colored zones of varying widths, some opaque, others transparent, according as they reflect the glowing tints of the lower, or the cooler lights of the upper sky.

And now and then a thunder-shower, in an afternoon when the sunlight gently shimmers over its breadth, comes to try its resources in color effects.   It sweeps low across it with slaty wings, and blots out the islands and blackens the water with its rough breath and angry shade.   Watch now, after the gusts of rain are spent, the inky darkness of the upper end of the lake. But the islands farther away, just coming into the returning light out of the cloud-fringe, show a white lustre as of new-fallen snow: And when the wrath of the tempest has retreated towards the sea, one can have the privilege, from the hills of Centre Harbor, of seeing a rainbow span the lake, succeeded, perhaps, by a sunset in which the whole surface of the water, responding to the hues above, outvies the rainbow with gorgeous flames.

A more sensitive eye will not fail to notice the variety of sunset effects by which Winnipiscogee is glorified. The great wreaths of gray and white cumuli, which sailed slowly around the skies' verge during the day, will sometimes melt into the uprising mists of evening, and belt the horizon with a delicate zone of violet and gray. What an exquisite veil is this for the shadowed parts of the hills around the southerly shores of the lake, and what a fascinating contrast to the fine pencillings of pale reddish hues on their sunward outlines! Another evening, the hills are not obscured thus. They stretch a long chain of azure and purple under the southern sky, which is filled over and back of them with masses of irregular, flaky, low clouds of orange, violet, and gray, that float before rich fields of creamy cirrus. These hues run an octave higher than those on the mountains below, and the sunbeams vivify them still more here and there with yellow curves and jagged lines of scarlet.

The abruptness and height of the hill to the northwest renders Centre Harbor comparatively unfavorable for seeing sunsets. Yet we now and then see a display there which the elevated and dark horizon seems to heighten rather than to mar. But let me quote here a passage from a letter of an artist friend, in which he describes a sunset that he once saw early in July during a visit to Centre Harbor. "The day had been cloudy, with scattered showers, and the effects, broad and massive, about the setting sun, were unspeakably rich in form and color. The tumultuous mingling of broad folds of half-exhausted rain clouds and rolling piles of cumuli near the sun, with their deep, though transparent colors, their wild dashes of gorgeous tertiaries, and jagged breaks of flaming orange and crinkling gold, showed me from what studies Rubens colored the 'Judgment of Paris' and the 'Plague of the Fiery Serpents.' The most beautiful feature of the evening's display came a little later, when the sun was down, and had withdrawn his fire from a large mass of the lower clouds, which now being purified, gathered into one towering form of priestly vapor, unsullied white, rising high above the murkiness and splendid impurity around into the tender golden blue of the upper sky. The most notable peculiarity about it, however, was the seemingly perfect whiteness of the great mass in shade, while the narrow edging of sunshine appeared white again in flame."

But we must not pass from a treatment of the color around Lake Winnipiseogee without referring to the October splendors that begird it, when the hues of sunset are spread permanently upon the hills. During July and August, a gradual change is slowly going on, by which the colors of June are not so much altered as deepened and enriched. September is the transition period, from the styles or effects of color in the season's time of growth, to those belonging to the period of decline and decay. As yet the landscape has lost nothing of the fulness of its summer foliage. But richer tints gradually steal into the shadows and darker tones of the landscape, warming the coolness, and breaking the monotony, with flashes of crimson and orange. More purple is shown in the distances of the lake, with richer browns and lighter olives and citrine upon the foregrounds. Nature seems to be carelessly running her hand over the notes, touching and indicating the great chords, before breaking into the full pomp of the autumn symphony.

And as October comes near, the pale green of the plentiful birches mounts into yellow. Some of the maples have turned to scarlet, others orange, others a dull or pale red. The oaks and hardier trees show deep crimson stains running among their dark green masses. The grass-grounds or pastures are becoming yellow. The bared edges and boulders, so quiet and shy in their light gray suits of summer, stand out conspicuous in blue and purple ; and the humble sumachs have advanced from their shadowed places, and are calling attention to their red and yellow plumes. On the borders of the little streams or pools in the meadows, the pink and purple clusters of the thoroughwort blossoms, the blue and white asters, and the epaulet flowers are in their prime ; a deep red mingles with the olive of the ferns, and the sweetbrier is hung thick with scarlet berries.

These colors mounting and growing richer in hue and mass give the tone to the landscape seen around Winnipiseogee in mid-October. Now indeed we may safely say that nothing in Europe can surpass it. The rose-tints on the snowy spires that shoot over the Königsee ; the flushes "which morn and crimson evening paint," that dye the steep crests which soar above the cultivated slopes around Lucerne ; the dreamy air and flickering lights that enhance the beauty of the Italian shores under which Como sleeps, are more than mated in the gorgeousness and the softness amid which the New England lake is pavilioned now. Whoever has the privilege of sailing on Winnipiseogee during the heart of October may say,

> My soul to-day
> Is far away,
> Sailing the Vesuvian Bay;
> My wingéd boat,
> A bird afloat,
> Swims round the purple peaks remote;—
>
> Round purple peaks
> It sails and seeks
> Blue inlets and their crystal creeks,
> Where high rocks throw
> Through deeps below,
> A duplicated golden glow.
>
> I heed not, if
> My rippling skiff
> Floats swift or slow from cliff to cliff;—
> With dreamful eyes
> My spirit lies
> Under the walls of Paradise.

Whence have these hues been distilled that surpass the richness of the Orient and the flames that are reflected in the Amazon ? Whence has overflowed upon the prosaic air of New England this luxurious sweetness through which the light transudes upon a pageant such as no poet has ascribed to the pastures and the hill-sides of Arcadia?

How near to us are the fountains of miracle ! How close the processes and magic of the Infinite art !

> Onward and on, the eternal Pan,
> Who layeth the world's incessant plan,
> Halteth never in one shape,
> But forever doth escape
> Like wave or flame, into new forms.
>
> . . . .
>
> The world is the ring of his spells,
> And the play of his miracles.

Besides the splendor and subtlety of the colors around Winnipiseogee in October, there is a continual changefulness in every part of the view, even the foregrounds ; and especially under the magic influence of the evening light, dolphin flushes seem to make the landscape unsteady, and the scenes as we look at them undergo

> a sea change
> Into something rich and strange.

A wooded cape or island, one moment blazing in bright yellow and green, orange and scarlet, is the next a mass of variegated gray and purple or faded green. The Ossipee range now displays over its extensive sides a lambent vesture of light purple and crimson, yellow, pale-green, and orange, softened and harmonized by a thin glazing of transparent azure ; but turn again and it sleeps calmly in a robe of the tenderest violet, and the nearer objects

> The woods erewhile armed in gold,
> Their banners bright with every martial hue,
> Now stand like some sad beaten hosts of old
> Withdrawn afar in time's remotest blue.

By the October haze, one considerable defect in the general lake views, to an artistic eye, is remedied. The somewhat harsh, spotty, or scattering effect of the irregular breaking in of so many dark points of land upon the light water, is concealed or softened.

> How fuse and mix, with what unfelt degrees,
> Clasped by the faint horizon's languid arms,
> Each into each, the hazy distances!

13

The softened season all the landscape charms;
Those hills, my native village that embay,
In waves of dreamier purple roll away,
And floating in mirage seem all the glimmering farms.

And the morning and evening effects now show more variety, as well as richness, than in the summer months. What added picturesqueness is given to the reflections by the many and various colors around the shores! And what joy to sail in the steamer when the evening sunlight pours upon the sides of Ossipee and Red Hill, falling here and there upon grassy slopes, running in golden streams to the water's edge, leaving broad spaces or stripes of deep emerald or purple shade between, over which some scattered maples and birches stand, kindled into torches of scarlet and yellow fire!

The birds with most splendid plumage are not attractive songsters. In the summer-time, the pleasure of morning and evening by the lake-side is enhanced by the songs of birds and the sounds of winds through the waving crops and the full strung harps of the woods. But now the appeal is to the eye, and the ear is unsolicited. It is the melodies of tint and the grand harmonies of color that appeal to us in the Autumn. There is seldom a breeze on the lake during the reign of the October haze. The tender whispers of the wind are hushed; the pulses of robin music, the shrill but sweet soprano of the fife-bird, and the whippoorwills' soft concert, do not enrich the air. The cricket's monotonous chant, " the insect's drowsy hum," is all the accompaniment allowed to the gorgeous pageantry of October, the sunset of the year.

It is a pity that tourists could not see the lake when it is thus enfolded in the pomp of purple and gold. But if we can learn to see it truly in its paler beauty of summer, we shall find ourselves drawn into sympathy with the charming poem written by Mr. Whittier as the antistrophe to the lines which introduce our description, entitled.

.

SUMMER BY THE LAKE-SIDE.

EVENING.

Yon mountain's side is black with night,
 While, broad-orbed, o'er its gleaming crown
The moon slow rounding into sight,
 On the hushed inland sea looks down.

How start to light the clustering isles,
 Each silver-hemmed! How sharply show
The shadows of their rocky piles,
 And tree-tops in the wave below!

How far and strange the mountains seem,
 Dim-looming through the pale, still light!
The vague, vast grouping of a dream,
 They stretch into the solemn night.

Beneath, lake, wood, and peopled vale,
 Hushed by that presence grand and grave   .
Are silent, save the cricket's wail,
 And low response of leaf and wav·

Fair scenes! whereto the Day and Night
 Make rival love, I leave ye soon,
What time before the eastern light
 The pale ghost of the setting moon

Shall hide behind yon rocky spines,
 And the young archer, Morn, shall break
His arrows on the mountain pines,
 And, golden-sandalled, walk the lake!

Farewell! around this smiling bay
 Gay-hearted Health, and Life in bloom
With lighter steps than mine, may stray
 In radiant summers yet to come.

But none shall more regretful leave
 These waters and these hills than I;
Or, distant, fonder dream how eve
 Or dawn is painting wave and sky:

13 *

How rising moons shine sad and mild
    On wooded isle and silvering bay;
Or setting suns beyond the piled
    And purple mountains lead the day;

Nor laughing girl, nor bearding boy,
    Nor full pulsed manhood, lingering here,
Shall add to life's abounding joy,
    The charmed repose to suffering dear

Still waits kind Nature to impart
    Her choicest gifts to such as gain
An entrance to her loving heart
    Through the sharp discipline of pain.

Forever from the hand that takes
    One blessing from us others fall;
And, soon or late, our Father makes
    His perfect recompense to all!

O, watched by Silence and the Night,
    And folded in the strong embrace
Of the great mountains, with the light
    Of the sweet heavens upon thy face,

Land of the Northland! keep thy dower
    Of beauty still, and while above
Thy solemn mountains speak of power,
    Be thou the mirror of God's love.

THE PEMIGEWASSET VALLEY.

PLYMOUTH, CAMPTON, AND FRANCONIA.

" We were thus entering the State of New Hampshire on the bosom of the flood formed by the tribute of its innumerable valleys. The river was the only key which could unlock its maze, presenting its hills and valleys, its lakes and streams, in their natural order and position. The Merrimack, or Sturgeon River, is formed by the confluence of the Pemigewasset, which rises near the Notch of the White Mountains, and the Winnipiseogee, which drains the lake of the same name. At first it comes on murmuring to itself by the base of stately and retired mountains, through moist primitive woods whose juices it receives, where the bear still drinks it, and the cabins of settlers are far between, and there are few to cross its stream; enjoying in solitude its cascades still unknown to fame; by long ranges of mountains of Sandwich and of Squam, slumbering like tumuli of Titans, with the peaks of Moosehillock, the Haystack, and Kiarsarge, reflected in its waters; where the maple and the raspberry, those lovers of the hills, flourish amid temperate dews;—flowing long and full of meaning, but untranslatable as its name Pemigewasset, by many a pastured Pelion and Ossa, where unnamed muses haunt,—tended by Oreads, Dryads, Naiads, and receiving the tribute of many an untasted Hippocrene.

> Such water do the gods distil,
> And pour down every hill
> For their New England men,
> A draught of this wild nectar bring,
> And I'll not taste the spring
> Of Helicon again.

Falling all the way, and yet not discouraged by the lowest fall. By the law of its birth never to become stagnant, for it has come out of the clouds, and down the sides of precipices worn in the flood, through beaver-dams broke loose, not splitting but splicing and mending itself, until it found a breathing-place in this low land. There is no danger now that the sun will steal it back to heaven again before it reach the sea, for it has a warrant even to recover its own dews into its bosom with interest at every eve."

THOREAU.

THE PEMIGEWASSET VALLEY.

ONE hour by steamer across Lake Winnipiseogee, and another hour by cars, will carry the traveller from Centre Harbor to Plymouth, from which the stages start with passengers for the Franconia mountains, at the head of the valley of the Pemigewasset. The distance from Centre Harbor, directly across to Plymouth by the county road, is only twelve miles. If this road were less hilly, it would offer one of the most delightful drives among the mountains. Although but twelve miles long, its measure, by the artist's estimate, must take into account the water-views that spot it so brilliantly. During a large portion of the drive the two lakes,—Great Squam, singularly striped with long, narrow, crinkling islands, and, like Wordsworth's river, winding in the landscape "at its own sweet will,"—and Little Squam, unbroken by islands, fringed and shadowed by thickets of the richest foliage, that is disposed around its western shore, in a long sweeping curve line which will be remembered as a delightful melody of the eye,—offer themselves in various aspects that often compel us to stop and quietly drink in their beauty. No wonder that the Indians were so strongly attached to this neighborhood. and fought so desperately before yielding the possession of it to the white intruders. The lower hills tempted them with abundance of game, and the calm water supplied them with unfailing stores of fish ; while Winnipiseogee was but six miles distant one way, and the Pemigewasset equally near on the west. And possibly the surpassing loveliness of the landscape served as a golden thread in the cord that bound them to this peaceful dell in the centre of New England. The larger Squam Lake, not a fourth part so large as Winni piscogee, is doubtless the most beautiful of all the small sheets of water in New England ; and it has been pronounced by one gentleman, no less careful in his words than cultivated in his taste, more charmingly embosomed in the landscape than any lake of equal size he had ever seen in Europe or America.

The whole Sandwich range is in view behind the lower hills that guard the lake. The most striking picture is gained about five miles from Centre Harbor, from the top of a hill on the road, where, as we look over the broadest portion of the lake, and across several parallel pars of narrow islands, the whole form of gallant Chocorua, with his steel-hooded head, fills the background to the northward, towering, without any intervening obstruction, twelve or fifteen miles away. We give an illustration of this view. But we can call attention in words only to a dark and massive mountain that stands also in the land scape, wearing a hue as of beaten metals and adamant. From whatever point it is observed near Centre Harbor, it is distinguished by its darker color from the main Sandwich range, back of which it looms. And from Squam Lake it shows scattered points, and short, jagged lines of glittering lights, (probably bare points of quartz,) which make its darkness sparkle as though it were sheathed in a coat of mail.

There are charming reliefs of forest-path in the road, which, though uneven, is of quite civilized smoothness. And it opens at last upon a splendid surprise in the rich meadows of Holderness and Plymouth, that are studded or overlooked by tasteful country residences, and adorned with clusters and avenues of grand old elms. Holderness, which lies opposite Plymouth on the eastern bank of the Pemigewasset, was founded by a company of English emigrants ardently devoted to the creed and worship of the Church of England, and with glowing anticipations of the future for the colony. The founders hoped and believed that they were laying the basis of the great city of New England, the rival of Puritan Boston, and destined to throw it in the shade. The head-quarters of heresy, they allowed, would have some *commercial* advantages, on account of its nearness to the ocean and its excellent harbor ; but, in population, refinement, dignity, and wealth, they supposed that Holderness was to be the chief city of the New England colonies. What a strange answer to their dream, that even the pretension with which the settlement was made is not noticed by history, and has scarcely wandered from the proprietors' records into any tradition !

Plymouth is one of the villages to which a day or two, at least, should be devoted on the way to the mountains. Many visitors will be glad to learn that the old building remains here in which Danie

14

Webster made his first argument before a court. It is now used as a wheelwright's shop. The statesman wrote his name in large letters with red chalk, a short time before his death, upon a wall of the room which vibrated to his first legal effort ; but the autograph, the most valuable one probably to be found in New England, has since been covered by a daub from a paint brush. In scenery, Plymouth is remarkable for the beauty of its meadows, through which the Pemigewasset winds, and for the grace of its elm-trees. Even the hurrying and careless visitor will have his attention arrested here and there

by a faultless one, standing out alone over its private area of shadow seemingly an over-gushing fountain of graceful verdure.

There are several moderate hills in the village from which delight

ful views of the river amply repay the small trouble it requires to
gain them. And Prospect Mountain, or North Hill, which is its true
name, commands a panorama so extensive and charming that an
ascent of it should be accounted one of the great privileges of this
route to the mountains. The surveyors tell us that it stands, higher
over the village than Red Hill over Centre Harbor; yet there is a
very good wagon road to the summit. The landscape, if less lovely
in one or two respects than that from Red Hill, has more variety, and
includes more pastoral beauty. The whole extent of Winnipiseogee
in its broadest part is visible, and the arms and creeks, which stretch
out from its body like claws and antennæ, seem to be separate water
gems scattered upon the landscape. The view of it, however, as a
whole, is not nearly so fine as from Red Hill, where the carvings and
adorning of its curiously scalloped shores are seen. Directly beneath
us are the two Squam lakes. And the track of the Pemigewasset,
here and there receiving a tributary stream through beautifully
guarded passes on the west, may be followed along widening
meadows, from the distant slopes that give birth to it, to the broader
and lordly current below, where it joins its cold tide with the warmer
stream that flows from Winnipiseogee, and takes the name of Merri
mack.

> I felt the cool breath of the North,
>   Between me and the sun,
> O'er deep, still lake, and ridgy earth,
>   I saw the cloud-shades run.
> Before me, stretched for glistening miles,
>   Lay mountain-girdled Squam;
> Like green-winged birds, the leafy isles
>   Upon its bosom swam.
>
> Aud, glimmering through the sun-haze warm,
>   Far as the eye could roam,
> Dark billows of an earthquake storm
>   Beflecked with clouds like foam,
> Their vales in misty shadow deep,
>   Their rugged peaks in shine,
> I saw the mountain ranges sweep ·
>   The horizon's northern line.

14 *

There towered Chocorua's peak; and west,
Moosehillock's woods were seen,
With many a nameless slide-scarred crest
And pine-dark gorge between.
Beyond them, like a sun-rimmed cloud,
The great Notch mountains shone,
Watched over by the solemn-browed
And awful face of stone!

It is indeed a grand view of Lafayette and Mount Cannon which Prospect Hill affords. And some portions of each of the ten counties of New Hampshire are within the range of our vision there. It is a question if the dome of Mount Washington itself is not visible on the north. Several of the noblest isolated mountains of the state show themselves to the best advantage,—the dark mass of Mooschillock heaving like a whale just beginning to dive, the amber colored sides of the desolate Cardigan, the blue declivities of the true Kiarsarge sloping off on the south in Merrimack county, and far below, the pale shapes which tell us where

Green-tufted, oak-shaded, by Amoskeag's fall
The twin Uncanoonucs rise stately and tall.

There are many persons who cannot make excursions that require horseback riding. The view from Mount Prospect should be especially noticed for their benefit, since it can be thoroughly enjoyed at the cost of no more exertion than a wagon ride, and an absence of four hours from the hotel.

Who that has driven on a clear day from Plymouth to Franconia can ever forget the ride ? Our most vivid impressions of its beauty are derived from a ride over it in the early summer, a year or two since. "The gold and the crystal cannot equal it ; and the exchange of it shall not be for jewels of fine gold." It was a perfect day of June.

And what is so rare as a day in June?
Then, if ever, come perfect days;
Then Heaven ·tries the earth if it be in tune,
And over it softly her warm ear lays:

Whether we look, or whether we listen,
We hear life murmur, or see it glisten;
Every clod feels a stir of might,
    An instinct within it that reaches and towers,
And, groping blindly above it for light,
    Climbs to a soul in grass and flowers;
The cowslip startles in meadows green,
    The buttercup catches the sun in its chalice,
And there's never a leaf nor a blade too mean
    To be some happy creature's palace;
The little bird sits at his door in the sun,
    Atilt like a blossom among the leaves,
And lets his illumined being o'errun
    With the deluge of summer it receives;
His mate feels the eggs beneath her wings,
And the heart in her dumb breast flutters and sings;
He sings to the wide world, and she to her nest,—
In the nice ear of Nature which song is the best?

It is to be regretted that the mountains are not visited during the splendid days of the early summer. From the middle of June to the middle of July, foliage is more fresh; the cloud scenery is nobler; the meadow grass has a more golden color; the streams are usually more full and musical; and there is a larger proportion of the "long light" of the afternoon, which kindles the landscape into the richest loveliness. The mass of visitors to the White Mountains go during the dogdays, and leave when the finer September weather sets in with its prelude touches of the October splendor. In August there are fewer clear skies; there is more fog; the meadows are apparelled in more sober green; the highest rocky crests may be wrapped in mists for days in succession; and a traveller has fewer chances of making acquaintance with a bracing mountain breeze. The latter half of June is the blossom season of beauty in the mountain districts; the first half of October is the time of its full-hued fruitage.

Let us hope that some of our readers will find opportunity to visit the Pemigewasset valley before the first of July, and have leisure enough also to devote a day or two, if no more, to the village of Campton. Where the bees persistently congregate, the honey must

be most plentiful. If the hovering and return of the artist bees is a
decisive test, the nectar of beauty must be secreted near Campton
on the Pemigewasset, and North Conway on the Saco, more freely
than along any other of the usually travelled stage-routes of the
mountains.

Some one has described the White Mountains as "the beam of a
pair of scales which drop some thirty miles, and hold on the East the
broad valley of Conway, balanced on the West by the charming intervales of Campton." This figure would be more applicable for con-
trasting the position and beauty of the scenery around Bethel and
North Conway. These villages do hang poised in position and in
loveliness from the curving beam of the Mount Washington range,—
the first depending from the eastern end of the chain on the line of
the Androscoggin, and the last from the western end on the line of
the Saco. Campton is not tethered to the Mount Washington chain,
but it may fairly be compared with North Conway for landscape
charm. It hangs a little lower down in latitude, and some artists
have maintained that, in the scale of beauty, it forces North Conway
to kick the beam. Others as stoutly deny this; and we, grateful
alike for the villages and artists, have no desire or intention, either
to adjust or mingle in the dispute.

Perhaps it is fair to say that the intervale alone in Campton is, in
proportion to its extent, more picturesquely effective than that of
North Conway. Being finely wooded, and better united to the bordering hills, it furnishes perfectly appropriate and beautiful foregrounds to the favorite views of valley and mountains, whose flitting
moods of superior beauty or grandeur have been promoted by many
painters, Mr. Durand and Mr. Gay especially, into the abiding
charm of art. The windings of the river in this intervale, with the
beauty, variety, and abundance of its trees, makes West Campton
rich in artists' "bits" of the utmost grace. Here, some elms, bordering large spaces of the smooth sward with green domed tops,
evenly poised upon their single columnar trunks, look, as an architectural friend once expressed it, like unwalled chapter-houses to the

cathedral groves. There, we find a sparkling group of varied foliage which we may call voluptuous, in which the golden plumes of the ash shine, perhaps, against the brown and olive darkness of the oak, and the butternut's pale yellow spray mingles with the shimmering gray of the beech, and the dull purple and emerald of the birch and wild cherry.

A visit to a place like Campton might be well employed in making the eye more sensitive to the colors and the characters of trees. Every painter sees how striking are the contrasts of hue between the oak and the beech, the elm and the lime, the aspen and the maple. They are not merely different kinds of green, but they take on absolutely different colors as a subtile effluence around their green, which is revealed to a careful and sensitive sight. And every one who delicately enjoys the colors on the hills, in the hour before sunset, finds that a mountain slope arrayed in birches dyes itself in floods of different splendor from one that is covered with larger or mixed growths of forest. Many persons who go to the mountains cannot distinguish a maple from a beech, an aspen from a birch, or a fir-tree from a pine. The pleasures of taste, as well as the pleasures of knowledge, begin and increase with the power of detecting fine differences, and of nicely discerning the individuality of objects. A man who should be thoroughly acquainted with the architecture of trees— the articulation of their boughs and branches, the angles or curves or arches which they describe, and which give each species a distinct character—the manner in which their foliage is set and massed, in which it plays with the wind or is swayed by it, and the hues in which their beauty or strength is draped, would find any landscape that presents a variety of trees perpetually attractive.

And the various hues of trees are no more marked than their various tones. The oak roars when a high wind wrestles with it; the beech shrieks; the elm sends forth a long, deep groan; the ash pours out moans of thrilling anguish. Perhaps a mind curious for analogies might detect some relation not entirely fanciful between the colors of trees in full sunlight, and their tones when thoroughly wak-

ened by the wind. Walter Scott once maintained that something
might be done by the union of poetry and music to imitate those
voices, giving a different measure to the oak, the pine, and the
willow. Our own poet, James Russell Lowell, has written some
charming interpretations of the characters of our prominent trees.
Let us listen to some of his verses on " The Birch " :—

> Rippling through thy branches goes the sunshine,
> Among thy leaves that palpitate forever;
> Ovid in thee a pining Nymph had prison'd
> The soul once of some tremulous inland river,
> Quivering to tell her woe, but, ah! dumb, dumb forever.

> Upon the brink of some wood-nestled lakelet,
> Thy foliage like the tresses of a Dryad,
> Dripping about thy slim white stem, whose shadow
> Slopes quivering down the waters dusky quiet,
> Thou shrinkst, as on her bath's edge would some startled Dryad

> Thou art the go-between of rustic lovers;
> Thy white bark has their secrets in its keeping;
> Reuben writes here the happy name of Patience,
> And thy lithe boughs hang murmuring and weeping
> Above her, as she steals the mystery from thy keeping.

> Thou art to me like my belovéd maiden,
> So frankly coy, so full of trembly confidences;
> Thy shadow scarce seems shade, thy pattering leaflets
> Sprinkle their gathered sunshine o'er my senses,
> And Nature gives me all her summer confidences.

> Whether my heart with hope or sorrow tremble,
> Thou sympathizest still; wild and unquiet,
> I fling me down, thy ripple, like a river,
> Flows valley-ward, where calmness is, and by it
> My heart is floated down into the land of quiet.

In many places on the river banks, or in the dried channels of
former freshets, and along the streams that feed the Pemigewasset,
plentiful studies are found of tufts and beds of grasses, sedgy banks,
weeds and flowering plants of the most splendid variety. Also fine
studies of " interiors," with wild passages of mountain brook and
cascade, can be made in some of the many ravines having their out-

lets here. Surrounded with such beauty as Campton presents, Goethe's subtle and seductive poem " Ganymede " interprets the feeling, half mystic, half voluptuous, which Nature inspires :—

How with morning splendor
Thou round upon me glowest,
Spring beloved!
With thousandfold love-rapture
How through my heart thrills
Thy warmth everlasting,
Holy and precious,
Infinite Nature.
Could I but compass thee
Within these arms!

Lo! on thy breast here
Prone I languish;
And thy flowers and thy grass
Press themselves on my heart.
Thou coolst the torturing
Thirst of my bosom,
Love breathing Morning wind!
Calleth the nightingale
Loving to me from the misty vale.
I come, I come;
Ah! whither away!

Up! Upward it draws!
The clouds are hovering
Downward, the clouds they
Condescend to passionate yearning!
Here! Here!
In your embraces
Upward!
Embraced and embracing,
Up! Up to thy bosom,
All loving Father!

Those that know this remarkable poem in the German will recognize, we are sure, in the rhythm and faithfulness of this version, never published before, the blended delicacy and vigor of a master's touch.

We have spoken on a former page of the beauty of the Welch Mountain, which forms the immediate background of the river view from Campton village. Its general shape is extremely picturesque.

15

Being nearly destitute of forest covering, and showing large masses of bare quartz, it presents very beautiful and striking harmonies of the grays with neutral hues of blue and white, and at sunrise and sunset exhibits proportional increase of splendor. The Sandwich

range, too, affords ample and important subjects to the dwellers in Campton for the enjoyment and study of mountain color and form. In all lights they are picturesque if not beautiful; but there is no limit to the softness, purity, and magnificence of color with which the setting sun sometimes floods their broad and rugged sides.

Of course the Franconia mountains form one of the leading attractions in the landscape here, West Campton being the southernmost point in the valley from which they can be advantageously seen. As they are visible from the meadow as well as from the hill-sides, the choice of several different combinations of middle and foregrounds is offered to all artists, and to those who love complex and proportioned beauty in the landscapes near their summer resting-place. We have known artists to say that the marvellous middle ground of belt and copse, and meadow and river, back of which the three sharp spires of Lafayette and his associates tower, to face the heavier rocky wall which forms the western rampart of the Notch, is the most enchanting scene of the kind which this valley and that of the Saco can offer.

In common daylight there is very little variety or picturesqueness in their aspect. No doubt persons who have seen mountains only under a dull sky, or through a very clear air, on a bright day, between the hours of nine and four, suppose that all descriptions of their splendor are either deliberately manufactured for the sake of fine writing, or illusions of fancy, proofs that

we receive but what we give,
And in our life alone does Nature live.

But let them study the Notch mountains of Franconia from the school-house in Campton, by the morning or evening light. They differ then from their ordinary aspects as much as rubies and sapphires from pebbles. See the early day pour down the upper slopes of the three easterly pyramids ; then upon the broad forehead of the Profile Mountain, kindling its gloomy brows with radiance, and melting the azure of its temples into pale violet ; and falling lower, staining with rose tints the cool mists of the ravines, till the Notch seems to expand, and the dark and rigid sides of it fall away as they lighten, and recede in soft perspective of buttressed wall and flushed tower,—and then say whether, to an eye that can never be satiated with the blue of a hyacinth, the purple of a fuschia, and the blush of a rose, the gorgeousness ascribed to the mountains is a mere exercise of rhetoric, or a fiction of the fancy. Or, towards evening of midsummer, at the same spot, see the great hills assume a deeper blue or purple ; see the burly Cannon Mountain stand, a dark abutment, at the gate of the Notch, unlighted except by its own pallor ; and, as the sun goes down, watch his last beams of crimson or orange cover with undevastating fire the pyramidal peaks of the three great Haystacks,

and then decide whether language can recall or report the pomp of the spectacle, any more than the cold colors of art can exaggerate what the Creator writes there in chaste and glowing flame.

> Then, as if the earth and sea had been
> Dissolved into one lake of fire, were seen
> Those mountains towering, as from waves of flame,
> Around the vaporous sun, from which there came
> The inmost purple spirit of light, and made
> Their very peaks transparent.

Have our readers considered this testimony of Mr. Ruskin ?   " In some sense, a person who has never seen the rose-color of the rays of dawn crossing a blue mountain twelve or fifteen miles away, can hardly be said to know what *tenderness* in color means at all. *Bright* tenderness he may, indeed, see in the sky or in a flower, but this grave tenderness of the far-away hill-purples he cannot conceive."

And now with the mountains in our mind's eye, from a point so favorable as Campton for enjoying their beauty, let us, before making a closer acquaintance with the Notch, raise the question of *their use.* Nothing is sublimer to the senses than a great mountain, though many other objects and forces of Nature are immeasurably more sublime to thought. A structure like Illimani or Aconcagua of the Andes, towering nearly five miles above the contented clods, bearing up the pine to look down upon the palm, defying the force of gravitation,

Standing alone 'twixt the earth and the heavens,
Heir of the sunset and herald of morn,

thrills the eye by the heroic energy with which the soaring mass seems to be vital, and by which of its own will it cleaves the air and converses with the sky. And yet what insignificant things they are, after all, when we measure them by our thought, in their relation to the surface and depth of the globe ! On the rim of a race-course a mile in circuit, if it could be lifted up as a great wheel, a pebble-stone three inches high would be larger in proportion than Mount Lafayette is, as a bunch on the planet itself. The thickness of a sheet of writing paper on an artificial sphere a foot in diameter, represents the eminence of the mountain chains. They are no more than the cracks in the varnish of such a ball. The roughnesses on the skin of an Havana orange are more marked than Chimborazo, Kinchin-Junga, and the valley of the Jordan, are upon the earth. And yet these trifling elevations and scratches reveal the heights and soundings of our knowledge of the planet.

What do we know of the four thousand miles radius of the earth ? What do we know of the air above the highest mountain tops ? It

grows rarer as we ascend; and but a few miles above the highest of
the Himalayas, no doubt, there is blackness of darkness, except to an
eye that should turn directly to the sun. The domain of light and of
knowledge lies within this petty film, whose top is nearly touched by
the little mountain heads that slightly roughen the roundness of the

world. Peel a pellicle from the planet, thinner in proportion than the
thinnest of the laminæ of an onion, and all our science and wisdom,
and all life, too, will be stripped off.

Yet, think of the uses of the little inequalities that we call mountains. Think of their service to the intellect. They are not excres-
cences on the globe's surface,—ridges of superfluous matter bolted
upon the original smoothness of our orb. Many of our readers pos-

sibly have seen pictures of mountains that look like mounds of putty, as though they had been stuck upon the landscape,—as though they had been *thumbed* into shape, and might be thumbed into any other form. But the mountains were heaved up from the planet's crust. It is in large measure by their help that the science of geology has advanced during the last century with rapid strides. They tell us something of what the earth's crust is made of, and the texture and thickness of its outer cuticles. By looking *up*, a man gains the same knowledge that he would acquire by sinking a mine of corresponding depth. The highest mountains are inverted shafts,—upspringing wedges of rock, flinging the garment of soil away, tilting and sepa-rating the strata through which they break, and standing bare for the scrutiny of science. Thus the highest mountain crests are tide lines of the force that slumbers in the planet's bosom. The most stiff and resistant features of the world to our senses, they are really the outbursts of the globe's passion, the witnesses of a pent fury that may yet break forth in violence not yet conceived, before which Ossa indeed is " but a wart," and Orizaba a mere toy.

Well has it been said, that " mountains are to the rest of the body of the earth what violent muscular action is to the body of man. The muscles and tendons of its anatomy are, in the mountain, brought out with fierce and convulsive energy, full of expression, passion, and strength ; the plains and the lower hills are the repose and the effort-less motion of the frame, when its muscles lie dormant and concealed beneath the lines of its beauty, yet ruling those lines in their every undulation." This vigor, this fierce vitality, in which they had their origin, is the source of much of the exhilaration which the sight of their wild outlines inspires, even when the beholder is unconscious of it. The waves of flame, that drove up the great wedges of granite in New Hampshire through ribs of sienite and gneiss, bolted them with traps of porphyry and quartz, crusted them with mica schist, and cross riveted them with spikes of iron, lead, and tin, suggest their power in the strength with which the mountains are organized into the landscape, just as the force of a man's temperament is shown in the lines of his jaw and nose.

The centre-fire heaves underneath the earth,
And the earth changes like a human face;
The molten ore bursts up among the rocks,
Winds into the stone's heart, outbranches bright
In hidden mines, spots barren river-beds,
Crumbles into fine sand where sunbeams bask—
God joys therein! The wroth sea's waves are edged
With foam, white as the bitten lip of Hate.
When, in the solitary waste, strange groups
Of young volcanoes come up, cyclops-like,
Staring together with their eyes on flame;—
God tastes a pleasure in their uncouth pride.

The uses of mountain ranges, in relation to the supply of water, are so evident that we need not dwell long upon them. It is plain that we could not live upon the globe in any state of civilization, if the surface had been finished as a monotonous prairie. Were it not for the great swells of land, the ridges and crests of rock, the wrinkles, curves, and writhings of the strata, how could springs of water be formed? what drainage could a country have? how could the rains be hoarded in fountains and lakes? where would be the storehouses of the snow and hail? " Every fountain and river, from the inch-deep streamlet that crosses the village lane in trembling clearness, to the massy and silent march of the everlasting multitude of waters in Amazon or Ganges, owe their play and purity and power, to the ordained elevations of the earth." Ah, how does the aqueduct masonry of Rome, or the Croton and Cochituate system of supply for cities, compare with Nature's chain of reservoirs,—the Rocky Mountains, the Andes, and the Alleghanies, and the service-pipes she gullies in their granite for pastures, towns, cities, and states!

The richest beauty that invests the mountains suggests this branch of their utility. The mists that settle round them, above which their cones sometimes float, aerial islands in a stagnant sea; the veils of rain that trail along them; the crystal snow that makes the light twinkle and dance ; the sombre thunder-heads that invest them with Sinai-like awe, are all connected with their mission as the hydraulic distributors of the world,—the mighty troughs that apportion to the land the moisture which the noiseless solar suction is ever lifting from the sea. Their peaks are the cradles, their furrows the first play-grounds, of the great rivers of the earth.

It is an equally obvious truth, that mountain chains diversify climates. By their condensing effect upon the wet sea-winds, they make some districts more moist than others, and so variegate fertilities and the products of vegetation. One side of a high mountain ridge receives much more rain than the other. For days together the valley of the Po is never clouded, because the Alps, shrouded in dense fogs, are drawing off the waters from the wet winds before they reach the Italian plains. And the Himalayas force the summer monsoons to wring out their bounty so thoroughly upon their southerly sides, that the steppes of inland Asia suffer to compensate for the bounteous rivers and rich vegetation of the Indian peninsula. The Pacific shore under the loftiest Andes is very dry and comparatively barren, because the trade winds, that blow across and enrich the countries of the Amazon from the Atlantic, are robbed of most of their bounty in scaling those cold summits from the East, and have little to disburse upon the western slopes. We are told that if a mountain system could be upheaved in Sahara, the hot breezes that sweep over it would be chilled and compelled to disgorge their booty, —so that the wilderness, sprinkled with rain and veined with rivers, would in time "blossom as the rose." As to our supply of water and our irrigation, we must, with David, "lift up our eyes to the hills, from whence cometh our help."

Mr. Ruskin notes it as one of the prominent uses of mountains, that they cause perpetual change in the soils of the earth. The physical geographers assure us that if the whole matter of the Alps were shovelled out over Europe, the level of the continent would be raised about twenty feet. And this process of levelling is continually going on. By a calculation, which he made in the valley of Chamouni, Mr. Ruskin believes that one of the insignificant runlets, only four inches wide and four inches deep, carries down from Mont Blanc

10

eighty tons of granite dust a year ; at which rate of theft at least eighty thousand tons of the substance of that mountain must be yearly transformed into drift sand by the streams, and distributed upon the plains below. On Whiteface Mountain, of the Sandwich group, a slide took place in 1820, which hurled down huge blocks of granite, sienite, quartz, felspar, and trap-rocks, and cut a deep ravine in the side of the mountain, several miles in extent. But compensation was made in part for its destructive fury. An extensive meadow at the base, which had borne only wild, coarse grasses, was rendered more fertile by the fine sediment, here and there four or five feet in depth, that was distributed upon it, and now produces excellent grass and white clover. Take a century or two into account, and we find the mountains fertilizing the soil by the minerals which they restore to it to compensate the wastes of the harvests. " The hills, which, as compared with living beings, seem everlasting, are, in truth, as perishing as they. Its veins of flowing fountain weary the mountain heart, as the crimson pulse does ours ; the natural force of the iron crag is abated in its appointed time, like the strength of the sinews in a human old age ; and it is but the lapse of the longer years of decay which, in the sight of its Creator, distinguishes the mountain range from the moth and the worm."

We see, then, in looking at a chain of lofty hills, and in thinking of their perpetual waste in the service of the lowlands, that the moral and physical worlds are built on the same pattern. They represent the heroes and all-beneficent genius. They receive upon their heads and sides the larger baptisms from the heavens, not to be selfish with their riches, but to give,—to give all that is poured upon them,—yes, and something of themselves with every stream and tide. When we look up at old Lafayette, or along the eastern slopes of Mount Washington, we find that the lines of noblest expression are those which the torrents have made, where soil has been torn out, and rocks have been grooved, and ridges have been made more nervous, and the walls of ravines have been channelled for noble pencillings of shadow, by the waste of the mountain in its patient suffering.

In its gala days of sunlight the artist finds that its glory is its character. All its losses are glorified then into expression. The great mountains rise in the landscape as heroes and prophets in history, ennobled by what they have given, sublime in the expressions of struggle and pain, invested with the richest draperies of light, because their brows have been torn, and their checks been furrowed by toils and cares in behalf of districts below. Upon the mountains is written the law, and in their grandeur is displayed the fulfilment of it, that perfection comes through suffering.

Let us again avail ourselves of Mr. Ruskin's help in unfolding the relations of mountains to changes of the air. " Change would, of course, have been partly caused by differences in soils and vegetation, even if the earth had been level ; but to a far less extent than it is now by the chains of hills, which, exposing on one side their masses of rock to the full heat of the sun, (increased by the angle at which the rays strike on the slope,) and on the other casting a soft shadow for leagues over the plains at their feet, divide the earth not only into districts, but into climates, and cause perpetual currents of air to traverse their passes, and ascend or descend their ravines, altering both the temperature and nature of the air as it passes, in a thousand different ways ; moistening it with the spray of their waterfalls, sucking it down and beating it hither and thither in the pools of their torrents, closing it within clefts and caves, where the sunbeams never reach, till it is as cold as November mists, then sending it forth again to breathe softly across the slopes of velvet fields, or to be scorched among sunburnt shales and grassless crags ; then drawing it back in moaning swirls through clefts of ice, and up into dewy wreaths above the snow-fields ; then piercing it with strange electric darts and flashes of mountain fire, and tossing it high in fantastic storm-cloud, as the dried grass is tossed by the mower, only suffering it to depart at last, when chastened and pure, to refresh the faded air of the far-off plains."

But we come to the highest use which mountains serve when we speak of their *beauty*. No farm in Coös county has been a tithe so serviceable as the cone of Mount Washington, with the harvests of color that have been reaped from it for the canvas of artists, or for the joy of visitors. Think of the loss to human nature if the summits of Mont Blanc and the Jungfrau could be levelled, and their jagged sides, sheeted with snow and flaming with amethyst and gold, should be softened by the sun and tilled for vines and corn. Pour out over them every year all the wine that is wrung from the vineyards of Italy and France, and what a mere sprinkling in comparison with the floods of amber, of purple, and of more vivid and celestial flames with which no wine was ever pierced, that are shed over them by one sunrise, or that flow up their cold acclivities at each clear sunset? The mountains are more grand and inspiring when we stand at the proper distance and look at them, than when we look from them. Their highest call is to be resting-places of the light, the staffs from which the most gorgeous banners of morning and evening are displayed. And these uses we may observe and enjoy among the moderate mountains of New Hampshire. They are huge lay figures on which Nature shows off the splendors of her aerial wardrobe. She makes them wear mourning veils of shadow, exquisite lace-work of distant rain, hoary wigs of cloud, the blue costume of northwest winds, the sallow dress of sultry southern airs, white wrappers of dog-day fog, purple and scarlet vests of sunset light, gauzy films of moonlight, the gorgeous embroidery of autumn chemistries, the flashing ermine dropped from the winter sky, and the glittering jewelry strewn over their snowy vestments by the cunning fingers of the frost. These are the crops which the intellect and heart find waiting and waving for them, without any effort or care of mortal culture, on the upper barrenness of the hills.

> So call not waste that barren cone
> Above the floral zone,
> Where forests starve:
> It is pure use;—
> What sheaves like those which here we glean and bind
> Of a celestial Ceres and the Muse?

And besides the beauty of light, let us hear Mr. Ruskin interpret the charm added to the earth by the geological relation of the hills to the country that is dependent from them, as well as upon them. This beauty is also part of their use. And it is to be accredited to the mountains as no small benefaction that they have been the means of adding the following passage to the treasury of English literature : " The great mountains *lift* the lowlands *on their sides.* Let the reader imagine, first, the appearance of the most varied plain of some richly cultivated country ; let him imagine it dark with graceful woods, and soft with deepest pastures ; let him fill the space of it, to the utmost horizon, with innumerable and changeful incidents of scenery and life ; leading pleasant streamlets through its meadows, strewing clusters of cottages beside their banks, tracing sweet footpaths through its avenues, and animating its fields with happy flocks, and slow wandering spots of cattle ; and when he has wearied himself with endless imagining, and left no space without some loveliness of its own, let him conceive all this great plain, with its infinite treasures of natural beauty and happy human life, gathered up in God's hands from one edge of the horizon to the other, like a woven garment ; and shaken into deep falling folds, as the robes droop from a king's shoulders ; all its bright rivers leaping into cataracts along the hollows of its fall, and all its forests rearing themselves aslant against its slopes, as a rider rears himself back when his horse plunges ; and all its villages nestling themselves into the new windings of its glens ; and all its pastures thrown into steep waves of greensward, dashed with dew along the edges of their folds, and sweeping down into endless slopes, with a cloud here and there lying quietly, half on the grass, half in the air; and he will have as yet, in all this lifted world, only the foundation of one of the great Alps. And whatever is lovely in the lowland scenery becomes lovelier in this change : the trees which grew heavily and stiffly from the level line of plain assume strange curves of strength and grace as they bend themselves against the mountain side ; they breathe more freely, and toss their branches more carelessly, as each climbs higher, looking to the clear light above the top-

most leaves of its brother tree ; the flowers which on the arable plain
fell before the plough, now find out for themselves unapproachable
places, where year by year they gather into happier fellowship, and
fear no evil ; and the streams which in the level land crept in dark
eddies by unwholesome banks, now move in showers of silver, and are
clothed with rainbows, and bring health and life wherever the glance
of their waves can reach."

THE FRANCONIA NOTCH.

Methinks ye take luxurious pleasure
In your novel western leisure;
So cool your brows and freshly blue,
As Time had nought for ye to do:
.   .   .   .
While we enjoy a lingering ray,
Ye still o'ertop the western day,
Reposing yonder on God's croft
Like solid stacks of hay;
So bold a line as ne'er was writ
On any page by human wit;
The forest glows as if
An enemy's camp-fires shone
Along the horizon.
Or the day's funeral pyre
Were lighted there;
Edged with silver and with gold,
The clouds hang o'er in damask fold,
And with such depth of amber light
The west is dight,
Where still a few rays slant,
That even Heaven seems extravagant.

The Franconia Notch, to which the lines just quoted furnish an
appropriate introduction, is a pass about five miles in extent between
one of the western walls of Lafayette and Mount Cannon. The valley is about half a mile wide ; and the narrow district thus inclosed

contains more objects of interest to the mass of travellers, than any other region of equal extent within the compass of the usual White Mountain tour. In the way of rock sculpture and waterfalls, it is a huge museum of curiosities. There is no spot usually visited in any of the valleys, where the senses are at once impressed so strongly and so pleasantly with the wildness and the freshness which a stranger instinctively associates with mountain scenery in New Hampshire. There is no other spot where the visitor is domesticated amid the most savage and startling forms in which cliffs and forest are combined. And yet there is beauty enough intermixed with the sublimity and the wildness to make the scenery permanently attractive, as well as grand and exciting.

The mountains are not nearly so high, or so noble in form, around the Franconia Pass as around the Glen; but the walls are much closer and more precipitous. The place where the Profile House is situated would be much more properly called a glen, than the opening which now bears that name by the Peabody River, at the base of Mount Washington. There is no wild and frowning rock scenery either visible or easily accessible from the Glen House. In the White Mountain Notch there is no hotel at which travellers stay. The Crawford House is situated just outside of it. And if there were a hotel so placed within it as to command its vast walls and its most powerful lines, the scene would be too terrific and desolate to win travellers to a visit of many days. The sides of the White Mountain Notch are many hundred feet higher than the highest cliff of Franconia. But they are torn with landslides and torrents; there is very little forest growth upon them; and their bare sand and gravel, and their scarred, grim ledges, overpower and awe sufficiently to overshadow the sense of pleasure and refreshment which one wants to feel in the scenery which he chooses to dwell in for several weeks or days. That which makes the White Mountain Notch the most astonishing spectacle, at the first visit, or on any short visit, which the whole region has to show, makes it the less welcome as a place to stay in.

The Franconia Pass is not oppressive. Large portions of the wall opposite the Profile House are even more sheer than the Willey Mountain, or Mount Webster, in the great Notch ; but it bends in a very graceful curve ; the purple tinge of the rocks is always grateful to the eye ; and instead of the sandy desolation over and around the Willey House, the forest foliage that clambers up the sharp acclivities, fastening its roots in the crevices and resisting the torrents and the gale, relieves the sombreness of the bending battlement by its color, and soften its sublimity with grace. Every one who has been driven into Franconia from Bethlehem or from Littleton, and who has had the privilege of an outside seat on the stage, must have been struck with the gentle crescent line of the vast outworks of Lafayette, suggesting the sweep of a tremendous amphitheatre, whose walls are alive with the ascending orders of the wilderness.

One of the most interesting portions of the steep easterly rampart of the Notch is the Eagle Cliff, immediately in front of the Profile House, which shoots up some fifteen hundred feet above the road. It derives its name from the fact that a pair of the winged " Arabs of the air " have kept far up on the cliff their " chamber near the sun." It is a charming object to study. Except in some of the great ravines of the Mount Washington range, which it costs great toil to reach, there is no such exhibition of precipitous rock to be found. And how gracefully it is festooned with the climbing birches, maples, spruces, and vines ! There are those to whom the sight of such a crag, sharply set at the angle of a mountain wall, is one of the most enjoyable and memorable privileges of a tour among the hills. Such will find the best points for appreciating the height and majesty of the Eagle Cliff, by ascending a few hundred feet on the Cannon Mountain opposite, or by walking to the borders of Profile Lake only a moderate distance from the hotel. If there were a pleasant boat on this small sheet of water, visitors would find it a most delightful use of the hour before sunset, to see from the further shore the ebbing of the ruddy light from the base of the cliff, till fainter contrasts of purple and green are left again in the evening shadow. In thinking of that view as it was given, towards sunset, while seated under the shadow of the dark firs that hem the western edge of the Profile Lake, the music of the good old abbot's evening meditation, in Longfellow's " Golden Legend," floats into our memory :—

Slowly, slowly up the wall
Steals the sunshine, steals the shade;
Evening damps begin to fall,
Evening shadows are display'd.
Round me, o'er me, everywhere,
All the sky is grand with clouds,
And athwart the evening air
Wheel the swallows home in crowds.
Shafts of sunshine from the west
Paint the dusky windows red;
Darker shadows, deeper rest,
Underneath and overhead.
Darker, darker, and more wan
In my breast the shadows fall,
Upward steals the life of man
As the sunshine from the wall.
From the wall into the sky,
From the roof along the spire;
Ah, the souls of those that die
Are but sunbeams lifted higher.

This cliff, and the whole wall with which it is connected, shows its height more impressively in some of the misty dogdays, when fogs play their tricks along its breastworks. Sometimes they break away above, and let the pinnacles of rock be seen disconnected from the base. Then we can hardly believe that Lafayette himself has not moved a little nearer, and pushed aside the curtains to look down at the Profile House. Sometimes they tear themselves into horizontal strips, through whose lines of gray the green and purple of the trees and rocks give peculiar pleasure to the eye. Sometimes they thicken below and break above, to show a dash or a long line of delicate amber light upon the edge of the wall. At last the whole texture gets mysteriously loosened, and the broad curtain begins at once to rise and melt. The sunshine pours unobstructed over the Notch, and

17

only here and there a shred of the morning fog is left to loiter upwards. Watch it, and think of Bryant's poem:

Earth's children cleave to Earth—her frail
Decaying children dread decay.
Yon wreath of mist that leaves the vale,
And lessens in the morning ray:
Look how, by mountain rivulet,
It lingers as it upward creeps,
And clings to fern and copsewood set
Along the green and dewy steeps;
Clings to the fragrant kalmia, clings
To precipices fringed with grass,
Dark maples where the wood-thrush sings,
And bowers of fragrant sassafras.
Yet all in vain—it passes still
From hold to hold, it cannot stay,
And in the very beams that fill
The world with glory, wastes away,
Till, parting from the mountain's brow,
It vanishes from human eye,
And that which sprung of earth is now
A portion of the glorious sky.

The most attractive advertisement of the Franconia Notch to the travelling public is the rumor of the " Great Stone Face," that hangs upon one of its highest cliffs. If its inclosing walls were less grand, and its water gems less lovely, travellers would be still, perhaps, as strongly attracted to the spot, that they might see a mountain which breaks into human expression,—a piece of sculpture older than the Sphynx,—an intimation of the human countenance, which is the crown of all beauty, that was pushed out from the coarse strata of New England thousands of years before Adam.

The marvel of this countenance, outlined so distinctly against the sky at an elevation of nearly fifteen hundred feet above the road, is greatly increased by the fact that it is composed of three masses of rock which are not in perpendicular line with each other. On the brow of the mountain itself, standing on the visor of the helmet that covers the face, or directly underneath it on the shore of the little lake, there is no intimation of any human features in the lawless rocks. Remove but a few rods either way from the guide-board on the road, where you are advised to look up, and the charm is dissolved. Mrs. Browning has connected a law of historical and social insight with a passage and a fancy, that many of our readers will be

glad to associate with their visit to the spot where the granite Profile is revealed to them :—

> Every age,
> Through being beheld too close, is ill-discerned
> By those who have not lived past it. We'll suppose
> Mount Athos carved, as Persian Xerxes schemed,
> To some colossal statue of a man:
> The peasants, gathering brushwood in his ear,
> Had guess'd as little of any human form
> Up there, as would a flock of browsing goats.
> They'd have, in fact, to travel ten miles off
> Or ere the giant image broke on them,
> Full human profile, nose and chin distinct,
> Mouth, muttering rhythms of silence up the sky,

And fed at evening with the blood of suns;
Grand torso,—hand, that flung perpetually
The largesse of a silver river down
To all the country pastures. 'Tis even thus
With times we live in,—evermore too great
To be apprehended near.

One of Mr. Hawthorne's admirable "Twice-told Tales" has woven
a charming legend and moral about this mighty Profile ; and in his
description of the face the writer tells us : " It seemed as if an enormous giant, or Titan, had sculptured his own likeness on the precipice. There was the broad arch of the forehead, a hundred feet in
height ; the nose, with its long bridge ; and the vast lips, which, if
they could have spoken, would have rolled their thunder accents
from one end of the valley to the other." We must reduce the scale
of the charming story-teller's description. The whole profile is about
eighty feet in length ; and of the three separate masses of rock which
are combined in its composition, one forms the forehead, another the
nose and upper lip, and the third the chin. The best time to see the
Profile is about four in the afternoon of a summer day. Then, standing by the little lake at the base and looking up, one fulfils the appeal
of our great transcendental poet in a literal sense in looking at the
jutting rocks, and,

through their granite seeming
Sees the smile of reason beaming.

The expression is really noble, with a suggestion partly of fatigue and
melancholy. He seems to be waiting for some visitor or message.
On the front of the cliff there is a pretty plain picture of a man with
a pack on his back, who seems to be endeavoring to go up the valley.
Perhaps it is the arrival of this arrested messenger that the old stone
visage has been expecting for ages. The upper portion of the mouth
looks a little weak, as though the front teeth had decayed, and the
granite lip had consequently fallen in. Those who can see it with a
thundercloud behind, and the slaty scud driving thin across it, will
carry away the grandest impression which it ever makes on the beholder's mind. But when, after an August shower, late in the after-

noon, the mists that rise from the forest below congregate around it, and, smitten with sunshine, break as they drift against its nervous outline, and hiding the mass of the mountain which it overhangs, isolate it with a thin halo, the countenance, awful but benignant, is " as if a mighty angel were sitting among the hills, and enrobing himself in a cloud vesture of gold and purple."

The whole mountain from which the Profile starts is one of the noblest specimens of majestic rock that can be seen in New Hampshire. One may tire of the craggy countenance sooner than of the sublime front and vigorous slopes of Mount Cannon itself—especially as it is seen, with its great patches of tawny color, in driving up from the lower part of the Notch to the Profile House. Yet the interest of the mountain to visitors has been so concentrated in the Profile, that very few have studied and enjoyed the nobler grandeur on which that countenance is only a fantastic freak. And many, doubtless, have looked up with awe to the Great Stone Face, with a feeling that a grander expression of the Infinite power and art is suggested in it than in any mortal countenance. " Is not this a place," we have heard it said, " to feel the insignificance of man ? " Yes, before God, perhaps, but not before matter. The rude volcanic force that puffed the molten rocks into bubbles, has lifted nothing so marvellous in structure as a human skeleton. The earthquakes and the frosts that have shaken and gnawed the granite of Mount Cannon into the rough semblance of an intelligent physiognomy, are not to be compared for wonder to the slow action of the chemistries that groove, chasten, and tint the bones and tissues of a human head into correspondence with the soul that animates it, as it grows in wisdom and moral beauty. The life that veins and girdles the noblest mountain on the earth, is shallow to the play of vital energies within a human frame.

> No mountain can
> Measure with a perfect man.

The round globe itself is only the background upon which the human face is chiselled. Each one of us *wears* more of the Infinite art,—is housed in more of the Infinite beneficence, than is woven into the whole material vesture of New Hampshire. And the mind that can sap the mountain, untwist its structure, and digest the truth it hides, —the taste that enjoys its form and draperies,—the soul whose solemn joy, stirred at first by the spring of its peaks, and the strength of its buttresses, mounts to Him who "toucheth the hills and they smoke,"—these are the voyagers for which the Creator built

> this round sky-cleaving boat
> Which never strains its rocky beams;
> Whose timbers, as they silent float,
> Alps and Caucasus uprear,
> And the long Alleghanies here,
> And all town-sprinkled lands that be,
> Sailing through stars with all their history.

The forenoon can be very profitably spent by guests in the Profile House who love mountain climbing, in scaling Mount Cannon,—after they have explored the track of the charming cascade, just back of the hotel, that flings its silver down with grace and music, to be stranded into the flashing tide of the Pemigewasset below. But towards evening a visit must without fail be paid to

ECHO LAKE.

When we begin to criticize, or make exceptions to, the scenery of the great White Mountain range, we speak at once of the lack of water. It makes the artistic sense quite thirsty to live several weeks near their base. If we had full power over the scenery near the highest range to alter or amend it, we should order a lake to appear forthwith in "The Glen." Then the spot would be perfect. To be able to sail about over a liquid mirror covering the whole gorge of the Peabody River in front of the Glen House ;—to see the clouds sweeping under you in a mighty bowl of blue ; to paddle around the bend of such a lake towards Gorham, and catch the Narcissus of the range, Mount Madison, secluded from his fellows, gazing at his own symmetry ; to look down at the pyramid of Adams, hanging soft and steady in an illusive sky ; to skim along in the shadow of Washington, observing the heavy roll of his shoulder like an arrested wave, or the delicate ambrotype of the nervous edge of the spur that bounds Tuckerman's ravine ; to be able to watch the speckled lights and shadows slowly shifting over the whole line of the sunken chain ;—or, more fascinating than all, to see a gorgeous October in such a magic glass, snowy summits with trailing mists dropping from bulky slopes that are gay with blooming forests,—what is there this side the Alps that could then compare with that spot ?   Oh ! for one rub on the lamp of Aladdin !   Oh, for the advent of some artist-Moses, whose rod might smite those rocks, and make the Peabody torrent swell and spread to the amplitude of such a silvery sheet, thus, far more than duplicating the beauty of the spot, while endowing the mountain chain with self-consciousness.

But enough of imaginary lakes.   Franconia is more fortunate in its little tarn that is rimmed by the undisturbed wilderness, and watched by the grizzled peak of Lafayette, than in the old Stone Face from which it has gained so much celebrity.   Echo Lake is the only sheet of still water that nestles near any one of the higher White Mountains.   How much joy has it fed in human hearts ! Something of its bounty expended upon the infant Pemigewasset is borne down into the Merrimack, and contributes to the power that moves the Wheels of Nashua and Lowell, and supplies a thousand operatives with bread.   But its more sacred use is not narrowed to the bounds of the stream which it supplies in part with gentle pulse. Thousands have seen it whose hearts its springs have fed with unwasting water, and in whose memory its beautiful surface, swept by the gentle edges of the summer breeze, and burnished by the sunlight, is a sweet and perennial symbol of purity and peace.

We have heard of persons that were called " embodied sympathies."   Is not this the true definition of a little mountain lake ?   It is a mirror, an interpreter of what enfolds and oversweeps it.   See what colors and forms it is stained with or hides! The little segment of beach it repeats. The rocks around it it sets below as part of the wall of its under stillness. The climbing trees and the shadow of the steep shores make a large section of its borders dim with dusky green. The sky hues, blue or gray, brilliant or sober, dull or joyous,

it clothes itself with. It answers to the temper of the wind, with smiling ripples, or slaty churlishness, or heaving petulance. It is glad in the colors of sunrise, and pensive as the flames of sunset cool in the west. Hardly a rod of its surface wears any color, when you look at it steadily, that can be said to belong to itself. And yet it does not merely mimic what is shown to it. It takes the moods of mountain, woods, and firmament into its own being, softly flashes their joy, or is saturated with their grief, and repeats to them their experience, as the heart of a friend returns the color of our fortunes or our moods. The mountains stand in Nature's eloquent hieroglyphics as the types of sturdy and suffering service ; the rivers, for unwearied, cheering, life-renewing charities ; the little lakes, for the beauty, the sweetness, the refreshment of that noiseless sympathy, not revealing itself in the new products of an active beneficence like the moving waters,—from the rills that gush through tiny lanes of grass to streams that over-flow bounty upon the meadows,—but which none the less belongs to the exquisite and sacred ministries of love upon the earth, without which the world would be " a dry and thirsty land where no water is." How delicate and graceful in suggestion, melody, and fancy, are these verses from the poet Milnes : —

Till death the tide of thought may stem,
There's little chance of our forgetting
The highland lake, the water gem,
With all its rugged mountain-setting.

Our spirits followed every cloud
That o'er it, and within it, floated;
Our joy in all the scene was loud,
Yet one thing silently we noted:

That, though the glorious summer hue
That steeped the heav'ns could scarce be brighter,
The blue below was still more blue,
The very light itself was lighter.

And each the other's fancy caught
By one instinctive glance directed;
How doubly glows the Poet's thought
In the belov'd one's breast reflected!

It is towards evening that visitors are usually drawn to the lake to sail upon it, and hear the echoes from which it derives its name. It is better worth visiting then, however, for its echoes of color than of sound.

18

> For now the eastern mountain's head
> On the dark lake throws lustre red;
> Bright gleams of gold and purple streak
> Ravine and precipice and peak—
> (So earthly power at distance shows;
> Reveals his splendor, hides his woes.)

But the echoes are interesting, whether repeating from the moun-tain walls the notes of the voice, or

> Replying shrilly to the well-tuned horns,

or rolling back on the shore the reports of the cannon that " tears the cave where Echo lies." These it returns in sevenfold reduplications of thunder, as wall behind wall of the mountain amphitheatre catches the sound on its crescent and tosses it up towards old Lafayette,

> Till high upon his misty side
> Languish'd the mournful notes, and died.
> For never sounds, by mortal made,
> Attain'd his high and haggard head,
> That echoes but the tempest's moan,
> Or the deep thunder's rending groan.

The last four lines our readers will not understand as referring to the noise of the cannon which, of course, must be clearly enough heard on the top of Lafayette. For all screams of the human voice or bugle notes, however, and such " sounds by mortals made," it is as true for Lafayette as for " stern old Coolin," in whose behalf Scott wrote it. Those of our readers who are familiar with Wordsworth's poems on the naming of places, will at once recall the passage which we here transcribe, as the most vivid description of mountain echoes in the compass of English literature.

> When I had gazed perhaps two minutes space,
> Joanna, looking in my eyes, beheld
> That ravishment of mine, and laughed aloud.
> The Rock, like something starting from a sleep,
> Took up the Lady's voice, and laughed again;
> That ancient Woman, seated on Helm-crag,
> Was ready with her cavern: Hammar-scar,
> And the tall Steep of Silver-how, sent forth
> A noise of laughter; southern Loughrigg heard.

And Fairfield answered with a mountain tone;
Helvellyn far into the clear blue sky
. Carried the Lady's voice,—old Skiddaw blew
His speaking-trumpet;—back out of the clouds
Of Glaramara southward came the voice;
And Kirkstone tossed it from his misty head.

Thus far, we have been held by the attractions in the upper part
of Franconia Notch that immediately surround the Profile House.
We must now follow the Pemigewasset a few miles below, to the
southern opening of the pass, where the Flume House commands
the widening valley. Those who would thoroughly enjoy a forenoon,
and taste with eye and ear the freshness of the forest, the glancing
light on a mountain stream, the occasional rare beauty of the mosses
on its banks, the colors at the bottom of its cool, still pools, the
overarching grace of its trees, or the busy babble of its broken and
sparkling tide, should walk from one hotel to the other, down the
river which runs parallel with the road, but which is for the most
part concealed from it by the forest. A real lover of Nature, who
has time at command, will no more consent to lose the pleasures
which these rambles give in unveiling the coy charms of Nature's
wildness, for the sake of the greater ease and speed of the stage,
than he would think of taking his "dinner concentrated in a
pill."

Rev. Henry Ward Beecher tells us: "I have always wished that
there might be a rock-spring upon my place. I could wish to
have, back of the house some two hundred yards, a steep and tree-
covered height of broad, cold, and mossy rocks — rocks that have
seen trouble, and been upheaved by deep inward forces, and are
lying in any way of noble confusion, full of clefts, and dark and
mysterious passages, without echoes in them, upholstered with pendu-
lous vines and soft with deep moss. Upon all this silent tumult of
wild and shattered rocks, struck through with stillness and rest, the
thick forest should shed down a perpetual twilight. The only glow
that ever chased away its solemn shadows should be the red rose-light
of sunsets, shot beneath the branches and through the trunks, lighting

up the gray rocks with strange golden glory." Mr. Beecher refers
to the light which Longfellow has described in Hiawatha : —   .

> Slowly o'er the simmering landscape
> Fell the evening's dusk and coolness,
> And the long and level sunbeams
> Shot their spears into the forest,
> Breaking through its shields of shadow,
> Rushed into each secret ambush,
> Searched each thicket, dingle, hollow.

" What light is so impressive as this last light of the day streaming
into a forest so dark that even insects leave it silent ? Yes, another
light is as strange—that rose-light of the afternoon, which shines
down a hill-side of vivid green grass, taking its hues, and strikes
through the transparent leaves into the forest below, and spreads
itself along the ground in a tender color for which we have no name,
as if green were just melting into rose color, and orange color were
just seizing them both.

" But to return to the spring. In such a rock forest as I have
spoken of, far up in one of its silent aisles, a spring should burst
forth, making haste from the seams of the rock, as if just touched
with the prophet's rod—cold, clear, copious, and musical from its
birth. All the way to the outer edge of the forest it should find
its own channels, and live its own life, unshaped by human hands.
But before the sun touched it, we should have a rock reservoir, into
which it should gather its congregation of drops now about to go
forth into useful life."

The Basin, about a mile from the Flume House, to which the walk
down the Pemigewasset leads us, is just what the poetic preacher
would desire to have transported to his grounds. The granite bowl,
sixty feet in circumference, is filled with water ten feet deep, that
is pellucid as air. The rocky shelf, twenty feet above, has been
grooved by a cascade that perpetually pours over ; and into the
depths of cool shadow below, golden flakes of light sink down like
falling leaves. If it did not lie so near the dusty road, or if a landscape gardener could be commissioned to arrange the surroundings of

it, it would be as rare a gem as the Franconia cabinet of curiosities could show.

> There is a silent pool, whose glass
> Reflects the lines of earth and sky;
> The hues of heaven along it pass,
> And all the verdant forestry
>
> And in that shining downward view,
> Each cloud, and leaf, and little flower,
> Grows 'mid a watery sphere anew,
> And doubly lives the summer hour.
>
> Beside the brink, a lovely maid
> Against a furrowed stem is leaning,
> To watch the painted light and shade
> That give the mirror form and meaning.
>
> Her shape and cheek, her eyes and hair,
> Have caught the splendor floating round;
> She in herself embodies there
> All life that fills sky, lake, and ground.
>
> And while her looks the crystal meets,
> Her own fair image seems to rise;
> And, glass-like, too, her heart repeats
> The world that there in vision lies.

The best way to enjoy the beauty of the Basin, is to ascend to the highest of the cascades that slide along a mile of the slope of the mountain at the west. Then follow down by their pathways, as they make the rocks now white with foam, now glassy with smooth, thin, transparent sheets, till they mingle their water with the Pemigewasset at the foot, and pouring their common treasury around the groove worn into the rocky roof, fall with musical splash into the shadowed reservoir beneath. Wordsworth has versified a tradition connected with such a pool among the Cumberland hills. We can enjoy the poetry of it by the Basin, if we are not allowed to associate its pathos with the air shadowed by that mossy granite, and moist with spray that broke not long before in rain upon the mountain-tops.

> A love-lorn Maid, at some far-distant time,
> Came to this hidden pool, whose depths surpass

In crystal clearness Dian's looking-glass;
And, gazing, saw that Rose, which from the prime
Derives its name, reflected as the chime
Of echo doth reverberate some sweet sound:
The starry treasure from the blue profound
She longed to ravish;—shall she plunge, or climb
The humid precipice, and seize the guest
Of April, smiling high in upper air?   ,
Desperate alternative! what fiend could dare
To prompt the thought? Upon the steep rock's breast
The lonely Primrose yet renews its bloom,
Untouched memento of her hapless doom!

If we were pained a little by the ill-framing of the Basin, we cannot withhold admiration and gratitude that the approach to

THE FLUME

has been so pleasantly preserved from everything that can intrude by discordant associations upon its romantic charms. From the travelled road we pass into a rough, winding wagon-road in the forest. Leaving the wagon, we mount by a footpath that leads nearer and nearer to the sweet melody, that gives a promise to the ear which is not to be broken to the hope. Soon we reach the clean and sloping granite floors over which the water slips in thin, wide, even sheets of crystal colorlessness. Above this, we meet those gentle ripples over rougher ledges that are embossed with green. Then, still higher up, where the rocks grow more uneven, we are held by the profuse beauty of the hues shown upon the bright stones at the bottom of the little translucent basins and pools. Still above, we come to the remarkable fissure in the mountain, more than fifty feet high, and several hundred feet long, which narrows, too, towards the upper end, till it becomes only twelve feet wide, and which, doubtless, an earthquake made for the passage of the stream which the visitors are now to ascend. We go up, stepping from rock to rock, now walking along a little plank pathway, now mounting by some rude steps, here and there crossing from side to side of the ravine by primitive little bridges, that bend under the feet and that are railed by birch-poles, and then climbing the rocks again, while the spray breaks upon us from the dashing and roaring stream, till we arrive at a little bridge which spans the narrowest part of the ravine.

How wild the spot is! Which shall we admire most,—the glee of he little torrent that rushes beneath our feet; or the regularity and smoothness of the frowning walls through which it goes foaming out into the sunshine; or the splendor of the dripping emerald mosses

that line them ; or the trees that overhang their edges ; or the huge
boulder, egg-shaped, that is lodged between the walls just over the
bridge where we stand,—as unpleasant to look at, if the nerves are
irresolute, as the sword of Damocles, and yet held by a grasp out of
which it will not slip for centuries ?   Was ever such an amount of
water put to more various and romantic use, in being poured down a
few hundred feet for calmer and prosaic service in the river below ?

> The struggling Rill insensibly is grown
> Into a Brook of loud and stately march,
> Crossed ever and anon by plank or arch;
> And, for like use, lo! what might seem a zone
> Chosen for ornament—stone matched with stone
> In studied symmetry, with interspace
> For the clear waters to pursue their race
> Without restraint. How swiftly have they flown,
> Succeeding—still succeeding! Here the Child
> Puts, when the high-swoln Flood runs fierce and wild,
> His budding courage to the proof; and here
> Declining Manhood learns to note the sly
> And sure encroachments of infirmity,
> Thinking how fast time runs, life's end how near!

One should remain at the Flume House a day or two, at least, in
order to have the privilege of visiting " The Flume " two or three
times.   Most persons see it only once, and then in connection with
large parties when there is too much confusion, distraction, and
chatter.   The early morning is the best time to seek it; and if not
more than three or four will go together, the beauty of the place will
open itself as it cannot in the first visit, and as it will not to a crowd.
In the Odyssey we read of

> a lovely cave,
> Dusky and sacred to the Nymphs, whom men
> Call Naiads.   .   .   .   .   .   .
>   In it, too, are long looms
> Of stone, and there the Nymphs do weave their robes,
> Sea-purple, wondrous to behold.   Aye-flowing
> Waters are there.   Two entrances it hath ;
> That to the north is pervious unto men;
> That to the south more sacred is, and there
> Men enter not, but 'tis the Immortals' path.

This southerly entrance to the Flume may be found by those who seek it quietly, and with reverence for the Spirit out of whose perennial bounty all beauty pours.

If we could visit Franconia in winter we should, no doubt, find scenery more startling than any which the summer has to offer. Those of our readers will believe it who have seen stereoscopic views of the Flume when

> those eagle-baffling mountains
> Slept in their shrouds of snow ;— beside the ways
>
> The waterfalls were voiceless — for their fountains
> Were changed to mines of sunless crystal now,
> Or by the curdling winds — like brazen wings
>
> Which clanged along the mountain's marble brow —
> Warped into adamantine fretwork, hung
> And filled with frozen light the chasm below.

The Flume is the chief attraction in the immediate neighborhood of the Flume House, as the Profile is of the narrower portion of the Notch five miles above. And the Pool is another of its resources,— a gloomy, natural well in the forest, a hundred fifty feet broad, and about as deep, which holds perpetually about forty feet of water.

> At noon-day here
> 'Tis twilight, and at sunset blackest night.

If this was hollowed out for Naiads, they must be of a very sullen temper, Nymphs of the Stygian order, that love

> some uncouth cell,
> Where brooding Darkness spreads his jealous wings
> And the night raven sings.

One of the grandest cascades of the mountain region has been discovered on Mooschillock River, the child of a hill unnamed as yet, which is climbed by a path about two miles below the hotel. It is in such a hurry to get away from home, that it goes on the jump, almost all the way, to join the Pemigewasset, making two leaps of eighty feet each, one immediately after the other, which, as we climb towards them, gleam as one splendid line of light through the trees

19

and shrubbery that fringe the rocky cleft. Is it not possible to give them a more appropriate name than "Georgiana Falls?" The view

from the summit of the ridge that nurtures this adventurous stream, has been pronounced by the native philosopher, whom many of our readers have heard discourse at the Pool about geology and the fate of Captain Symmes, " the stalwartest prospect in all Franconi'."

But the view from the Flume House itself is a perpetual refreshment, and one needs not seek by hard climbing or wandering for any increased temptation to contentment. No scenes can be more strongly contrasted in spirit and influence than those around the two hotels, five miles apart. From the Flume House the general view is cheerful and soothing. There is no place among the mountains where the fever can be taken more gently and cunningly out of a worried or burdened brain. So soft and delicate are the general features of the outlook over the widening Pemigewasset valley! So rich the gradation of the lights over the miles of gently sloping forest that sweeps down towards Campton! So pleasant the openings here and there that show a cluster of farm-houses, and the bright beauty of cultivated meadows inclosed by the deeper green of the wilderness! How can the eye ever drain, or the mind ever weary of the loveliness in form and color of those hills that bubble off to the horizon? And here, too, we can have more of the landscape beauty of the larger mountains than the greater nearness of the Profile House to them would allow. The three peaks of the highest Haystacks, Lafayette, Pleasant, and Liberty, are in view, and at evening one can see the glorious purple mount the forests that hang shaggy on their sides,—extinguishing the green as completely as if the trees for miles had suddenly been clothed with leaves of amethyst,—and then chased by the shadow retreat upwards till it dyes the rocks with its harmless fire, and still upwards to the peaks, and then leaps to the clouds above, where

> slowly from the scene
> The stooping sun upgathers his spent shafts,
> And puts them back into his golden quiver.

Or, by an easy climb of half an hour up Mount Pemigewasset directly back of the hotel,—a climb not at all difficult in dry weather to ladies,—the sunset view will be far more impressive. The spurs and hollows of Lafayette and his associates will be lighted up by the splendor that pours into them from the west. It searches and reveals all the markings of the torrents ; it gilds the tautness of the rocky tendons that stretch from the summits to the valleys, and that run some-times in hard lines and sometimes in curves full of rebellious energy, like a tough bow strung to the utmost tension ; and it pours upon the

innumerable populace of trees which the mountain sides support one wide blaze of purple, which slowly burns off upward, leaving twilight behind it, and gleaming on the barren crests, long after the valley, which stretches in view for twenty miles, is dimmed with shade.

> As we clomb,
> The Valley, opening out her bosom, gave
> Fair prospect, intercepted less and less,
> O'er the flat meadows, far off,
> And yet conspicuous, stood the old Church-tower
> In majesty presiding over fields

And habitations seemingly preserved
From the intrusion of a restless world
By rocks impassable and mountains huge.

Soft heath this elevated spot supplied,
And choice of moss-clad stones, whereon we couched
Or sate reclined; admiring quietly
The general aspect of the scene; but each
Not seldom over-anxious to make known
His own discoveries; or to favorite points
Directing notice, merely from a wish
To impart a joy, imperfect while unshared.
That rapturous moment never shall I forget
When these particular interests were effaced
From every mind!—Already had the sun,
Sinking with less than ordinary state,
Attained his western bound; but rays of light—
Now suddenly diverging from the orb
Retired behind the mountain tops or veiled
By the dense air—shot upwards to the crown
Of the blue firmament—aloft and wide:
And multitudes of little floating clouds,
Through their ethereal texture pierced—ere we,
Who saw, of change were conscious—had become
Vivid as fire; clouds separately poised,—
Innumerable multitude of forms
Scattered through half the circle of the sky;
And giving back, and shedding each on each,
With prodigal communion, the bright hues
Which from the unapparent fount of glory
They had imbibed, and ceased not to receive.

We have thus far been engaged with the aisles and galleries, the fonts and crypts, of this mountain cathedral of Franconia, but have not attempted to mount the spire which springs from a corner of the northerly entrance. Mount Lafayette, which is now ascended by a bridle path that winds into the forest about midway between the two hotels, is a little over five thousand feet in height—higher therefore than the loftiest of the mountains of Scotland. In form and character it is unlike Mount Washington, although in geological structure it is essentially similar. It differs in expression, to the eye of an artist who studies its outlines from the occasional openings along the steep ascent, as a keen, nervous temperament differs from a square-shouldered, burly, and bilious frame.

It does not require so long a ride on horseback to reach the peak of Lafayette as to scale Mount Washington; but the average ascent is more steep, and after heavy rains the mud will be found more troublesome than the sharpness of the angles that must be climbed. One unacquainted with mountain paths, and the trustworthy competence of the ponies, whose hoofs get used to striking fire from the primeval granite of their upper stairways, would imagine, on the first ascent to the peak, that there was great danger in the expedition, and would think, no doubt, that it was a remarkable chance or Providence that returned him safely. But the peril is not worth thinking of. The mules of the Andes are not more surefooted than the horses prove to be that mount far above the nests of the eagles, on the sharp fin-like ridges of Lafayette, from which, on one side, tremendous gorges sweep, and on the other the most lovely of level landscapes are displayed. Any man with two legs that can sit upright on a horse needs have no fear of making the adventure. Indeed, even the bipedal condition is not essential. When we made our last ascent of the mountain, a friend was of the party whom accident had robbed of one of the natural supports which are impartially supplied to the human race. His genius, however, has supplied the deficiency not only in his own case, but for a multitude of others, whose gratitude is a noble part of his reward, by a limb almost as good for walking as nature furnishes, and relieved from numberless inconveniences and ills which we must take with the more supple organism of flesh and blood. He mounted the horse at the Profile House, and did not dismount till he could put Dr. Palmer's artificial leg, in company with the real limb which Nature gave him, on the rocky apex of Lafayette. We could add graceful testimony to the attractions of Franconia, as well as to the versatility of our companion, if we could print the poem which he wrote on the excursion, that falls under our notice as these pages are passing through the press.

Ah, the pleasure, if we have been long pent in the city, of tasting the freshness of the mountain air by the ascent of the steep wilderness on horseback ! Each cell of the lungs is a breathing and joyous palate. Cheerily we cross the trees which brutal winter tempests have uprooted and tilted over to die athwart the path ! And how charmingly the sounds of the wilderness fall on the ear,—the twitter of the birch leaves, the deeper tone of the beech, the sigh of the hemlock, and the long-drawn moan of the pine ! When the horse atops for rest, listen to the tap of the woodpecker on some withered trunk, a death drum to nests of bugs and knots of worms, that think themselves safe against such detective police ; next to the whirr of a startled partridge ; soon to the slender, long-drawn, honeyed whistle of the fife-bird, ending with a clear and thrice-repeated dactyl, as if calling some distant friend by the name of " Peabody ; " and then to the hysteric chatter of scatter-brained squirrels, and the brisk clock-winding which they parody in their throats ! Have our readers ever seen Mr. Thoreau's vivid description of a squirrel ? We will quote part of it. " One would approach at first warily by fits and starts, like a leaf blown by the wind, now a few paces this way, with wonderful speed and waste of energy, making inconceivable haste with his ' trotters ' as if it were for a wager, and now as many paces that way, but never getting on more than half a rod at a time. Then suddenly pausing with a ludicrous expression and a gratuitous somerset, as if all the eyes in the universe were fixed on him,—for all the motions of a squirrel, even in the most solitary recesses of the forest, imply spectators as much as those of a dancing girl,—wasting more time in delay and circumspection than would have sufficed to walk the whole distance,—I never saw one walk,—before you could say ' Jack Robinson,' he would be in the top of a young pitch-pine, winding up his clock and chiding all imaginary spectators, soliloquizing and talking to all the universe at the same time " And to this inspiration of the lungs and ear in the forest, must be added the expectation of grand scenery towards which we are riding, and the zest which the ever-shifting network of light and shadow over the tree trunks and the leaves affords to the eye.

Lafayette is so differently related to the level country, as the Duke of western Coös, that the view from his upper shoulders and summit has an entirely different character from that which Mount Washington commands. In the first place, the Mount Washington range itself is prominent in the landscape, and the sight of it with all its northerly and western braces certainly does much to make up for the large districts which it walls from vision. Of course, with the exception of this range, there is no other mountain whose head intercepts the sweep of the eye. But it is the lowlands that are the glory of the spectacle which Lafayette shows his guests. The valleys of the Connecticut and Merrimack are spread west and southwest and south. With what pomp of color are their growing harvests inlaid upon the floor of New England! Here we see one of Nature's great water-colors. She does not work in oil. Every tint of the flowers; all the gradations of leaf-verdure; every stain on the rocks; every shadow that drifts along a mountain slope, in response to a floating cloud; the vivid shreds of silver gossamer that loiter along the bosom of a ridge after a shower; the luxurious chords of sunset gorgeousness; the sublime arches of dishevelled light,—all are Nature's temptation and challenge to the intellect and cunning of the artist to mimic the splendor with which, by water and sunbeams, she adorns the world.

When we can see them from the proper height and in their relations, common facts wear a ravishing beauty. It is so in the realm of science when we mount to a grand generalization; it is so when we merely rise in space, and see the common fields and farms reduced to patches of color on the earth's robe. There is no house on the summit of Lafayette, and therefore we cannot hide a moment from whatever grandeur or loveliness the day supplies.

> See yonder little cloud, that, borne aloft
> So tenderly by the wind, floats fast away
> Over the rocky peaks ! It seems to me
> The body of St. Catherine, borne by angels!

It is the precursor of others that roll out of the northwest, to wrap the peak in cold gray mist for a few moments. But it is only that they may be torn away again, and that we may be surprised by the contrast of their ashy gloom with the new created world that soon spreads over and beneath us

> Its floors of flashing light,
> Its vast and azure dome,
> Its fertile, golden islands,
> Floating on a silver sea.

Yes, it is the semblance of a vaguely tinted ocean that is produced by the obscure and tender colors that stretch over hundreds of square miles to the horizon. What a privilege it would be to be removed far enough into space to observe the motion without losing the color of the globe,—to see the morning break upon the Himalayas, and the vast blue of the ocean under the noon, and sunset flood the Andes with violet and gold,—to watch the creeping of spring over the northern latitudes, and

> Summers, like blushes, sweep the face of earth.

This is the privilege with which the great German poet endows the angels. He makes them sing, in the opening hymn of " Faust,"

> And fleetly, thought surpassing, fleetly
> The earth's green pomp is spinning round;
> Where Paradise alternates sweetly
> With night terrific and profound.

Surely, no man ever earned his sight seeing. It is reward enough for an angel to be able simply to read the geography of this globe through its delicate sapphire-tinted vesture, as it rolls noiselessly to bathe its checkered lands with light.

> The sight gives angels strength, though greater
> Than angels' utmost thought sublime;
> And all thy wondrous works, Creator,
> Are glorious as in Eden's prime.

But why should we attempt in prose, or in random passages, any description of the view from Lafayette, when one of Bryant's poems interprets for us the relations of the mountain to the glen, the sharpness of its outlines, the beauty of the Pemigewasset that flows from its base to wind through fat farms, and the emotions which the com-

bined grandeur and loveliness inspire ?   It is difficult to believe that
it was not written expressly for the spot.

> There, as thou stand'st,
> The haunts of men below thee, and around
> The mountain summits, thy expanding heart
> Shall feel a kindred with that loftier world
> To which thou art translated, and partake
> The enlargement of thy vision. Thou shalt look
> Upon the green and rolling forest tops,
> And down into the secrets of the glens,
> And streams, that with their bordering thickets strive
> To hide their windings. Thou shalt gaze, at once,
> Here on white villages, and tilth, and herds,
> And swarming roads, and there on solitudes
> That only hear the torrent, and the wind,
> And eagle's shriek. There is a precipice
> That seems a fragment of some mighty wall,
> Built by the hand that fashioned the old world,
> To separate its nations, and thrown down
> When the flood drowned them. To the north, a path
> Conducts you up the narrow battlement.
> Steep is the western side, shaggy and wild
> With mossy trees, and pinnacles of flint,
> And many a hanging crag. But, to the east,
> Sheer to the vale go down the bare old cliffs,—
> Huge pillars, that in middle heaven upbear
> Their weather-beaten capitals, here dark
> With the thick moss of centuries, and there
> Of chalky whiteness where the thunderbolt
> Has splintered them. It is a fearful thing
> To stand upon the beetling verge, and see
> Where storm and lightning, from that huge gray wall
> Have tumbled down vast blocks, and at the base
> Dashed them in fragments; and to lay thine ear
> Over the dizzy depth, and hear the sound
> Of winds, that struggle with the woods below,
> Come up like ocean murmurs. But the scene
> Is lovely round; a beautiful river there
> Wanders amid the fresh and fertile meads,
> The paradise he made unto himself,
> Mining the soil for ages. On each side
> The fields swell upward to the hills.

THE SACO VALLEY.

CHOCORUA, NORTH CONWAY, AND THE NOTCH.

Farewell, ye streets! Again I'll sit
On crags to watch the shadows flit;
To list the buzzing of the bee,
Or branches waving like a sea;
To hear far off the cuckoo's note,
Or lark's clear carol high afloat,
And find a joy in every sound,
Of air, the water, or the ground
Of fancies full, though fixing nought,
And thinking—heedless of my thought.

Farewell! and in the teeth of care
I'll breathe the buxom mountain air,
Feed vision upon dyes and hues
That from the hill-top interfuse,
White rocks, and lichens born of spray,
Dark heather tufts, and mosses gray,
Green grass, blue sky, and boulders brown,
With amber waters glistening down,
And early flowers, blue, white, and pink,
That fringe with beauty all the brink.

MACKAY.

WE once heard of a traveller who went down to New Orleans, every spring, and came North just fast enough to keep pace with the strawberries. He managed to rise on the degrees of latitude at even speed with the bounteous vines, and, ascending village by village, and city after city, plucked and ate, and thus extended the spring-time for his palate all the way from the Gulf of Mexico to Montreal. How charming it would be to follow the fresh foliage and the apple blossoms in their northern march from Charleston to Eastport! What a rich year in which one should have nearly three months of the heart of spring, by riding thus on the crest of the earliest quickening wave, that breaks in green and white over the fields and farms of half a continent!

We have sometimes duplicated the opening season of the year by a visit to the White Mountains through the Saco valley, after the blossoms had faded from the lower districts of New England. Indeed, about the last of May one can have a faint touch of the charm of Switzerland, by driving through North Conway and The Glen to Gorham.

> The sun looks o'er, with hazy eye,
> The snowy mountain-tops which lie
> Piled coldly up against the sky:
>
> Dazzling and white! save where the bleak,
> Wild winds have bared some splintering peak,
> Or snow-slide left its dusky streak.
>
> Yet green are Saco's banks below,
> And belts of spruce and cedar show
> Dark fringing round those cones of snow.

The earth hath felt the breath of spring,
Though yet on her deliverer's wing
The lingering frosts of winter cling.

Fresh grasses fringe the meadow-brooks,
And mildly from its sunny nooks
The blue eye of the violet looks.

And odors from the springing grass,
The sweet birch and the sassafras,
Upon the scarce-felt breezes pass.

Her tokens of renewing care
Hath Nature scattered everywhere,
In bud and flower and warmer air.

We can recall a most singular combination of such freshness of
bloom in the Saco valley, with one of the very wildest aspects
which the mountains ever assume. Just where we expected the cul-
minating pleasure of the ride from Centre Harbor to Conway,—that
is on the top of the hill in Eaton, we experienced a singular disappointment. The snow-capped ridge of Washington ought to have
risen out of the north : the whole horizon should have been thunder-
clouded with dark and rugged domes. But though the sky had not
a cloud, there was nothing to be seen. Fires in the neighboring forests had thickened the air to the north with smoke, and cancelled the
hills from the landscape as completely as if they had been annihilated.
It was interesting, however, to see them start out by turns from their
pall, as we rode along. First the Motes outlined themselves ; next,
the graceful spectre of Kiarsarge peered from the golden smoke to
keep us company ; but even when our wagon rattled into the level
street on which North Conway is built, the same veil hid every trace
of Mount Washington from sight. The meadows of North Conway,
however, with their elms arching in fresh drapery, their maple groves
not yet impenetrable by the eye with thickets of verdure, and the
orchards, that nestled under the banks of the village, snowy with
bloom, were more charming than in summer,—perhaps more charming in contrast with the Day-of-Judgment atmosphere that invested
the hills.

But in order not to lose the contrast of spring in the valleys with winter on the mountain crests, we drove from North Conway by the Ellis River through Jackson to the Glen. What glorious sweeping lines the ridges in Jackson, half revealed to us through the sultry dusk of the afternoon! The smoke was something to be grateful for, when we saw those stupendous amphitheatres, seemingly doubled in height, towering into gloom. After a while we could detect the craggy spurs of Washington outlined as a faint etching. And soon we seemed to be looking at the shade of the mighty monarch in an unsubstantial landscape of Hades—the phantasm of a mountain, like that awful Phantasm of Jupiter which Shelley, in the " Prometheus Unbound," called up from the shadowy world that mimics all that is real on the earth,

> where do inhabit
> The shadows of all forms that think and live.
> . . . .
> Vast, sceptred phantoms; heroes, men, and beasts;
> And Demogorgon, a tremendous gloom.

Cheerily the brooks, fed from the melting snows of the invisible summits near us, foamed along the road-side,—their waves stained by the golden light, as though they were hurrying tributaries of some Pactolus. How cool the air of the forests through which the latter portion of the Pinkham road twists its way,—assuring us, as well as the remnants of snow-banks did, directly under the nearest trees, that Winter is not far off in time, and is still lingering on the neighboring heights! It was a ride to call up the charming passage on Spring from Goethe's " Faust : "—

> Spring's warm look has unfettered the fountains,
> Brooks go tinkling with silvery feet;
> Hope's bright blossoms the valley greet;
> Weakly and sickly up the rough mountains
> Pale old Winter has made his retreat.
> Thence he launches, in sheer despite,
> Sleet and hail in impotent showers,
> O'er the green lawns as he takes his flight;
> But the sun will suffer no white,
> Everywhere waking the formative powers,
> Living colors he yearns to spread.

And then when we ride out of the woods into the glorious Glen, we find the contrast for which we had made the early spring journey to the hills. We see the forest green up to a snow line. We stand in an almost tropical afternoon and look up to February. We see snow-fields thirty and fifty feet deep clinging in the ravines, and literally blazing upon the brown barrenness that relieves them. There is no smoke hanging around those peaks, and no suggestion of fire in those fortifications of the frost. Up there the summer does not come with

> thief-like step of liberal hours,
> Thawing snow-drift into flowers.

It is almost a drawn battle between the sun and the snow-banks that are packed into the clefts of Tuckerman's ravine, and around the dome of the stubbed, square-shouldered Jefferson ; for it is not till the last of August that the whole of it is dislodged. But now, standing by a brook in front of the Glen House, one may have the sense of Spring in the sweet, warm air, and the rustle of the young birch leaves that overhang the water ; and yet may *see* Winter by lifting the eye, and *feel* it by dipping the hand into the ice-water, into which that whiteness aloft is slowly dying, to be repeated in the snowy caps which the rocks will force upon the stream, as it goes brawling and dashing over them towards the Androscoggin.

But we are travelling too fast. We should not have been tempted into such a smoky atmosphere for the sake of escaping from it so delightfully. We ought to have ridden along more leisurely by the Sandwich mountains, under which the earthquake force must once have played with dolphin-like frolic, to have rolled the central mass, as it did, in so many smooth and heavy domes. And then we should have reined up by the shore of the little lake, two or three miles off from the regular Conway road, to see the two Chocoruas that are nearer alike than the Siamese twins. One is a rocky, desolate, craggy-peaked substance, crouching in shape not unlike a monstrous walrus (though the summit suggests more the half-turned head and beak of an eagle on the watch against some danger) ; the other is the wraith of the proud and lonely shape above.

How rich and sonorous that word Chocorua is ! Do not, O reader, commit the sin of which the Yankee inhabitants are guilty, and into which stage-drivers will tempt you, of flattening the majestic roll and melancholy cadence of the word into " Corway." Does not its rhythm suggest the wildness and loneliness of the great hills ? To our ears it always brings with it the sigh of the winds through mountain pines. We have said in a former chapter that no mountain of New Hampshire has interested our best artists more. It is everything that a New Hampshire mountain should be. It bears the name of an Indian chief. It is invested with traditional and poetic interest. In form it is massive and symmetrical. The forests of its lower slopes are crowned with rock that is sculptured into a peak with lines full of haughty energy, in whose gorges huge shadows are entrapped, and whose cliffs blaze with morning gold. And it has the fortune to be set in connection with lovely water scenery,—with Squam, and Winnipiscogee, and the little lake directly at its base. Its pinnacle, too, that looks so sheer and defiant, is a challenge to adventurous pedestrians among the mountains, which is accepted now and then by parties every summer. Although it is but thirty-four hundred feet in height, the steepness of its ledges and the absence of any path make the scaling of it a greater feat than a walk to the top of Mount Washington by any of the bridle roads.

On one side of its jagged peak a charming lowland prospect stretches east and south of the Sandwich range, indented by the emerald shores of Winnipiseogee, which lies in queenly beauty upon the soft, far-stretching landscape. Pass around a huge rock to the other side of the steep pyramid, and you have turned to another chapter in the book of nature. Nothing but mountains running in long parallels, or bending, ridge behind ridge, are visible, here blazing in sunlight, there gloomy with shadow, and all related to the towering mass of the imperial Washington.

With the exception of Mount Adams of the Mount Washington
21

range, there is no peak so sharp as Chocorua. And there is no other summit from which the precipices are so sheer, and sweep down with such cycloidal curves. One must stand on the edge of the Grand Gulf, a thousand feet below the summit of Mount Washington, to see ravine lines so full of force, and spires of rock so sharp and fearful. It is so related to the plains on one side, and the mountain gorges on the other, that no grander watchtower except Mount Washington can be scaled to study and enjoy cloud scenery. The sketch we give of the peak is copied from studies made on the spot. The engraving loses not only all the charm of color, but very much of the spirit, which belongs to the original in oil by Mr. Coleman. It is possible that the accomplished artist, who has passed so many hours near the summit, could decide for us, out of his own recollections, the accuracy of this brilliant description, by an American poet, of sunrise seen from such a mountain top.

> Before me rose a pinnacle of rock,
> Lifted above the wood that hemmed it in,
> And now already glowing.
>
> .   .   .   .
>
> I scaled that rocky steep, and there awaited
> Silent the full appearing of the sun.
> Below there lay a far-extended sea,
> Rolling in feathery waves. The wind blew o'er it
> And tossed it round the high-ascending rocks,
> And swept it through the half-hidden forest tops,
> Till, like an ocean waking into storm,
> It heaved and weltered. Gloriously the light
> Crested its billows, and those craggy islands
> Shone on it like to palaces of spar
> Built on a sea of pearl. Far overhead,
> The sky, without a vapor or a stain,
> Intensely blue, even deepened into purple,
> Where, nearer the horizon, it received
> A tincture from the mist, that there dissolved
> Into the viewless air,—the sky bent round,
> The awful dome of a most mighty temple,
> Built by omnipotent hands for nothing less
> Than infinite worship. There I stood in silence:—
> I had no words to tell the mingled thoughts
> Of wonder and of joy that then came o'er me,
> Even with a whirlwind's rush. So beautiful.

So bright, so glorious! Such a majesty
In yon pure vault! So many dazzling tints
In yonder waste of waves —so like the ocean

21 *

With its unnumbered islands there encircled
By foaming surges, that the mounting eagle,
Lifting his fearless pinion through the clouds
To bathe in purest sunbeams, seemed an ospray
Hovering above his prey; and yon tall pines,
Their tops half mantled in a snowy veil,
A frigate with full canvas, bearing on
To conquest and to glory. But even these
Had round them something of the lofty air
In which they moved; not like to things of earth,
But heightened, and made glorious, as became
Such pomp and splendor.
            Who can tell the brightness
That every moment caught a newer glow,
That circle, with its centre like the heart
Of elemental fire, and spreading out
In floods of liquid gold on the blue sky
And on the opaline waves, crowned with a rainbow
Bright as the arch that bent above the throne
Seen in a vision by the holy man
In Patmos! who can tell how it ascended,
And flowed more widely o'er that lifted ocean
Till instantly the unobstructed sun
Rolled up his sphere of fire, floating away,—
Away in a pure ether, far from earth,
And all its clouds,—and pouring forth unbounded
His arrowy brightness! From that burning centre
At once there ran along the level line
Of that imagined sea a stream of gold,—
Liquid and flowing gold, that seemed to tremble
Even with a furnace heat,—on to the point
Whereon I stood. At once that sea of vapor
Parted away, and, melting into air,
Rose round me; and I stood involved in light,
As if a flame had kindled up, and wrapped me
In its innocuous blaze. Away it rolled,
Wave after wave. They climbed the highest rocks
Poured over them in surges, and then rushed
Down glens and valleys, like a wintry torrent
Dashed instant to the plain. It seemed a moment,
And they were gone, as if the touch of fire
At once dissolved them. Then I found myself
Midway in air; ridge after ridge below
Descended, with their opulence of woods,
Even to the dim-seen level, where a lake
Flashed in the sun, and from it wound a line,
Now silvery bright, even to the farthest verge
Of the encircling hills. A waste of rocks

Was round me,—but below, how beautiful,
...s .sch the plain! a wilderness of groves
And ripening harvests; while the sky of June,
The soft blue sky of June, and the cool air,
That makes it then a luxury to live,
Only to breathe it, and the busy echo
Of cascades, and the voice of mountain brooks,
Stole with such gentle meanings to my heart.
That where I stood seemed heaven.

And Chocorua is the only mountain whose peak is crowned with a legend. Would that the vigorous pen which has saved for us many of the fragmentary traditions of the early Indian life in New England, and set them to the music of such terse and vigorous lines as " The Bridal of Pennacook," " Mogg Megone," and " The Funeral Tree of the Sokokis," had enshrined thus the story of Chocorua's Curse, and in this way given the mountain added glory in the landscape of New Hampshire ! Mr. Whittier has not told it in verse ; but our readers will be glad that we can give it to them in such vivid prose as the following, by Mrs. Child : —

" A small colony of hardy pioneers had settled at the base of this mountain. Intelligent, independent men, impatient of restraint, they had shunned the more thickly-settled portions of the country, and retired into this remote part of New Hampshire. But there was one master-spirit among them who was capable of a higher destiny than he ever fulfilled.

" The consciousness of this had stamped something of proud humility on the face of Cornelius Campbell,—something of a haughty spirit, strongly curbed by circumstances he could not control, and at which he seemed to murmur. He assumed no superiority ; but, unconsciously, he threw around him the spell of intellect, and his companions felt, they knew not why, that he was ' among them, but not of them.' His stature was gigantic, and he had the bold, quick tread of one who had wandered frequently and fearlessly among the terrible hiding-places of nature. His voice was harsh, but his whole countenance possessed singular capabilities for tenderness of expression ; and sometimes, under the gentle influence of domestic excite-

ment, his hard features would be rapidly lighted up, seeming like the
sunshine flying over the shaded fields in an April day.

" His companion was one calculated to excite and retain the
deep, strong energies of manly love. She had possessed extraordinary beauty, and had, in the full maturity of an excellent judgment,
relinquished several splendid alliances, and incurred her father's
displeasure, for the sake of Cornelius Campbell. Had political circumstances proved favorable, his talents and ambition would unques-
tionably have worked out a path to emolument and fame ; but he
had been a zealous and active enemy of the Stuarts, and the restora-
tion of Charles II. was the death-warrant of his hopes. Immediately flight became necessary, and America was the chosen place of
refuge. His adherence to Cromwell's party was not occasioned by
religious sympathy, but by political views too liberal and philosophical
for the state of the people ; therefore, Cornelius Campbell sought a
home with our forefathers, and, being of a proud nature, he withdrew
with his family to the solitary place we have mentioned.

" A very small settlement in such a remote place was, of course,
subject to inconvenience and occasional suffering. From the Indians
they received neither injury nor insult. No cause of quarrel had
ever arisen ; and, although their frequent visits were sometimes
troublesome, they never had given indications of jealousy or malice.
Chocorua was a prophet among them, and, as such, an object of
peculiar respect. He had a mind which education and motive would
have nerved with giant strength ; but, growing up in savage freedom, it wasted itself in dark, fierce, ungovernable passions. There
was something fearful in the quiet haughtiness of his lips ; it seemed
so like slumbering power—too proud to be lightly roused, and too
implacable to sleep again. In his small, black, fiery eye, expression
lay coiled up like a beautiful snake. The white people knew that his
hatred would be terrible ; but they had never provoked it, and even
the children became too much accustomed to him to fear him.

" Chocorua had a son, nine or ten years old, to whom Caroline
Campbell had occasionally made such gaudy presents as were likely

to attract his savage fancy. This won the child's affections, so that he became a familiar visitant, almost an inmate of their dwelling; and, being unrestrained by the courtesies of civilized life, he would inspect everything, and taste of everything which came in his way. Some poison, prepared for a mischievous fox, which had long troubled the little settlement, was discovered and drunk by the Indian boy, and he went home to his father to sicken and die. From that moment jealousy and hatred took possession of Chocorua's soul. He never told his suspicions; he brooded over them in secret, to nourish the deadly revenge he contemplated against Cornelius Campbell.

"The story of Indian animosity is always the same. Cornelius Campbell left his hut for the fields early one bright, balmy morning in June. Still a lover, though ten years a husband, his last look was turned towards his wife, answering her parting smile; his last action a kiss for each of his children. When he returned to dinner, they were dead—all dead! and their disfigured bodies too cruelly showed that an Indian's hand had done the work !

" In such a mind grief, like all other emotions, was tempestuous. Home had been to him the only verdant spot in the desert of life. In his wife and children he had garnered up all his heart; and now that they were torn from him, the remembrance of their love clung to him like the death-grapple of a drowning man, sinking him down into darkness and death. This was followed by a calm a thousand times more terrible—the creeping agony of despair, that brings with it no power of resistance.

> ' It was as if the dead could feel
> The icy worm around him steal.'

" Such, for many days, was the state of Cornelius Campbell. Those who knew and reverenced him feared that the spark of reason was forever extinguished. But it rekindled again, and with it came a wild, demoniac spirit of revenge. The death-groan of Chocorua would make him smile in his dreams; and, when he waked, death seemed too pitiful a vengeance for the anguish that was eating into his very soul

"Chocorua's brethren were absent on a hunting expedition at the time he committed the murder, and those who watched his movements observed that he frequently climbed the high precipice, which afterwards took his name, probably looking out for indications of their return. Here Cornelius Campbell resolved to effect his deadly purpose. A party was formed, under his guidance, to cut off all chance of retreat, and the dark-minded prophet was to be hunted like a wild beast to his lair.

"The morning sun had scarce cleared away the fogs, when Chocorua started at a loud voice from beneath the precipice, commanding him to throw himself into the deep abyss below. He knew the voice of his enemy, and replied, with an Indian's calmness, ' The Great Spirit gave life to Chocorua, and Chocorua will not throw it away at the command of the white man.' ' Then hear the Great Spirit speak in the white man's thunder!' exclaimed Cornelius Campbell, as he pointed his gun to the precipice. Chocorua, though fierce and fearless as a panther, had never overcome his dread of fire-arms. He placed his hands upon his ears, to shut out the stunning report ; the next moment the blood bubbled from his neck, and he reeled fearfully on the edge of the precipice. But he recovered himself, and, raising himself on his hand, he spoke in a loud voice, that grew more terrific as its huskiness increased, ' A curse upon ye, white men ! May the Great Spirit curse ye when he speaks in the clouds, and his words are fire ! Chocorua had a son, and ye killed him while the sky looked bright ! ' Lightning blast your crops ! Winds and fire destroy your dwellings ! The Evil Spirit breathe death upon your cattle ! Your graves lie in the war-path of the Indian ! Panthers howl and wolves fatten over your bones ! Chocorua goes to the Great Spirit,—his curse stays with the white man ! '

"The prophet sank upon the ground, still uttering inaudible curses, and they left his bones to whiten in the sun. But his curse rested on that settlement. The tomahawk and scalping-knife were busy among them ; the winds tore up trees, and hurled them at their dwellings ; their crops were blasted, their cattle died, and sickness came upon their strongest men. At last the remnant of them departed from the fatal spot to mingle with more populous and prosperous colonies. Cornelius Campbell became a hermit, seldom seeking or seeing his fellow-men ; and two years after he was found dead in his hut."

During many years the cattle in the town of Burton, now called Albany, at the base of Chocorua, were afflicted with a strange disease. Science has discovered that the trouble is in the water, which contains a weak solution of muriate of lime. The disease of the cattle was for years attributed to Chocorua's dying curse. Whether that curse sank into the mountain and poisoned with muriate of lime the springs from which the Burton cows were to drink, or the muriate of lime at the base generated the story of the sachem's imprecation on the summit, let us not too curiously inquire. Let us only recall the fact with gratitude that, since science has provided a remedy for the suffering cattle in common soap-suds, the superstitious dread has nearly disappeared. Some charming cultivated intervales in the village of Albany now add to the beauty of the prospect from the battered crest of the mountain, and intimate, either that the sachem's wrongs have been expiated, or that his dusky spirit is appeased.

NORTH CONWAY.

But now let us listen to an appeal of seductive cadence in music of a gentler key.

Come down, O maid, from yonder mountain height;
What pleasure lives in height, (the shepherd sang,)
In height and cold, the splendor of the hills?
But cease to move so near the Heavens, and cease
To glide a sunbeam by the blasted pine,
To sit a star upon the sparkling spire;
And come, for Love is of the valley, come,
For Love is of the valley, come thou down
And find him; by the happy threshold, he,
Or hand in hand with Plenty in the maize,
Or red with spirted purple of the vats,
Or foxlike in the vine; nor cares to walk

22

With Death and Morning on the Silver Horns,
Nor wilt thou snare him in the white ravine,
Nor find him dropt upon the firths of ice,
That huddling slant in furrow-cloven falls
To roll the torrent out of dusky doors:
But follow; let the torrent dance thee down
To find him in the valley; let the wild
Lean-headed Eagles yelp alone, and leave
The monstrous ledges there to slope, and spill
Their thousand wreaths of dangling water-smoke,
That like a broken purpose waste in air;
So waste not thou; but come; for all the vales
Await thee; azure pillars of the hearth
Arise to thee; the children call, and I
Thy shepherd pipe, and sweet is every sound,
Sweeter thy voice, but every sound is sweet;
Myriads of rivulets hurrying through the lawn,
The moan of doves in immemorial elms,
And murmuring of innumerable bees.

Such is the invitation with which North Conway coaxes us from the gaunt and grizzly peak which peers over one of its south-westerly walls. It is a short task to give the topographical dimensions and to describe the mountain framing of this village. We can easily say that it is a level bank about thirty feet above the channel and the meadows of the Saco River, extending some four or five miles, and measuring, perhaps, three miles in breadth. On the west, the long and noble Mote Mountain guards it; on the east, the rough, less lofty, and bending Rattlesnake ridge helps to wall it in,—unattractive enough in the ordinary daylight, but a great favorite of the setting sun which loves to glorify it with Tyrian drapery. On the south-west, as we have said, Chocorua manages to get a peep of one corner of its lovely meadows. Almost the whole line of the White Mountains proper, crowned in the centre by the dome of Mount Washington, closes the view on the north-west and north,—only some twelve or fifteen miles distant by the air. And nearer, on the north-east, its base but two miles distant, swells the symmetrical Kiarsarge, the queenly mountain of New Hampshire, which, when the Indian titles were expunged from the great range, should have been christened "Martha Washington." The true Indian name of this charming pyramid is Pequawket. And far to the south, the hills " soften away in a series of smaller and smaller darkening mounds or humps, that answer to the description of the sea-serpent's back."

But what suggestion of the exquisite loveliness of the village is given by the most accurate report of its meadow farms and mountain guards ? We well remember driving into it from the north, by the Jackson road, some three years since, about sunset, under waving hangings of vermilion and gold. The sinking sunlight was shedding yellow splendor over the meadows, tinging the higher edges of the azure mists that settle in the ravines of Mount Washington with tender rose-color, and flooding the upper half of the Rattlesnake ridge with purple, sharply ruled from a basis of deep bronze green. Our wagon was stopped on the borders of the bank, about three miles north of the centre of the village, on the edge of Bartlett, where the meadows look most fascinating ; and one of our party, who was thus for the first time introduced to the quiet and the luxuriant loveliness of this village, said, " I did not suppose that there was on the earth a landscape so exquisite as this." The only other comment that was made, while the sun was setting, was the quotation of the lines from Wordsworth,—

> full many a spot
> Of hidden beauty have I chanced to espy
> Among the mountains; never one like this;
> So lonesome, and so perfectly secure;
> Not melancholy—no, for it is green,
> And bright, and fertile, furnished in itself
> With the few needful things that life requires.
> In rugged arms how softly does it lie,
> How tenderly protected! Far and near
> We have an image of the pristine earth,
> The planet in its nakedness; were this
> Man's only dwelling, sole appointed seat,
> First, last, and single, in the breathing world,
> It could not be more quiet; peace is here
> Or nowhere; days unruffled by the gale
> Of public news, or private; years that pass
> Forgetfully; uncalled upon to pay
> The common penalties of mortal life,
> Sickness, or accident, or grief, or pain.

22 *

One always finds, we think, on a return to North Conway, that his recollections of its loveliness were inadequate to the reality. Such profuse and calm beauty sometimes reigns over the whole village, that it seems to be a little quotation from Arcadia, or a suburb of Para-dise. Who can tell how it is that the trees here seem of more aristocratic elegance,—that the shadows are more delicately pen-cilled,—that the curves of the brooks are more seductive than elsewhere ? Why do the nights seem more tender and less solemn ? What has touched the ledgy rocks with a grace that softens the impression of sublimity and age ? What has made the " twi-light parks " of pine dim with a pensive rather than a melancholy dusk ?

Certainly, we have seen no other region of New England that is so swathed in dreamy charm. A few years ago, the Mote Mountains were ravaged with fire ; and yet their lines give such delight, that few mountains look so attractive in verdure as they in desolation. The atmosphere and the outlines of the hills seem to lull rather than stimulate. There are no crags, no pinnacles, no ramparts of rock, no mountain frown, or savageness brought into contrast, at any point, with the general serene beauty. Kiarsarge is a rough and scraggy moun-tain when you attempt to climb it ; but its lines ripple off softly to the plain. Mount Washington does not seem so much to stand up, as to lie out at ease across the north. The leonine grandeur is there, but it is the lion not erect, but couchant, a little sleepy, stretching out his paws and enjoying the sun. And tired Chocorua appears as if looking wistfully down into

> a land
> In which it seemed always afternoon.

Indeed there is no place in New England which better fits one to read and enjoy Tennyson's Lotus-Eaters. The lines of the land-scape have something of the luscious delay and lingering undulation which the poem has.

> There is sweet music here that softer falls
> Than petals from blown roses on the grass,

Or night-dews on still waters between walls
Of shadowy granite, in a gleaming pass;
Music that gentlier on the spirit lies
Than tired eyelids upon tired eyes;
Music that brings sweet sleep down from the blissful skies
Here are cool mosses deep,
And through the moss the ivies creep,
And in the stream the long-leaved flowers weep,
And from the craggy ledge the poppy hangs in sleep.

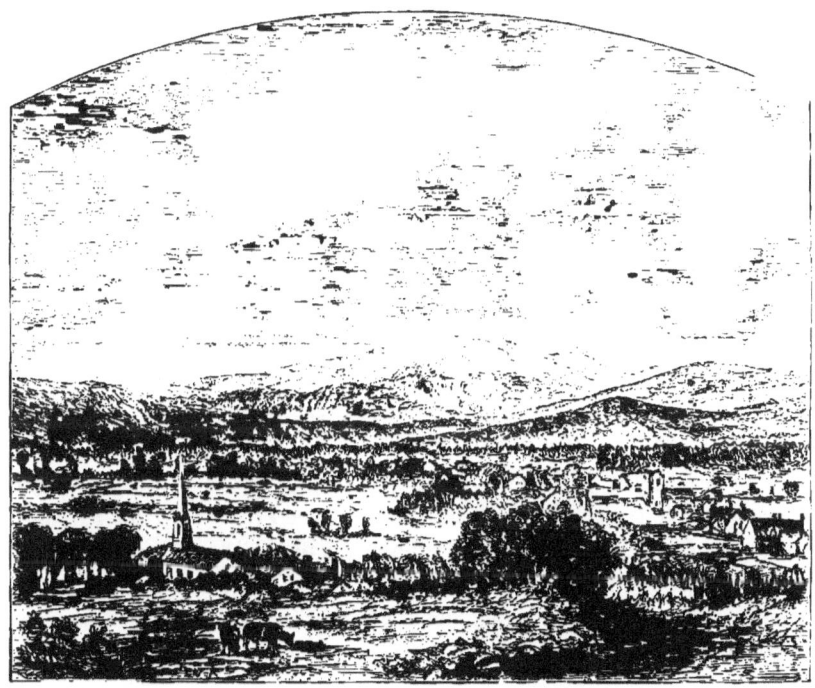

And then the sunsets of North Conway! Coleridge asked Mont
Blanc if he had " a charm to stay the morning star in his steep
course." It is time for some poet to put the question to those
bewitching elm-sprinkled acres that border the Saco, by what sorcery

they evoke, evening after evening, upon the heavens that watch them, such lavish and Italian bloom. Nay it is not Italian, for the basis of its beauty is pure blue, and the skies of Italy are not nearly so blue as those of New England. One sees more clear sky in eight summer weeks in Conway, probably, than in the compass of an Italian year. The air of Italy is more opalescent, and seems to hold the light in luscious repose, and yet a little unsteady in tint. But for pomp of bright, clear, contrasted flames on a deep and transparent sky, the visitors of North Conway, on the sunset bank that overlooks the meadows, enjoy the frequent privilege of a spectacle which the sun sinking behind the Notch conjures for them, such as he rarely displays to the dwellers by the Arno or the inhabitants of Naples. How often have we seen such shows from that bank, while the evening song of birds came up from the near orchards and the distant maple-groves of the meadows below, as it seemed too wasteful in Nature to have prepared for the fading canopy of one small village and of one summer evening! Then was the time for the miracle of Joshua—for some artist-priest, like Turner, to bid the sun stand still, that such gorgeousness might be a garniture of more than a few rapid moments upon the cloud-flecked pavilion of the air. And as the brightness burned off from the hills behind, and the hastening fire mounted from the lower clouds to stain the cirrus, and the west began to glow with the upcast beams of the sunken sun, one could not but feel the aspiration connected with the fleeting magnificence of sunset, which is not the least marvellous passage of Goethe's Faust. We are indebted for the translation to the kindness of a friend, whose knowledge of German is equalled only by his artistic command of English, and who has given a full equivalent of the original in rhythm and grace.

> He yields, he vanishes, the day is gone,
> Yonder he speeds, and sheds new life forever.
> O! had I wings to rise and follow on
> Still after him with fond endeavor!
> Then should I see beneath my feet
> The still world's everlasting vesper,
> Each summit tipp'd with fire, each valley's silence sweet
> The silver brook. the river's molten jasper.

And nought should stay my God-competing flight,
Though savage mountains now with all their ravines,
And now the ocean with its tempered havens,
Successive greet the astonished sight.
The God at length appears as he were sinking;
But still the impulse is renewed,
I hasten on, the light eternal drinking,
The day pursuing, by the night pursued,
The heavens above, and under me the billows.
A pleasant dream! Meanwhile the sun has fled.
In vain, alas! the spirit's wings are spread,
Never will bodily wings appear as fellows.

Of course it must not be understood that North Conway is always thus beautiful. The sunshine, even when the days are clear, sometimes produces only journey-work. Besides the prismatic beams and the actinic ray, there is the artistic quality in the light which, at times, refuses to leave its fountains, and the scene is prosaic. Now and then the Saco, swelled by the bounty of a score of mountain heights, overflows its bed, sweeps the whole surface of the intervale, and mounts to the very edge of the bank on which the village is built. We cannot prophesy these baptisms. So we cannot tell when the spiritual heights from which Nature issues will unseal their opulence, and send the freshet of bloom,—when the " finer light in light " will break its bounds and give us

one of the charméd days
When the genius of God doth flow,

and the whole valley will turn into a goblet, brimming with beauty too liberal to be contained by the mountain walls that are tinted with its weird waves. By hurrying through the mountains, we may lose the luxury and revelations of one of these ineffable atmospheres, when Italy and New England seem interfused, and the light is a compound of molten diamond and opal.

In his drawing of North Conway, too, our artist has softened and improved the village portion of its physiognomy. One cannot help being struck with its capacity of improvement. If some duke, or merchant-prince with unlimited income, could put the resources of landscape taste upon it, adorn it with cottages, hedge the farms upon

the meadows, span the road with elms, cultivate the border-hills as
far up as there is good soil, the village might be made as lovely a
spot as it would be possible to combine out of the elements of New
England scenery. The beauty of the place may be measured by the
fact, that, when it was first sought for summer boarding or residence,
people seldom noticed the inversion of taste which was shown in the
arrangement of the houses and grounds. The barns in the most
sightly places, the ugly fences on the intervale, the sandy banks that
begged for sods to prevent them from fretting and heating the eyes,
which on a sultry day turn towards the cool verdure below, were
drowned out of offending prominence by the overpowering loveliness
that enveloped them.

One can hardly conceive what heightened charm a very little cultivation on the sides of a mountain will add to the landscape. Mr.
Emerson has interpreted the friendship of Nature for human art, in
those lines that sing themselves now through the whole cultivated
mind of our country :—

> Earth proudly wears the Parthenon
> As the best gem upon her zone;
> And Morning opes with haste her lids,
> To gaze upon the Pyramids;
> O'er England's abbeys bends the sky
> As on its friends a kindred eye;
> For out of Thought's interior sphere,
> These wonders rose to upper air;
> And Nature gladly gave them place,
> Adopted them into her race,
> And granted them an equal date
> With Andes and with Ararat.

We have seen a common rye-field of some fifty acres on the slope of
Mount Moriah, in the Androscoggin Valley, which made a visit to the
village of Gorham a greater delight, by the addition of its strong and
lively green to the drapery of the mountain, and the exquisite contrast, at evening, of its gold with the tender purple of the forests
above. Nature had plainly been longing for the necessity of the
agriculture that would bind a new sheaf for her harvest of hues, and

suggest how the monotonous mountain robe might be changed for the brocade of art. This change has commenced in North Conway. Tasteful residences have already begun to sprinkle the village ; and although we may not live to see Kiarsarge draped with farms, or the desolation of the Mote Mountain blossom as the rose, it is possible that the general charm of the " Invitation " which one of our own poets, who is a faithful lover of North Conway, has inwoven with his verse, may yet in our lifetime be added to the natural enticements of the landscape :—

> The warm wide hills are muffled thick with green,
> And fluttering swallows fill the air with song.
> Come to our cottage-home. Lowly it stands,
> Set in a vale of flowers, deep fringed with grass.
> The sweetbrier (noiseless herald of the place)
> Flies with its odor, meeting all who roam
> With welcome footsteps to our small abode.
> No splendid cares live here—no barren shows.
> The bee makes harbor at our perfumed door,
> And hums all day his breezy note of joy.
>
> Come, O my friend! and share our festal month,
> And while the west wind walks the leafy woods,
> While orchard-blooms are white in all the lanes,
> And brooks make music in the deep, cool dells,
> Enjoy the golden moments as they pass,
> And gain new strength for days that are to come.

When the time comes that this poetry by Fields shall be the type of the cultivation in the village, North Conway will be lifted out of the New Hampshire county in which it is taxed, and be the adytum of a temple where God is to be worshipped as the Infinite Artist, in joy.

We may catch a glimpse of the life which the scenery of the village was created to enclose, through an extract from a letter which once enriched the columns of the Boston " Journal of Music." Of course it is from the pen of the accomplished editor, whose fine sense for natural beauty is in chord with his cultured appreciation of the most spiritual of the arts. " Sit down with us upon the door-step here of our friend's hospitable summer home, just as the sun of a most gorgeous day goes down behind the long level ridge of the

superb Mote Mountain, that bounds the scene before us, its wooded
wall upreared as for the walk of some angel sentinel that shall keep
holy watch and ward all night over the lovely mountain-girded scene.
A little later, one may almost fancy he perceives the sheen of the

colossal armor gleaming up there in the starlight! Now the sun
sends mingled light and lengthened shadows over the picturesque
labors of the haymakers, in the broad, green, beautiful meadows that
spread, a mile wide, waving with grass and grain and patches of

glistening corn, clear to the mountain's feet, to the hieroglyphic rocky faces of the curious ledges, that form its outposts in front, and to the winding Saco River, whose course is marked with gracefully overhanging elms and oaks and maples, that also stud the plain in scattered groups, and shade the brooks that ramble, musically gurgling, to the river. A lovelier plain was never spread before a poet's feet, to woo the willing thoughts abroad. A scene of plenty, purity, and peace. On our right, in the north, loom the White Mountains, blue and misty and yet boldly outlined. There is Mount Washington, rearing his broad Jove-like throne amid his great brothers and supporters; these, with innumerable lesser mountains, (each Olympian enough when clouds cap and conceal the grander ones behind them,) gaze solemnly and serenely down our broad valley, and look new meanings in the ceaseless changes of the air and light.

. . . .

" In the forenoon, when every leaf and blade of grass was stirring before the strong, purifying west wind, and when all this motion strangely contrasted with the clear still blue sky above, and with the exquisitely white fleecy clouds that rested on the summits of Mount Washington and of his lower neighbors, we strolled away over the meadows alone. It was a magnificent scene; the tall ripe grass, the corn and oats and bearded barley, bending and tossing in the wind about us, and running in incessant waves, which it was an inexhaustible delight to watch, and try to seize the outline of the law of such infinitely varied and yet unitary motion. It was Nature's best type of the Fugue in music; the same perpetual pursuit and tendency of many to one end, yet never ending.

" Our friend's house, which is just back from the road by which the crowded stage-loads of scenery seekers pass through the Notch of the White Mountains, stands on a raised plateau that rims the meadow foresaid; and here now, on the door-step sit we in the cool of the evening, filling sight and soul with all this beauty. The sun has gone down, and the new moon has lifted her pure silvery crescent from behind the Mote. We gaze upon it through the leafy

23 *

arches of three tall, stately elms, that stand on guard upon the road-side just before the house. The world without makes music to the world within ; the outward scene is like a glowing reflex of the soul's ideal and harmonious moods. Nature and conscious life are one. It seems just the spot where one—with fitting company—might realize a perfectly artistic life. Poetry might bathe her visionary eyes in ever new and quickening light, and choose her language out of the words which God's finger has traced in innumerable forms and types of beauty and of meaning all around her. Philosophy might medi-tate the problems of life and eternity, with every report of the five outward senses loyally conspiring, not disturbing. Art might illus-trate and complete all with a human meaning, and realize the pictures and the statues and the noble edifices which it sees hinted in the landscape. For one, we would contribute far more readily, extrava-gant as it might be, to some colossal marble statue or architectural pile, that should cast its shadow yonder from the ridge of the Mote Mountain, than to that civilized absurdity of the Washington monu-ment scheme at the Capitol. Music, of the rarest, highest, most artistic, would sound as fitting and as truly home-like here, as do the native birds and waterfalls. And worship finds a solemn, heaven-suggesting altar in each mountain height.

"What music-lover has not often longed that he might hear the fine strains of the masters in the summer, in the open air, amid nature's free and grand surroundings, and not be doomed to know such chiefly in the ungrateful artificial limits of the concert room, with gas light and unsympathetic crowds. Here, by a rare luck, we taste this pleasure, this doubly perfect harmony. A piano, almost a rarer wonder here to simple villagers than the first locomotive, has but this day arrived, nor are there wanting cunning fingers to woo forth its music ; and as our eyes range the meadows and the mountains, deli-cate strains of Chopin, notturnes, preludes, and mazourkas, steal from the house and float like the voice of our own soul's selectest, inmost thoughts and feelings over the whole scene. And hark! now sister voices blend : the angel trio from ' Elijah,' *Lift thine eyes !* Were we not already lifting them, and to the mountains ? And melodies of Robert Franz, (*Nun die Schatten dunkeln*, &c.,) as fresh and genuine and full of soul, and free from hacknied commonplace, as if they had been born among these mountains, sing to us and sing for us, and bridge over that awkward chasin of conscious dumbness, which sometimes so painfully separates us from the life and soul of that outward beauty which seems to challenge us for something corresponding on our part. The fairest landscape dies and turns cold before us, and looks ghost-like and unreal, often, as the moon pales before the sun, for the want of something *more* than nature, such as friends, or Art, or intellectual study, or true worship, or some creative action or expression on our own part, which shall meet Nature half way and fulfil the purpose of her invitation. Such is Music to our idle group (and yet how richly occupied) beneath the moon and stars here this sweet evening."

After some hours kindred in artistic privilege with those which our friend has thus described, it was our fortune, in returning under a dark sky to the hotel, to see a remarkable exhibition over the North Conway meadows, produced by a very humble cause. The hot evening had brought out the fire-flies by the acre over the intervale ; and looking down and off from the banks, forty feet in the dusk, while the bottom was invisible, it was a grander spectacle than we can describe, to see two or three miles of darkness sparkling with winged stars. It required but little fancy to catch the outline of mimic constellations— momentary Dippers, ephemeral Pleiades, evanescent parodies in the insect phosphorus of colossal Orion with his club of suns. And let us not think that the boundless and persistent splendor of the skies is insulted by this comparison. For let us remember that, to the in-seeing eye, the Infinite Art is shown no less in the veining of insect wings, and that vital energy which shed those twinkles of a second over the evening fields, than in the whirl of the monstrous balls that sprinkle light through the deeps of a firmament, and which, in the measure of His large purposes, may be only flickers of a moment on a larger tract of gloom. Is it not written, " All of them shall wax

old like a garment ; as a vesture shalt thou change them, and they
shall be changed " ?

> " There's nothing great
> Nor small," has said a poet of our day,
> (Whose voice will ring beyond the curfew of eve
> And not be thrown out by the matin's bell)
> And truly, I reiterate, . . . nothing's small!
> No lily-muffled hum of a summer bee,
> But finds some coupling with the spinning stars;
> No pebble at your foot, but proves a sphere;
> No chaffinch, but implies the cherubim:
> And,—glancing on my own thin, veinéd wrist,—
> In such a little tremor of the blood
> The whole strong clamor of a vehement soul
> Doth utter itself distinct. Earth's crammed with heaven,
> And every common bush afire with God:
> But only he who sees, takes off his shoes.

If now, turning in another direction, we seek to explain the difference in charm between North Conway and other villages of the mountains, we must bear in mind that there is the same difference between
scenes in nature, that there is between words when put together at
random and words arranged in sentences.   Ordinarily, hills and
streams, trees and fields, convey by their arrangement no definite
impression, and hold attention by no intellectual charm.   They simply supply the scattered vocabulary of line and flash, tint and form,
by means of which the artist rewrites his symmetrical thought.
Truth, for the purposes and order of science, is furnished by one tree
as well as another ; by a stream, whether it leap in musical cascade
or flow calmly to the sea ; by the mountain, regardless of the slope
of its wall, or the shape of its crest.   But for purposes of art and
artistic joy, the disposition and proportion of materials are all important ; for thus only is land lifted into landscape.   It is pleasant to
find in any scene one or two instances of combination—rock with
stream, meadow and hill, dip and cone—that will satisfy the eye, and
offer a sentence or a rhyme of the omnipresent Artist.   It is delightful when we find a paragraph or a long passage, that obeys the gram-
mar of beauty, and prints a rounded conception of the Creator.   Then
the day is too short for the ever-renewing joy of vision.   The distinc-

tion of North Conway is, that it is a large natural poem in landscape. Up to the limit where art can come in as improvement, it is finished by the natural forces with a fine pencil. Every arc of the circle which the eye breaks off by a direct gaze,—from the scarred gorges of the range that closes the view on the northwest, to the cheerful openness of the southerly outlook,—is a picture ready for the canvas, having definite sense, sentiment, and rhythm. When one enters it, it is the opening of a volume of divine verse, with strophe and antistrophe of mountain majesty, with eclogues, and idyls, and sonnets, and lyrics, wrought out of meadows and groves, and secluded nooks and leaping streams.

It would require more space than our volume will allow, to do justice to the various charms into which this wide circle of beauty is broken by walks and· excursions and drives. One of the prominent pleasures of a clear and cool day is to find different points for studying Mount Washington. In what novelties of shape, dignity and effect he may be thrown by the rambles of a morning! We may see his steep, torn walls rising far off beyond a hill which we are ascending, and which hides from us most of the foreground in the village and the base on which the mountain stands; or may catch a glimpse of him through a couple of trees that stand sentinel to keep other mountains of the range from an intrusion that will reduce his majesty; or may seek a position over a grove whose breezy plumes afford the most cheerful contrast of motion and color to set off his gray grandeur and majestic rest; or from different points near the Saco may relate him, by changing angles, into fresh combinations with the level verdure of the meadows, or with some curve of its brooks, or some graceful thicket of its maples. Such a walk upon the meadows over its roughnesses, its occasional rods of marsh, its ditch here and there, useful to the farmer but not delightful to feet in search of the picturesque, its rickety fences to be climbed,—and all for the sake of catching a new attitude, or a new expression of the monarch hill of New England, certainly tempts one who is familiar with Stirling's poems to repeat to himself the lines—

I looked upon a plain of green,
    That some one called the Land of Prose
Where many living things are seen,
    In movement or repose.

I looked upon a stately hill
    That well was named the Mount of Song,
Where golden shadows wait at will
    The woods and streams among.

But most this fact my wonder bred,
    Though known by all the nobly wise,
It was the mountain streams that fed
    The fair green plain's amenities.

But let us remember that a climbing of Mount Washington, along the very track of those delicate dimples and golden-edged shadows, would make it seem intensely enough the "Land of Prose," while the poetry and the gold would have floated off upon the meadow, to efface all suggestion of ditches and marsh, and make it one strip of shaven and fascinating lawn. And we need not go so far as the nearest outwork of the White Mountain wall to see this poetry, which the lowlands always refer to the mountains, flung back again. The sunset bank, near the Kiarsarge House in the centre of Conway village, or still better, the roadside, near the little Methodist church on the edge of Bartlett, opens the meadow in such loveliness, that one might believe he was looking through an air that had never enwrapped any sin, upon a floor of some nook of the primitive Eden. What more appropriate reverence can we pay to this intervale, beyond all question, as seen from the point last mentioned, the most entrancing piece of meadow which New England mountains guard, or upon which the setting sun lavishes his gold, than to connect with it Mr. Ruskin's analysis of the beauty and apostrophe to the uses of the grass ?

"Gather a single blade of grass, and examine for a minute, quietly, its narrow sword-shaped strip of fluted green. Nothing, as it seems there, of notable goodness or beauty. A very little strength, and a very little tallness, and a few delicate long lines meeting in a point,— not a perfect point neither, but blunt and unfinished, by no means a

creditable or apparently much cared for example of Nature's work
manship; made, as it seems, only to be trodden on to-day and to-
morrow to be cast into the oven; and a little pale and hollow stalk,
feeble and flaccid, leading down to the dull brown fibres of roots.
And yet, think of it well, and judge whether of all the gorgeous
flowers that beam in summer air, and of all strong and goodly trees,
pleasant to the eyes and good for food,—stately palm and pine, strong

ash and oak, scented citron, burdened vine,—there be any by man so
deeply loved, by God so highly graced, as that narrow point of feeble
green. . . . .

"Consider what we owe merely to the meadow grass, to the covering of the dark ground by that glorious enamel, by the companies of
those soft, and countless and peaceful spears. The fields! Follow
but forth for a little time the thoughts of all that we ought to recog-

nize in those words. All spring and summer is in them,—tne walks
by silent scented paths,—the rests in noonday heat,—the joy of herds
and flocks,—the power of all shepherd life and meditation,—the life
of sunlight upon the world, falling in emerald streaks, and failing in
soft blue shadows, where else it would have struck upon the dark
mould, or scorching dust,—pictures beside the pacing brooks,—soft
banks and knolls of lowly hills,—thymy slopes of down overlooked
by the blue line of lifted sea,—crisp lawns all dim with early dew, or
smooth in evening warmth of barred sunshine, dinted by happy feet,
and softening in their fall the sound of loving voices ; all these are
summed in those simple words ; and these are not all. We may not
measure to the full the depth of this heavenly gift, in our own land ;
though still, as we think of it longer, the infinite of that meadow sweetness, Shakespeare's peculiar joy, would open on us more and more, yet
we have it but in part. Go out in the spring time, among the meadows
that slope from the shores of the Swiss lakes to the roots of their
lower mountains. There, mingled with the taller gentians and the
white narcissus, the grass grows deep and free ; and as you follow
the winding mountain paths, beneath arching boughs all veiled and
dim with blossom,—paths that forever droop and rise over the green
banks and mounds sweeping down in scented undulation, steep to the
blue water, studded here and there with new-mown heaps, filling all
the air with fainter sweetness,—look up towards the higher hills,
where the waves of everlasting green roll silently into their long inlets
among the shadows of the pines ; and we may, perhaps, at last know
the meaning of those quiet words of the 147th Psalm, " He maketh
grass to grow upon the mountains."

One of the favorite excursions of those who remain long in North
Conway is to the " Ledges," Thompson's Falls, and Echo Lake, on
the other side of the Saco, the extreme distance being only some
three miles. The Falls flow down a spur of the Mote Mountain, just
in the rear of the lower Ledge. The loose rocks are thrown about in
such complete confusion that it strikes the eye, fresh from the finished

andscape around the meadows, as a patch of chaos too obstinate to be organized into the general *Cosmos*. The highest of the Ledges, which are bold, broad granite bluffs, rises about nine hundred and sixty feet above the Saco. The river must be forded twice to reach them, which adds greatly to the charm of the excursion. The lower Ledge is almost perpendicular, and the jagged face of the rock, richly weather-stained, reminds one of the Saguenay Cliffs, which it strongly resembles also in the impression it makes by its soaring gloom. An easy climb of a hundred feet carries one to a singular cavity in this Ledge, which visitors have named " The Cathedral." And truly the waters, frosts and storms that scooped and grooved its curves and niches, seemed to have combined in frolic mimicry of Gothic art. The cave is forty feet in depth and about sixty in height, and the outermost rock of the roofing spans the entrance with an arch, which, half of the way, is as symmetrical as if an architect had planned it. Was it skill or patience that the gnomes failed in, that excavated or heaved it ; or did they design to produce in their wild sport merely *torsos* of the majesty of a great minster ?

> From this deep chasm, where quivering sunbeams play
> Upon its loftiest crags, mine eyes behold
> A gloomy *Niche*, capacious, blank, and cold;
> A concave, free from shrubs and mosses gray;
> In semblance fresh, as if, with dire affray,
> Some statue, placed amid these regions old
> For tutelary service, thence had rolled,
> Startling the flight of timid Yesterday!
> Was it by mortals sculptured?—weary slaves
> Of slow endeavor! or abruptly cast
> Into rude shape by fire, with roaring blast
> Tempestuously let loose from central caves?
> Or fashioned by the turbulence of waves,
> Then, when o'er highest hills the Deluge pass'd?

The whole front of the recess is shaded by trees, which kindly stand apart just enough to frame off Kiarsarge in lovely symmetry,— so that a more romantic resting place for an hour or two in a warm afternoon can hardly be imagined. We have said that the measure and spirit of " The Lotos Eaters " harmonize with the summer air

and landscape of North Conway. But think of driving across those
meadows in a breezy afternoon and taking a poem fresh from the lips
of Tennyson ! No, we do not pretend that such has ever been our
fortune ; but we do say that in a wagon, as we drove across the intervale, under the shadow of the maple groves, and twice through the
hurrying river which nearly buried the wheels with its merry flood,
we caught the first echo that had fallen on our ears, this side the sea,
from the richest strain of the Laureate's silver bugle. It was when a
lady chanted in joyous soprano to a delighted party,—

> The splendor falls on castle walls
> And snowy summits old in story;
> The long light shakes across the lakes,
> And the wild cataract leaps in glory.
> Blow, bugle, blow, set the wild echoes flying;
> Blow, bugle; answer, echoes, dying, dying, dying.
>
> O hark, O hear! how thin and clear,
> And thinner, clearer, farther going;
> O sweet and far, from cliff and scar,
> The horns of Elfland faintly blowing!
> Blow, let us hear the purple glens replying ;
> Blow, bugle; answer, echoes, dying, dying, dying.
>
> O love, they die in yon rich sky,
> They faint on hill or field or river;
> Our echoes roll from soul to soul,
> And grow forever and forever.
> Blow, bugle, blow, set the wild echoes flying,
> And answer, echoes, answer, dying, dying, dying.

Is not that an association to glorify forever in memory the soft
and drooping clouds that overhung the Saco, the lights and shadows
that skimmed, widening, melting, ever-renewing their fruitless but joyous chase over the billowy grass, and the sombre patience of Mount
Washington, himself flecked with mottled light and gloom? Of
course the echoes from Echo Lake, which lies in front of " The
Cathedral," sounded that afternoon more mellow, floating back from
" Elfland," rather than from the face of a granite wall. And yet
one visit to the lake by moonlight lies even more softly and winningly

in memory. The savage twin-cliffs and the wooded link that unites them, like the bond of the Siamese pair, reflected in that little sheet of water, seemed a picture rather than a reality—a dream lying yet before the imagination of the Creator, rather than the embodiment of it in the rough elements of nature. An evening spent there when the full rising moon silvers " The Ledges," and burnishes the bosom of the lake, and sheds its beams among its dark pine fringes, to slip slowly down the stately columns of the larger trees, will long be remembered as a sweet midsummer night's dream.

But we must now pass with only a word of greeting " Diana's Baths," which also belong to the resources of the visit to " The Cathedral,"—the valley views offered from the ride on the Dundee road,—the excursion to Jackson with the cascade pictures on a branch of the Ellis River—the wild glen to be found in the drive to Sligo—the triple cascades of Wildwood Brook, not long since discovered—the glorious excursion to Fryeburg, with the views gained of Jockey Cap, and the Saco intervales of that village, and Lovell's Pond which has the distinction of being more deeply dyed with tradition than any other sheet of water in New England. Gould's Pond and the ride to Chocorua Lake we have spoken of in a former chapter.

The " Artist's Brook " in the village itself is the only feature of the scenery that we can delay with now. Its true celebration is to be found in the artists' studios, or in the galleries, for which it has furnished exquisite tangles of foliage and light ; rough boulders around whose clinging mosses the water slips with a flash that can be painted but with a voice that cannot be entrapped ; curves through diminutive glens, half in shadow and sprinkled on the other side with light through fluttering birch leaves, or an over-hanging beech with marbled stem, such as Kensett loves to paint ; and more open passages, where the water brawls, and the thinner trees of the sides show the bulk of distant Washington. Sitting down on the meadow where the brook loiters over its sandy bed, and sometimes stops to cool itself in the green shadow of an elm before it moves on to join the

Saco near at hand, does it not sing essentially the same song to us
that the brook did which Tennyson has thus translated ?

I come from haunts of coot and hern
  I make a sudden sally
And sparkle out among the fern,
  To bicker down a valley

By thirsty hills I hurry down,
  Or slip between the ridges,
By twenty thorps, a little town,
  And half a hundred bridges.

Till last by Philip's farm I flow
　　To join the brimming river,
For men may come and men may go,
　　But I go on forever.

I chatter over stony ways,
　　In little sharps and trebles
I bubble into eddying bays,
　　I babble on the pebbles.

With many a curve my banks I fret
　　By many a field and fallow,
And many a fairy foreland set
　　With willow-weed and mallow

I chatter, chatter, as I flow
　　To join the brimming river,
For men may come and men may go
　　But I go on forever.

I wind about, and in and out,
　　With here a blossom sailing,
And here and there a lusty trout,
　　And here and there a grayling.

And here and there a foamy flake
　　Upon me, as I travel,
With many a silvery waterbreak
　　Above the golden gravel.

And draw them all along, and flow
　　To join the brimming river,
For men may come and men may go
　　But I go on forever.

I steal by lawns and grassy plots,
　　I slide by hazel covers;
I move the sweet forget-me-nots
　　That grow for happy lovers.

I slip, I slide, I gloom, I glance,
　　Among my skimming swallows
I make the netted sunbeam dance
　　Against my sandy shallows.

I murmur under moon and stars
In brambly wildernesses;
I linger by my shingly bars,
I loiter round my cresses;

And out again I curve and flow
To join the brimming river,
For men may come and men may go
But I go on forever.

A sonnet of Wordsworth's also, written evidently in praise of some
English stream, that in quality and character is cousin to this gem of
North Conway, ought to be quoted here.

Brook! whose society the Poet seeks,
Intent his wasted spirits to renew;
And whom the curious Painter doth pursue
Through rocky passes, among flowery creeks,
And tracks thee dancing down thy waterbreaks;
If wish were mine·some type of thee to view,
Thee, and not thee thyself, I would not do
Like Grecian Artists, give thee human cheeks,
Channels for tears; no Naiad shouldst thou be,—
Have neither limbs, feet, feathers, joints, nor hairs;
It seems the Eternal Soul is clothed in thee
With purer robes than those of flesh and blood,
And hath bestowed on thee a better good;
Unwearied joy, and life without its cares.

We have already said that the dreaminess which pervades the air
and hangs around the walls of North Conway, rests upon the slopes
of Kiarsarge and veils the roughness and barrenness of its acclivities. Seen through the haze of a genial afternoon it seems as though
it would be pastime to mount its cone, carpeted then to the eye with
a plushy depth and indistinctness of mellow and cross-lighted air.
One cannot see then how he could require more than half an hour to
gain its summit from the base, although it stands twenty-seven hundred feet above the valley. Many persons have been tempted by
this illusion to ascend on foot, and have thus been brought to a permanent conviction that a mountain is something very different in *genus*
from a hill.

Do not some of our readers recall the fascination of the diorama exhibited to those whom Kiarsarge allows to pass above its elegant shoulders ? Do they not call to mind the mob of mountains that first storms the sight from the north and west, as though Mount Washington had given a party, and all the hills were hurrying up to answer the invitation ? Can they not see again with the mind's eye the different effects of color and shadow upon the lines of hills, according to their distance, height, and the position of the sun, and how they soon group themselves in relation to the two great centres— the notched summit of Lafayette and the noble dome of Washington? Do they not recall the soothing contrast to these shaggy surges of the land in the far stretching open country of the south, gemmed with lakes and ponds, brilliant with cultivation, sweeping out like a vast and many colored sea to

> the grim gray rounding
> Of this bullet of the earth
> On which we sail,

over which, far to the southwest, the filmy outline of Monadnoc gleams like a sail just fading out upon a vaster sea ? Did they ascend for the purpose of passing the night in the house that is clamped to the rocks of the sharp summit, and can they not call up the picture of the glorious purple light, dyed into the hills behind them by the level rays of the sinking sun ? Can they not repeat by recollection the contrast of the heavy shadows of the highest ranges with a heaven of molten gold,

> with light and heat intensely glowing,
> While, to the middle height of the pure ether,
> One deepening sapphire from the amber spread?

Or was the evening so clear that the shadow of Kiarsarge itself stretched slowly towards Portland, and faded out when the point of its unsubstantial triangle had climbed half up the slope of Pleasant Mountain in Maine ? Or was it the cloud scenery of sunset that was the prominent splendor of the spectacle, and did

23

                    masses of crimson glory,
Pale lakes of blue, studded with fiery islands,
Bright golden bars, cold peaks of slaty rock.
Mountains of fused amethyst and copper,
Fierce flaming eyes, with black o'erhanging brows,
Light floating curls of brown or golden hair,
And rosy flushes, like warm dreams of love
Make rich and wonderful the failing day,
That, like a wounded dolphin, on the shore
Of night's black waves, died in a thousand glories ?

Perhaps they saw the full moon rise after the flames of sunset had faded. Perhaps they recollect how slowly its red and swollen disc loomed up the East through the thick vapors, and then, as soon as its light became clear, left a streak of silver on the horizon which must have been a strip of the ocean. And they renew in memory the delight it gave them to watch those gentle beams leap down from mountain tops into the vales, and waken by successive flashes the sleeping lakes that gem the vicinity of Kiarsarge. Or, if the moonlight did not give this picture of a new-created world, they may remember how, after sunset, the poet's picture was interpreted to them : —

                    Repentant day
Frees with his dying hand the pallid stars
He held imprisoned since his young, hot dawn.
Now watch with what a silent step of fear
They'll steal out one by one, and overspread
The cool delicious meadows of the night.
And lo, the first one flutters in the blue
With a quick sense of liberty and joy!

And then the sunrise repeated the effects of light and gloom,—the purple on the hills, the gigantic shadows, the conflict between the radiance on the summits and the dusk in the valleys, which the previous evening had shown. And again the clearly defined outline of Kiarsarge, they will remember, lay before them—but on the hills at the west now—sharper than when the sunset created it, and slowly shrunk towards the foot of the mountain.

    And if these visions have been seen, as a human being should see them, they have become staple of wisdom and a well of joy. They describe almost the full circle of the privilege amid which the senses are set If the spectacles could be shown as miracles, the first cre-ations of the spirit that quickeneth all things, what wonder and rapture would respond to them! Are they of less meaning and worth because they are visions that have been renewed and varied perpetually for ages by the indwelling Life ?

> Alas! thine is the bankruptcy
> Blessed Nature so to see.
>
> . . . . . .
>
> Ever fresh the broad creation,
> A divine improvisation,
> From the heart of God proceeds,
> A single will, a million deeds.

North Conway, as we have said in a former chapter, lies at the proper distance from the hills that inclose it, and from the Mount Washington range, to command various and rich landscape effects. And this no doubt is the great charm of the place to scores of those that pass several weeks of the summer in the village, who perhaps could not explain to themselves the secret of their fascination. A great many persons think of mountain scenery as monotonous. If you live directly under a savage mountain wall, like one side of the Notch, it may be. If you stay a few miles off from a great range in full view, nothing can be less monotonous.

" When the lofty and barren mountain," says a legend I have somewhere read, " was first upheaved into the sky, and from its ele-vation looked down on the plains below, and saw the valley and the less elevated hills covered with verdant and fruitful trees, it sent up to Brahma something like a murmur of complaint,—' Why thus bar-ren ? why these scarred and naked sides exposed to the eye of man ?' And Brahma answered, ' The very light shall clothe thee, and the shadow of the passing cloud shall be as a royal mantle. *More ver-dure would be less light*. Thou shalt share in the azure of heaven, and the youngest and whitest cloud of a summer's sky shall nestle in thy bosom. Thou belongest half to us.'

"So was the mountain dowered. And so too," adds the legend, "have the loftiest minds of men been in all ages dowered. To lower elevations have been given the pleasant verdure, the vine, and the olive. Light, light alone,—and the deep shadow of the passing cloud,—these are the gifts of the prophets of the race."

The glory of the mountains is *color*. A great many people think that they see all that there is to be seen of the White Hills in one visit. Have they not been driven from Conway to the Notch, and did they not have an outside seat on the stage on a clear day? Have they not seen the Glen when there were no clouds, and ascended Mount Washington, and devoted a day and a half to Franconia, and crossed Winnipiseogee on their way home? At any rate, if they have staid a week in one spot, they cannot understand why they may not be said to have exhausted it; and if they have passed one whole season in a valley, it might seem to them folly to go to the same spot the next year.

But how is it in regard to a great gallery abroad? Is a man of true taste satisfied with going once to see a Claude, to see the coloring of a Titian, the expression of a Madonna, the sublime torso of Hercules, or the knotted muscles of the Laocoön? Is one visit enough to satisfy a man of taste with a collection that has three or four first-rate pictures, each by a Church, a Durand, a Bierstadt, a Gignoux?

But what if you could go into a gallery where the various sculpture took different attitudes every day? where a Claude or a Turner was present and changed the sunsets on his canvas, shifted the draperies of mist and shadow, combined clouds and meadows and ridges in ever-varying beauty, and wiped them all out at night? or where Kensett, Coleman, Champney, Gay, Church, Durand, Wheelock, were continually busy in copying from new conceptions the freshness of morning and the pomp of evening light upon the hills, the countless passages and combinations of the clouds, the laughs and glooms of the brooks, the innumerable expressions that flit over the meadows, the various vestures of shadow, light, and hue, in which they have

seen the stalwart hills enrobed ? Would one visit then enable a man
to say that he had seen the gallery ? Would one season be sufficient
to drain the interest of it ? Thus the mountains are ever changing.
They are never two days the same. The varying airs of summer,
the angles at which, in different summer months, the light strikes
them, give different general character to the landscapes which they
govern. And then when we think of the perpetual frolic of the
sun blaze and the shadow upon them, never twice alike ; the brilliant
scarfs into which the mists that stripe or entwine them are changed ;
the vivid splendors that often flame upon them at evening,

> Like the torrents of the sun
> Up the horizon walls;

the rich, deep, but more vague and modest hues, which we try in
vain to bring under definition, that glow upon them in different airs ;
and the evanescent tints that touch them only now and then in a long
season, as though they were something too rare and pure to be shown
for more than a moment to dwellers of the earth, and then only as a
hint of what may be displayed in diviner climes,—we see that it is the
landscape-eye alone, and the desire to cultivate it, which is needed to
make the mountains, from any favorable district such as North Conway, an undrainable resource and joy.

Those who seek a sort of melodramatic astonishment by the height
of their peaks and the gloomy menace of sheer and desolate walls,
will be disappointed at first, and will not find that the mountains
" grow upon them." But it is not so with color. That is a perpetual surprise. The glory of that, even upon the New Hampshire
mountains, cannot be exaggerated. They should be sought for their
pomp, far more than for their configuration.

" The fact is," says Mr. Ruskin, " we none of us enough appreciate the nobleness and sacredness of color. Nothing is more common than to hear it spoken of as a subordinate beauty,—nay, even as
the mere source of a sensual pleasure ; and we might almost believe
that we were daily among men who

Could strip, for aught the prospect yields
To them, their verdure from the fields;
And take the radiance from the clouds
With which the sun his setting shrouds.

But it is not so. Such expressions are used for the most part in thoughtlessness ; and if the speakers would only take the pains to imagine what the world and their own existence would become if the blue were taken from the sky, and the gold from the sunshine, and the verdure from the leaves, and the crimson from the blood which is the life of man, the flush from the cheek, the darkness from the eye, the radiance from the hair,—if they could but see, for an instant, white human creatures living in a white world,—they would soon feel what they owe to color. The fact is, that of all God's gifts to the sight of man, color is the holiest, the most divine, the most solemn. We speak rashly of gay color and sad color, for color cannot at once be good and gay. All good color is in some degree pensive, the loveliest is melancholy, and the purest and most thoughtful minds are those which love color the most.

"I know that this will sound strange in many ears, and will be especially startling to those who have considered the subject chiefly with reference to painting ; for the great Venetian schools of color are not usually understood to be either pure or pensive, and the idea of its preëminence is associated in nearly every mind with the coarseness of Rubens, and the sensualities of Correggio and Titian. But a more comprehensive view of art will soon correct this impression. It will be discovered, in the first place, that the more faithful and earnest the religion of the painter, the more pure and prevalent is the system of his color. It will be found in the second place, that where color becomes a primal intention with a painter otherwise mean or sensual, it instantly elevates him, and becomes the one sacred and saving element in his work. The very depth of the stoop to which the Venetian painters and Rubens sometimes condescend, is a consequence of their feeling confidence in the power of their color to keep them from falling. They hold on by it, as by a chain let down from heaven, with one hand, though they may sometimes seem to gather dust and ashes with the other. And, in the last place, it will be found that so surely as a painter is irreligious, thoughtless, or obscene in disposition, so surely is his coloring cold, gloomy, and valueless. The opposite poles of art in this respect are Frà Angelico and Salvator Rosa ; of whom the one was a man who smiled seldom, wept often, prayed constantly, and never harbored an impure thought. His pictures are simply so many pieces of jewelry, the colors of the draperies being perfectly pure, as various as those of a painted window, chastened only by paleness, and relieved upon a gold ground. Salvator was a dissipated jester and satirist, a man who spent his life in masking and revelry. But his pictures are full of horror, and their color is for the most part gloomy-gray. Truly, it would seem as if art had so much of eternity in it, that it must take its dye from the close rather than the course of life. ' In such laughter the heart of man is sorrowful, and the end of that mirth is heaviness.'

" These are no singular instances. I know no law more severely without exception than this of the connection of pure color with profound and noble thought. The late Flemish pictures, shallow in conception and obscure in subject, are always sombre in color. But the early religious painting of the Flemings is as brilliant in hue as it is holy in thought. The Bellinis, Francias, Peruginos painted in crimson, and blue, and gold. The Caraccis, Guidos, and Rembrandts, in brown and gray. The builders of our great cathedrals veiled their casements, and wrapped their pillars with one robe of purple splendor. The builders of the luxurious Renaissance left their palaces filled only with cold, white light, and in the paleness of their native stone."

The inexperienced eye has no conception of the affluent delight that is kindled by the opulence of pure and tender colors on the mountains. A ramble by the banks of the Saco in North Conway, or along the Androscoggin below Gorham, will often yield from this cause what we may soberly call rapture of vision. A great many

persons, in looking around from Artist's Hill, would say at first that
green and blue and white and gray, in the foliage, the grass, the sky,
the clouds, and the mountains, were the only colors to be noticed,
and these in wide, severely contrasted masses. We should go entirely beyond their appreciation in speaking of the light brown and
olive plateaus rising from the wide flats of meadow green, the richer
and more subtle hues on the darker belt of lower hills, the sheeny
spaces of pure sunshine upon smooth slopes or level sward, the glimmer of pearly radiance upon pools of aerial sapphire brought from the
distant mountains in the wandering Saco, the blue and white mistiness from clouds and distant air gleaming in the chasms of brooks
fresh from the cool top of Kiarsarge, and the gold or silver glances
of light upon knolls or smooth boulders scattered here and there upon
the irregular and tawny ground, and upon the house-roofs beyond.
Yet let a man who thinks these particulars are imaginary hold his
head down, and thus reverse his eyes, and then say whether the delicacy and variety of hues are exaggerated in such a statement. There
are those who have such perception of colors with their eyes upright.
And they will know that the tints just noted are only hints of a great
color-symphony to be wrought out upon the wide landscape. They
know how the rich or sombre passages of shade, and the olive strips and
slaty breadths of darkness will be transformed in some glorious afternoon, when the landscape assumes its full pomp, into masses of more
etherial gloom, and made magnificent by the intermixture of gorgeous
tones of purples, emeralds and russets with cloudy azure and subtle gray along the second part of the mountain outworks. They
know how those flecks of pearl and sapphire upon the meadow will
mingle and spread with shifting azure and amethyst upon the lower
parts of the great mountains ; and how the spaces of sunshine, the
blue and white mistiness, and the golden and silver glances of light,
will assume new beauty and larger proportions amid the gleaming hues
of the looming azure ridge, the waving gray and purple of cloud-en-
wrapped peak, the tender flashes of changeful light and tint in sky
and cloud, and the tremulous violet and aerial orange of the myste

rious ravines, with their wondrous sloping arras, on whose striped folds, inwrought with gold and silver upon pale emerald ground, are, one might think, the mystical signs of some weird powers that work from within the earth.

But those who cannot detect this range and harmony of hues upon a complicated landscape like that seen from Artist's Hill, have no doubt noticed and enjoyed the simpler and stronger contrasts revealed upon one or two features of such a scene. They have watched, perhaps, the shadow of a wandering cloud thrown over a towering mountain a few miles off, and covering it with a dusk that conceals all its variety of form, as if a purple mantle had been suddenly cast upon it; and they remember how splendidly it made the sparkling gladness of the waters contrast with its undisturbed breadth of gloom. They have rejoiced, when the shadow passed, in seeing the soft, cloudy blue show here and there flakes and lines of tender green and russet and pale orange, that just hint peaks and ridges, which in another change of light may fill the mountain surface with many purple tents tipped and edged with gold. They know how grand is the effect upon the mountains, when there are only a few broken lines of dim light near their tops to show the depth of the shade that drapes them—as though they were themselves darker shadows of soaring earth transformed to cloud! Or possibly their memory reports to them how, in the rich light of evening, a great pyramid will stand up, as we have sometimes seen the charming Mount Madison, draped in a gorgeous tunic whose warp seemed to be aerial sapphire overshot with threads of gold. And they can understand that the visitor is still more fortunate who has an evening provided for him when the light is clear, but interrupted by struggling masses of bright cumuli. Ah, how the light breaking through the shifting openings brings out a continual succession of scenic effects! The clouds break and pass, and the sunshine and shadows ever changing place, reveal, each instant, along the mountain sides, new wonders of soaring ridge, jutting crags delicately veined, and rounded slopes declining to pale depths of winding

26

ravines, down whose shadowed sides crinkle the narrow, silvery lines of the landslides, like faint lightning in far-off clouds. The next instant, perhaps, the clouds, closing together, leave a monotonous breadth of purple darkness over all. And then, drifting irregularly apart, they open the opportunity for a sunbeam to slip through upon the broad fields of cold shadow. And like a brand of white flame, it hastens to kindle a running fire which consumes the darkness, mantles over the sloping terraces and flashing pinnacles, and leaves a magnificent symbol of the "Allegro" of Milton, where a moment before "Il Penseroso" was suggested by the stately gloom.

The spectacles that, in some rare week of summer, are shown within the compass of a score of hours in one of the White Mountain valleys, interpret for us the passage of our great poet : "How does Nature deify us with a few and cheap elements ! Give me health and a day, and I will make the pomp of emperors ridiculous. The dawn is my Assyria ; the sunset and moon-rise my Paphos, and unimaginable realms of faerie ; broad noon shall be my England of the senses and the understanding ; the night shall be my Germany of mystic philosophy and dreams." And we cannot better close these pages on the privilege of sight in a village like North Conway than with another charming passage by Mr. Emerson which he kindly con sented to extract for us from a manuscript lecture. "The world is not made up to the eye of figures,—that is only half ; it is also made of color. How that mysterious element washes the universe with its enchanting waves ! The sculptor had ended his work,—and behold ! a new world of dream-like glory. This is the last stroke of nature ;— beyond color we cannot go. In like manner, life is made up not of knowledge only, but of love also. If thought is form, sentiment is color. It clothes the poor skeleton world with space, variety, and glow. The hues of sunset make life great and romantic to a wretch ; so the affections make some pretty web of cottage and fireside details bright, populous, important, and claiming the high place in our history."

In Scotland, a highland pass, so wild and romantic as that **from**
Upper Bartlett to the Crawford House, would be overhung with
26 *

traditions along the whole winding wall of its wilderness; and legends that had been enshrined in song and ballad would be as plentiful as the streams that leap singing towards the Saco, down their rocky stairs. But no hill, no sheer battlement, no torrent that ploughs and drains the barriers of this narrow and tortuous glen, suggests any Indian legend. One cascade, however, about half a mile from the former residence of old Abel Crawford, is more honored by the sad story associated with it, than by the picturesqueness of the crags through which it hurries for the last mile or two of its descending course. It is called " Nancy's Brook;" and the stage-drivers show to the passengers the stone which is the particular monument of the tragedy, bearing the name " Nancy's Rock."

Here, late in the autumn of the year 1778, a poor girl, who lived with a family in Jefferson, was found frozen to death. She was engaged to be married to a man who was employed in the same family where she served. She had intrusted to him all her earnings, and the understanding was, that in a few days they should leave for Portsmouth, to be married there. But during her temporary absence in Lancaster, nine miles from Jefferson, the man started with his employer for Portsmouth, without leaving any explanation or message for her. She learned the fact of her desertion on the same day that her lover departed. At once she walked back to Jefferson, tied up a small bundle of clothing, and in spite of all warnings and entreaties, set out on foot to overtake the faithless fugitive. Snow had already fallen ; it was nearly night ; the distance to the first settlement near the Notch was thirty miles ; and there was no road through the wilderness but a hunter's path marked by spotted trees. She pressed on through the night, as the story runs, against a snow-storm and a northwest wind, in the hope of overtaking her lover at the camp in the Notch, before the party should start in the morning. She reached it soon after they had left, and found the ashes of the camp-fire warm.

It was plain to those, who, alarmed for her safety, had followed on from Jefferson to overtake her, that she had tried in vain to rekindle the fire in the lonely camp. But the fire in her heart did not falter, and she still moved on, wet, cold, and hungry, with resolution unconquered by the thirty miles' tramp through the wilderness, on the bitter autumn night. She climbed the wild pass of the Notch which only one woman had scaled before—for it was then a matter of great difficulty to clamber over the steep, rough rocks—and followed the track of the Saco towards Conway. Several miles of the roughest part of the way she travelled thus, often fording the river. But her strength was spent by two or three hours of such toil ; and she was found by the party in pursuit of her, chilled and stiff in the snow, with her head resting upon her staff, at the foot of an aged tree near "Nancy's Bridge," not many hours after she had ceased to breathe. When the lover of the unhappy girl heard the story of her faithfulness, her suffering, and her dreadful death, he became insane ; and, after a few weeks, as one account informs us, after a few years, as another states it, died, a raving madman. And there are those who believe that often in still nights the valley walls near Mount Crawford echo the shrieks and groans of the restless ghost of Nancy's lover.

THE NOTCH.

Beware the pine-tree's withered branch!
Beware the awful avalanche!

The leaves are falling, falling,
  Solemnly and slow;
Caw! caw! the rooks are calling,
  It is a sound of woe,
    A sound of woe!

Through woods and mountain passes
  The winds, like anthems, roll;
They are chanting solemn masses,
  Singing: "Pray for this poor soul.
    Pray,—pray!"

And the hooded clouds, like friars,
        Tell their beads in drops of rain,
        And patter their doleful prayers;—
        But their prayers are all in vain,
        .   All in vain!

In North Conway we were surrounded by mountain splendor, cheer, and peace ; the gradually darkening pass through Bartlett, and the pathos of the story murmured by Nancy's Brook, prepare us for the impression of mountain wrath and ravage when we reach those awful mountain walls whose jaws, as we enter them, seem ready to close together upon the little Willey House, the monument of the great disaster of the White Hills.

There is no Indian tradition connected with the Notch. We have no record that any Indians ever saw it. It was discovered in 1772 by a hunter named Nash, who had climbed a tree on Cherry Mountain. The farmers of Jefferson and Bethlehem were very glad to learn that there was a prospect of a more direct and speedy communication with the towns below, and with Portsmouth, than by winding around the easterly base of the great range. But the early experiments of passing through the Notch to reach the lowlands seemed to cost in toil and peril more than an equivalent for the gain in time.

Huge terraces of granite black
        Afforded rude and cumber'd track;
        For from the mountain hoar,
        Hurl'd headlong in some night of fear,
        When yell'd the wolf and fled the deer,
        Loose crags had toppled o'er.

        .   .   .   .

        For all is rocks at random thrown,
        Black waves, bare crags, and banks of stone,
        As if were here denied
        The summer sun, the spring's sweet dew,
        That clothe with many a varied hue
        The bleakest mountain-side.

Horses were pulled up the narrowest and most jagged portion of the Notch between Mount Webster and Mount Willard, and let down again by ropes. And the primitive method of transporting any commodities was to cut two poles some fifteen feet in length, nail a couple of bars across the middle, on which a bag or barrel could be fastened, then harness the horse into the smaller ends which served as thills, and let the larger ends, which had no wheels under them, drag on the ground. The first article of commerce that was carried in this way from the sea-shore, through the solemn walls and over the splintered outlet of the Notch, was a barrel of rum. It was taxed heavily, in its own substance, however, to ensure its passage, and reached the Amonoosuc meadows in a very reduced condition. The account between highlands and lowlands on the large ledger of traffic was balanced, soon after, by a barrel of tobacco, raised on the meadows of Lancaster, which, by horse-power and ropes, was let down the pass under Mount Willard, and, after crossing the Saco thirty-two times before reaching Bartlett, was sent on its smoother way to Portsmouth.

The Willey House, Mr. Spaulding tells us, was built as early as 1793. In 1803 a road was laid out through the Notch to Bartlett, at a cost of forty thousand dollars ; and so many teams passed through with produce that it was quite necessary and not unprofitable to keep a house and stable in the Notch for their accommodation. In the autumn of 1825, Mr. Samuel Willey, Jr., with his family, moved into this little tenement, which has derived such tragic interest from his name. During the following winter, we are told that his hospitable kindness and shelter were greeted with as much gratitude by travellers who were obliged to contend with the biting frost, the furious storms, and the drifted snows of the Notch, as the monks of St. Bernard receive from the chilled wanderers of the Alps. The teamsters used to say, that when a furious northwester blew through the Notch in winter, it took two men to hold one man's hair on.

In the spring of 1826, Mr. Willey began to enlarge the conveniences of the little inn for entertaining guests. And in the early summer the spot looked very attractive. There was a beautiful meadow in front, stretching to the foot of the frowning wall of Mount Webster, and gemmed with tall rock-maples. To be sure, Mount

Willey rose at a rather threatening angle, some two thousand feet behind the house ; but it was not so savage in appearance as Mount Webster opposite, and pretty much the whole of its broad, steep wall was draped in green. In a bright June morning the little meadow farm, flecked with the nibbling sheep, and cooled by the patches of shadow flung far out over the grass from the thick maple foliage, must have seemed to a traveller pausing there, and hearing the pleasant murmur of the Saco and the shrill sweetness of the Canada Whistler, as romantic a spot as one could fly to, to escape the fever and the perils of the world.

Late in June, Mr. Willey and his wife, looking from the back windows of their house in the afternoon of a misty day, saw a large mass of the mountain above them sliding through the fog towards their meadows, and almost in a line of the house itself. Rocks and earth came plunging down, sweeping whole trees before them, that would stand erect in the swift slide for rods before they fell. The slide moved under their eye to the very foot of the mountain, and hurled its frightful burden across the road. At first they were greatly terrified, and resolved to remove from the Notch. But Mr. Willey, on reflection, felt confident that such an event was not likely to occur again ; and was satisfied with building a strong hut or cave a little below the house in the Notch, which would certainly be secure, and to which the family might fly for shelter, if they should see or hear another avalanche that seemed to threaten their home.

Later in the summer there was a long hot drought. By the middle of August, the earth, to a great depth in the mountain region, was dried to powder. Then came several days of south wind betokening copious rain. On Sunday the 27th of August, the rain began to fall. On Monday the 28th, the storm was very severe, and the rain was a deluge. Towards evening, the clouds around the White Mountain range and over the Notch, to those who saw them from a distance, were very heavy, black, and awful. It was plain that they were to be busy in their office as a

Factory of river and of rain.

Later in the night they poured their burden in streams. Between nine o'clock in the evening and the dawn of Tuesday, the Saco rose twenty-four feet, and swept the whole intervale between the Notch and Conway.

, The little Rocky Branch in Bartlett, a feeder of the Saco, brought down trees, rocks, and logs from the hill-side, and formed a dam near a log-cabin on its meadow, which made in a little time a pond of water that undermined and floated the house, so that the family could not escape. They climbed into the upper part of the cabin, and for hours were tossed on the mad flood, hearing the roar of the water and the storm, and expecting every moment to be crushed or drowned. The cabin, however, held together, and when the water subsided, they were rescued from their ark. Near by, on the Ellis River, which also pours into the Saco, a herd of colts were swept from a yard where they were penned, and their dead bodies were found mangled by rocks and roots several miles below. Around Ethan Crawford's house, just beyond the Notch, a pond of over two hundred acres was formed in a few hours ; a bridge was dashed against a shed and carried away ninety feet of it ; many of the sheep were drowned, and those which escaped " looked as though they had been washed in a mud-puddle." The water came within eighteen inches of the door, and between the house and stable a river was running. And the channel of the Ammonoosuc, near by, which on Sunday morning was a few yards wide, and overhung by interlaced trees of the ancient forest, was torn out ten times as wide by a mighty torrent that whirled off the banks and trees, and filled the broader bed with boulders, amid which in summer now the river is almost lost. In the little settlement of Gilead, also, thousands of tons of earth, rocks, and forest were loosened from the overhanging hills The roar of the slides was far more frightful than the thunder, and the trails of fire from the rushing boulders more awful than the lightning. For hours the inhabitants were in consternation. Their houses trembled as though an earthquake shook them, and they ex-pected, every moment, to be buried under an avalanche.

27

At Abel Crawford's, six miles from the Willey House, the river overflowed its banks, beat down the fences, tore up the grain, dashed to pieces a new saw-mill, swept the logs, boards, and ruins into the sand, and then circling the house, flooded the cellar, sapped part of the wall, and rose about two feet on the lower floors. Mr. Crawford was not at home ; but the heroic wife placed lighted candles in the windows, and to prevent the house from being demolished by the jam that was threatening it, stood at a window near the corner, and, in the midst of the tempest, pushed away with a pole the timber, which the mad current would send as a battering ram against the walls. And now and then the lightning would show her the drowning sheep, bleating for help, which were hurried past the house in the flood.

On the morning of Tuesday the sun rose into a cloudless sky, and the air was remarkably transparent. The North Conway farmers, busy in saving what they could from the raging flood of the Saco, saw clearly how terrible the storm had been upon the Mount Washington range. The whole line was devastated by landslides. Great grooves could be distinctly seen where the torrents had torn out all the loose earth and stones, and left the solid ledge of the mountain bare. Wherever there was a brook, stones from two to five feet in diameter were rolled down by thousands, in tracks from ten to twenty rods wide, dashing huge hemlocks before them, and leaving no tree nor root of a tree in their path. Soon after, a party ascending by the Ammonoosuc counted thirty slides along the acclivity they climbed, some of which ravaged thus more than a hundred acres of the wilderness,—not only mowing off the trees, but tearing out all the soil and rocks to the depth of twenty and thirty feet. And on the declivities towards North Conway, it was thought that this one storm dismantled more of the great range, during the terrible hours of that Monday night, than all the rains of a hundred years before.

What had been the fate of the little house in the Notch, and of the Willey family, during the deluge ? All communication with them on Tuesday morning was cut off by the floods of the Saco. But at four

o'clock in the afternoon of Tuesday, a traveller passing Ethan Crawford's, some seven miles above the Willey House, desired, if possible,
to get through the Notch that night.   By swimming a horse across

the wildest part of the flood, he was put on the track.   In the narrowest part of the road within the Notch, the water had torn out
huge rocks, and left holes twenty feet deep, and had opened trenches,

27 *

also, ten feet deep and twenty feet long. But the traveller, while daylight lasted, could make his way on foot over the torn and obstructed road, and he managed to reach the lower part of the Notch just before dark. The little house was standing, but there were no human inmates to greet him. And what desolation around! The mountain behind it, once robed in beautiful green, was striped for two or three miles with ravines deep and freshly torn. The lovely little meadow in front was covered with wet sand and rocks intermixed with branches of green trees, with shivered trunks, whose splintered ends " looked similar to an old peeled birchbroom," and with dead logs, which had evidently long been buried beneath the mountain soil. Not even any of the bushes that grew up on the meadow in front of the house were to be seen. The slide from the mountain had evidently divided, not many rods above the house, against a sharp ledge of rock. It had then joined its frightful mass in front of the house, and pushed along to the bed of the Saco, covering the meadow, in some places thirty feet, with the frightful debris and mire.

The traveller entered the house and went through it. The doors were all open ; the beds and their clothing showed that they had been hurriedly left ; a Bible was lying open on a table, as if it had been read just before the family had departed. The traveller consoled himself, at last, with the feeling that the inmates had escaped to Abel Crawford's below, and then tried to sleep in one of the deserted beds. But in the night he heard moanings which frightened him so much, that he lay sleepless till dawn. Then he found that they were the groans of an ox in the stable, that was partly crushed under broken timbers which had fallen in. The two horses were killed. He released the ox, and went on his way towards Bartlett.

Before any news of the disaster had reached Conway, the faithful dog " came down to Mr. Lovejoy's, and, by moanings, tried to make the family understand what had taken place. Not succeeding, he left, and after being seen frequently on the road, sometimes heading north, and then south, running almost at the top of his speed, as though bent on some absorbing errand, he soon disappeared from the region, and has never since been seen."

On Wednesday evening suspicions of the safety of the family were carried down to Bartlett and North Conway, where Mr. Willey's father and brothers lived. But they were not credited. The terrible certainty was to be communicated to the father in the most thrilling way. At midnight of Wednesday, a messenger reached the bank of the river opposite his house in Lower Bartlett, but could not cross. He blew a trumpet, blast after blast. The noise and the mountain echoes startled the family and neighborhood from their repose. They soon gathered on the river bank, and heard the sad message shouted to them through the darkness.

On Thursday the 31st of August, the family and many neighbors were able to reach the Notch. Tall Ethan Crawford left his farm which the floods had ravaged, and went down through the Notch to meet them. " When I got there," he says, " on seeing the friends of that well-beloved family, and having been acquainted with them for many years, my heart was full and my tongue refused utterance, and I could not for a considerable length of time speak to one of them, and could only express my regards I had to them in pressing their hands—but gave full vent to tears. This was the second time my eyes were wet with tears since grown to manhood." Search was commenced at once for the buried bodies. The first that was exhumed was one óf the hired men, David Allen, a man of powerful frame and remarkable strength. He was but slightly disfigured. He was found near the top of a pile of earth and shattered timbers with " hands clenched and full of broken sticks and small limbs of trees." Soon the bodies of Mrs. Willey and her husband were discovered— the latter not so crushed that it could not be recognized.

No more could be found that day. Rude coffins were prepared, and the next day, Friday, about sunset, the simple burial-service was offered. Elder Samuel Hasaltine, standing amidst the company of strong, manly forms, whose faces were wet with tears, commenced the service with the words of Isaiah: " Who hath measured the waters in the hollow of his hand, and meted out heaven with a span, and comprehended the dust of the earth in a measure, and weighed the mountains in scales, and the hills in a balance." How fitting this language in that solemn pass, and how unspeakably more impressive must the words have seemed, when the mountains themselves took them up and literally responded them, joining as mourners in the burial liturgy! For the minister stood so that each one of these sublime words was given back by the echo, in a tone as clear and reverent as that in which they were uttered. We may easily believe that the "effect of all this was soul-stirring beyond description."

The next day the body of the youngest child, about three years old, was found, and also that of the other hired man. On Sunday, the eldest daughter was discovered, at a distance from the others, across the river. A bed was found on the ruins near her body. It was supposed that she was drowned, as no bruise or mark was found upon her. She was twelve years old, and Ethan Crawford tells us " she had acquired a good education, and seemed more like a gentleman's daughter, of fashion and affluence, than the daughter of one who had located himself in the midst of the mountains." These were buried without any religious service. Three children,—a daughter and two sons,—were never found.

It seems to us that nothing can interpret so effectively the terror of this tragedy as the connected statement of the simple facts so far as they are known. We are indebted for the facts to Rev. Benjamin Willey's interesting " Incidents in White Mountain History," and to the story of Ethan Crawford's life, now out of print. But the horror of that night to the doomed family,—who can imagine that? The glimpses given us of the fury of the storm, by the peril of Abel Crawford's family, and by the experience of the settlers that were tossed in their hut upon the flood of the Rocky Branch, furnish but faint coloring of the awfulness of the tempest, as the Willey family must have seen and felt it. About two years after, a man who had moved into the same house witnessed a thunder-tempest in the night, which was not nearly so terrible as the storm of 1826, but which supplies us with better means of conceiving the tremendous passion of the elements amid which the Willey family were overwhelmed, and what must have been their consternation and despair. We are told that the "horror of great darkness" that filled the Notch would be dispelled by the blinding horror of lightning, that now and then kindled the vast gray wall of Mount Webster opposite the house, opened

> The grisly gulfs and slaty rifts
> Which seam its shiver'd head,

and showed the torrents that were hissing down its black shelves and frightful precipices. Next a rock, loosened by a stream or smitten by a thunderbolt, would leap down the wall, followed all the way by a trail of splendor that lighted the whole gorge, and waking a reverberating noise by its concussions, more frightful than the roar of the thunder, which seemed to make the very ground tremble. To this was added the rage of the river and the fury of the rain,—and all united to produce a dismay which we may well believe prevented the inmates from speaking for half an hour, and caused them "to stand and look at each other almost petrified with fear."

For several hours the Willey family were enveloped in

> Such sheets of fire, such bursts of horrid thunder,
> Such groans of roaring wind and rain,

as flamed and roared in the storm that beat upon Lear. The father and mother, anxious for their young children, doubtless saw, with their mind's eye, that fearful land-slide of June more vividly than any horror which the lightning showed them on the walls of their gigantic prison. In every pause of the thunder they were straining to hear the more fearful sound of the grinding avalanche. And what must have been the concentrated agony and dread, when they heard the moving of the loosened ridge; heard nearer and nearer its accumulating roar; heard, and saw perhaps, through one flaming sheet of the lightning, that it was rushing in the line of their little home;

and, unable to command their nerves, or hoping to outrun its flood, rushed from their security into

> The tyranny of the open night too rough
> For nature to endure.

The relatives who studied the ground closely after the disaster were unable to cónjecture why the family could not have outrun the land-slide, or crossed its track, if they left the house as soon as they' heard its descent far up the mountain. Some of them at least, they thought, should thus have been able to escape its devastation. Mr. James Willey informs us that the spirit of his brother appeared to him in a dream, and told him that the family left the house sometime *before* the avalanche, fearing to be drowned or floated off by the Saco, which had risen to their door. They fled back, he said, farther up the mountain to be safe against the peril of water, and thus, when the land-slide moved towards them, were compelled to run a greater distance to escape it than would have been required if they had staid in their home ; while they would have been swept off by the flood, if they had kept the line of the road which could have conducted them out of the Notch. It is a singular fact, Mr. Benjamin Willey tells us, that this explanation accounts for more known features of the catastrophe than any other which has been formed. It explains why the eldest daughter was found without a bruise, as though she had been drowned ; and also the fact that a bed was found near her body, with which certainly the family would not have encumbered themselves, if they had rushed from the house with the single hope of escaping destruction when the avalanche was near. It accounts for the appearance of the body of the hired man, who was first discovered. And, by connecting the terror of a sudden flood with the other horrors of the night, it brings the picture into harmony with what we know of the ravage and disaster along the line of the Saco below.

The Bible was open on the table in the Willey House when it was entered the next day. The family were then secure from the wrath of elements that desolate the earth. At what place could the book have been found open more fitting than the eighteenth psalm, to ex press the horrors of the tempest and the deliverance which the spirit finds ? " The Lord also thundered in the heavens, and the Highest gave his voice ; hailstones and coals of fire. Then the channels of waters were seen, and the foundations of the world were discovered

at thy rebuke, O Lord, at the blast of the breath of thy nostrils. He sent from above, he took me, he drew me out of many waters. He brought me forth also into a large place ; he delivered me, because he delighted in me."

Upon the spot where a portion of the family were buried, it was a custom during several years for each visitor to cast a stone. Thus a large monument was reared out of the ruins of the slide. One visitor, Dr. T. W. Parsons of Boston, has cast an offering upon the grave, that will last longer than the solid pile, in the following ballad, one of the most powerful expressions of his genius, and which might have obviated the necessity of the long description which we have given.

THE WILLEY HOUSE.

A BALLAD OF THE WHITE HILLS.

I.

Come, children, put your baskets down,
 And let the blushing berries be;
Sit here and wreathe a laurel crown,
 And if I win it, give it me.

'Tis afternoon—it is July—
 The mountain shadows grow and grow;
Your time of rest and mine is nigh—
 The moon was rising long ago.

While yet on old Chocorua's top
 The lingering sunlight says farewell,
Your purple fingered labor stop,
 And hear a tale I have to tell.

II.

You see that cottage in the glen,
 Yon desolate forsaken shed—
Whose mouldering threshold, now and then,
 Only a few stray travellers tread.

No smoke is curling from its roof,
 At eve no cattle gather round,
No neighbor now, with dint of hoof,
 Prints his glad visit on the ground.

A happy home it was of yore:
 At morn the flocks went nibbling by,
And Farmer Willey, at his door,
 Oft made their reckoning with his eye.

Where you rank alder-trees have sprung,
 And birches cluster thick and tall,
Once the stout apple overhung,
 With his red gifts, the orchard wall.

Right fond and pleasant, in their ways,
 The gentle Willey people were;
I knew them in those peaceful days,
 And Mary—every one knew her.

III.

Two summers now had seared the hills,
 Two years of little rain or dew;
High up the courses of the rills
 The wild rose and the raspberry grew;

The mountain sides were cracked and dry,
 And frequent fissures on the plain,
Like mouths, gaped open to the sky,
 As though the parched earth prayed for rain

One sultry August afternoon,
 Old Willey, looking toward the West,
Said—" We shall hear the thunder soon;
 Oh! if it bring us rain, 'tis blest."

And even with his word, a smell
 Of sprinkled fields passed through the air
And from a single cloud there fell
 A few large drops—the rain was there.

Ere set of sun a thunder-stroke
 Gave signal to the floods to rise;
Then the great seal of heaven was broke!
 Then burst the gates that barred the skies!

While from the west the clouds rolled on,
 And from the nor'west gathered fast;
" We'll have enough of rain anon,"
 Said Willey—" if this deluge last."

For all these cliffs that stand sublime
 Around, like solemn priests appeared,
Gray Druids of the olden time,
 Each with his white and streaming beard.

Till in one sheet of seething foam
 The mingling torrents joined their might:
But in the Willeys' quiet home
 Was naught but silence and " Good night!
28 *

For soon they went to their repose,
  And in their beds, all safe and warm,
Saw not how fast the waters rose,
  Heard not the growing of the storm.

But just before the stroke of ten,
  Old Willey looked into the night,
And called upon his two hired men,
  And woke his wife, who struck a light,

Though her hand trembled, as she heard
  The horses whinnying in the stall,
And—" children! " was the only word,
  That woman from her lips let fall.

" Mother! " the frighted infants cried,
  " What is it? has a whirlwind come? "
Wildly the weeping mother eyed
  Each little darling, but was dumb.

A sound! as though a mighty gale
  Some forest from its hold had riven,
Mixed with a rattling noise like hail,
  God! art thou raining rocks from heaven

A flash! O Christ! the lightning showed
  The mountain moving from his seat!
Out! out into the slippery road!
  Into the wet with naked feet!

No time for dress—for life! for life!
  No time for any word but this:
The father grasped his boys—his wife
  Snatched her young babe—but not to kiss.

And Mary with the younger girl,
  Barefoot and shivering in their smocks,
Sped forth amid that angry whirl
  Of rushing waves and whelming rocks.

For down the mountain's crumbling side,
  Full half the mountain from on high
Came sinking, like the snows that slide
  From the great Alps about July.

And with it went the lordly ash,
  And with it went the kingly pine,
Cedar and oak amid the crash,
  Dropped down like clippings of the vine.

Two rivers rushed—the one that broke
His wonted bounds and drowned the land,
And one that streamed with dust and smoke,
A flood of earth, and stones and sand.

Then for a time the vale was dry,
The soil had swallowed up the wave;
Till one star looking from the sky,
A signal to the tempest gave:

The clouds withdrew, the storm was o'er,
Bright Aldabaran burned again;
The buried river rose once more,
And foamed along his gravelly glen.

IV.

At morn the men of Conway felt
Some dreadful thing had chanced that night,
And some by Breton woods who dwelt
Observed the mountain's altered height.

Old Crawford and the Fabyan lad
Came down from Amonoosuc then,
And passed the Notch—ah! strange and sad
It was to see the ravaged glen.

But having toiled for miles, in doubt,
With many a risk of limb and neck,
They saw, and hailed with joyful shout,
The Willey House amid the wreck.

That avalanche of stones and sand,
Remembering mercy in its wrath,
Had parted, and on either hand
Pursued the ruin of its path.

And there, upon its pleasant slope,
The cottage, like a sunny isle
That wakes the shipwrecked seaman's hope,
Amid that horror seemed to smile.

And still upon the lawn, before,
The peaceful sheep were nibbling nigh;
But Farmer Willey at his door
Stood not to count them with his eye.

And in the dwelling—O despair!
The silent room! the vacant bed!
The children's little shoes were there—
But whither were the children fled?

That day a woman's head, all gashed,
  Its long hair streaming in the flow,
Went o'er the dam, and then was dashed
  Among the whirlpools down below.

And farther down, by Saco's side,
  They found the mangled forms of four,
Held in an eddy of the tide;
  But Mary, she was seen no more.

Yet never to this mournful vale
  Shall any maid, in summer time,
Come without thinking of the tale
  I now have told you in my rhyme.

And when the Willey House is gone,
  And its last rafter is decayed,
Its history may yet live on
  In this your ballad that I made.

There is little need now of any detailed or elaborate description of the wildness and majesty of the Notch. Its tremendous walls are touched with a terror, reflected from the Willey calamity, which is not explained by the abrupt battlements of Mount Willey and Mount Webster, and the purple bluff of Mount Willard, which stands in the way between them to forbid any passage through. It is well to remind visitors of the Crawford House, however, that the most impressive view of the Notch, after all, is not gained by riding up through it from Bartlett, but by riding down into it from the Crawford House through the narrow gateway. This excursion should, without fail, be made from the Crawford House by all persons who have only ascended through it from Conway, by the stage. They will find a turn in the road, not a mile from the gateway, where three tremendous rocky lines sweep down to a focus from Mount Willard, Mount Webster, and Mount Willey. There is more character in this view than in the aspect of the open gorge at the Willey House. This is the Notch in bud, with its power concentrated and suggested to the imagination. At the Willey House it is all open; you stand between walls two miles long, and there are no ragged, nervous lines of rock running down from a cloud, or lying sharp against the blue distance.

Especially if one can take a walk or drive to the point we speak of, near the Crawford House, late in a clear afternoon, he will be doubly repaid by the sight of one of these mountain edges sweeping down in shadow to the haggard ruins at its base, and of the other glistening in delicate and cheerful gold. A moonlight view at the same spot gives

the contrast no less marked and impressive, in blackness on one side and silver on the other.

But to know the Notch truly, one must take the drive from the Crawford House to the top of Mount Willard, and look down into it. A man stands there as an ant might stand on the edge of a huge turccn. We arc lifted twelve hundred feet over the gulf on the brink of an almost perpendicular wall, and see the sides, Webster and Willey, rising on either hand eight hundred feet higher still, and running off two or three miles towards the Willey House. The road below is a mere bird-track. The long battlements that, from the front of the Willey House, tower on each side so savagely, from this point seem to flow down in charming curves to meet at the stream, which looks like the slender keel from which spring up the ribs that form the hold of a tremendous line-of-battle ship on the stocks. But perhaps we suggest a more exact and noble comparison if we speak of its resemblance to the trough of the sea in a storm. They are earth-waves, these curving walls that front each other. They were flung up thus, it may be, in the passion of the boiling land, and stiffened before they could dash their liquid granite against each other, or subside by successive oscillations into calm.

Mr. Ruskin has called attention by drawings in the fourth volume of the Modern Painters, to the picturesque characters of the lines of projection and escape among the *debris* of the Swiss mountains. They are almost always found to represent portions of infinite curves ; and in spite of breaks and disturbances, their natural unity is so sweet and perfect, that we have little difficulty in turning the sketches of them into the outlines of a bird's wing, slightly ruffled, but still graceful, and very different from any that we should suppose would be designed or drawn by a land-slide, or the rage of a torrent. Standing over the Notch, also, we are struck with the grace that curbed the rage of the murderous avalanches. We remember talking once with a man who was very indignant at all poetic descriptions of natural scenery. " Now," said he, " what can be honestly said of this Willey Notch, but. ' Good Heavens, what a rough hole ! ' " Yet, on Mount Willard, it is the delicacy of slope and curve, and not the roughness, that is prominent. " Strength and beauty are in his sanctuary," and it is beauty which the savage forces serve at last. The waste of the mountains is not destructive, but creative. In the long run the ravage of the avalanche is beneficent. And here we see how, as its apparent cruelty is overruled by the law of love, its apparent disorder is overruled by the law of loveliness. " The hand of God, leading the wrath of the torrent to minister to the life of mankind, guides also its grim surges by the law of their delight ; and bridles the bounding rocks, and appeases the flying foam, till they lie down in the same lines that lead forth the fibres of the down on a cygnet's breast."

The view of the summits of the Mount Washington range, too, from Mount Willard—the only point within some miles of the Notch where any of them can be seen—is a reward for the short excursion, almost as valuable as the view of the Gulf of the Notch. And let us again advise visitors to ascend Mount Willard if possible, late in the afternoon. They will then see one long wall of the Notch in shadow, and can watch it move slowly up the curves of the opposite side, displacing the yellow splendor, while the dim green dome of Washington is gilded by the sinking sun " with heavenly alchemy."

Those who love mountain cascades, and especially those who love to climb to them through the undisturbed wilderness, will find now a new temptation to a drive into the Notch and through it from the Crawford House. The Flume and the Silver Cascade pouring down from Mount Webster have gladdened the eyes of almost all the visitors to the hotel, for they are visible from the road. The windings and leapings of the Silver Cascade, whose downward path for more than a mile is in view, suggest the movement and in part the picture of Shelley's lines :—

> Arethusa arose
> From her couch of snows
> In the Acroceraunian mountains,—
> From cloud and from crag,
> With many a jag,
> Shepherding her bright fountains,
> She leapt down the rocks
> With her rainbow locks
> Streaming among the streams ;—
> Her steps paved with green
> The downward ravine

29

Which slopes to the western gleams:
And gliding and springing,
She went ever singing,

In murmurs as soft as sleep;
    The Earth seemed to love her,
    And Heaven smiled above her,
As she lingered towards the deep.

But a more wild and beautiful waterfall than any hitherto seen on the western side of the mountains, was discovered on Mount Willey in September, 1858, by Mr. Ripley of North Conway, and Mr. Porter of New York. An old fisherman had reported at the Crawford House that he had once seen a wonderful cascade on a stream that pours down that mountain, and empties into the Saco below the Willey House. These gentlemen drove through the Notch to the second bridge below the Willey House, which crosses a stream with the unpoetical name of Cow Brook, and followed up this rivulet into the wild forest. An ascent of nearly two miles revealed to them the object of their search inclosed between the granite walls of a very steep ravine, whose cliffs, crowned with a dense forest of spruce, are singularly grand. They saw the cascade leaping first over four rocky stairways, each of them about six feet high, and then gliding, at an angle of forty-five degrees, a hundred and fifty feet with many graceful curves down a solid bed of granite into a pool below. The Cascade is about seventy-five feet wide at the base, and fifty at the summit.

Exploring the stream nearly a mile higher, other falls were discovered, each one deserving especial notice, and one or two of most rare beauty. The finest of these upper falls was christened, we believe by the discoverers, the "Sparkling Cascade," and the larger one below, the "Sylvan-Glade Cataract." The brook itself has been named since in honor of Mr. Ripley, and the ravine, of Mr. Porter. We hope, however, that the name "Avalanche Brook," which we believe the explorers first gave to it, may be the permanent title of the stream, since it flows near the track of the fatal land-slide of 1826, and that Mr. Ripley's name may be transferred to the Cataract.

Child of the clouds! remote from every taint
Of sordid industry thy lot is cast;
Thine are the honors of the lofty waste:

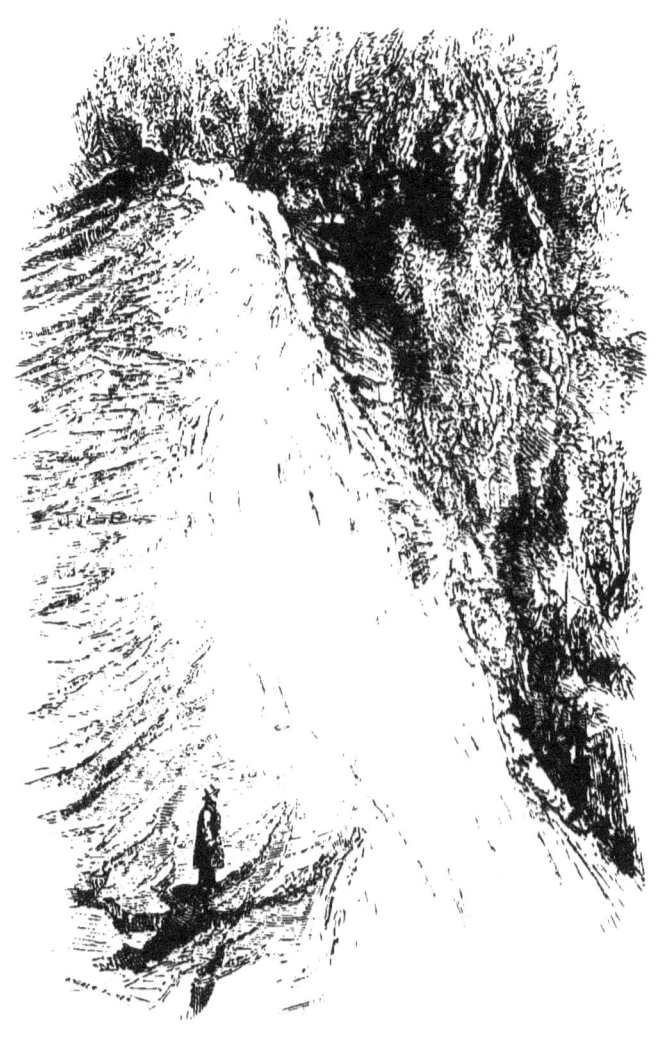

Not seldom when with heat the valleys rainr.
Thy handmaid Frost with spangled tissue quaint

Thy cradle decks;—to chant thy birth, thou hast
No meaner Poet than the whistling Blast,
And Desolation is thy Patron-Saint!
She guards thee, ruthless Power! who would not spare
Those mighty forests, once the bison's screen,
Where stalked the huge deer to his shaggy lair
Through paths and alleys roofed with sombre green;
Thousands of years before the silent air
Was pierced by whizzing shaft of hunter keen!

Mr. Champney, who visited these falls about a fortnight after their discovery, is inclined to ascribe to them a nobler beauty than any others thus far known among the mountains. He describes the picturesque rock-forms as wonderful, and their richness in color and marking, in mosses and lichens, as more admirable than any others he has had the privilege of studying in the mountain region. And this cascade is only a sample, probably, of the uncelebrated beauties in the wilderness around the White Hills. With the exception of the hunter who gave the rumor of them at the Crawford House, they had not, probably, been looked upon by human eyes until Mr. Ripley and his party detected them. When Mr. Champney came down from his first study of their picturesqueness, to which we are indebted for the sketch here given, the comet was blazing above the jagged rocks of Mount Webster. And when that comet, on its preceding visit, hung over a world upon which no representatives of our race had appeared, to admire the majestic curve of its trail and to compute its orbit, the music of the waterfall was still flowing, it may be;

Through the green tents, by eldest Nature drest,

and its cool spray was sprinkled, as now, upon

*
the unplanted forest floor, whereon
The all-seeing sun for ages hath not shone;
Where feeds the moose, and walks the surly bear,
And up the tall mast runs the woodpecker.

Indeed, only a short distance from the Crawford House, not more than a fifteen minutes' walk through the woods, a succession of little cascades were discovered, in the same month, which Nature had cunningly kept from human knowledge. These being so easily accessible, and yet so wild and charming, must add very much to the attractions of the hotel at the Notch. Perhaps it is these cascades that feed the " Basin," which has attained celebrity from Rev. Henry Ward Beecher's bath in it, after his return from the top of Mount Washington. Indeed, it is possible, that, without knowing it, Mr. Beecher was the discoverer of these falls. If so, they found their poet when they first gave hospitality in their crystal bowl to a human figure, as the following passage, which is as good as a bath to the mind, will abundantly testify :—

" We went toward the Notch, and, turning to the right at the first little stream that let itself down from the mountains, we sought the pools in which we knew such streams kept their sweetest thoughts, expressing them by trout. The only difficulty was in the selection. This pool was deep, rock-rimmed, transparent, gravel-bottomed. The next was level-edged and rock-bottomed, but received its water with such a gush that it whirled around the basin in a liquid dance of bubbles. The next one received a divided stream, one part coming over a shelving rock and sheeting down in white, while the other portion fell into a hollow and murmuring crevice, and came gurgling forth from the half-dark channel. Half way down, the rock was smooth and pleasant to the feet. In the deepest part was fine gravel and powdered mountain, commonly called sand. The waters left this pool even more beautifully than they entered it ; for the rock had been rounded and grooved, so that it gave a channel like the finest moulded lip of a water-vase ; and the moss, beginning below, had crept up into the very throat of the passage, and lined it completely, giving to the clear water a green hue as it rushed through, whirling itself into a plexus of cords, or a kind of pulsating braid of water. This was my pool. It waited for me. How deliciously it opened its flood to my coming. It rushed up to every pore, and sheeted my skin with an aqueous covering, prepared in the mountain water-looms. Ah, the coldness ;—every drop was molten hail. It was the very brother of ice. At a mere hint of winter, it would change to ice again ! If the crystal nook was such a surprise of delight to me, what must I have been to it, that had, perhaps, never been invaded, unless by the lip of a moose, or by the lithe and spotted form of sylvan trout! The drops and bubbles ran up to me and broke about my neck and ran laughing away, frolicking over the mossy margin, and I could hear them laughing all the way down below. Such a monster had never, perhaps, taken covert in the pure, pellucid bowl before!

" But this was the centre-part. Not less memorable was the fringe. The trees hung in the air on either side, and stretched their green leaves for a roof far above. The birch and alder, with here and there a silver fir, in bush form, edged the rocks on either side. As you looked up the stream, there opened an ascending avenue of cascades, dripping rocks bearded with moss, crevices filled with grass, or dwarfed shrubs, until the whole was swallowed up in the leaves and trees far above. But if you turned down the stream, then through a lane of richest green, stood the open sky, and lifted up against it, thousands of feet, Mount Willard, rocky and rent, or with but here and there a remnant of evergreens, sharp and ragged. The sun was behind it, and poured against its farther side his whole tide of light, which lapped over as a stream dashes over its bounds and spills its waters beyond. So it stood up over against this ocean of atmospheric gold, banked huge and rude against a most resplendent heaven! As I stood donning my last articles of raiment, and wringing my over-wet hair, I saw a trout move very deliberately out from under a rock by which I had lain, and walk quietly across to the other side. As he entered the crevice, a smaller one left it and came as demurely across to *his* rock. It was evident that the old people had sent them out to see if the coast was clear, and whether any damage had been done. Probably it was thought that there had been a *slide* in the mountain, and that a huge icicle or lump of snow had plunged into their pool and melted away there. If there are piscatory philosophers below water half as wise as those above, this would be a very fair theory of the disturbance to which their mountain homestead had been subjected. As I had eaten of their salt, of course I respected the laws of hospitality, and no deceptive fly of mine shall ever tempt trout in a brook which begets pools so lovely, and in pools that yield themselves with such delicious embrace to the pleasures of a mountain bath."

About five miles from the Crawford House, driving on a downward grade, on a road more pleasantly bordered with foliage, perhaps, than any other among the hills, we come to another resting-place for travellers, called " The White Mountain House." The White Mountain range itself, though it is ascended from the public-house at the Notch, is not visible from that point. It is only when we drive out into the open plain, from which the huge mound rises, called " The Giant's Grave," not far from the White Mountain House, that the chain itself comes into view. Here every summit but one is in sight, and a very favorable opportunity is afforded for observing the effects of the land-slides, which seem to have plundered the lower mountains of the range of a large proportion of their substance, and have left traces of ravage in fantastic lines, deeply engraved upon their thin sides.

The distance, in a straight line from the plain at the foot of The Giant's Grave to the top of Mount Washington, is nearly seven miles and a half. The height of the summit over this level area is less than five thousand feet, although it rises more than six thousand two hundred feet above the sea. A very noble view of Mount Washington itself is gained by approaching near its base on this area, and seeing it separated from the rest of the ridge.

> The mighty pyramids of stone,
> That, wedge-like, cleave the desert airs,
> When nearer seen and better known,
> Are but gigantic flights of stairs.
>
> The distant mountains, that uprear
> Their solid bastions to the skies,
> Are crossed by pathways, that appear
> As we to higher levels rise.

From the Notch, the ascent of Mount Washington is made by mounting gradually the steps of Clinton, Pleasant, Franklin and Munroe,—each rising higher than the last, and all of them destitute of trees,—which lead to the crest of the ridge. From the White Mountain House there is a carriage-road on which visitors are carried some ways up on Mount Washington itself, to within about two miles of the summit. Here horses are taken for the remainder of the ascent. The views, by both roads, when the day is clear, give compensation that makes the toil a trifle. But we must reserve what we have to say of the views which the summit gives, for the next chapter, and we have no intention of assuming to decide which of the three routes by which the ascent is made is preferable.

The rambles in the neighborhood of the White Mountain House are exceedingly interesting. There are many hills of moderate height which may be scaled, from which views of the great range are gained, that, especially towards evening, are very impressive and rich. We must remember that the neighborhood of this hotel supplies the nearest access to the White Mountain range on the western side ; in fact it is the only point where, from the level of the road, the range is even visible, after we leave North Conway.

Then, too, the falls and cliffs of the Ammonoosuc lie not far from the hotel. This river, one of the principal feeders of the Connecticut, is undoubtedly the wildest stream in New England. The water, which it receives from the cone of Mount Washington, and from the Blue Ponds, near the summit of Mount Munroe, dashes down the mountain side, often in leaps of thirty to forty feet at a time,—pours over the gray granite shelves near the White Mountain House, where, after every heavy rain the water is tossed into heaps as high as haycocks,— catches only for a moment the deep shadows of the balsam fir, white pine, and spruce, which the grand cliffs of its right bank throw upon it, and will not stop to play with the flickering lights and shades that dance upon its ripples through the birches that rustle on the flat ledges which guard it on the left,—but in a hurry along its whole course of thirty miles, during which it descends over five thousand feet, is calmed in the current of the sober Connecticut that moves with a lordly leisure towards the sea.

> Fast by the river's trickling source I sit,
>   And view the new-born offspring of the skies;
> Cradled on rocky felt, a nursling yet,
>   Fed by his mother-cloud's soft breast, he lies.
>
> But lo! the heaven-born streamlet swelling flows,
>   Dreaming e'en now of fame, the woods adown,
> And as his bosom heaves with longing throes,
>   His wavelets rock the mirrored sun and moon.
>
> And now he scorns beneath the firs to creep,
>   Or hemmed by narrow mountain walls to flow,
> But tumbles headlong down the rocky steep,
>   And foams along the pebbly vale below.
>
> " Come on! come on! " he every brookling hails,
>   " Here suns exhaust and sands absorb your force,
> Ye brothers come! through smiling fields and dales
>   I lead you down to your primeval source."

The children of the rain obey, and hurl
  Applause, as they the young adventurer meet.
With kingly pride his swelling billows curl,
  And woods and rocks fall prostrate at his feet.

Now to the plains, in triumph he descends
  With dark blue train and state that homage claim;
Parched fields his breath revives, as on he bends
  His course, baptizing nations with his name.

And bards in strain divine his praises sing,
  Tall ships are on his bosom borne away,
Proud cities court him, flowery meadows cling
  Around his knees and sue him to delay.

But they detain him not—with ceaseless haste
  Fair fields and gilded towns he hurries by
Nor slacks his tide impetuous, till at last
  He on his father's bosom falls to die.

The name of Crawford is associated with the Giant's Grave and the neighboring meadow. And we ought not to leave the spot until we have paid respect to the memory of the early settlers of the wilderness which is upborne on the flanks of the White Hills. We can now breakfast in Boston, and reach the base of Mount Washington, on the eastern or the western side, in season for supper. It is difficult for us to conceive the hardships of the pioneers who, seventy or eighty years ago, invaded " the forest primeval," and determined to wring a livelihood from lands upon which, at evening or morning, the shadow of Mount Washington was flung. Whether we read the accounts of the first settlers in Jackson, Conway, Bartlett, Albany, Bethlehem or Shelburne, the stories are essentially the same. The perils of isolation, the ravages of wild beasts, the wrath of the mountain torrents, the obstacles to intercourse which the untamed wilderness interposed,—every form of discomfort and of danger was visibly threatened by the great mountains to guard their immediate slopes and valleys from intrusion, but in vain. Whether we study history on a large or a small scale, we find that the movements of population, carrying the threads of civilization to new districts, new climates, and foreign shores, furnish the most mystic chapters in the revelation of an Intellect that works through human folly as through human wisdom for generous ends.

When there was so much land within the bounds of civilization already unoccupied and unclaimed, what could have induced families eighty years ago, to move from a great distance in order to colonize the banks of the Ellis River, or the wild borders of the upper Ammonoosuc, or the glen through which above North Conway the Saco rushes? The very horses of the settlers on the Bartlett meadows, in 1777, would not stay, but struck over the hills due south, in the direction of Lee from which they had been taken. They all perished in the forest before the succeeding spring. And many of the pioneers, as if to taste hardship in its bitterest flavor, started for their new homes in the winter. One couple travelled eighty miles on snow-shoes, the husband carrying a pack of furniture on his back, in order to enjoy the privilege of nearly starving in Conway. Joseph Pinkham and his family removed to Jackson in 1790, when the snow was five feet deep on a level. Their hand-sled, on which their provisions, furniture, and clothing were packed, was drawn by a pig which they compelled to work in harness. John Pendexter and wife made a triumphal entry into Bartlett in the winter. She rode a large part of the way from Portsmouth, on a feeble horse, with a feather-bed under her and a child in her arms, while the husband dragged the rest of their worldly wealth over the snow. Their child was cradled in a sap-trough, and became the mother of a family, "all of whom do honor to their parentage."

Several of the earliest settlers lived for years without any neighbors within many miles. The pioneer in the village of Jackson was obliged to go ten miles to a mill, and would carry a bushel of corn on his shoulder, and take it back in meal, without removing the burden during the whole distance ; and Ethan Crawford tells us that his grandfather went once to a lower settlement for a bushel of salt, the scarcity of which produced a great deal of distress and sickness in the cabins of the forest, and returned with it on his back, eighty miles through the woods. And it was not from the lack of salt alone that these bold people suffered. Not all the families scattered along the course of a mountain stream owned cows, and could have so rich a diet as milk-porridge. Water and meal, with dried trout without salt, were their dependence when game was shy, or long storms prevented hunting. Sometimes when famine threatened, they were obliged to send deputations thirty, fifty, sixty miles to purchase grain. And we read that now and then, in times of great scarcity, the most hardy settlers wore a wide strap of skin, which. as they grew more emaciated was drawn tighter, to mitigate the gnawings of hunger, that they might hold out till relief came. Often we are told the buckle was drawn almost to the last hole. In the early history of Conway, we read of a man who had tightened his strap thus, and was lying down thinking that he should never rise again. A neighbor, almost as weak, and who did not own a gun crept to his door to say that a moose was not far from the cabin. The news excited the famishing pioneer so that he was able to cut a new hole in the strap and gird it tighter. He then crept out and was fortunate enough, by resting the gun, to kill the moose. The skeleton men soon had a bountiful repast, and it is pleasant to read the assurance that before thirty-six hours their straps would hardly reach round them.

Besides occasional famine, these families were tried by the fresh-ets that tore up their rude bridges, swept off their barns, and even floated their houses on the meadows. On the Saco intervale, in the year 1800, a heavy rain swelled the river, so that it floated every cabin and shed that had been built on it, and bore them quietly down the current, " the cocks crowing merrily as they floated on." Let us be grateful for this note of cheer in the story. The year before this the few settlers in Bethlehem attempted to build a bridge over the Ammonoosuc. The laborers, who worked all day in the water, had nothing to eat but milk-porridge, which was carried to them hot by their wives. At last they were obliged to cut and burn wood enough in the forest to make a large load of potash, which they sent to Concord, Mass., a distance of a hundred seventy miles, to be bar-tered for provisions. The teamster was absent four weeks, and dur-ing part of this time the settlers cooked green chocolate roots and a few other wild plants, to save them from starvation.

When the settlers accumulated anything worth stealing which the mountains could not destroy by natural ravage, the bears were un-loosed upon them. If nuts and berries failed, and there was a famine in the woods, down came an irruption of black barbarians upon the cattle, especially upon the pigs. Often a huge bear would make his appearance near a settler's house, steal a good-sized pig with his forepaws, and run off with him, eating as he ran. And sometimes the personal contests of the squatters with these aboriginal tenants, would be such as are decidedly more pleasant in history than in experience. What a charming surprise, for instance, to an early settler under Chocorua, when he ascended a hill near his cabin, on a very dark night, and came suddenly into the embrace, more warm than friendly, of a big bear that was waiting for him at the top. Then commenced a wrestling-match which it is delightful to contemplate. The bear was an adept in hugging, but the man understood the art of tripping, and by a dexterous movement threw the bear from her feet. The two rolled down the hill in the darkness, over and over, and tumbled into a pond at the foot. Here the bear let go, and both, crawling wet out of the water, were content to consider it a drawn battle, and retired to their respective places of abode.

The first things, of course, which the settlers did when a dozen families had collected within the compass of a few miles, were to organize a church, and establish a school. By the time two dozen families were gathered in a valley, it was almost certain that a second church of a different sect would be started. Ministers toiled all the week on their meadow or wood-lot, and, if they did not preach without notes, wrote their sermons at night by the blaze of pitch-knots. The school-house was built of rough hemlock logs, covered with rude boards and the bark of trees, and was lighted by two or three panes of glass placed singly in its wall. " The something that answered for a fireplace and chimney was constructed of poor bricks and rocks, together with sticks, laid up so as to form what was called a ' catting,' to guide the smoke." And to this cabin the scholars went in paths cut through the thick forests. Yet in many an instance the passion for learning was kindled within these rude hovels as intensely as it has ever been in the most shapely academy. A son of one of these pioneers, now a clergyman, who attended such a school, assures us that many an excited contest in spelling and ciphering took place within its walls, and that " many tears have been shed, and bursts of applause shaken the very bark on its roof at the successful performance of the ' Conjuror ' and ' Neighbor Scrapewell.' " Such rough churches, and wigwam schools, have been the cell-germs from which the organizing power of civilization in our cold north has poured.

From one of these " locations," or " grants," the story runs that a man once made his appearance in the State Legislature, and took a seat. He was asked for proof that he was the choice of the people.

" Whom could they put up against me ? " he said ; " I am the only man in my town." His claim to a seat was allowed. There must have been a few more inhabitants in the settlement in upper Coös which was legally warned to have training. After the officers were chosen, there was but one soldier. And he said, " Gentlemen, I hope you will not be too severe in drilling me, as I may be needed another time. I can form a solid column, but it will rack me shockingly to display."

The hardships of which we have been writing are forcibly suggested at the Giant's Grave. Abel Crawford lived in a log hut on that mound some months, alone. But in 1792. the Rosebrook family moved into it when it was buried in snow, so that the entrance to it could be found with difficulty. For six weeks neither the sun, nor the heat from the cabin, would make a drop of water fall from the caves. During the whole winter they were dependent upon the game they could catch, and often, from fear that the father might return empty, the children would be sent down through the Notch twelve miles, to Abel Crawford's, to obtain something for sustenance. Good Mrs. Rosebrook often lay awake late in the night, waiting anxiously for the children's return through the snows and winds of the awful Notch, and when they arrived would " pour out her love in prayer and thankfulness to her heavenly Father, for preserving them, and that she was permitted to receive them again to her humble mansion."

Abel Crawford, in his old age, was never tired of telling stories of the hardships and adventures of the pioneers. He was well named the " veteran pilot " of the hills ; for he was the first guide that introduced visitors to the grandeur of the scenery so easily reached now, and he saw the gradual process of civilization applied to the wilderness between Bethlehem and Upper Bartlett. When he was about twenty-five years old, he wandered through the region alone for months, dressed in tanned mooseskin, lord of the

> Cradle, hunting-ground, and bier
> Of wolf and otter, bear and deer.

He assisted in cutting the first footpath to the ridge, and at seventy-five, in the year 1840, he rode the first horse that climbed the cone of Mount Washington. During the last ten years of his life he was a noble object of interest to thousands of visitors from all parts of the United States, for whom the whole tour of the hills had been smoothed into a pastime and luxury. He died at eighty-five.

He had been so long accustomed to greet travellers in the summer, that he longed to have his life spared till the visitors made their appearance in Bartlett, on their way to the Notch. He used to sit in the warm spring days, supported by his daughter, his snow-white hair falling to his shoulders, waiting for the first ripple of that large

tide which he had seen increasing in volume for twenty years. Not
long after the stages began to carry their summer freight by his
door, he passed away. We have a very pleasant recollection of
the venerable appearance of the patriarch in front of his house
under Mount Crawford, in the year 1849, when we made our first
visit to the White Hills. A large bear was chained to a pole near
the house, and the stage load of people had gathered around, equally
interested in seeing a specimen of the first settlers and of the aboriginal tenants of the wilderness. The old man handed the writer a
biscuit, and said : " Give it to the beast, young man, and then tell
when you go back to Boston, that a bear ate out of your hand up in
these mountains." The difference between an experience in the
mountain region, as our party were then enjoying it for a week, and
his early acquaintance with its hardships and solitude, was the difference between feeding a fettered bear with a biscuit, and wrestling in
a tight hug with a hungry one alone in the forest.

In 1803 the first rude public-house for straggling visitors to the
White Mountains, was erected on the Giant's Grave itself. And in
1819 the first rough path was cut through the forest on the side of
the Mount Washington range to the rocky ridge. Ethan Allen
Crawford, who lived on the Giant's Grave, marked and cleared this
path in connection with Abel Crawford, his father, who was living
eight miles below the Notch. A few years after, Ethan spotted and
trimmed a footpath on the side of Mount Washington itself, along
essentially the same route by which carriages are driven now from
the White Mountain House to the Cold Spring. And it ought not to
be forgotten that it was by Ethan Crawford, that the first protection
for visitors was built under the cone of Mount Washington. It was
a stone hut, furnished with a small stove, an iron chest, a roll of sheet
lead, and a plentiful supply of soft moss and hemlock boughs for
bedding. The lead was the cabin-register on which visitors left their
names engraved by a piece of sharp iron. Every particle of this
camp and all the furniture, was swept off on the night of the storm
by which the Willey family were overwhelmed.

Noble Ethan Crawford ! we must pause a few moments before the career of this stalwart Jötun of the mountains, in the story of whose fortunes the savageness and hardships of the wilderness and the heroic qualities they nurse are shown in one picture. He was born in 1792. His early childhood was passed in a log hut a few miles from the Notch ; and in his manhood, after a fire in 1818 had burned the comfortable house on the Giant's Grave, he lived again in a log house with but one apartment and no windows. In 1819, he had built a rough house of a larger size, with a stone chimney, in which during the cold spells of winter, more than a cord of wood would be burned in twenty-four hours. He tells us that he never owned a hat, mittens, or shoes until he was thirteen years old ; yet could harness and unharness horses in the biting winter weather with bare head, hands, and feet, " and not mind, or complain of the cold, as I was used to it." As to what is called comfort in the lowlands, he found that

> Naught the mountain yields thereof,
> But savage health and sinews tough.

He grew to be nearly seven feet in height, and rejoiced in a strength which he would show in lifting five hundred weight into a boat ; in dragging a bear that he had muzzled to his house, that he might be tamed ; or in carrying a buck home alive, upon his shoulders. What a flavor of wild mountain life, what vivid suggestions of the closest tug of man with nature,—of raw courage and muscle against frost and gale, granite and savageness, do we find in his adventures and exploits ;—his leaping from a load of hay in the Notch when a furious gust made it topple, and catching it on his shoulder to prevent it from falling over a precipice ; his breaking out the road, for miles, through the wild winter drifts ; his carrying the mail on his back, after freshets, to the next settlement, when a horse could not cross the streams ; his climbings of Mount Washington with a party of adventurers, laden like a pack-horse, without suffering more fatigue than ordinary men would feel after a level walk of ten miles ; his returns from the summit bearing some exhausted member of a

31 *

party on his back ; his long, lonely tramps, on snow-shoes, after moose, and his successful shooting of a pair of the noble beasts, two miles back of the Notch, about dark, and sleeping through the cold night in their warm skins, undismayed by the wolf howls that serenaded him !

The tribe of bears in a circumference of twenty miles knew him well. Many a den he made desolate of its cubs by shaking them, like apples, from trees into which they would run to escape him ; then tying his hankerchief around their mouths he would take them home under his arm to tame them. Many a wrestle did he have with full grown ones who would get their feet in his traps. Scarcely a week passed while he lived among the mountains which was not marked by some encounter with a bear.

With the wolves also, he carried on a war of years. So long as he kept sheep he could not frighten the wolves into cessation of hostilities. The marauders showed the skill of a surgeon in their rapine and slaughter. Ethan found, now and then, a sheepskin a few rods from his house with no mark upon it except a smooth slit from the throat to the fore legs, as though it had been cut with a knife. The legs had been taken off as far as the lowest joint ; all the flesh had been eaten out clean, and only the head and backbone had been left attached to the pelt. When the feat was accomplished, the wolves would give him notice by a joint howl, which the Washington range would echo from their " bleak concave," so that all the woods seemed filled with packs of the fierce pirates. Once in a December night four wolves made a descent upon his sheep, which fled among the carriages near the house, for safety. Ethan went out in. his nightdress and faced them in the bright moonlight. He had no weapon, and so they rose on their haunches to hear what he might have to say. He harangued them, to little purpose for some time, and at last " observed to them that they had better make off with themselves," with the intimation that an axe or gun would be soon forthcoming. They then turned about and marched away, " giving us some of their lonesome music." But Ethan found, the next morning, that they had enjoyed his hospitality, by digging up carcasses of bears back of the stable, and gnawing them close to the bone.

He thinned the sables from the region by his traps. The banks of the neighboring brooks he depopulated of otters. Yet he had an affection for all the creatures of the wilderness, and loved to have young wolves, and tame bucks, and well-behaved bears, and domesticated sable, around his premises : while the collecting of rare alpine plants from the snowy edges of the ravines on the ridge, where Nature had "put them according to their merits," was "a beautiful employment, which I always engaged in with much pleasure." But his most remarkable adventures were his contests with the wild-cats, the fiercest animals which the mountains harbored. The hills that slope towards the Ammonoosuc were cleared by him of these furious freebooters, that made great havoc with his geese and sheep. His greatest exploit was his capture of one of these creatures in a tree within the Notch, by a lasso made of birch sticks, which he twisted on the spot. He slipped it over the wild-cat's neck, and jerked the animal down ten feet. The noose broke. He repaired it instantly, fastened it once more around the creature's head, pulled him down within reach, and after a severe battle, killed him. He seems to have possessed a magic fetter, like that which the dark elves of the Scandinavian myths wove to bind the wolf Fenrir, and which was plaited of six things into a cord smooth and soft as a silken string : the beards of women, the noise of a cat's footfall, the roots of stones, the sinews of bears, the spittle of birds, and the breath of fish.

What extremes in Ethan's experience ! He entertained many of the wisest and most distinguished of the country under his rude roof, and was gratefully remembered for his hospitality, and his faithful service in guiding them to the great ridge. He would come home from a bear-fight, to find in his house, perhaps, "a member of Congress, Daniel Webster," who desired his assistance on foot to the summit of Mount Washington. There was a couple whose talk would have been worth hearing ! Ethan says that they went up "without meeting anything worthy of note, more than was common for me to find, *but to him things appeared interesting.* And when we arrived there, he addressed himself in this way, saying : ' Mount Washington, I have come a long distance, and have toiled hard to arrive at your summit, and now you give me a cold reception. I am extremely sorry, that I shall not have time enough to view this grand prospect which lies before me, and nothing prevents but the uncomfortable atmosphere in which you reside.' " How accurately Ethan reported the address, we cannot certify ; but as the rostrum was the grandest, and the audience the smallest, which was ever honored with a formal speech by the great orator, the picture should not be lost. The snow from a sudden squall froze upon the pair as they descended the cone. The statesman was evidently interested in his guide, for Ethan says that, " the next morning, after paying his bill, he made me a handsome present of twenty dollars."

And Ethan's life was perpetually set in remarkable contrasts. From struggles with wild-cats in the forests of Cherry Mountain, to the society of his patient, faithful, pious wife, was a distance as wide as can be indicated on the planet. Mount Washington looked down into his uncouth domicile, and saw there

Sparta's stoutness, Bethlehem's heart.

Lucy taught him how to meet calamity without despair and repining. When his house burned down, and left him with no property but one new cheese and the milk of the cows, his wife, though sick, was not despondent. When his debts, caused by this fire, pressed heavy, and he staggered under difficulties as he never did under the heaviest load in the forest, she assured him that Providence had some wise purpose in their trouble. When his crops were swept off, and his meadows filled with sand by freshets, Lucy's courage was not crushed. He knocked down a swaggering bully, once, on a muster-field in Lancaster, and was obliged to promise Lucy that he would never give way to an angry passion again. When death invaded their household, and his own powerful frame was so shaken by disease and pain, that a flash of lightning, as he said, seemed to run from his spine to the ends of his hair, his wife's religious patience and trust proved an undrainable cordial. And after he became weakened by sickness, if he staid out long after dark, Lucy would take a lantern and go into the woods to search for him. He was put into jail at last in Lancaster for debt. Lucy wrote a pleading letter to his chief creditor to release him, but without effect. This, says Ethan, "forced me, in the jail, to reflect on human nature, and it overcame me, so that I was obliged to call for the advice of physicians and a nurse." Other forms of adversity, too, beset him,— opposition to his public-house when travellers became more plentiful, which destroyed his prospects of profit; the breaking of a bargain for the sale of his lands; foul defamation of his character to the post-office authorities in Washington, from whom he held an appointment. Broken in health, oppressed by pecuniary burdens, and with shattered spirits, he left the plateau at the base of Mount Washington for a more pleasant home in Vermont, accompanied by Lucy, whose faith did not allow her to murmur. But he experienced hard fortune there, too, and returned to die, within sight of the range, an old man, before he had reached the age of fifty-six years.

Since the breaking up of his home on the Giant's Grave, the mountains have heard no music which they have echoed so heartily as the windings of his horn, and the roar of the cannon which he used to load to the muzzle, that his guests might hear a park of artillery reply. Few men that have ever visited the mountains have done more faithful work or borne so much adversity and suffering. The cutting of his heel-cord with an axe, when he was chopping out the first path up Mount Washington, was a type of the result to himself of his years of toil in the wilderness; and his own quaint reflection on that wound, which inflicted lameness upon him for months, is the most appropriate inscription, after the simple words, " an honest man," that could be reared over his grave: " So it is that men suffer various ways in advancing civilization, and through God, mankind are indebted to the labors of men in many different spheres of

life." And does he not have part in this general eulogy by Mr.
Emerson ?

Many hamlets sought I then,
Many farms of mountain men;
Found I not a minstrel seed,
But men of bone, and good at need.
Rallying round a parish steeple
Nestle warm the highland people,
Coarse and boisterous, yet mild,
Strong as giant, slow as child,
Smoking in a squalid room
Where yet the westland breezes come.
Close hid in those rough guises lurk
Western magians,—here they work.
Sweat and season are their arts,
Their talismans are ploughs and carts;
And well the youngest can command
Honey from the frozen land;
With sweet hay the wild swamp adorn,
Change the running sand to corn;
For wolves and foxes, lowing herds,
And for cold mosses, cream and curds;
Weave wood to canisters and mats;
Drain sweet maple juice in vats.
No bird is safe that cuts the air
From their rifle or their snare;
No fish, in river or in lake,
But their long hands it thence will take;
And the country's flinty face,
Like wax, their fashioning skill betrays,
To fill the hollows, sink the hills,
Bridge gulfs, drain swamps, build dams and mills,
And fit the bleak and howling place
For gardens of a finer race.

There is a tradition that an Indian maniac once stood on the
Giant's Grave, and swinging a blazing pitch-pine torch, which he
had kindled at a tree struck by lightning, shouted in the storm the
prophecy,—

The Great Spirit whispered in my ear
No pale-face shall take deep root here.

Fabyan's large hotel, built at the foot of the Giant's Grave, has been
burned to the ground. Two public-houses on the mound itself have
been destroyed; the meadow has been ravaged by freshets; and

two hotels at the gate of the Notch have also been consumed by fire. Were these fires kindled by sparks from the dusky prophet's torch ? We are happy that we can leave this question with those of our readers who love the atmosphere of wild traditions around mountains, better than the evening light that glows on their tops, or the rare flowers and plants that climb their ravines.

And we must not forget to speak of the range, before we lose sight of it here, as a soaring garden of plants, a vast conservatory of Flora. We are told that the distinct zones of vegetation on this range are scarcely surpassed on the flanks of Mount Etna or the Pyrenees. Mount Washington is a gigantic thermometer of botanic life, and the creative forces, enfeebled as they ascend towards the zero of perpetual snow, pass by degrees entirely out of the temperate lines, and indicate by plant, lichen, or moss, the levels of Lapland, Siberia, and Labrador.

But let us not anticipate any of the valuable details of the chapter on the vegetation of the mountains from a thoroughly competent hand, with which we are able to enrich this volume. Prof. Edward Tuckerman, of Amherst College, has been for many years a lover of the scenery, an explorer of the wildest glens and gorges, and a student of the botanic riches of the Mount Washington range. Mr. Emerson's description of a forest seer may be well applied to him.

A lover true, who knew by heart
Each joy the mountain dales impart;
It seemed that Nature could not raise
A plant in any secret place,
In quaking bog, or snowy hill,
Beneath the grass that shades the rill,
Under the snow, between the rocks,
In damp fields known to bird and fox,
But he would come in the very hour
It opened in its virgin bower,
As if a sunbeam showed the place,
And tell its long descended race.

The chapter which follows has been prepared by Prof. Tuckerman for these pages.   32

THE VEGETATION OF THE WHITE MOUNTAINS.

THE predominant LIFE in mountains is always Vegetable Life. This, in itself, or in its manifold bearings on the landscape, is sure to be beheld and felt,—and studied, too, by those who seek the inner truth of the outward,—

> Unfolded still the more, more visible,
> The more we know.

In the higher, alpine tracts, there is little beside this. A hare, two or three birds, and a very few insects, are all the animals as yet certainly known to inhabit the highest region of the White Hills.[*] But that region is furnished with a peculiar and interesting vegetation; and the relations of this vegetation to that of the lower parts of the mountains, and of the low country, may first occupy, very briefly, our attention.

No one can observe carefully the plants of a high mountain, without seeing that those which occur in the higher parts are, to a considerable degree, different from those at the foot; and still further that this difference presents itself, with more or less evident distinctness, as a series of zones, each with vegetable features of its own. And these distinct zones of vegetation on mountains have been found by botanists to correspond with a like succession in the low country, one set of plants being followed here, in like manner, by another, as we go northward, and that which characterizes the highest mountain

---

[*] " Fourteen species of insects " were caught by Dr. J. W. Robbins on the summit of Mount Adams, and some water insects in the little alpine lake under the peak, towards Mount Madison. And he saw on the summit a small quadruped, " probably a mouse," (MS. journal.) Gray squirrels have more than once been seen on the rocky summit of Mount Washington. Several butterflies, two of them of much rarity, occur, about the upper regions.

region, below perpetual snow, occurring again in the low country, as soon as we reach a sufficiently northern latitude. It is thus that an alp may offer a reduced, but on that very account more easily estimated picture of a number of differing (perhaps vast) districts of vegetable life, or be compared, as it is by Mr. A. De Candolle, to a series of degrees of latitude condensed ; in which the same phe- nomena which are dilated, so to say, in the plain country over hundreds of leagues, are compressed within certain hundreds of yards.* The study of these remarkable conditions of plant life has been pursued with much attention in Europe, and has furnished, or at least suggested, a large part of the most important knowledge that we have, of Botanical Geography ; but the limitation of the region has complicated as well as facilitated inquiry, and a great deal, therefore, still remains to be done, even where the questions at issue have been longest considered.†

Here, the succession of zones was observed by Cutler in 1784, and its more general features stated at length by Bigelow in 1816 ;— but an approximate determination of the superior and inferior limits of species has yet to be accomplished.‡ and will doubtless require, as it will reward, the observation of many years.

The immediate base of the highest group of the White Mountains has an elevation at the Giant's Grave, on the west side, and at the Glen House, on the east, of about sixteen hundred feet. This height increases, as we approach the base of Mount Clinton, at the gate of the Notch, where it exceeds eighteen hundred feet, and probably falls off on the north side. Many trees, and other plants, are thus exclu- ded. The linden appears only as a very rare (possibly introduced)

---

* A. De Cand. Geogr. Bot. I. p. 249.　　　　　　　† 3 Ibid.

‡ Even in Europe these limits have been well verified as yet, in only a very small num- ber of species. Ibid. I. p. 268. It is evident that the above remarks apply only to moun- tains of a certain height; and that mountains in warmer latitudes must be proportionally higher, to exhibit the interesting phenomena of which mention has been made. The few hundred feet by which the highest summits of the Carolina mountains surpass Mount Washington, are far from sufficient to give them the same importance in Botanical Geog- raphy.

tree on the warm burnt lands of Mount Crawford. The sumachs are wanting The vine is unknown, as are the hawthorns, and the Canada plum. There is no sassafras; nor slippery elm; nor hackberry; nor buttonwood; nor hickory; and the butternut comes no nearer than ten or fifteen miles off. Only the red oak occurs, and that below the Notch. The chestnut is wanting. Beech begins only below the Notch on the west side, but is found a little higher on the east. The black birch is unknown, as is pitch pine. Red pine occurs about Mount Crawford, but not beyond, northward, till we pass the mountains. The larch, the arbor vitæ, and the junipers, occur scarcely at all, except at the outskirts.

Other trees and herbs approach near to the mountains, but cease before we ascend them. Such are white maple, along the rivers; red maple, in swampy lands not far from the mountains on the west side, and coming still nearer on the east; black cherry, in the intervals, with the choke cherry; juneberry, as a tree (called sugar-tree), at the foot of Mount Crawford; the white and the black ash; the American elm, following the rivers, and ascending the Ammonoosuc three or four miles above Giant's Grave; the red oak, reaching perhaps highest in the woods between the Notch and Mount Crawford; the hornbeam, in the intervals, not far from Mount Crawford; the black birch, so far as it occurs in the immediate neighborhood of the hills; and the balsam (and perhaps also the balm of Gilead) poplar.

And this brings us to the ascent. The country people recognize loosely two of the zones of which mention has been made above, distinguishing the hard wood, or green growth, which is the lower forest from the *black growth*, or upper forest, in which evergreens are predominant; and beside these, botanists designate the highest, bald district, with the heads of ravines descending from it, as the *alpine region*, and have sometimes spoken of a small tract, intermediate between the last two, but still very imperfectly characterized, as the *subalpine region*. Let us traverse these regions. The place where we enter, with its elevation and other features, will determine the character of the forest at the very foot. If it be a cold moun-

tain swamp, as between Giant's Grave and Mount Clinton, there will
be less variety of trees, and the evergreens will play a larger part,
even at the base. But as we ascend, these differences become less
striking, and at length greatly disappear. Sovereign of trees of the
lower forest was the white pine. Douglas, the author of " The Present State of the British Settlements in North America," 1749–1753,
speaks of a white pine cut near Dunstable in 1736, " straight and
sound, seven feet eight inches in diameter at the butt." * Before the
Revolution, all these trees, excepting those growing in townships
granted before 1722, were accounted the King's property in New
Hampshire, (as they were also in Maine,) and the books of the royal
contractors for masts furnished Douglas and Belknap with some interesting items of the size and value of the sticks thus sent home. The
dimensions of those mentioned by Belknap as exported by Mark
Hunking Wentworth, Esq., run from 25 to 37 inches through ; and
Colonel Partridge, it appears, sent home a few of 38 inches, and two
of 42 inches ; these being all hewn before they were measured. And
Dr. Dwight heard from a gentleman of Lancaster that he had seen
a white pine which measured two hundred and sixty-four feet in
height.† Straight columns of this princely tree rise here and there,
and spread the few strong limbs which make its crown, above the
lower forest ; but the day of its pride, still witnessed to by the
enduring stumps ("it is a common saying that ' no man ever cut
down a pine, and lived to see the stump rotten ' " ‡) has long gone
by. Beside the white pine, the first class of forest trees is made up
of the rock maple, the beech, and the hemlock, at the foot ; and,
ascending a little higher, the white birch, the yellow birch, and the
spruce. The fir, white spruce, the two aspens, the witch hazel, and
the mountain ash make the second class. Of these the hemlock is
perhaps second in size. It loves low, moist lands, but often ascends

* Belknap, N. H. III. p. 80.
† Travels, II. p. 34. Williamson says: " Has been seen six feet in diameter at the butt,
and two hundred and forty feet in height." Hist. of Maine, II. p. 110.
‡ Belknap, III. p. 81.

the mountain side. Its trunk is as straight as that of the pine, but
is deformed by numerous dead limbs. " It rises," says Mr. Emerson,
" with an uniform shaft, sixty or eighty feet, with its diameter but
slightly diminished until near the top, when it tapers very rapidly,
and forms a head, round, and full of branches."* The rock maple is
scarcely less than the hemlock, and was particularly abundant in the
country about the mountains, where it is still one of the finest trees.
The beech belongs undoubtedly to the first class of our forest trees,
but it hardly equals the others of this rank, in the White Mountains ;
nor does it reach above the foot, being scarcely met with on the west
side indeed, above the Notch, though becoming very common below.
Its erect, even, smooth-barked trunk, with " long diverging arms,
stretching outwards at a large angle," † is almost always covered with
a gay patchwork of lichens, and though the tree be often low and
irregular, its firm, shining leaves, and handsome bole make it sure to
be looked at and remembered.

The yellow birch is another striking tree of the lower woods. The
bark, at first yellowish, but becoming grayish with age, separates into
large, thick, irregular scales, the raised edges of which give the
ragged look which distinguishes the huge trunk. This rises to the
utmost height of the forest, dividing only, like a sort of *candelabrum*,
into a few bulky limbs at the top. Equal in size, but much more
elegant is the canoe birch, " the points of light from its white trunk
producing a brilliant effect in the midst of its soft but glittering foliage,
hanging, as we often see it, over some mountain stream, or sweeping
up with a graceful curve from the side of its steep bank." ‡

And last of the trees of this rank, the black spruce rises to the
height of the lower forest, but adds to the general effect perhaps as
much by its sombre masses of color as by its outline, the peculiar
symmetrical elegance of which this is capable, being commonly
not attained, to any great perfection, in the woods. This spruce

---

* Trees and Shrubs of Massachusetts, p. 80, a book which cannot be too highly com-
nended to every lover of trees.　　　　　　　　　† Ibid. p. 158.
‡ Emerson, Trees and Shrubs, p. 210.

makes forests itself, redolent of healing perfume, and carpeted inim-
itably with dense mats of fresh moss, in which the pretty creeping
snowberry often hides its flowers and fruit. In such woods the tree
has sometimes reached a great size. Josselyn tells us in his " New
England's Rarities," 1672, of spruce-trees " three fathom," or
eighteen feet about ; and in his " Voyages," the same writer speaks
of one spruce log " at Pascataway, brought down to the water-side by
our mast-men, of an incredible bigness, and so long that no skipper
durst ever yet adventure to ship it,''—a statement which might well
have been made more particular. But the tree occurs for the most
part only scatteringly on the central group of mountains.

Of the forest trees of second rank, the fir is by far the finest. It
possesses the smoothest trunk, and the most beautiful foliage of all the
evergreens, and none equals it in the singular elegance of its form.
No one spot in the mountains was so rich in handsome firs, a few
years since, as the neighborhood of the Giant's Grave ; and many
trees remain there still. The white spruce is another of the smaller
evergreens, differing from the black spruce in its more graceful habit,
and lighter color. The American aspen, very nearly resembling the
aspen of Europe and of poetry, and the somewhat larger and handsomer great aspen, occur frequently along roadsides in the lower
forest, and the former ascends the mountains several thousand feet,
in burnt lands. Here and there in moister spots, the slender rowan
or mountain ash displays its tufts of feathered leaves, and climbs the
hills even to the region of perpetual shrubs. More common, and
confined to the lower forest is the American witch hazel, a pleasing,
" bushy tree," which does not need its autumnal wealth of blossoms
to attract the eye of lovers of nature. The striped maple or moose-
wood, so called because its bark is a favorite winter food of our
noblest deer, and the mountain maple, are two still smaller trees,
common in the lower woods. " The latter," says the instructive
writer already cited, " assumes towards autumn various rich shades
of red, and as sometimes seen, eighteen or twenty feet high, hanging
over the sides of a road through woods, with its clusters of fruit

beneath the leaves, turning yellowish when the leaf-stalks are scarlet, it has considerable beauty." * The red cherry, with sour fruit growing in little bunches, is another small tree, particularly common in burnt lands. The alternate cornel, a conspicuous, large shrub, sometimes almost a tree, with elegant, oval, dark-green leaves, and creamy heads of flowers, is frequent on roadsides Here, too, occurs, much more rarely, the cranberry-tree, of which the favorite Gelder-rose, or snowball, is only a garden variety. The hoary alder reaches sometimes to a height of almost thirty feet, and is one of the more constant and familiar of the lower draperies of the hills. The mountain alder is more elegant, in its fruit at least, but begins rather higher, and is never anything but a shrub. There are several tree-like willows in the lower region, of which perhaps the beaked willow is the most noticeable.

Of lesser shrubs there is only room to speak of a few of the more conspicuous or important. The brambles attract everybody with their pleasant fruits. Of these the wild red raspberry and the high blackberry are sufficiently known. The latter is the more tender shrub, and often fails to perfect its berries; but the former climbs the mountains even to the upper precipice of Giant's Stairs, offering, in such secluded nooks, to latest autumn its welcome cheer. And the purple-flowering raspberry, frequent in rocky places in the lower region, and attracting the eye with its large leaves and rose-like blossoms, is perhaps the very pride of its race. A mountain gooseberry, with ungrateful fruit, but handsome, deeply-cut leaves, is found in swampy places, from the Notch to the alpine region. The garden red currant has occurred to me rarely in the lower valley of Mount Washington River; but the mountain currant, much like the other, except that the fruit is hairy and has a slight unpleasant odor, which does not however diminish its wholesomeness, is confined, perhaps entirely, to the upper region. The common elder and red-berried elder are both frequent at the foot of the mountains; but only the latter ascends them. The witherod is also confined to the lower

* Emerson, Trees and Shrubs, p. 498.

region; bu; the hobble-bush accompanies or impedes the climber far up the mountain sides. Both these species of viburnum produce fruit that may be eaten when ripe, and that of the hobble-bush is rather pleasant, to wayfarers at least. There is no fruit of its kind that appears to surpass the Canada blueberry, when eaten in perfection on the summits of the lower ridges or spurs, as especially of Mount Crawford; and this, which does not grow so far south as Massachusetts, is also remarkably good as a dried fruit. Nor must we fail to glance, in passing, at the rhodora,

> Spreading its leafless blooms in a damp nook
> To please the desert;

still, as when Bigelow wrote, beautiful in the Notch, in June, and on the mountains, later; at the cheerful but modest mountain holly, with its clean, smooth, light-green leaves and crimson berries; and last, not least, at our American yew, than which there is no handsomer undershrub, in leaf or berry.

The foregoing may perhaps serve as some introduction to the plants which are most likely to attract the eye in the lower forest. But as we ascend, many of these disappear, and the trees of the green growth, or hard wood, become fewer and smaller, till they are lost at length in the solemn evergreen woods. This is the second zone of vegetation, which the people of the country call, fitly enough, the black growth. The trees are spruce and fir, with, here and there, a yellow or a canoe birch, or a mountain ash. Fraser's balsam fir has also occurred to me in this region, but I know not what proportion it makes of the growth. These woods are almost silent, and very few flowers vary the sameness of the thick mat of mosses which covers the earth. The mountain aster and the mountain golden-rod, the white orchis, the white hellebore, clintonia, and more rarely the three-leaved Solomon's seal, are among these; but what surpasses all other herbs in abundance, and really characterizes the region, is the delicate wood-sorrel.

The upper forest diminishes constantly as the elevation increases, till at the height of about four thousand feet it becomes a close

33

thicket of dwarf trees, the lengthened and depressed limbs of which, strong enough to support a man, make a natural, often impenetrable hurdle, or *chevaux de frise*, to shut in the alpine solitudes. A few flowers still adorn the more barren soil, especially in moist places, and are less likely to be passed over than below. The dwarf cornel or bunchberry, the creeping snowberry, the bluets, Little's wild liquorice, the dwarf orchis, the twayblade, the purple and the painted trilliums, and clintonia, make most of these, which cease, nearly all, as the shrubs grow less. At length the shrubs come suddenly to an end, and the wide wilderness of the alpine region opens before us. Barren rocks, it seems, varied only with green patches here and there, or hollows, where dwarf firs and birches still ·struggle up. But this " tumultuous waste of huge hill-tops " is less barren than we think. The plants have, many of them, to be looked for; but these reward, abundantly, the search. The largest part of the vegetation here is like nothing that we have seen below, nor shall we find it in the low country much short of the coast of Labrador. Perhaps it is the mountain sandwort, a delicate, little grass-like herb with starry white blossoms, that first catches the eye ; or the evergreen cowberry with its bell-shaped, pinkish flowers and blood-red fruit ; or the strange, thick-leaved Labrador tea ; or the heath-like crowberry with black fruit ; or the mountain bilberry. These are all at home here, and true mountain plants ; but they are not peculiar to the region, and can and do grow at much lower elevations. But the Lapland diapensia, which is met with almost as soon, will be sought probably in vain, except on the highest summit of the Adirondack, near Lake Champlain, and doubtless Katahdin, till a much more northern latitude than ours is reached. The thick tufts of this plant are composed of many, closely packed simple stems, densely clad below with fleshy evergreen leaves, and making above a flat cushion, out of which rise. in July and after, short stalks bearing showy white flowers. " Of all more perfect plants," says Wahlenberg, " this is most patient of cold, and preserves its greenness through the direst (Lapland) winter. As I journeyed through the alps in the intensest

frost, I saw the leafy sods of diapensia as bright as in summer."[*]
The dwarf birch, first described by Linnæus in his Flora of Lapland,
and noticeable for its small, rounded leaves, is another truly alpine
plant, which occurs in moist places, with one or two shrub-willows.
Another, still smaller willow, loves rather the rocks, and bears the
name of the first botanist who explored the mountains. Some other
shrubs, of more interest, come gradually into view, in little nooks of
the rocky region. Such are the Lapland rhododendron, a spreading,
small shrub with leathery, evergreen leaves, dotted with rusty, resin-
ous points, and bearing open-bell-shaped, deep purple flowers in July
and after. In Europe, with the exception of a single Norwegian
station, this is confined to Lapland ; but extends here through all the
vast solitudes from Labrador to the Polar Sea. Rather more rare,
and much smaller is the alpine azalea, with procumbent trunk and
spreading branches, clothed with elegant, also evergreen oblong
leaves, and small, bell-shaped, rosy blossoms. Linnæus says no
plant is more common in the alps of Lapland than this. It is not
known at any other station in the United States, but occurs in New-
foundland, and northward. The alpine bear-berry is still more rare.
This has larger, net-veined, wrinkled leaves, which are not evergreen,
and bears a few egg-shaped, pale, flesh-colored blossoms, which are
followed by a black fruit, of no account, says Linnæus, among the
Laps. At once more curious, and more easily to be found, as we
approach the rocky brink of the ravines, which descend from the
high plain to the southeast of the peak of Mount Washington, and
especially from that grassy expanse which is known as Bigelow's
Lawn, is the moss-like cassiope, with tufted, thread-like stems, covered
with crowded, appressed, needle-shaped leaves, and sending up on
solitary stalks a most graceful, nodding, open-bell-shaped flower,
contained .in a purple calyx. Wonderfully does it charm the beholder, exclaims Linnæus, in the most barren regions of our (Lapland) alps ! But the cassiope is surpassed in beauty by the alpine
heath. We have no other American plant so well entitled to be

[*] Wahl. Fl. Lapp. 58.

called a heath as this. Like the last, it loves especially the rocky brinks of the ravines,—a low shrub, with heath-like evergreen leaves, the arrangement of which reminds one also of the firs, and bearing, in July and August, from two to five " oblong-urn-shaped," purple flowers, which, as is common in alpine species, are large for the plant.

We are at the edge of the gulfs and ravines, perhaps the most striking inner feature of Mount Washington. The great depth and headlong descent of these valleys, fill, at once, the eye, nor is it always easy to restrict it to the humbler quests of Flora. But those patches of verdure that make glad the rocky walls, offer a more luxuriant vegetation than has yet, anywhere, occurred to us. Here grows the daisy-leaved lady's smock ; the alpine violet ; the moss campion ; the alpine willow-herb, speedwell, and painted cup ; the eyebright ; Peck's geum ; the dwarf bilberry, and rarely, along rivulets, the alpine saxifrage. And below, close to the lingering snows, are the rare mountain cudweed, and mountain sorrel. It is in these tiny pastures that we find the grasses of the alps, most of them of singular beauty. Southwest of Mount Washington, about the Lake of the Clouds, and on the side of the peaks of Monroe, are spots a good deal like those just described, and more easily reached ; and near by the latter is a stony plain, the peculiar home of the alpine cinquefoil, and a few other plants. The southwestern summits are lower, and less generally interesting than the regions already described, but the cloudberry is confined to them, and they also possess the alpine bear-berry, and, very abundantly, the two mountain rattlesnake-roots.

Some few plants of the lower country ascend the valleys, and mingle with the alpine vegetation at their heads. Such are the cow-parsnip, and the hellebore, the linnæa, the bluets, the chickweed-wintergreen, the dwarf cornel, the clintonia, the twisted bellwort, and the rosy bellwort.

Nor should this sketch be dismissed without mention of a handsome stranger from the Southern Alleghanies, which, within a few years,—so at least it seems,—has appeared and established itself in the slides of the Notch. The silver whitlow-wort was first observed by Mr. Oakes, in 1844, in the Notch, where it is now very common; and the same year the writer discovered it, in soil similar to that of its other station, on the summit of the ridge of Mount Crawford. It well deserves admiration. If possible, we shall give further particulars of the botany of the mountains, in a catalogue at the end.

Mountain gorses, ever golden!
Cankered not the whole year long!
Do you teach us to be strong,
Howsoever pricked and holden
Like your thorny blooms, and so
Trodden on by rain and snow
Up the hill-side of this life, as bleak as where ye grow?

Mountain blossoms, shining blossoms'
Do ye teach us to be glad
When no summer can be had,
Blooming in our inward bosoms?
Ye whom God preserveth still,
Set as lights upon a hill,
Tokens to the wintry earth that Beauty liveth still!

Mountain gorses, do ye teach us
From that academic chair
Canopied with azure air,
That the wisest word Man reaches
Is the humblest he can speak?
Ye who live on mountain peak,
Yet live low along the ground, beside the grasses meek!

Mountain gorses! since Linnæus
Knelt beside you on the sod,
For your beauty thanking God,—
For your teaching, ye should see us
Bowing in prostration new.
Whence arisen,—if one or two
Drops be on our cheeks—O world! they are not tears, but dew

THE ANDROSCOGGIN VALLEY.

BETHEL, GORHAM, BERLIN, AND THE GLEN.

" *No scenes have given me more lasting pleasure. The mountains, it is said, are not lofty enough for sublimity. But as the light and cloud play on them, and they arise around you in dark, or silver, or purple masses, the effect is very magical—under certain lights, even perfectly sublime. Scenes more spiritual Switzerland itself could hardly produce. But all comparisons are futile. We grow to love a country, as we grow to love a person, because we have there exercised our faculty of loving. Nowhere to me has nature been more kindly beautiful. And who has not noticed how all the pleasing accessories of a fertile and homely landscape gain infinitely by their union with the mountain ranges? The streams run conscious of the purple hills ; every tree and flower has something more than its own beauty, when it grows in the shadow, or in the light, of the glorious mountains. Wherever they rear their mystic summits to the clouds, there is an indescribable commingling of heaven and of earth. The mountain is the religion of the landscape.*"

THORNDALE.

THE railroad from Portland to Montreal meets the Androscoggin River at Bethel in Maine, twenty miles distant from Gorham. Bethel itself is the North Conway of the eastern slope of the mountains, and would well reward a visit of a few days. It has no single patch of meadow that is so fascinating as the broad emerald floor under the Mote Mountain, which has excited in artists such joy and such despair. But its river-scenery is much richer than that of the Saco ; and it has so many pleasant strips of meadow, like the " Middle Intervale," relieved by the broad winding Androscoggin in front, and by ample hills in the rear, brightly colored to the summit with fertile farms, that, for drives, it is a question if North Conway would not be obliged to yield the palm.

Before many years it is to be hoped that there will be a larger overflow from the regular track, into the more lonely aisles and the side-chapels of the grand cathedral district of New Hampshire. Then the wonder will be that Bethel was not from the first more celebrated. As we write about it, we have a picture in mind which Paradise Hill showed to us in a showery noon, on our first visit to the village. The height is fitly named. We can see now the wide array of gentle hills swelling so variously that the verdure of the forests, or the mottled bounty of the harvests, drooped from them in almost every curve of grace. Some of these hills were partially lighted through thin veils of cloud ; some were draped with the tender gray of a shower, which now and then would yield to flushes of moist and golden sunshine ; not far off rose a taller summit in slaty shadow ; and between, on the line of the river, the different greens

34

of the intervale would gleam in the scattered streams of light that forced their way, here and there, through the heavy and trailing curtains of the dogday sky. In the morning or evening light that horizon must inclose countless pictures which only need selection, and not improvement, for the canvas.

The ride in the cars from Bethel to Gorham is very charming. If the railroad approached no nearer to Gorham than this point, a stage-ride along the same route could hardly be rivalled in New Hampshire. What a delightful avenue to the great range it would be! The brilliant meadows, proud of their arching elms; the full broad Androscoggin, whose charming islands on a still day rise from it like emeralds from liquid silver ; the grand, Scotch-looking hills that guard it ; the firm lines of the White Mountain ridge that shoot, now and then, across the north, when the road makes a sudden turn ; and at last, when we leave Shelburne, the splendid symmetry that bursts upon us when the whole mass of Madison is seen throned over the valley, itself overtopped by the ragged pinnacle of Adams ;—it is, indeed, hard to say that any approach to the mountains could be finer than from Conway through Bartlett up the Saco Valley,—but we honestly think that, if the distance between Bethel and Gorham were traversed by stage, travellers would confess that it must take the first rank, among all the paths to Mount Washington.

In the introductory chapter we called attention to the fact, that around the village of Gorham some of the most impressive landscapes to be found in New England, are combined from the Androscoggin River, its meadows, the lower hills that inclose it, and one or two of the great White Mountains proper that overlook the valley. This is the only region where we can see one of the four highest mountains of the chain standing alone ; and so there is no point from which such an impression of height is obtained as on the banks of the Androscoggin within two or three miles of Gorham, or from some of the hills around the village.

In order to call attention to one of the most striking of these landscapes in which Mounts Madison and Adams are the dominant figures, we will quote a portion of a letter by the writer of these pages to a friend. As it was sent fresh from an enjoyment of the scene, on the evening of a hot summer day, just after the long railroad ride from Boston, it may have less feebleness than a copy of the scene from memory.

" Shall I write you a *Miserere* over the journey to Gorham to-day or an *Exultemus* at the arrival ? It has been a dreadful avenue to the temple—the long hours of heat and dust, of roar and cinders ; but it is all past, and, while it made the pleasure of the day's end

34 *

sweeter, will not drag out any length of repetitious misery in the
memory. We chew the cud of our purer pleasures, not of the pains
that ushered them. They are digested in the first experience.

.   .   .   .

" The second relief came to us in the afternoon, when our train
struck a shower that hurried to meet us from the mountains. It was
a grand welcome, after the morning heat. A sweeping northwest
ʼgust, rushing towards us down the river, flung its dim drapery across
the whole breadth of the Androscoggin, letting it droop heavily, here
and there, in thick thunderous folds, that thinned themselves in fire
and rain, and left the air sweet and fresh in the track of their wrath.
Thus the twenty miles from Bethel to Gorham˙gave us an hour of
delicious poetry. Vapors flitted over the rough and sturdy hills,
among which we twisted our way. The meadows were jewelled with
the recent shower. The river lay glassy in the quiet light ; and the
trees stood as pensive and cool in the moist, sweet air, as their
motionless ambrotypes in the liquid mirror by which they grew. I
should have been willing to stay in the cars another hour.

"But the punctual ' Grand Trunk' landed us in Gorham just
when we were due, at quarter past five, P. M.—in time to get washed
and rested before the supper of strawberries and trout, and then to
have a *dessert* ride. During supper, another and lighter shower
trailed down the valley, and bequeathed to us a rich feast of sunset
beauty. A soft-tinted rainbow spanned all the southerly intervale between the mountain bulwarks of the valley. Brittle mists were
breaking over the whole breastworks of Moriah, Imp, and Carter,
showing to fine advantage the dark masses of their healthy green.
Clouds of exquisite pearly and fawn hues were piled over the west ;
and beneath them, scudding shreds of fog on the Pilot Hills, would
be smitten with the subtle silver and gold of the dying sun. It was
a rich renewal of my acquaintance with Gorham, and a rare evening
for a ride. I turned the horse's head northward, to let him trot
along the Androscoggin banks, in the hope of getting a clear view of
some of the White Mountain summits, from the point where I think

they look grandest. Of course, I could not sleep without paying respects to those masters of the manor.

" The yellow and sparkling light on the grass would have been payment enough for the ride, after yesterday's sirocco in Boston, and the matted misery of the railroad journey. The music and majesty of the Androscoggin, briskly sweeping the curves of its downward grade with so strong a tide, would, at any time, reward a visit. But my eyes were hungry for a grander spectacle. Should I be disappointed ? I turned my head at the proper spot, with some misgiving, but the shower had been propitious,—the summits I longed for were not shrouded.

" Hail, glorious ridges and princely peaks ! Hail to your stubborn masonry of tilted strata ! Hail to your shaggy belts of pine, and the arctic shrubbery of your breasts ! Hail to your black ravines, your savage gorges, channelled with torrents and gnawed with frosts ; your granite throats scarred with thunder ; your foreheads bare and defiant to all the batteries of storm ! *There* you stand, the glory of New England, rooted, massive, majestic as in all the years since the first tired pioneer gazed with awe upon you,—as in all the years since Adam ! When I last looked at you, your twin heads rose out of the golden robes which Autumn weaves ;—now, the forests are green again, and you are swarthy with the ' inky cloak ' which the spent thunderclouds are dropping over your stout frames. How has the winter fared with you ? Not a line of your rugged symmetry have the ruffian tempests of January and March softened. A thousand winters, doubtless, open fruitless cannonades upon your cones. Still you look down, patient and sublime, repeating in granite hieroglyphic, to the pleasure-seekers that flit in summer around your solemn base, the old story of Titan Prometheus, tormented, silent, and victorious for the good of man ! Do they not seem to say to the Prince of the powers of the air, as Shelley makes the Titan demi-god say to Jupiter,—

> Let alternate frost and fire
> Eat into me, and be thine ire

Lightning, and cutting hail, and legioned forms
Of furies, driving by upon the wounding storms.

See, old Adams wears one little knot of snowy ribbon on his breast,
—a modest trophy which the sun has not yet stolen from him,—the
only sign he gives of his triumph over another year! That narrow,
silky sparkle is, no doubt, a snow-drift, some rods in length, that is
dying gradually into a trout-stream.

"Ah, what refreshment in that sight! the horse shall walk slowly
in returning, that the mountain grandeur may be deliberately tasted.
Fatigues vanish before it. The throat is stronger; the nerves are
strung anew; the brain is recharged with power. Many a time,
during the last eight months, I have found myself breathing the sublimity they shed, as they have risen in the dreamy atmosphere of
memory. But, this evening, I have looked again upon their walls
and buttresses, and a week of rest has been concentrated in the joy
of the hour."

The close of this quotation leads us to say that, apart from the
physical refreshment which change of air and rest from business
afford, the great value of a tour among the mountains is found in the
stock it supplies for "pleasures of memory." The labor and fatigue
of journeyings, the excursions, the climbings, the fishing-expeditions,
the drives, with all the pictures that are thus brought before the eye,
are the *capital*, of which after-thoughts, reviving recollections, the
occasional resurrection of some exquisite view in our reveries, are the
interest. The rough facts of a landscape that impresses us renew
themselves, like hill-shores in a lake, in dream pictures, when we
have receded from them. That journey is the most profitable one
which affords the largest number of those scenes whose lovely appa-
ritions will rise afterwards before the musing eye. And that day, or
that confederacy of mountain-forms, proves the richest resource or
investment, that is found to exhale most freely the pictures which
enlarge the mental treasury—which pays most liberally these ideal
dividends.

In this respect Adams and Madison, of which we have just been speaking, furnish the most profitable acquaintance. Their Doric majesty, when first seen, makes an impression so strong and so simple, that the beholder feels he shall never lose it. One cannot see how the substance upheaved in them could be sculptured into forms that would blend more powerfully the effect of height and mass. They completely shut out every other mountain of the range, and every suggestion that there is a range behind them,—except one climbing spur of Mount Washington,—so that we have a greater height than that of Mount Washington itself seen from the Giant's Grave, shown, not in the centre of a long chain, but in two peaks enthroned over a base not more than three miles broad. The height of Mount Adams is about five thousand eight hundred feet; the height of Mount Washington nearly six thousand three hundred. But the valley in Gorham is only about eight hundred feet above the sea, while the plain near the Giant's Grave, or the plateau in the Glen, is elevated more than sixteen hundred feet. When seen, therefore, near the bend of the Androscoggin, about a mile and a half above the Alpine House in Gorham, Mount Adams not only makes a greater impression of height than Mount Washington does from the Glen, or from the Giant's Grave, but is actually several hundred feet higher above the road than the monarch of the range measures from either of those points. It is really the highest elevation which we can look at in New England from any point within a few miles of the base. Indeed, it is the highest point of land overlooking a station near the base, that can be seen east of the Mississippi. For, though there are several mountains in North Carolina that are higher from the sea than Mount Washington, there are none of them that rise so high over the immediate table-land from which they spring, while their forms are far less picturesque. And then, as we have said, the forms and isolation of these easterly outworks of the New Hampshire ridge make their height more powerfully felt.

It is worth while to stay two or three days in Gorham, in order to study these burly pyramids from various points, by climbing the hill-sides ; or to see them striped midway with cloud ; or to catch the sublime picture they make when a heavy shower sweeps near them without enveloping their summits in fog, and hides with thick rain all their surface, and makes them, in mid-day, monotonous blue-black piles, kindled now and then into momentary color by a sudden stream or sheet of sulphurous glare.

But the most vivid impression which these two mountains' can make upon visitors who have only a day to pass in Gorham, will be gained by a drive to Randolph Hill, which is about five miles from the hotel. The road rises nearly six hundred feet in this distance. After the first mile the summits are in view all the way. As the sides of the mountains are more and more clearly seen, attention is arrested by the correspondent lines that run northwest from Adams, and southeast from Madison. They are alike in almost all their details. These earthquake rhymes are more interesting for the intellect than the granite physiognomy in Franconia. And the lower outworks and braces of Mount Madison repeat, in reduced form and reverse order, the shapes of the two great hills. There is no drive more valuable than this for a close study of the multitudinous details that make up the foreground of a vast mountain—the abutments, the water-lines, the ravine walls and edges, the twistings of rock beneath the soil, that give character to a view ten miles off, which almost every eye feels, but which only a critical one can explain. Here is a lesson in drawing which shows very quickly what a complicated piece of art a noble mountain is, even in form, leaving the richness and complexity of color out of the account.

And then the general aspect of these mountains during this drive. How proud and secure ! What weight and what spirit ! They are not dead matter,—they live. So solid, yet soaring ! They seem to lift themselves to that glorious height. When we gain the summit of Randolph Hill, and ride to the edge where it slants down to the .eft, we stand where we can put our hand upon the mane of a mountain without reaching so far as Byron was obliged to in his poem, when he laid his hand upon the mane of the sea,—for he stood in fancy on the Alban Mount, some miles away from the ocean, when he stretched out his arm to touch it thus.   Here we see the northeastern wall of the White Mountain chain declining sharply to the valley.   From Randolph Hill we look down to the lowest course of its masonry, and up to the two noblest spires of rock which the ridge supports.   How lonely and desolate it looks, aloft there !   And yet

those pinnacles, that are scarcely fanned by a breath of summer, and that feel such storms as the valleys never know and could not bear,—is it not wholesome to look at them and think what they undergo for the good of New England ?   Must we not summon Emerson's lines, that stand at the portal of his stirring pages on Heroism, to express the feeling which these granite types of Puritan pith and sturdiness awaken, when we look up to their storm-scarred brows ?

Ruby wine is drunk by knaves
Sugar spends to fatten slaves
35

Rose and vine leaf deck buffoons;
Thunder-clouds are Jove's festoons,
Drooping oft, in wreaths of dread,
Lightning-knotted round his head;
The hero is not fed on sweets,
Daily his own heart he eats;
Chambers of the great are jails,
And head-winds right for royal sails.

It seems, however, to be true that no mountain is a hero to its
valley, although the proverb may be false in regard to men. Many,
no doubt, will sympathize with the antipathy of the English writer
who says : "If they look like Paradise for three months in the
summer, they are a veritable Inferno for the other nine ; and I
should like to condemn my mountain-worshipping friends to pass
a whole year under the shadow of Snowden, with that great black
head of his shutting out the sunlight, staring down in their garden, overlooking all they do, in the most impertinent way, sneez-
ing and spitting at them with rain, hail, snow, and bitter, freezing
blasts, even in the hottest sunshine. A mountain ? He is a great,
stupid giant, with a perpetual cold in his head, whose highest ambition is to give you one also. As for his beauty, no natural object
has so little of its own. He owes it to the earthquakes that reared
him up, to the rains and storms which have furrowed him, to every
gleam and cloud which passes over him. In himself, he is a mere
helpless stone-heap."

We once asked a good-natured old farmer who lived on Randolph
Hill, if he did not find it inspiring to dwell on a spot where two such
forms as Madison and Adams towered so grandly before his eyes.
"Blast 'em," said he, "I wish they was flat ; I don't look at 'em
for weeks at a time." "But," said we, "the great summits must
look peculiarly grand in winter." "Guess not," he said, "it's too
'tarnal cold. You come and see the same clouds whirling round them
peaks three weeks at a time, and you'd wish the hills was moved off
and dumped somewhere else." The good old fellow's flesh shuddered
like jarred jelly, while he told us of the hardships of winter there, as
though he began to feel already the biting nor'westers which the

next January would unleash upon the hills. Moreover he couldn't understand what so many people from Gorham, especially of the "female sect," that often, he said, "covered them rocks six and eight at a time," came to Randolph Hill to see.

Every symphony should have a sportive movement. But it must not close with a Scherzo. As we turn back from Randolph Hill, and descending, lose sight of the base which the summits of Adams and Madison crown, let us hear Wordsworth interpret what such hills should be in a long acquaintance :—

> I could not, ever and anon, forbear
> To glance an upward look on two huge peaks,
> That from some other vale peered into this.
> "Those lusty twins," exclaimed our host, "if here
> It were your lot to dwell, would soon become
> Your prized companions.—Many are the notes
> Which, in his tuneful course, the wind draws forth
> From rocks, woods, caverns, heaths, and dashing shores;
> And well these lofty brethren bear their part
> In the wild concert—chiefly when the storm
> Rides high; then all the upper air they fill
> With roaring sound, that ceases not to flow,
> Like smoke, along the level of the blast,
> In mighty current; theirs, too, is the song
> Of stream and headlong flood that seldom fails;
> And, in the grim and breathless hour of noon,
> Methinks that I have heard them echo back
> The thunder's greeting. Nor have nature's laws
> Left them ungifted with a power to yield
> Music of finer tone; a harmony.
> So do I call it, though it be the hand
> Of silence, though there be no voice;—the clouds,
> The mist, the shadows, light of golden suns,
> Motions of moonlight, all come thither—touch,
> And have an answer—thither come, and shape
> A language not unwelcome to sick hearts
> And idle spirits:—there the sun himself,
> At the calm close of summer's longest day,
> Rests his substantial orb;—between those heights
> And on the top of either pinnacle,
> More keenly than elsewhere in night's blue vault,
> Sparkle the stars, as of their station proud.
> Thoughts are not busier in the mind of man
> Than the mute agents stirring there:—alone
> Here do I sit and watch."

We have already said that the noble scenery for which Gorham should be visited is not to be seen from the hotel. For this reason many tourists, not attracted strongly by the views from the platform where the cars land them, hurry away in the stage to the Glen, and lose the enjoyment of some of the richest landscapes which New England holds, that would be shown to them by short drives, or even by walks that may be taken without fatigue. There is no hint at the public-house of any such picture as we have just attempted to describe. There is no suggestion of any ridge, or bulwark, or crag, of Mount Madison and Mount Adams. Yet a level walk of a mile, on the road along the Androscoggin, brings out both the mountains from base to crown. If they were visible in such majesty from the piazza of the hotel, we feel sure, that, spacious as it is, it would not be large enough to accommodate the travellers that would crowd to it. No portion of Mount Washington is in sight from its grounds ; yet a walk of half a mile below, or into a pasture near, with an easy slope, is repaid by one of the most impressive views of its dome and ravines that can be gained.

It is by a low and uninteresting hill, which rises directly in front of the hotel, that the mountains of the Washington chain are thus concealed. Back of the house, across the Androscoggin, swells the broad-based Mount Hayes. Numerous picturesque spurs, broken by jutting ledges, whose base the river washes in its downward sweep, run out from it to the intervale, and fascinate the artists by the " silver colonnades " of birch which they uprear, and by the contrasts of light and verdure on their higher turrets of rock.

The sky along the northwest is cut by the grand outline of the Pilot Mountain wall. This ridge is remarkable for the splendid shadows from clouds that wander over it in the forenoons, when the northwest wind rolls heavy masses of the cumuli towards Mount Washington. It has one other distinction, too, which should be known by all visitors of the valley. The deep chasm which is plainly seen, in a clear morning, from the piazza of the Alpine House, cut about midway of the long battlement, and from which the cloud·

shadows that dip into it often spread each way upon the mountain, like the wings of a tremendous condor, is the only hiding-place we have ever found in the region, where the winter is not dislodged by the fogs and sun of August. The hollows under the rocks in the upper portions of the ravine are ice-houses that never fail. On the 8th day of September, 1858, the most oppressive day of the season in the Androscoggin Valley, the writer explored this cleft, and found its shadowed side so cold that it was dangerous to rest there even for a few moments,—so chilly was the breath from the ice-blocks between the immense boulders, which the winter hides there in the hope, perhaps, of defying the sun yet with a *glacier* in New Hampshire.

Southward from the hotel, Mount Moriah and Mount Carter, separated from each other by another eminence called " The Imp," tower pretty sharply, and form one of the walls of the Glen. The portions of this range that rise from the Peabody Valley, flare out towards their tops somewhat like a half tunnel, as from a common centre below. When the mists or fog-wreaths ascend from it in the morning, we see what an immense caldron is rimmed there by walls of matted wilderness; and in the evening, when a storm breaks away, and mists pour up like incense from those deeps to the level of the thin summits of the chain, one can hardly see a more gorgeous show of color than is given in the green shadows, held by the deep-cut stairways of Mount Carter, the strong and brilliant purple that floods its crest, and the amber and rose with which the mists are dyed as they float upward to thin away and melt into the blue.

Mount Moriah itself should be seen from the bend of the Androscoggin River, a little more than a mile north of the hotel. Here its charming outline is seen to the best advantage. Its crest is as high over the valley as Lafayette rises over the Profile House ; and, with the exception perhaps of the Mote Mountain in North Conway, the long lines of its declivity towards the east, flow more softly than any others we can recall. They wave from the summit to the valley in

curves as fluent and graceful as the fluttering of a long pennant from
a masthead.   The whole mass of the mountain, moreover, is clothed
with the richest foliage, unscarred by any land-slide, unbroken by
any ravages of storm and frost, even in its ravines.

These lines look peculiarly charming if they can be seen when a

southerly rain is just commencing, or when a light shower falls upon
them, but does not wrap the ridge in cloud.   Does the reader
remember Leigh Hunt's description of a sudden shower in the
country ?

> As I stood thus, a neighboring wood of elms
> Was moved, and stirred, and whispered loftily

Much like a pomp of warriors with plumed helms,
When some great general, whom they long to see,
Is heard behind them, coming in swift dignity;
And then there fled by me a rush of air,
That stirred up all the other foliage there,
Filling the solitude with panting tongues;
At which the pines woke up into their songs,
Shaking their choral locks; and on the place
There fell a shade, as on an awe-struck face;
And overhead, like a portentous rim
Pulled over the wide world, to make all dim,
A grave, gigantic cloud came hugely uplifting him

It passed with its slow shadow; and I saw
Where it went down beyond me on a plain,
Sloping its dusky ladders of thick rain;
And on the mist it made, and blinding awe,
The sun reissuing in the opposite sky,
Struck the all-colored arch of his great eye,
And the disburdened country laughed again,
The leaves were amber; the sunshine
Scored on the ground its conquering line;
And the quick birds, for scorn of the great cloud,
Like children after fear, were merry and loud.

Frequently it has been our fortune to see a shower thus sweep down the Androscoggin Valley, and as it thinned out, trail the softest veils over the Moriah range. And how much more gentle and soothing its outline appeared when the warm rain-drops were woven into broad webs of gossamer to mark the ridges more distinctly, line behind line, and show their figure in more refined pencilling against the damp sky !

As a general thing, Gorham is the place to see the more rugged sculpturing and the Titanic brawn of the hills. Turning from North Conway to the Androscoggin Valley is somewhat like turning from a volume of Tennyson to the pages of Carlyle; from the melodies of Don Giovanni to the surges of the Ninth Symphony; from the art of Raffaello to that of Michel Angelo. But nothing can be more graceful and seductive than the flow of these lines of Mount Moriah seen through such a veil. They do not suggest any violent internal forces. It should seem that they rose to melody, as when Amphion played his lyre, and saw the stones move by rhythmic masonry to the place where they were wanted. And the beauty is the more effective by contrast with the sternness and vigor of the lines of Adams and Madison, that can be seen from the same point near the Androscoggin, where we suppose ourselves to look at Mount Moriah. They are Ebal, representing the terrors of the law ; this is Gerizim, the hill of blessing. Or shall we not rather contrast Mount Adams and Mount

Moriah by the aid of a charming sonnet of Percival, which one might think had been written at evening, in full view of these rivals in the landscape, where the Androscoggin bends around Mount Hayes.

> Behold yon hills. The one is fresh and fair;
>   The other rudely great. New-springing green
> Mantles the one; and on its top the star
>   Of love, in all its tenderest light, is seen

Island of joys! how sweet thy gentle rays
  Issue from heaven's blue depths in evening's prime
But round yon bolder height no softness plays,
  Nor flower nor bud adorns its front sublime.
Rude, but in majesty, it mounts in air,
  And on its summit Jove in glory burns;
  'Mid all the stars that pour their radiant urns,
None with that lordly planet may compare.
But see, they move; and, tinged with love's own hue,
Beauty and Power embrace in heaven's serenest blue.

The charming picture of the marriage of these planets reminds us that we must not pass without notice the loveliness of the nights, when the full moon rises over the ridge of Mount Moriah and looks down into the valley, "shut out from the rude world by Alpine hills."

See yonder fire! it is the moon
Slow rising o'er the eastern hill.
It glimmers on the forest tips,
And through the dewy foliage drips
In little rivulets of light,
And makes the heart in love with night.

We do not know any other resting-place near the Washington range, where one of the higher hills is so fortunately related to the landscape, as Mount Moriah, for showing the peculiar effect of the moon upon the mountain lines, and the witcheries of its refulgence upon the mountain sides and ravines. Kiarsarge is the most favorable eminence from which to look *down* upon a moonlight landscape ; Gorham gives the best position for enjoying the moonlight upon the hills.

Many persons imagine that the mountains must seem higher under the moon than in the daylight, when the sun shows all their foreground. But the moonlight strangely flattens them. They do not look half so high under a zenith moon as in the noontime of a clear day. A thick air, or a shower streaming before them and taking out much of their robustness, has the effect of lifting them much higher ; but when all color is drawn from them, and they stand in mere pencillings of black shadow and silver, their outlines are less firm, and they are lowered into mounds.

36

Yet, to an artist's eye, the effects of moonlight, when it climbs from behind and overflows a mountain, are unspeakably fascinating There is quite a large log-house on the thin crest of Mount Moriah, and once in the season the full moon rises directly over that hut,—

suggesting, before its silver edge appears, the mediæval picture of the dark head of a saint or martyr, circled by a golden nimbus.

She cometh,—lovelier than the dawn,
    In summer, when the leaves are green,
More graceful than the alarmed fawn,
    Over his grassy supper seen;
Bright quiet from her beauty falls.

After it climbs above the hut, the deep blue darkness of the mountain begins to catch delicate tinges of the pale, weak light which flows

wider and freer down the long steep slopes. The meadows beneath look level as a floor, and are laid with a carpet which seems to be an illusion of tender green grass, and light gray ground. The head of the Imp catches cool tinges of the pallid lustre, which slowly wanders down and off into the great caldron we have spoken of under the Carter Mount. And as it descends, the exhalations from the dusky depths, born from the invisible streams, that sing along the rugged beds of the ravines, rise and drink the moonlight to fulness, and hang before the mountains as though they might be woven of the very texture of the chaste beams that are falling over the wilderness.

And now in the daylight let us make an excursion to

BERLIN FALLS.

If there were no other attraction in the Gorham Valley, part of a day, at least, out of the mountain journey, should be devoted to the village for the sake of the drive to this, the most powerful cataract of the mountain region. Cascades we can see in other districts of the hills. The Ammonoosuc Falls are very powerful after a heavy rain, though the turbidness of their flood gives them little beauty then. But here we have a strong river that shrinks but very little in long droughts, and that is fed by the Umbagog chain of lakes, pouring a clean and powerful tide through a narrow granite pass, and descending nearly two hundred feet in the course of a mile.

The ride to the Berlin Falls is charming. The road is on the western bank of the Androscoggin all the way. The river moves now and then in such sweeping curves, and is overhung for most of the distance by a mountain with foliage so massive and varied, and the gradual descent of the river-bed gives the current, during a great portion of the way, so much briskness, while the mountain views behind are so majestic, that the six miles, if we drive in an open wagon, do not seem long enough, however eager we may have been to see the cataract. There is no hard climbing or long walking required, after leaving the vehicle. The Falls are close by the road. It is a

winding granite gorge through which the river rushes, over the narrowest part of which a stout bridge is thrown. Visitors should alight at the lowest part of the cataract, and go out through a little thicket of trees upon a mossy ledge, about fifteen feet above the current, where they can face the sweeping torrent. How madly it hurls the deep transparent amber down the pass and over the boulders,—flying and roaring like a drove of young lions, crowding each other in furious rush after prey in sight. On the bridge, we look down and see the current shooting swifter than the " arrowy Rhone," and overlapped on either side by the hissing foam thrown back from each of the rock walls. Above the bridge, we can walk on the ledge of the right-hand bank, and sit down where we can touch the water and see the most powerful plunge of all, where half of the river leaps in a smooth cataract, and, around a large rock which, though sunken, seems to divide the motion of the flood, a narrow and tremendous current of foam shoots into the pass, and mingles its fury at once with the burden of the heavier fall.

We do not think that in New England there is any passage of river passion that will compare with the Berlin Falls. But if we stay long on the borders of the gorge, as we ought to, we shall find that the form and the rage of the current are subordinate in interest to its beauty and to the general surrounding charm. Who can tire of gazing at the amber flood, from the point first described, to see the white frostwork start out over its whole breadth, and renew itself as fast as it dies ? Fix the eye upon the centre of that flood, and it seems to be a flying sheet of golden satin, with silver brocade leaping out to overshoot it, as it hurries from its loom. An artist, with whom more than once we have rested on the bank to catch the short-lived effects on the shifting currents of the river, speaks of the charm of " the foam foliage, white and prismatic, that crests the leaping waves, running from fall to fall, and circling dark domes of water that revolve over submerged stones." He recalls the grace of " the fountain jets of silver spray, and of the ever-falling crystal fringes that hang around the black rocks." And he tells us that, at such a spot, " by joining somewhat of the poet's contemplation to the artist's study, we may see glimpses of sylphic shapes, shining in the darkness of some thin-curtained arch, or, glancing along the liquid coils from pool to pool, nimbly working out those rapidly changing designs, whose wondrous beauty and inexhaustible variety are not inherent in material things, but are possible only to fairy or supernatural powers."

The sides of the rocks through which the Androscoggin thus pours are charmingly colored with lichens and weather-stains. In the crannies and little juttings on the sides where soil has lodged, grasses, small bushes, and wild flowers have taken root, and unfold their verdure and beauty undisturbed by the wrath below. Out to the very edge of the walls, young birches and pines, too, have stationed themselves to catch the fresh mists that rise. It was a cataract in Switzerland for which Wordsworth wrote the following sonnet; but how could it be more appropriate if it had been written as a description of the torrent in whose praise we quote it? What more can we say than that its fitness is equal to its beauty?

> From the fierce aspect of this River, throwing
> His giant body o'er the steep rock's brink,
> Back in astonishment and fear we shrink:
> But, gradually a calmer look bestowing,
> Flowers we espy beside the torrent growing;
> Flowers that peep forth from many a cleft and chink,
> And, from the whirlwind of his anger, drink
> Hues ever fresh, in rocky fortress blowing:
> They suck—from breath that, threatening to destroy,
> Is more benignant than the dewy eve—
> Beauty, and life, and motions as of joy:
> Nor doubt but He to whom yon Pine-trees nod
> Their heads in sign of worship, Nature's God,
> These humbler adorations will receive.

Those who have passed a delightful hour or two of the afternoon by Berlin Falls, and who read these pages, will be tempted to ask us, as we now turn from them, " Why do you not say something of the inspiring view of Mounts Madison and Adams, whose peaks, seen from the bridge, soar with such proud strength in the western sky? Why do you not call attention to the glorious lines that support their crests,—those of Madison a little more feminine than those of Adams, but both majestic,—a lioness and lion crouched side by side, half resting, half watching, with muscles ready in a moment for vigorous use ? Why do you not try to report the singular charm of looking down the broad stream, roughened with foamy rapids, as it hurries towards the base of those twin crests, and of the rich colors that combine in the harmony of the picture,—the snowy caps on the blue river, the green banks, the gray and gold of the mountain slopes and crowns ? " We certainly would not overlook these features of the landscape at Berlin Falls ; but we have a richer pleasure in store for our readers by inviting them to take with us

A DRIVE TO MILAN.

It disturbs our geographical prejudices a little, perhaps, to be told that only six or seven miles divide settlements with such distinguished names. But it will help us to discriminate if we learn to pronounce these names as the Yankees do, with the accent strong on the first syllable. We should look in vain for any imperial palace as we drive through *our* Berlin ; and instead of a university we shall see only a cluster of saw-mills, where part of the forests of Umbagog are prepared for service to civilization. So too, if we should ride to the very borders of Milan, we might not find in the red spire of the village church that would greet us, the artistic satisfaction which one would anticipate from the first glimpse of the *Duomo*, which we associate with the capital of Lombardy. (A wicked friend of ours who took the drive with us, when the village first saluted our eyes remarked, that this Milan seemed to be set in the plain of Lumber-dy.)

But we will not drive so far as the village. We will "follow the road" about two miles above Berlin Falls, cross the large, covered bridge of the Androscoggin, and drive about two miles above that on the eastern bank of the river. Then we will turn the horses' heads again towards Gorham. Now look down the river towards the moun-

tains !   Do we see the two peaks that were so fascinating at the
Falls below ?   They have received an addition to their company.
There are three now.   Mount Washington has lifted his head into
sight behind Madison, and has pushed out the long outline of the

ridge that climbs from the Pinkham forest, and by all the stairways
of his plateaus, to his cold and rugged crown.   What a majestic
trio !   What breadth and mass, and yet what nervous contours !
The mountains are arranged in half circle, so that we see each summit perfectly defined, and have the outline of each on its character-

istic side lying sharp against the sky,—Adams as it is braced from the north, Madison from the southeast, Washington from the south. They hide the other summits of the range completely. And from our position we look down the long avenue of hills that guard the Androscoggin, and over the wilderness from which they spring, and see them from a height very favorable for revealing their elevation, and through a sufficient depth of air to give them both distinctness and bloom.

Is it not something to mourn over, that the spectacle of this *bivouac* of hills should have been so seldom seen by tourists in New Hampshire? Many thousands visit the White Mountains in the summer weeks, and not fifty have as yet looked upon this land-scape, so easily attained by a drive of an hour and a half from the hotel in Gorham. Up to the time of our writing these pages, more people in England have enjoyed this view through a painting of it by the artist whose sketch is here presented to our readers, and who sent it abroad in answer to an order, than in our own country have seen the Creator's original. We shall be glad if anything in this unworthy description proves a temptation to future visitors of the eastern valley of the mountains to take this drive towards Milan in a clear afternoon, and thus add such a powerful combination of the mountain forms, dimpled and flushed too with countless shadows and tints, to the treasures of their memory.

It is worth while to take the additional few miles of ride above Berlin Falls to the point where we are now resting, in order to see the river so calm. On a still afternoon it sleeps here as though it had not been troubled above, and had no more hard fortune to en-counter below. This level passage in its history, where it coaxes the grasses and trees of its shores down into its silence, as the water-spirit of Goethe's ballad seduced the Fisher into the stream, is kin-dred with the quiet of the English river, above its cataract, which Wordsworth thus describes :—

The old inventive Poets, had they seen,
Or rather felt, the entrancement that detains

Thy waters, Duddon! 'mid these flowery plains;
The still repose, the liquid lapse serene,
Transferred to bowers imperishably green,
Had beautified Elysium! But the chains
Will soon be broken;—a rough course remains,
Rough as the past; where Thou, of placid mien,
Innocuous as a firstling of the flock,
And countenanced like a soft cerulean sky,
Shalt change thy temper; and with many a shock
Given and received in mutual jeopardy,
Dance, like a Bacchanal, from rock to rock,
Tossing her frantic thyrsus wide and high!

But our readers, whom we have specially invited as guests on this excursion, must not be kept out after dark. We shall have the late hours of the afternoon for a slow drive down to Gorham, and a short call again upon the falls in Berlin on the way. Of course our readers all know that about six in the evening of a midsummer day is the time for a drive. From five to half-past seven is worth all the rest of the day. Nature, as Willis has charmingly said, pours the wine of her beauty twice a day,—in the early morning, and evening, when the long shadows fall. In the mountain region the saying is more strictly true,—not only as to shadows, but in regard to colors. Her richest flasks are reserved for the *dessert-hour* of the day's feast. Then they are bountifully poured.

Then flows amain
The surge of summer's beauty; dell and crag,
Hollow and lake, hill-side, and pine arcade,
Are touched with genius.

Yes indeed, it is the wine of beauty that is poured out around the valley now. Who can give the key to that magic of the evening sun by which he sheds over the hills the most various juices of light from his single urn? Those substantial twin majesties, Madison and Adams, have a steady preference for the brown-sherry hues,—though round their bases they are touched with an azure that is held in dark sapphires, but never was caught by any wine. The Androscoggin hills take to the lighter and brilliant yellows, the hocks and champagne ; the clarets, the Red Hermitage, the purple Burgundies, seem to be monopolized by the ridge of Mount Carter and Mount Moriah.

Would that it could be our fortune to see on the Mount Moriah range, before we reach the hotel, a counterfeit such as we once saw at sunset, of the majesty and splendor of Mont Blanc at evening ! The clouds piled themselves over the long range as if they were organized into the mountain,—as if they were ridges and pinnacles draped with snow. Back of them lay a sky perfectly clear, but not blue ; it was green,—such green as you see in the loop of a billow about to break in foam on a shelving, rocky shore. The west was drenched in peach bloom ; and over the whole mass of the towering fleece that mimicked Mont Blanc, was spread a golden flush just ready to flicker into rose-color, that was as glorious as any baptism of splendor upon Chamouni ; and which faded away to leave a death pallor as mournful as the upheaved snows of Switzerland can show, after the soul of sunshine has mounted from their crests.

And let us have the privilege of describing what we cannot hope to see again, a spectacle upon one portion of the Mount Moriah range, which has made one return ride to Gorham, from Berlin Falls, an enduring pleasure. Thus we wrote of it at the time :—

" The vapors hung in heavy masses over the principal ridges, but the west was clear. There was evident preparation for a magnificent display,—a great banquet by the sun to the courtier clouds, on retiring from office that day,—a high carnival of light. As I turned the horse towards Gorham, taking the Moriah range full in view, a slight shower began to fall down the valley of Mount Carter, and a patch of rainbow flashed across the bosom of the mountain. From point to point it wandered, uncertain where to ' locate,' but at last selected a central spot against the lowest summit, and concentrated its splendors.

" The background of the mountain was blue-black. Not a tree was visible, not an irregularity of the surface. It was one smooth mass of solid darkness, soft as it was deep. And the iris was not a bow, but a *pillar* of light. It rested on the ground ; its top did not quite reach to the summit of the mountain. With what intense delight we looked at it, expecting every instant that its magic texture would dissolve ! But it remained and glowed more brightly. I can give you no conception of the brilliancy and delicacy, the splendor and softness, of the vision. The rainbow on a cloud, in the most vivid display I ever saw of it, was pale to this blazing column of untwisted light. The red predominated. Its intensity increased till the mountain shadow behind it was black as midnight. And yet the pillar stood firm. ' Is not the mountain on fire ? ' said my companion. ' Certainly that is flame.' Five minutes, ten minutes, fifteen minutes, the gorgeous vision staid, and we steadily rode nearer. Really we began to feel uneasy. We expected to see smoke. The color was so intense that there seemed to be real danger of the trees kindling under it. We could not keep in mind that it was celestial fire we were looking at,—fire cool as the water-drops out of which it was born, and on which it reclined. It lay apparently upon the trees, diffused itself among them, from the valley to the crown of the ridge, as gently as the glory in the bush upon Horeb, when ' the angel of the Lord appeared unto Moses in a flame of fire, out of the midst of a bush ; and he looked, and behold the bush burned with fire, and the bush was not consumed.'

" It seemed like nothing less than a message to mortals from the internal sphere,—the robe of an angel, awful and gentle, come to bear a great truth to the dwellers in the valley. And it was, no doubt. It meant all that the discerning eye and reverent mind felt it to mean. That Arabian bush would have been vital with no such presence, perhaps, to the gaze of a different soul. ' To him that hath shall be given.' A colder, a skeptical spirit would have said, possibly, ' there is a curious play of the sunbeams in the mist about that shrub,' or, it may be, would have decided that he was the victim of an optical illusion, and so would have missed the message to put the shoes from his feet, because the place was holy ground. Nearly twenty minutes the pillar of variegated flame remained in the valley of Mount Carter, as if waiting for some spectator to ask its purpose, and listen for a voice to issue from its mystery. Then, lifting itself from its base, and melting gradually upwards, it shrunk into a narrow strip of beauty, leaped from the mountain summit to the cloud, and vanished.

"It seems difficult to connect such a show, in memory, with 'Gorham,'—so hard a name, a fit title for a rough, growing Yankee village. But such is the way the homeliest business is glorified here; such is the way the ideal world plays out visibly over the practical, in all seasons, and every day. Only have an eye in your head competent to appreciate the changes of light, the richness of shadows, the sport of mists upon the hills, and you can look up every hour, here, from the rough fences and uncouth shops of Yankee land, to the magic of fairy land. While that show was in the height of its splendor, I asked an old farmer, who was hauling stones with his oxen, what he thought of it. He turned, snatched the scene with his eye, and said indifferently, 'It's nice, but we often have 'em here; gee-haw, wo-hush!' Yes, that's just the truth. 'We *often* have 'em,'—*often* have the glories of the Divine art, passages of the celestial magnificence, playing over our potato fields; therefore the us pay no attention to them,—count them as matters of course, keep coolly at our digging, and wait for something more surprising to jar us from our skepticism, shatter the crusts of the senses, wake us to a feeling of mystery, and startle us, through fear, into a belief or consciousness of God.

"The iris-pillar suggested the burning bush on Horeb. As I close this letter, that passage broadens to my thought, into a symbol of a mightier truth. What statement is so competent as that to set forth the relation of the Creative Spirit to the universe? In Moses' time, nature, in the regard of science, was a mere bush, a single shrub. Now it has grown, through the researches of the intellect, to a tree. The universe is a mighty tree; and the great truth for us to connect

with the majestic science of these days, and to keep vivid by a relig
ious imagination, is, that from the roots of its mystery to the silver-
leaved boughs of the firmament, it is continually filled with God, and
yet unconsumed."

 ˙At the commencement of this chapter we alluded to the beauty of
the drive from Bethel to the hotel in Gorham. One of the prominent resources of a visitor who stays a week or two at the Alpine
House, is a ride of ten or twelve miles down the Androscoggin on its
right-hand bank, through Shelburne to Gilead, and then up the river
on the easterly bank, crossing it again at Lead-Mine bridge. This
drive can be taken before sunset on a long summer day, by leaving
the Alpine House just after dinner. And no drive of equal length
among the mountains offers more varied interest in the beauty of the
scenery, the historic and traditional associations involved with the
prominent points of the landscape, and the scientific attractions connected with some portions of the road.

In Shelburne, a small village six miles below Gorham, the driver
will point out the remains of a boulder, which, before it was blown
for use on the railroad track, overhung a ledge that has received the
name of "Granny Starbird," or as it is sometimes spelled, "Granny
Stalbird." She was the first woman who climbed through the great
White Mountain Notch, from Bartlett,—a feat which she accomplished
in 1776, on her way to Dartmouth (now Jefferson) to serve in the
family of Col. Whipple. Many years afterwards, when a widow, she
became very skilful as a doctress, and often travelled great distances
on horseback to visit the scattered settlers in their sickness. When
she was very old, she was sent for to visit a sick person below Shelburne, but was overtaken in the night by a tremendous thunderstorm.
The rain and wind were so furious that it was impossible for her to
keep the road against it, and she drove her horse under the boulder
that overhung this ledge, and stood by him, holding the bridle, all
night. The wind howled frightfully around her, and the lightning
showed her rivulets tearing across the road to swell the Androscog-

gin ; but the hardy old heroine faced it without dismay, and did not leave the rude shelter until noon of the next day, when the storm abated. The builders of the Grand Trunk Railway through Shelburne ought to be indicted for blasting that rock, which belonged to the poetry of the mountains, when any common granite of the neighborhood could as easily have served their prosaic needs.

The history of Shelburne, as of Bartlett and Bethlehem, startles us with the records of suffering which the pioneers in the mountain valleys were willing to undergo in establishing homes there. In 1781, a man, with a wife and three children, moved into Shelburne when the snow was five feet deep on the ground, and the Androscoggin was a bed of ice. The mother carried the youngest child, nine months old, in her arms ; a boy of four and a girl of six trudged by her side. Their shelter was a wretched cabin with just enough rough shingles laid across some poles on the top, to cover a space large enough for a bed. Their cow was provided with a large square hole in the snow covered with poles and boughs.

The stories of the ravages of bears and wolves in the neighborhood of Shelburne are more striking than those recorded of any other portions of the mountains. On the drive from Gorham to Gilead, the wagon passes a portion of the road where a pack of wolves attacked an Indian, and killed and devoured him, but not till they had lost seven of their starving band in the encounter ; and to their other afflictions, the early settlers of this neighborhood were troubled, as those in the Bartlett Valley were not, by Indian invasions. They experienced not only the hardships of isolation and cold, and the plunder of wild beasts, and the ravage of mountain torrents, and the desolation of freshets, but they knew the terror of the war-whoop, and some of their number felt the scalping-knife and tomahawk, as well as the horrors of Indian captivity. The last of the outrages by the savage tribes in New Hampshire broke upon the settlements along the Androscoggin above Bethel. In August of 1781 a band of Indians made an attack upon Bethel, and after plundering some of the settlers, and taking others with them as captives, came up through Gilead, murdered one of the hardy settlers there, robbed the cabin of the family that had moved into Shelburne on the snow, and carried their prisoners by Umbagog Lake into Canada. When the poor captives were so worn down with the march through the wilderness, and the loads which the savages laid upon them, that they were ready to faint with fatigue and hunger, the brutes would broil old moccasons of mooseskin, tainted by the heat, for their food. One of the party who escaped describes the hideousness of a war-dance in which the Indians disported themselves, in one of the rocky passes through which they were taken. He says, " It almost made our hair stand upright upon our heads. It would seem that Bedlam had broken loose, and that hell was in an uproar." During one of the carousals the Indians amused themselves with throwing firebrands at a negro called Black Plato, whom they set up as a mark. The man who gives us this account returned to the old neighborhood on the Androscoggin, and lived many years to tell of the hardships of the first settlers, and to see pleasant villages and fruitful fields adorn and enrich a large portion of the valley, through which he and his party were hurried in 1781.

And yet no Indian tragedy is so frightful as the civilized one which is connected with Gilead below Shelburne, and whose date is as recent as June, 1850. Here a Mr. Freeman lived, with a young and beautiful wife and three children. He was a blacksmith, and was employed in the service of the company that were building the railroad from Portland to Montreal. A contractor on the railroad boarded in his family. This man succeeded in alienating the affection of the young wife from her husband, and soon after left the village for New York. The young husband, who was passionately devoted to his wife, found very soon that she had lost all interest in him and in her children. At last, after insisting on a divorce, to which he would not listen, she told him that she should leave his house, and commenced preparations for a journey. A trunk arrived, which Mr. Freeman intercepted, in which he found beautiful dresses and jewelry for his wife, and a letter from the contractor making an appointment to meet her in Syracuse in New York. Mrs. Freeman did not learn of the arrival of the trunk or letter. But she still insisted on leaving her husband, and even informed him on what day she should depart. On the night previous the young husband sat up very long in conversation with his wife, and after she went to her chamber, he left the house. But who is that peering into the window when the light is out, and all is still? About midnight, the piercing shriek rose from her room, " I am murdered!" She was found with her arm shattered, and her head wounded by a charge of buckshot, that had been fired through the window from a musket which had evidently been aimed with care at her heart. " It was my husband," she said to those that gathered in the room. " And will he not come? Oh, George, my dear husband, shall I not see him to be forgiven?" She died before dawn, without any reproaches for her murderer, and with his name on her lips. Many hours after, the husband was found dead, about a mile from his house, and in his hand the fatal razor that had relieved his agony. The tragedy was deliberately planned; for in his house were found letters that contained directions in regard to his children, and the disposition of his property.

Let us drive now across the river, with the horses' heads towards Gorham again, and make our first halt near the house of Mr. Gates in Shelburne, under the shadow of Baldcap Mountain. If we had time to speak of the view from the summit, which requires about two hours' climbing, we should need words more rich than would come at our bidding. But how grand and complete is the landscape that stretches before us as we look up the river seven or eight miles to the base of Madison and to the bulk of Washington, whose majestic dome rises over two curving walls of rock, that are set beneath it like wings! Seen in the afternoon light, the Androscoggin and its meadows look more lovely than on any portion of the road between

38

Bethel and Gorham, and more fascinating than any piece of river
scenery it has ever been our fortune to look upon in the mountain
region. The rock and cascade pictures in the forests of Baldcap

well reward the rambles of an hour or two. Boarders for the summer, at moderate price, have been taken at Mr. Gates's, and we do
not know of any farm-house where the view from the door offers so
many elements of a landscape that can never tire.

THE LEAD-MINE BRIDGE

is reached by driving two miles in the direction of Gorham. The mine itself from which the bridge is named is about a mile distant, in a ravine of mica-slate rocks. Although the ore is quite plentiful, and contains three pounds of silver to the ton, it seems that it cannot be profitably wrought, and it is abandoned now. But in the afternoon of a sunny day, when the mountain summits are not covered, every ravine on the distant sides of Madison and Washington is a quarry of beauty. The whole substance of these mountains seems then to be literally precious stones. They stand out in the same shape as when seen from the Gates cottage two miles back. We do not have so much of the river and meadows in view as from the high bank there; but we are close to the stream on the bridge; we see it before us breaking around several charming islands, and then flowing with deep and melodious gurgle into one tide again, which hurries down towards Gilead.

This is one of the favorite excursions from Gorham. The bridge is only four miles distant from the hotel, and the drive is easily made in three quarters of an hour. The best time to make the visit is between five and seven of the afternoon. Then the lights are softest, and the shadows richest on the foliage of the islands of the river, and on the lower mountain sides. And then the gigantic gray pyramid of Madison with its pointed apex, back of which peers the ragged crest of Adams, shows to the best advantage. It fills up the whole distance of the scene. The view is one of uncommon simplicity and symmetry. The rolling slopes upon the base of Mount Moriah on one side, and the jutting spurs of Mounts Hayes and Baldcap on the other, compose an effective avenue through which the eye roams upward to the higher mountain that sits back as on a throne. Our readers will remember that a sketch of it is given in the introductory chapter, on the ninth page. But if the sketch were thrice as good, it could not give adequate suggestion of a view which at once takes the eye captive, and not only claims front rank among the richest landscapes that are combined in New Hampshire out of the White Mountains and the streams they feed, but impresses travellers that are fresh from Europe as one of the loveliest pictures which have been shown to them on the earth. For the artist's purpose, the middle distance is not sufficiently effective, and the river is nowhere quiet enough to balance the ripples and broken lights of the foreground ; but for eye-landscape, to be enjoyed without reference to the demands of the canvas, it would be difficult to conceive a scene where greater beauty of river and islands is crowned with a mountain so bold and yet so tenderly tinted, so symmetrical and still so masculine, so satisfactory in height without losing on the surface clearness and vigor of detail.

Ah, what charming effects have we not seen on Mount Madison from this bridge, conjured by the clouds and sun ! The gold on the sharp apex of its pyramid in the early morning ; the ever-shifting perplexity of lights and gloom investing it in a sultry noon when thunder-clouds sail over it ; and at sunset once or twice in dogdays, volcano-pictures, when piles of vapor that towered over it and buried the summit were lurid around the lower edges, and seemed to burst from a fiery heart within, as the sides of the mountain were kindled almost to a ruby hue by the last beams of day ! It is not a single mountain, but a gallery of pictures, that Madison stands for in our memory. See it in a clear and tender afternoon, and how delicately every lower ridge in its foreground is hinted by the western light, that reveals no shrub, no forest, no precipice, but only symmetry and softness, and a proud height in perfect proportion with its mass and slope, piercing an azure heaven with a double peak of tender brown ! We may measure its altitude now in feet by our angles, and find that its summit is nearly a mile from the level where we stand ; we may exhaust what science can tell of its substance and strata ; but all the truths of its structure are nothing to the *expression* it wears in this favorable air. As it sits enthroned thus over the stream and farms whose green and silver wind up to its base, can it be the mountain which looks so desolate in the ride to the Glen, that is pathless and savage to the feet of the climber, that stands out so ugly in the forenoon light, which, lying stern upon it, makes its harsh crest look covered with soiled sole-leather ? Now, as we gaze upon it, we see what it was really made for. Although it wears no snow, it recalls Tennyson's lines :—

> How faintly flushed, how phantom fair
> Was Monte Rosa, hanging there
> A thousand shadowy pencilled valleys
> And snowy dells in the golden air.

Its divine gala-dress is upon it. Its desolate rocks have ripened. Art has flowered out of the bitter geological stem. Its strata and truth, and all its endowments for use, are merely the rough touches of the brush, intended to be viewed, not near the canvas, but a few miles distant, that they may be smoothed and shaded into unspeakable beauty. And the colors, too ! What nettings of pale gold upon the sloping edges of its lesser peaks of azure, when the late afternoon light glances down its eastern side ! Or, if a large mass of cloud has covered it in deep blue shade, and the sun finding a small opening, pours through a widening cone of rays, how will the lower towers and domes of the mountain temple blaze out in splendid radiance, like gilded roofs with gemmy walls ! It is as if the sun had said,

> O thou afflicted, beaten with the storm!
> Behold I lay thy stones in cement of vermilion,
> And thy foundations with sapphires.
> And I will make thy battlements of rubies,
> And thy gates of carbuncles,
> And all thy borders full of precious stones!

One spectacle which it was our fortune to witness from the Bridge repeats itself more frequently than any other before our eyes :—a sudden shower driving down the valley, completely hiding the mountain with gusts of rain,—the gradual thinning of the wet veil, till the outline of the beautiful pyramid of Madison is seen dim and lofty on its pedestal,—the soft blue sky of evening revealed again through the cloudy west behind it,—and when the rain entirely ceased, the rising of most delicate mists from the surface of the mountain, to be smitten by the sun, which breaks through a cloud-rift, so that they hang over the broad pile as a veil of silver gossamer, say rather, a texture of light itself—light condensed into a gleaming web, almost too bright for a steady gaze! The mountain seemed transfigured. It was not so much swathed with splendor, as translucent. One might have thought he was looking through some rent in the curtain of matter, upon a celestial hill, sacred as Tabor once was, with " garments white and glistening."

Yet we ought not to be so engrossed with the distant magnificence as to overlook the beauty of the ledge in front of the Lead-Mine Bridge, around which the river sweeps with strong and melodious swirl. If we will sit down upon it and study it carefully for a few minutes, our eyes may be opened to the beauty of rock scenery in many a mountain walk or climb, especially if we let light fall upon it from this passage of Ruskin : " When a rock of any kind has lain for some time exposed to the weather, Nature finishes it in her own way ; first, she takes wonderful pains about its forms, sculpturing it into exquisite variety of dint and dimple, and rounding or hollowing it into contours, which for fineness no human hand can follow ; then she colors it ; and every one of her touches of color, instead of being a powder mixed with oil, is a minute forest of living trees, glorious in strength and beauty, and concealing wonders of structure, which in all probability, are mysteries even to the eyes of angels. Man comes and digs up this finished and marvellous piece of work, which in his ignorance he calls a ' rough stone.' He proceeds to finish it in *his* fashion, that is, to split it in two, rend it into ragged blocks, and, finally, to chisel its surface into a large number of lumps and knobs, all equally shapeless, colorless, deathful, and frightful. And the block, thus disfigured, he calls ' finished,' and proceeds to build therewith, and thinks himself great, forsooth, and an intelligent ani-

mal. Whereas, all that he has really done is, to destroy with utter
ravage a piece of divine art, which, under the laws appointed by the
Deity to regulate his work in this world, it must take good twenty
years to produce the like of again. This he has destroyed, and has
himself given in its place a piece of work which needs no more intelligence to do than a pholas has, or a worm, or the spirit which
throughout the world has authority over rending, rottenness, and decay. I do not say that stone must not be cut ; it needs to be cut
for certain uses ; only I say that cutting it is not ' finishing,' but *un-*
finishing, it ; and that so far as the mere fact of chiselling goes, the
stone is ruined by the human touch. It is with it as with the stones
of the Jewish altar, ' If thou lift up thy tool upon it thou hast polluted
it.' In like manner a tree is a finished thing. But a plank, though
ever so polished, is not. We need stones and planks, as we need
food ; but we no more bestow an additional admirableness upon stone
in hewing it, or upon a tree in sawing it, than upon an animal in
killing it."

One could sit on this rock and watch the curves, and listen to the
luscious tones of the Androscoggin, and find that the hours glide
away like minutes. Is it a lurking feeling of the analogy between
life and a river that makes a mountain stream so fascinating to us
all ? The Androscoggin has its source in distant lakes of Maine.
Our life is at first a tiny

> silver stream,
> Breaking in laughter from the lake divine
> Whence all things flow.

It flows narrow and babbling under the leafy shelter of home. It
swells like the Androscoggin into rapid and noisier youth, with headlong dashes of adventure, and the iris-tinged hours of poetic enthusiasm and hope. It settles, as its tributaries increase, into the fuller
and calmer stream, hiding more force, and serving nobler uses ; and
so, bearing down on its bosom and in its depths the qualities and the
energy of its earlier hours and experience, it tends steadily towards
the sea.

A friend of ours once said, when he stood with us on a lovely afternoon upon the Lead-Mine Bridge, that the supreme luxury of a summer life to him would be realized, if he could own a cottage, with a
well selected library, two or three miles below this bridge on the Androscoggin, and could float at evening in a boat down the stream from
the foot of Berlin Falls, while the sun was " flattering the mountain
tops," reaching his house in season to have an hour or two before
bedtime with Tennyson and Shelley.   Mr. Trench, the English poet
and theologian, has enlarged the conception which our friend had
shaped.   He tells us that he believes nature has no ampler dower of
sights and solemn shows than would be disclosed

> to them, who night and day —
> An illimitable way—
> Should sail down some mighty river,
> Sailing as to sail forever.
>
> .   .   .   .
>
> Morn has been—and lo! how soon
> Has arrived the middle noon,
> And the broad sun's rays do rest
> On some naked mountain's breast,
> Where alone relieve the eye
> Massive shadows, as they lie
> In the hollows motionless;
> Still our boat doth onward press:
> Now a peaceful current wide
> Bears it on an ample tide;
> Now the hills retire, and then
> Their broad fronts advance again,
> Till the rocks have closed us round.
> And would seem our course to bound
> But anon a path appears,
> And our vessel onward steers,
> Darting rapidly between
> Narrow walls of a ravine.
>
> Morn has been and noon—and now
> Evening falls about our prow:
> 'Mid the clouds that kindling won
> Light and fire from him, the Sun
> For a moment's space was lying,
> Phœnix in his own flames dying!
> And a sunken splendor still
> Burns behind the western hill:

Lo! the starry troop again
Gather on the ethereal plain;
Even now and there were none
And a moment since but one;
And anon we lift our head,
And all heaven is overspread
With a still-assembling crowd,
With a silent multitude—
Venus, first and brightest set
In the night's pale coronet,
Armed Orion's belted pride,
And the Seven that by the side
Of the Titan nightly weave
Dances in the mystic eve,
Sisters linked in love and light.
'Twere in truth a solemn sight,
Were we sailing now as they,
Who upon their western way
To the isles of spice and gold,
Nightly watching might behold
These our constellations dip,
And the great sign of the Ship
Rise upon the other hand,
With the Cross, still seen to stand
In the vault of heaven upright,
At the middle hour of night—
Or with them whose keels first prest
The huge rivers of the West,
Who the first with bold intent
Down the Orellana went,*
Or a dangerous progress won
On the mighty Amazon,
By whose ocean-streams they told
Of the warrior-maidens bold.

But the Fancy may not roam;
Thou wilt keep it nearer home,
Friend, of earthly friends the best
Who on this fair river's breast
Sailest with me fleet and fast,
As the unremitting blast
With a steady breath and strong
Urges our light boat along.
We this day have found delight
In each pleasant sound and sight
Of this river bright and fair,

* See Garcilasso's Conquest of Peru.
39

And in things which flowing are
Like a stream; yet without blame
These my passing song may claim,
Or thy hearing may beguile,
If we not forget the while,
That we are from childhood's morn
On a mightier river borne,
Which is rolling evermore
To a sea without a shore:
Life the river, and the sea
That we seek—eternity.
We may sometimes sport and play,
And in thought keep holiday,
So we ever own a law,
Living in habitual awe,
And beneath the constant stress
Of a solemn thoughtfulness—
Weighing whither this life tends,
For what high and holy ends
It was lent us, whence it flows,
And its current whither goes.

There are two or three other excursions to be made from Gorham, which deserve more copious treatment than our limits will permit. The ascent of Mount Madison, and the drive to the village of Jefferson, and thence over Cherry Mountain to the Notch, we shall have occasion to describe in another connection.   We must devote a page or two, however, to

MOUNT SURPRISE.

Mr. Eastman's Guide-book calls attention to this eminence, and it does not exaggerate the interest of the ride, or the beauty of the view which the summit discloses.   It is a portion of the general mass of Mount Moriah, but has acquired a separate name from the fact that it has a distinct summit which, a few years ago, was generously cleared of trees for visitors by fire and gale.   The distance to the top is two miles and a quarter from the hotel, requiring a horseback ride of an hour, or a walk of an hour and a half.   The forest-path itself—unequalled so far as we know in the whole mountain tour—is lovely enough to tempt a visitor, independently of the prospect from the crown.

Looking up the valley of the Peabody, we see the five highest peaks of the Washington range, but a full view is given of two only,— Madison, the Apollo of the highlands, and the Herculean structure of Washington, with his high, hard shoulders and. stalwart spurs. There are very few hills of moderate height accessible by bridle-paths, from which a good view of any portion of the great range can be gained,—positions near enough to reveal the extent and freshness of the forests, and yet far enough to allow the effect of height and symmetry. We know of none so favorable in both these respects as Mount Surprise. It ought to be to Gorham what Mount Willard is to the Notch. Possibly, if a good wagon-road were constructed to the summit, it might become in time the rival excursion to that on the eastern side. Certainly after several visits to Mount Willard, when the senses have become used to the impression, at first so start-ling, made by looking over the cliff into the awful gulf of the Notch, the view gained there of the summits of the Washington chain, espe-cially of Mount Jefferson, is more fascinating to an artistic taste. And Mount Surprise gives a still more striking spectacle. Plain prose, however eloquent, is no fit medium to describe that proud smooth swell of Madison from the Peabody Valley to a peak that pricks the sky. It needs rhythm ; it needs the buoyant surge of a blank verse like that of Coleridge, to ensoul the fascination of that soaring beauty, which spires at last into granite grandeur. There is no point among the New Hampshire hills where the " hymn in the valley of Chamouni " breaks from the heart to the lips so readily as here.

And if one wants to see forest-costume in the utmost richness of folds and retinue, let him look at the broad miles of wilderness that flow down the opposing sides of Carter and Madison. Was it for the sake of mountain outlines chiefly, or rather to exhibit such a luxu-riant drapery of blended birch, maple, and evergreen, that the tumult

39 *

was first stirred beneath this soil ?   One is tempted to believe that those two points—the tops of Carter and Madison—were lifted up gently from the level land at first, and held off from each other just far enough to let the forests droop in the most gracious folds from them, and meet with trails soft as velvet upon the valley.   Can we wonder that the love of elegant dress is a permanent passion in half the human race, when the dumb hills are attired in apparel so shapely, and so richly and variously hued ?   The ballrooms of Saratoga could not outshine the splendors of color displayed in a season upon Mount Carter.   And is human nature to be abased by the gorgeous costumes that counterfeit the most precious satins, cloths, and shawls, which the tilted granite is allowed to wear ?

Ah, and what intensity of expression in the ragged crest of Adams, which starts out, it may be, from a melting fog, and overtops the gentler slopes of Madison ; and what energy in those far-running southward braces of Washington, engraved perhaps upon a white cloud-background,—each worn to the rocky bone by the torrents of summer, and the slower but more penetrative wrath of winter cold ! It is indeed rich music for the eye that is afforded by the quintette of summits seen from Mount Surprise ; and one who can detect some dim analogy between tones and forms will find increased delight here in seeing how, in the mountain choir, the sharp soprano of Madison is brought into contrast and balance with the heavy bass of Washington, and how the body of the harmony is filled up by the tenor of Adams, the baritone of Jefferson, and the alto of Clay, whose bulk and lines are merely suggested by their crests that jut into view.

But a sweeter melody still is offered to the eye that turns from the great hills to the Androscoggin intervale.   It is the strength that " setteth fast the mountains " which appeals to us on the west ; on the east we have the smile of the landscape, the fluent curves of a river moving " like charity among its children dear," the sweet phrases which man has added to the wild natural music, the colors vivid and tender that glow upon winding miles of shorn grass and ripening grain.   No mountain so high as Washington can offer, in its comprehensive pageant, any one passage so lovely as this nearer view from Mount Surprise of the farms that border the Androscoggin. Here the infinite goodness responds by appropriate symbols to the infinite majesty which is represented by the barren hills. The spirit of the eighteenth psalm seems to brood over the torn and desolate ridge where the thunder-clouds crouch; but it is the eloquence of the sixty-fifth that streams from the softer section of the scene below : " Thou visitest the earth, and waterest it : thou greatly enrichest it with the river of God, which is full of water : thou preparest them corn, when thou hast so provided for it. Thou waterest the ridges thereof abundantly : thou settlest the furrows thereof : thou makest it soft with showers : thou blessest the springing thereof. Thou crownest the year with thy goodness ; and thy paths drop fatness. They drop upon the pastures of the wilderness ; and the little hills rejoice on every side. The pastures are clothed with flocks ; the valleys also are covered over with corn ; they shout for joy ; they also sing."

It is often true, however, so far as the stimulant of the poetic mood is concerned, that a part is greater than the whole. One subordinate feature of a landscape may prove more fruitful of inspiration than the general splendor in which it is inclosed. In the forest of Mount Surprise we meet, here and there, a pine or spruce veiled with drooping moss. The last walk it was our fortune to enjoy through the ascending aisle of the woods, was in company with the writer of the following exquisite poem, to which, however, we must take this exception,—that if its wish were fulfilled, a life would be cancelled from the conscious world, strong in its native stock as the oak, and graceful in its culture as the elm. The author is Rev. Dr. Hedge of Brookline, to whom also we are indebted for the translations from Goethe on pp. 93 and 154.

> I would I were yon lock of moss
> Upon the tresséd pine,
> Free in the buxom air to toss,
> And with the breeze to twine.

High over earth my pendent life
From care and sorrow free,
Should reck no more the creature's strite
With time and Deity.

No thought to break my perfect peace,
Born of the perfect whole,
From thought and will a long release,—
A vegetable soul.

Thus would I live my bounded age
Far in the forest lone,
Erased from human nature's page,
Once more the Godhead's own.

And now we must ask the reader's attention to the view from the summit of

MOUNT HAYES,

which is so remarkable that it should by no means be passed by. This is part of the record which the writer once made of his first acquaintance with that view, in company with the artist whose sketches are engraved for this volume.

"Mount Hayes takes its name from the excellent woman whom visitors in Gorham, some three years since, have occasion to remember with gratitude as a hostess of the hotel. It is now her monument. You remember it, doubtless, as the scarred and savage eminence that rises pretty sharply from the eastern bank of the Androscoggin, and directly overlooks the Alpine House. Its height is probably not far from twenty-five hundred feet. Two huge ledges of bare and jagged rock, some two miles apart, that clamp it to the valley, look like the carved paws of a colossal lion in repose. Over it the desolate crest soars like a bald eagle's head and beak; so that it sits a monstrous griffin overlooking the village, and commanding the sweep of the river for twenty miles. The ancient mythology pictures the griffin as the guardian of hidden treasures; and in this sense also the mountain admirably fulfils the symbolism of its form.

" I had heard frequently from some of the old settlers here that the mountain was remarkable for bears, blueberries, and views, and desired to make the ascent of it last year ; but no good opportunity offered when a guide could go. The other day, an artist friend of mine here was told that if we could get across the Androscoggin, about a mile above the Alpine House, we should find a sled-path to

the summit, and could easily reach it in an hour and a half. This determined my friend and myself to start about ten in the hot fore-noon, with the hope of bringing back a memory full of beauty to a rather late dinner. The paddling across the hurrying river by a backwoods-Charon, in a boat of quite primitive structure,—being three pieces of rough pine board nailed together, with liberal provision for

leaks,—was decidedly intresting, especially for the picture it gave us
of Mount Moriah, rising directly from the cool and curving flood,
that seems to bend out of its track to meet the stream which pours
down from those deep green dells.   No excursion could have a more
charming commencement.

"On the other side of the Androscoggin, we found the hint of a
path that led us to the first ledge ; but there all trace of it ceased.
The heat was torrid.   Should we return ?   We had taken no lun-
cheon ; we were not sure of finding water ; we had no guide ;—before
us was a wall of forest, with here and there a patch of ledge protruding through it, from which we might make an observation.   So
in the hope of a large dividend at the summit, we determined to invest liberally in a scramble, and started on a ' bee-line ' for the crest.
My dear editorial friend, a young forest looks poetic in the distance,
especially if it is a birch one, and steeps itself every evening in yellow sunset light.   But attempt to go through one, where no path has
been bushed out, and your admiration will be cut down, as Carlyle
would say, ' some stages.'   What with dead trunks that promise
foothold, and in which you slump to the knees ; *chevaux de frise* of
great charred logs that bristle with sharp black spikes ; openings of
tall purple fireweed, hiding snags that pierce through your boots ;
snaky underbrush that trips you ; intertangled young limbs that fly
back and switch your eyes ; rocks half covered with moss that wrench
the ankles ; slanting sticks that lie in wait for your pantaloons, and
force you to deduct a large *tare* before you get your accurate *net*
benefits from the expedition ;—the poetry of wild forest-clambering
turns out pretty serious prose.   It is about like fighting a phalanx of
porcupines.   For nearly three hours of a sultry midday, we were
wrestling thus with the wilderness, without water, in order to win
the secret of its summit.

"But we were trebly rewarded by the vision that burst upon us,
as we stood on the crown of the rocky precipice that plunges from
the mountain peak.   The rich upland of Randolph, over which the
ridges of Madison and Adams heave towards the south, first holds

the eye. Next the singular curve in the blue Androscoggin around the Lary farm, arching like a bow drawn taut. Directly beneath us lay two islands in the river,—one of a diamond shape, the other cut precisely like a huge kite, and fringed most charmingly with green. Down the valley, Shelburne, Gilead, West Bethel, and Bethel were laid into the landscape with rich mosaics of grove, and grass, and ripening grain,—needing, as my artist companion said, a brush dipped in molten opal to paint their wavering, tremulous beauty. Directly opposite, seemingly only an arrow-shot's distance, were the russet ravines of Moriah and the shadow-cooled stairways of Carter.

"But such sights as these I have often had before. The great reward of the scramble was that it gave me my *first view* of Mount Washington. I mean to say that, from no other point where I have had the fortune to stand, does it rise before you from valley to crown in imperial estate. Perhaps you remember Punch's advice to the splendid Koh-i-noor jewel in the Crystal Palace, which did not flash as it should have done, among the other gems : 'If you are the great diamond of the world, why don't you behave *as such?*' Mount Washington is the sovereign dome of New England, but it is very difficult to make him behave ' as such.' In the Glen, Mount Adams looks higher and more proud. Seen from North Conway, he is not isolated from the rest of the range, and wears no grandeur about the summit. At Lancaster he looks humpbacked. In Shelburne he appears heavy and dowdy. From Bethlehem he shows grand height, but unsatisfactory form. The village of Jefferson, on the Cherry Mountain road, about thirteen miles from Gorham, furnishes the best position for studying his lines and height in connection with the rest of the range. But Mount Hayes is the chair set by the Creator at the proper distance and angle to appreciate and enjoy his kingly prominence.

"All the lower summits are hidden, and you have the great advantage of not looking along a chain, but of seeing the monarch himself soar alone, back of Madison and Adams and seemingly disconnected with them, standing just enough to the south to allow an

40

unobstructed view of the ridges that climb from the Pinkham road up over Tuckerman's ravine, to a crest moulded and poised with indescribable stateliness and grace. It completely dimmed the glory of Mount Adams. The eye clung ever fascinated and still hungry upon those noble proportions and that haughty peace. We were just far enough removed to get the poetic impression of height which vagueness and airy tenderness of color give. The day was perfect for such effects. If I had been told that the dome was ten or twelve thousand feet high, I should not have been disappointed. Arithmetic was out of the account. It was satisfactory, artistic, mountain-eminence and majesty that we were gazing upon. Ah, what ripples of mystic light, waking colors uncertain, momentary, but ecstatic, would run in the warm noon, over that serene pinnacle! And yet we knew that feet were climbing, tired and faint, up its jagged desolation, and savage gales, possibly, were howling over the rocks, as though art and joy have no right on this rough globe! How delicately the shadows were tinted, to our eyes, in dimples of that crest, which were fissures scarred with land-slides and threatened by tottering crags! Was not the pleasure the more subtle to us because we knew that the splendor was illusion? And yet was not the seeming illusion nobler truth than the near and accurate reality? In the Creator's estimate of this globe, is it not probable that Mount Washington is a picture, rather than some thousands of cubic rods of rock?"

We have alluded frequently to the riches of color with which the mountains are dowered, and to the rare spectacles with which visitors in a valley are rewarded for their patient sojourn. Now that we must turn from Gorham and the landscapes which excursions from the village and hotel command, we can hardly do better than to carry with us one of the most gorgeous visions, interpreting Tennyson's phrase, " The low sun makes the color," which a summer residence of several years in the Androscoggin Valley has left in the writer's memory Thus runs the cold record which we made of the brilliant fact.

" We have had some compensation, my dear friend, for the recent hot weather, in two ways : for the body, in the breezes of the evening, which have breathed down the valley, after sunset, bearing something of the coolness that crowns the hills on the north, fanning the long passage-ways of the hotel, and making a seat on the western piazza an incomparable luxury ;—for the eye, in the soft haze which has benetted all the hills. If our days lately have been as hot as those of Southern Italy, we have enjoyed sunset hours when the scenery has been un-Yankee-ized,—when the air was full of sentiment, and, instead of affording free passage for the sunbeams, seemed to melt them, and mix itself with them, to form a new element, ' half languish and half light.' It swathed the ridges with a vague and tender blue, that took out all their ruggedness ; it gave a creamy quality to the yellow that streamed over the meadow-grass ; it threw a halo around the Titan hills, which cheated the eye as to their real character, and made them look as though they had no duties, but had been lifted up to dream the year away in unruffled joy.

" The cool weather gives us brain-landscape. The hills are cut sharply. Every scar and rock is exposed. We are trained by it to clear seeing. The scenery is severe, obtrudes geology on the attention, and suggests all kinds of scientific truth to the intellect. This hazy tone of the atmosphere gives heart-landscape. Wherever we look, it is not form, so much as hue and emotion, that nature shows. Rich opaline lights flush the prominent objects, changing every hour. Nature seems to have been created to inspire feeling. All the *ologies* are subordinate to artistic impression. The clouds mingle, with undecided outlines, into the tender leaden blue of the sky. The mountain peaks seem ready to dissolve into the air. The clearings of light among the shadows on the hillsides make the green of the forests seem like large masses of *chenille*. You can't think of strata, or forces, or metals, in looking at the chief mountains, any more than you would think of the texture of the canvas, or of the chemistry of pigments, in looking at one of Turner's masterpieces. Rocks, forests.

land-slides, earthquakes, are simply the material for a *landscape* that stimulates the imagination, educates the sense of beauty, and gladdens the heart.

" Is it possible, do you think, that Nature is ever conscious of human observation, and that she can change at all, can blush into rarer loveliness, when an eye that has a passion for beauty studies her ?   I have sometimes fancied, standing on the sea-shore after a storm, with an enthusiastic party, that the waves caught the excitement of the company, as actors feel the applause of the audience, and that they redoubled their efforts in answer to our cheers.   And often it has seemed to me that the mountains know when critical and appreciative visitors come to be refreshed and invigorated by their grandeur.   They will rise in apparent height, or mottle themselves with a richer complexity of hues, or select a rarer vestment from their aerial wardrobe, or look more solemn than usual or more sublime. If it is one of the great purposes of nature to get transmuted into human thought and emotion, and to reappear in human character, why may we not conjecture that the presence of a gifted guest has occult power enough, sometimes, to charm the most reverent look out of a hill, and induce the light to pour its most cunning splendors on the air,—so that the glory of the Creator may pass into the feeling of genius ?   If the world is for the education of man, why may not stars glow more alluringly, now and then, to the gaze of a Newton, or the Alps be shown in their most gorgeous possible apparel because Turner is looking at them ?   If the principle is true in the general, why not sometimes in the particular ?   Does not Mr. Emerson make Mount Monadnoc confess that his

> gray crags
> Not on crags are hung,
> But beads are of a rosary
> On prayer and music strung?

And does he not assure us, in the mountain's behalf, that, as soon as the seer or poet comes who carries the secret in his brain of which the granite pile is but the hieroglyph, its roots will be unfixed and its cone will spin ? Why then may the hills not respond *in part* to the presence of genius, though it carry not the full faith which is able to bid them float ?

" It seemed to me last night, that such a law might account for the marvellous spectacle which the sunset prepared for us. We have had few magnificent sunsets this season. Just enough of the purple has been poured over Mount Moriah in July to tempt us, by the recollection of its splendor, to watch, evening after evening, for the prospect of an unclouded western horizon. But, during a fortnight, no clouds would hang over the declining sun to catch his legacies of amber and crimson ; while just enough fog would bar the line of the west to intercept the magnificence that was intended for Mount Moriah. We had begun to drop the calculation of glowing evening skies from the category of the delights of the season.

" Last evening, however, we had a new visitor in Gorham, who is worthy to see the best which the region can reveal. I drove with him, in a single wagon, down the southerly road, to show him one of our grandest mountain-views, and to let the pure breeze take the heats of New York out of his portly frame,—when, lo ! a gorgeousness was conjured in the west such as I never saw in this valley before. Before touching the summits of the Pilot Hills, which bar the northwest, the sun, behind a cloud from which he was about to emerge, poured a strangeness and splendor of color down their blueblack mass which no brush could mock. The soft, leaden blue haze that lay off a little way from the mountains, was filled with a flood of flaming plum color and gold. It was a curtain of glory dropped before the long range. The gold was there, and seemed, when you looked exclusively at it, to cover the whole line. It was there in a broad and apparently simple tissue. The plum hue was just as plain, and seemed also to be an unmixed sheet of splendor.

" But how the two hues were so interblended in such changeable and blazing atmospheric silk, and how, in rifts through this magical drop-scene, the blue-black of the mountain was also distinctly visible, confounded the senses like a miracle. For some five minutes the

vision lasted in full brilliancy. And, as it began to fade, the unbroken mass of Mount Madison was adorned with a lustrous purple
sash, that fell athwart his breast from the shoulder to the waist.
That was an investiture with knightly honor, by the sovereign sun,
for which the mountain might well look high and proud. He seemed
to say,—is it not worth while to stand up here and be buffeted by
gales, and bitten by frosts, and pelted by hail, and harassed by torrents, and bleached by snows, to get, now and then, such an honor
as this for my patience and my scars,—a baldric fresh from the loom
of light, and woven of its most imperial hues? So always the hero's tasks are paid by the hero's glory. Was not that spectacle a
leaf from the gospel of nature, saying that the sunset hues,—the
peace and triumph of a noble life, more than atone for the noonday
trials and the chilly clouds?

" I had never before seen the dolphin flushes of evening thrown
upon either the Pilot Hills or the White Mountain range, and I had
never anywhere seen them so ravishing and mystical in their pomp
and charm. Was it not on account of my companion in the wagon,
a stranger to the scenery, who arrived in the afternoon train? Did
not nature know that all the richness of the shows she displayed to
his eye would be woven again into splendors of eloquence that outrun
her reach? Was not the sunset, was not that purple-belted pyramid,
eager to become material for imagery through his passionate and
poetic genius,—imagery sure to be vivid as that shining bloom, mystic as the interblending of those hues, soaring as that granite column,
tender and pathetic, too, as that all-soothing and loving haze? No
doubt, that spectacle will be transmuted, some day, in speech, or
hymn, or sermon, into the richer purple and gold which genius
weaves out of memory and experience, by my gifted companion,
whose broad fame as a Christian orator has recently been crowned by
Harvard with honors that are modestly worn."

> The life of man has wondrous hours
> Revealed at once to heart and eye,
> When wake all being's kindled powers,

And joy, like dew on trees and flowers,
 With freshness fills the earth and sky.
. . . .
The distant landscape glows serene;
 The dark old tower with tremulous sheen
Pavilion of a seraph stands.
 The mountain rude, with steeps of gold,
 And mists of ruby o'er them rolled,
Up towards the evening star expands.
. . . .
 And those who walk within the sphere,
 The plot of earth's transfigured green,
 Like angels walk, so high, so clear,
With ravishment in eye and mien.
 For this one hour no breath of fear,
 Of shame or weakness wandering near
Can trusting hearts annoy:
 Past things are dead, or only live
 The life that hope alone can give,
And all is faith and joy.
 'Tis not that beauty forces then
 Her blessings on reluctant men,
But this great globe, with all its might,
Its awful depth and heavenward height,
 Seems but my heart with wonder thrilling
And beating in my human breast;
 My sense with inspiration filling,
Myself—beyond my nature blest.
 Well for all such hours who know,
 All who hail, not bid them go,
If the spirit's strong pulsation
 After keeps its nobler tone,
And no helpless lamentation
 Dulls the heart when rapture 's flown;
If the rocky field of Duty,
 Built around with mountains hoar,
Still is dearer than the Beauty
 Of the sky-land's colored shore.

THE GLEN.

The road to the Glen lies through the forest between Mount Carter and Mount Madison along the brawling Peabody River. Rev. H.

White, in a book of remarkable incidents from the history of New England, tells us that a visitor from Massachusetts, by the name of Peabody, passed a night, many years ago, in an Indian's cabin on the height of land between the Saco and Androscoggin rivers. It must have been very near the spot where a clearing has been made in the Pinkham woods beyond the Glen House, under the walls of Tuckerman's ravine. The inmates of the Indian cabin, we are told, were roused in the night by a singular and dreadful noise, and in their terror rushed from the hut just in time to save their lives ; for the cabin was swept away by a furious torrent that had burst from the hillside where there had been no spring before. No date is given in connection with the story. One of the mountain books informs us that this was, possibly, the origin of the branch of the Peabody River that runs in front of the Glen House. But as long as Washington, Adams, Carter, and Madison have received baptisms of rain and been sheeted with snow, the Peabody River has not ceased to wind through the Glen, and hurry with its increasing burden of water eight hundred feet down to the Androscoggin in Gorham. Doubtless a convulsion may have opened a pathway for some feeder of the Ellis River which flows into the Saco, or of the Peabody that pays tribute to the Androscoggin. But the river itself, whose curves we see and whose brawl we hear on the ride to the Glen House, was fed from the broad shoulders of Mount Washington, from the gorges of Jefferson, from the more even desolation of the pyramid of Madison, and from rains distilled more slowly through the deep forest soil of Carter, ages before any settler lifted an axe upon its bordering trees, or any Indian looked up from its banks with awe to the craggy seat of Manitou,—yes,

> Ere Adam wived,
> Ere Adam lived,
> Ere the duck dived,
> Ere the bees hived,
> Ere the lion roared,
> Ere the eagle soared.

We are able to give a sketch of the Peabody stream from a point

where it is watched by one of the great White Mountain summits.
The following poem, which the accomplished author's kindness allows
us to transfer to type from manuscript, was written after a morning
visit from Gorham to the lower part of the Peabody, by Rev. William
R. Alger of Boston :—

My way in opening dawn I took,
Between the hills, beside a brook.
The peaks one sun was climbing o'er,—
The dew-drops showed ten millions more.

The mountain valley is a vase
Which God has brimmed with rarest grace

41

And, kneeling in the taintless air,
I drink celestial blessings there.

Behold that guiltless bird! What brings
Him here? He comes to wash his wings.
Let me, too, wash my wings, with prayer,
And cleanse them from foul dust and care.

. To one long time in city pent,
The lesson seems from heaven sent:—
For pinions clean yon bird takes care,
Of soul defiled do thou beware!

It is certainly a startling view that bursts upon us when we enter the Glen, either from Gorham or from Jackson, by the ' Pinkham road. No other public-house in the mountains, except those in North Conway, is so situated that Mount Washington is in view from its grounds. But North Conway is twenty miles distant. The Glen House is at the very base of the monarch ; and Adams, Jefferson, Clay, and Madison bend around towards the east, with no lower hills to obstruct the impression of their height,—so that from the piazza and front chamber windows of the hotel, the forest clothing of the five highest mountains of New England is distinctly seen, with all the clefts and chasms and the channelling of the rains, up to the bare ridge from which the desolate cones or splintered peaks ascend.

In the Glen we are a little too near the mountains for the best landscape effects ; and as the sun sets behind the great ridge, we cannot see the splendors and changes of the evening light poured over the range as from Jefferson, Bethlehem, and Lancaster. The best time for the effects of light on the peaks is early in the morning, when the rocky portions of the ridge are often burnished with surpassing beauty, or from four to six in the afternoon of midsummer, when the lights and shadows are most powerfully contrasted. A misty day, too, is a great privilege, when the fogs are not heavy and sulky, but break around the peaks in the graceful witcheries of their languid and unceasing change ; or when, in preparation for a storm, heavy clouds roll up the ravines and pack themselves between the cones of the ridge, and pour over into the caldron-like gulfs to whirl around their sides, and, now and then, suffer one of the mountains to show itself seemingly doubled in height, while all its companions are smothered by the towering vapors. It was during such a scene that

our first acquaintance with the Glen was made, many years ago, about sunset on a summer evening. The clouds had hidden Washington, Madison, Jefferson, and Clay, and had piled their inky folds behind Mount Adams. But not a shred of vapor spotted its foreground or flitted across its crest. The dusky outline of its pyramid, more than four thousand feet from the valley to the apex, rose alone, mimicking the Swiss Jungfrau in shape, so symmetrical and beautiful that the storm seemed to spare its proportions, and allow it for our delight to shoot its keen edges and spire into the black sky.

Mount Adams looks the highest at all times from the Glen House; and in fact, although it is nearly five hundred feet lower than Mount Washington, a greater elevation on one steady slope is seen in look- ing at it than Mount Washington reveals. The summit of Mount Washington lies back of the shoulder seen from the Glen, so that the effect of a thousand feet of height is really lost. And yet, after the first surprise has passed, there is no comparison between the two mountains for grandeur, as they tower above the hotel. Wash- ington is more massive. The lines that run off to the southeast from the summit, and especially those that sweep around the Great Gulf and Tuckerman's Ravine, are far more grand and fascinating, to the eye of an artist, than the symmetry of the slim pyramid of Ad- ams. One can never tire of looking at their sharp, curving edges, into whose steely hardness the torrents and rock-slides have torn steep dykes, that in the afternoon are delicate engravings of graceful shadow. And seen through a southerly air or a light shower, that shows, much more plainly than clear air does, the number and the graceful flow as well as vigor of these lines, we learn that the great privilege of the Glen is the opportunity it gives for studying from below the granite braces of the cone of Mount Washington.

It is very difficult, even after twenty opportunities of study, to copy from memory the outline of a well-formed mountain. And if not outlines, *a fortiori* not details of mass, which have all the com- plexity of the outline multiplied a thousand-fold, and drawn in fainter colors. "Nothing is more curious," says Mr. Ruskin, "than the state of embarrassment into which the unfortunate artist must soon be cast, when he endeavors honestly to draw the face of the simplest mountain cliff—say a thousand feet high, and two or three miles dis- tant. It is full of exquisite details, all seemingly decisive and clear;

but when he tries to arrest one of them, he cannot see it,—cannot find where it begins or ends,—and presently it runs into another; and then he tries to draw that, but that will not be drawn, neither, until it has conducted him to a third, which, somehow or another, made part of the first; presently he finds that, instead of three, there are in reality four, and then he loses his place altogether. He tries to draw clear lines, to make his work look craggy, but finds then that it is too hard; he tries to draw soft lines, and it is immediately too soft; he draws a curved line, and instantly sees it should have been straight; a straight one, and finds when he looks up again that it has got curved while he was drawing it. There is nothing for him but despair, or some sort of abstraction and shorthand for cliff. Then the only question is, which is the wisest abstraction; and out of the multitude of lines that cannot altogether be interpreted, which are the really dominant ones; so that if we cannot give the whole, we may at least give what will convey the most important facts about the cliff."

We have alluded in a former chapter to the grand contrast, in spring, of the snowfields on Mount Washington with the infant green of the forests below. But October is the best season for a visit to the Glen. In the middle of that month, the summits are often entirely covered with their winter whiteness. We have in our mind's eye now the spectacle which a ride from Gorham to the Glen, about the middle of October, has added to the gallery of our memory. For a large part of the way, Mount Washington was in sight more plainly than in summer, on account of the dropping of the leaves from many of the trees that border the road. It looked higher than in July or August. Around the base, orange, pale yellow, and brown were intermixed with evergreens; above these hues was a zone of dark purple; and over this, where in summer rises the gray or gray-green barrenness, a great dome of white, as though its sheathing might have been mother-of-pearl, swelled towards the heavy and rolling clouds. But as we emerged from the woods, and, from the hill where the Glen House is first seen, turned to get a sight of Mount Adams, the view was really startling. The sun was shining upon it, and it flashed above the gorgeous hues of its lower forest like a silver spire. The air was cool and transparent, the clouds were flying, there was no rain, and yet the effect was as though something was falling from the clouds over the mountain,—as though an emerald dust was sifting upon the sparkling crest and slope. After a while, the clouds settled a little lower and touched the mountain-tops, and for an hour or two would let their vapors droop a little below the crests, then draw them back till they just touched their tips, and thus allowed them to sway and waver for several hours. The flushes of the sunset on the Wetterhorn or Monte Rosa, the gorgeousness of tropic vegetation around the base and on the first acclivities of Chimborazo, are worth as pictures all the labor and expense which it costs to see them. Yet it is not impossible that one might find, in such a view of the Glen as October sometimes provides, a richer combination of colors than can be displayed by any landscape, unspeakably grander in proportion, in the great mountain districts of the globe.

And now shall we climb a few hundred feet of Mount Carter behind the Glen House, in order to obtain a more impressive view of the great hills we have been speaking of, and to enjoy the pleasures that reward such exertion. While we are shut in by the forest, we may turn our attention to the symmetry and varieties of the leaves, and try to learn something of Nature's wealth of resources as to graceful form, within narrow boundaries. An eye that is sensitive to the grace of curves and parabolas and oval swells will marvel at the feast which a day's walk in the woods will supply from the trees, the grasses, and the weeds, in the varying outlines, the notchings, veinings, and edgings of the leaves. They stand for the art of sculpture in Botany, representing the intellectual delight of Nature in form, as the flowers express the companion art of painting. Leaves are the Greek, flowers the Italian phase of the spirit of beauty that reveals itself through the Flora of the globe.

An exhaustive collection of leaves would form one of the most attractive museums that could be gathered. It would be a privilege that could not but unseal in some measure the dullest eye, to look in one day over the whole scale of Nature's foliage-art, from the feathery spray of the moss, to the tough texture on the Amazon lily's stem that will float a burden of a hundred weight; from the bristles of the pine-tree to the Ceylon palm leaf that will shield a family with its shade. Would it not astonish us into something like reverent admiration, if we could sweep the gradations of Nature's green as it is distilled from arctic and temperate and tropic light, and varied by some shade on every leaf that grows; if we could scan all the textures of the drapery woven out of salts and water in botanic looms, from the softest silk of the corn to the broad tissue of the banana's stock; if we could see displayed in wide masses all the hues in which Autumn dyes the leaves of our own forests, as though every square mile had been drenched in the aerial juices of a gorgeous sunset And then when we should see how the general geometry of the verdure is broken into countless patterns, we should find our museum of leaves as engaging a school for the education of the intellect as a collection of all vertebræ, or a representative conservatory of the globe.

.A careful and eloquent observer of Nature describes the leaf as a sudden expansion of the stem that bore it; an uncontrollable expression of delight, on the part of the twig, that Spring has come, shown in a fountain-like expatiation of its tender green heart into the air. And to hold this joy, Nature moulds the leaves as vases into the most diverse and fantastic shapes,—of eggs, and hearts, and circles, of lances and wedges, and arrows and shields. She cleaves, and parts, and notches them in the most cunning ways, combines their blades into subtle and complicated varieties, and scallops their edges and points into patterns that involve seemingly every possible angle and every line of grace.

Mr. Agassiz, from a single scale, is able to draw the form of the fish to which it belongs. It is possible that we may yet find in the leaf the whole character of the tree. A recent writer on botany maintains that a leaf with a leaf-stalk implies that the tree to which it belongs has naturally a bare trunk for a certain distance ; but that a leaf without a leaf-stalk shows that its parent tree is naturally branched from the ground. Also that there is a correspondence between the disposition and distribution of the leaf-veins and the disposition and distribution of the branches of the trees. Still further, that the angle at which the lateral veins in the leaf go off shows the angle at which the branch goes off, and that the curve of the vein shows the curve of the corresponding branch. Mr. Ruskin tells us that " the numbers of any great composition, arranged about a centre, are always reducible to the law of the ivy leaf, the best cathedral entrances having five porches corresponding in proportional purpose to its five lobes ; while the loveliest groups of lines attainable in any pictorial composition are always based on the section of the leaf-bud, or on the relation of its ribs to the convex curve inclosing them." And in a grander architecture than any human one, the laws of the arrangement of leaves around their stem are repeated. For it is found that the relations between the times of the revolutions of the planets in the solar system around the sun, are expressed by the same series of fractions which show the combinations most frequently observed in the arrangement of leaves, in spirals around their stems. ' The Maker of this earth but patented a leaf.'

And those five huge mountains, that face us as we rise out of the woods of Mount Carter into a little clearing—Washington, Clay, Jefferson, Adams, Madison, which seem to tower far more grandly when seen from this height than from the plateau in the Glen—are not the lines of the leaf shown to us in the veins of their ravines, and in the curves that bound many of their spires of rock, or that show the grace into which their landslides have subsided ? Only we must remember that these five huge lobes of earth, seen at the proper distance, are petals rather, of a mighty flower, whose bloom is not fixed for certain seasons, but flushes and fades by incalculable laws. And it is not fixed hues, such as a rose or a dahlia or a tulip bears, that this corolla of

earth is appointed to
display; but every
tender dye, which
the sun's pencil
leaves upon the Flo-
ra of New England,
glows upon them at
morning or at sun-
set, and their bloom
is the richest when
the vital forces of
the garden and the
forest are checked by
the winter frosts and
buried in the snow.

We shall have a very grand view of Mount Washington on the
way from the Glen House to visit the two cascades, a few miles dis-

42

tant in Pinkham Pass. In the Autumn of 1858, a clearing was made about three miles from the Glen, which opens the nearest view of the whole summit and shoulders of Mount Washington, which can ever probably be obtained from the base. It is near a small fountain whose water flows two ways—from one side into a branch of the Saco, from the other into a branch of the Androscoggin,—that we gain the view of the deep hollows and rocky ruins over which the dome of the great mountain is so serenely set. On one of those hard ridges, four thousand feet above us, three drops of rain may fall in company, one of which may trickle off towards the Ammonoosuc, to be borne into the Connecticut; while the other two, sinking into the invisible veins that feed this fountain, and bubbling up into it, may part company again,—on one side for the Peabody River, on the other for the Ellis,—and thus be received into the sea at different openings on the coast of Maine. Is not this a hieroglyphic lesson in the great spiritual laws?

> So from the heights of Will
> Life's parting stream descends,
> And as a moment turns its slender rill,
> Each widening torrent bends,—
>
> From the same cradle's side,
> From the same mother's knee,—
> One to long darkness and the frozen tide,
> One to the peaceful sea!

The waterfalls we are to seek are not at a great distance from the road, as many of the others are, which we have described; and on our way to the

CRYSTAL CASCADE,

let us bear in mind that "of all inorganic substances, acting in their own proper nature, and without assistance or combination, water is the most wonderful. If we think of it as the source of all the changefulness and beauty which we have seen in clouds; then as the instrument by which the earth we have contemplated was modelled into

symmetry, and its crags chiselled into grace ; then as, in the form
of snow, it robes the mountains it has made, with that transcendent
light which we could not have conceived if we had not seen ; then as
it exists in the form of the torrent,—in the iris which spans it, in the
morning mist which rises from it, in the deep crystalline pools which
mirror its hanging shore, in the broad lake and glancing river ; finally,
in that which is to all human minds the best emblem of unwearied,
unconquerable power, the wild, various, fantastic, tameless unity of
the sea ; what shall we compare to this mighty, this universal element, for glory and for beauty ? or how shall we follow its eternal
changefulness of feeling ?   It is like trying to paint a soul."

We never look at the Crystal Cascade without revering and re-
joicing over the poetry with which Nature invests the birth of so
common a thing as water.   The making of the most costly wine,
after the sun has ceased to tinge the grape with purple, and to
infuse sweetness into its pulp, has no such poetic charm connected
with it as encircles the advent of pure water.   The gentle and invisible suction of it in vapor fresh from the salt fountains of the sea ; its
dropping in crystal snow piled in fantastic drifts and pinnacles upon
the lofty mountain ridges, to melt there under the climbing summer
sun ; its descent in showers, or in tempests driven by howling winds
and flashing electric fire ; and then the passages of its earthly history,—its trickling from the hard rocks of lofty summits, flavored with
the cold pure breath of mountain winds, its leaping in rills, and their
marriage into brooks, its plunging in cascades, that laugh joyously
through sloping forests, its calmer flow through green nooks and over
mossy rocks, its soft " complaining " creep, " making the meadows
green," while it bears its burden to a river's treasury, or its untiring
bubble from the ground in springs,—what process of nature has so
much to stimulate and engage the imagination as the biography of
water, from its birth out of the ocean to its presence on our summer
tables to assuage our thirst !   If wine were our ordinary drink, and
water were as rare and expensive as our richest wine, and there were

only one elevation on the globe,—some ice-coned Chimborazo, some jagged Jungfrau,—where it was collected, condensed, and distributed in streams, what gorgeous poetry would be dedicated to the rare and gracious fluid, what eagerness to get draughts of it, what sums would be paid for transparent ice-blocks of it, what enthusiastic pilgrimages be made to the majestic crystal distillery piercing the heavens, whence the cloud-vapor was given in trickling beauty and melody to man! Yet every mountain is such a distillery, and the rocky bed of every leaping rivulet the vein of such a mysterious and poetic mercy to the world. We lack the insight to connect the processes and weave the history of the gift into marvel and beauty.

It requires about half an hour to reach the Crystal Cascade, with a party of ladies, from the side of the road where the wagon is left. And visitors should not forget that the proper point from which to see it is not the foot of the fall itself, but the top of the little cliff directly opposite. No contrast more striking can be found among the mountains than that of age and youth, which is furnished from that point. The cliff is richly carpeted with mosses that have been nourished and thickened by centuries, and that never till within ten years have yielded to any pressure more rude than the step of a partridge, or the footfall of a fawn. The rocks of the neighboring precipices look old. They are cracked and seamed as though the forces of decay had wound their coils fairly around them, and were crumbling them at leisure. The lichens upon them look bleached and feeble. These protruding portions of its anatomy indicate that Mount Washington has passed the meridian of his years. But the waterfall gives the impression of graceful and perpetual youth. Down it comes, leaping, sliding, tripping, widening its pure tide, and then gathering its thin sheet to gush through a narrowing pass in the rocks,—all the way thus, from under the sheer walls of Tuckerman's Ravine, some miles above, till it reaches the curve opposite the point where we stand, and winding around it, sweeps down the bending stairway, shattering its substance into exquisite crystal, but sending

off enough water to the right side of its path to slip and trickle over
the lovely, dark green mosses that cling to the gray and purple rocks
For how many thousand years has it enlivened the mountain side
thus with its flashes and its dance? Perhaps long enough to have

fulfilled one of the great Platonic years,—long enough for the very
water which in one summer week has poured down its channels, to be
returned from the sea by the clouds, to the very same spot over the
mountain ridge, and to repeat their journey.

But there is no suggestion of age in its curves and color, or in the sprightliness of its voice. Beautiful plunderer, it has made the mountain more meagre, and has torn out thousands of tons from his bulk, to find a more easy pathway down which it might move. But it is not only undimmed youth, it is feminine grace and freshness and charm which it expresses,—

> Laugh of the mountain! lyre of bird and tree
> Pomp of the meadow! mirror of the morn!
> The soul of April, unto whom are born
> The rose and jassamine, leaps wild in thee!

The mountain has yielded without murmur to the humors of the stream in choosing and channelling its path. The scene is the story told in a mightier sculpture than art can manage, of Ariadne riding the panther,—beauty resting gracefully on the submissive brute. And yet, when we forecast the service of these beautiful crystal sheets, born in part of snows packed in the shadowed caverns above, in carrying coolness to the Saco and North Conway, let it remind us of Longfellow's verses :—

> God sent his messenger the rain,
> And said unto the mountain brook,
> " Rise up and from thy caverns look
> And leap, with naked, snow-white feet,
> From the cool hills into the heat
> Of the broad, arid plain."
>
> God sent his messenger of faith,
> And whispered in the maiden's heart,
> " Rise up and look from where thou art
> And scatter with unselfish hands
> Thy freshness on the barren sands
> And solitudes of Death."

The surroundings of

THE GLEN ELLIS FALL

are more grand than those of the cascade just spoken of. In fact, if we wished to take a person into a scene that would seem to be the

very heart of mountain wildness, without wishing to make him climb
into any of the ravines, we should invite him to visit this fall of the
Ellis River. The best view of the fall is obtained by leaning against
a tree that overhangs a sheer precipice, and looking down upon the
slide and foam of the narrow and concentrated cataract to where it

splashes into the dark green pool, a hundred feet below. And then
as we look off from this point above the fall, we see the steep side of
Mount Carter crowded to the ridge with the forest. It is not the
sense of age, but of grim, almost fierce wildness, that is breathed
from the scenery, amid which this cataract takes a leap of eighty

feet to carry its contribution to the Saco. But we must be careful how we talk of the leap of the river, or we shall have Mr. Ruskin after us. He tells us that artists seldom convey the characteristic of a powerful stream that descends a long distance through a narrow channel, where it has a chance to expand as it falls. The springing lines of parabolic descent are apt to be the controlling feature of the picture. The stream is made to look active all the way, not supine. " Now water will leap a little way, it will leap down a weir or over a stone, but it *tumbles* over a high fall like this; and it is when we have lost the parabolic line, and arrived at the catenary,—when we have lost the *spring* of the fall, and arrived at the *plunge* of it, that we begin really to feel its weight and wildness. Where water takes its first leap from the top, it is cool, and collected, and uninteresting, and mathematical, but it is when it finds that it has got into a scrape, and has farther to go than it thought for, that its character comes out ; it is then that it begins to writhe, and twist, and sweep out zone after zone in wilder stretching as it falls, and to send down the rocket-like, lance-pointed, whizzing shafts at its sides, sounding for the bottom."

It is feminine and maidenly grace that is illustrated by the crystal cascade ; it is masculine youth, the spirit of heroic adventure, that is suggested by this stream, which flows for a long way level over a rocky bed before it breaks from its mountain-prison into a broader life.

Take, cradled Nursling of the mountain, take
This parting glance, no negligent adieu!
A Protean change seems wrought while I pursue
The curves, a loosely scattered chain doth make;
Or rather thou appear'st a glittering snake,
Silent, and to the gazer's eye untrue,
Thridding with sinuous lapse the rushes, through
Dwarf willows gliding, and by ferny brake.
Starts from a dizzy steep the undaunted Rill
Robed instantly in garb of snow-white foam;
And laughing dares the Adventurer, who hath clomb
So high, a rival purpose to fulfil;
Else let the dastard backward wend, and roam,
Seeking less bold achievement, where he will'

THE ASCENT OF MOUNT WASHINGTON.

Every morn I lift my head,
Gaze o'er New England underspread,
South from Saint Lawrence to the Sound,
From Catskill east to the sea-bound.

. . . .

Oft as morning wreathes my scarf,
Fled the last plumule of the Dark,
Pants up hither the spruce clerk
From South Cove and City Wharf.
I take him up my rugged sides,
Half repentant, scant of breath, —
Bead-eyes my granite chaos show,
And my midsummer snow;
Open the daunting map beneath, —
All his country, sea and land,
Dwarfed to measure of his hand;
His day's ride is a furlong space,
His city-tops a glimmering haze.
I plant his eyes on the sky-hoop bounding:
" See there the grim gray rounding
Of the bullet of the earth
Whereon ye sail,
Tumbling steep
In the uncontinented deep."
He looks on that, and he turns pale.
'Tis even so; this treacherous kite,
Farm-furrowed, town-incrusted sphere,
Thoughtless of its anxious freight,
Plunges eyeless on forever;
And he, poor parasite,
Cooped in a ship he cannot steer, —
Who is the captain he knows not,
Port or pilot trows not, —
Risk or ruin he must share.
I scowl on him with my cloud,
With my north-wind chill his blood;
I lame him, clattering down the rocks;
And to live he is in fear.
Then, at last, I let him down
Once more, into his dapper town.
To chatter, frightened, to his clan,
And forget me if he can.

EMERSON

WE have thus far been describing the appearance of Mount Washington and of the range as they are seen in the landscape, or directly from the base. Now let us hear the call :

> Up! where the airy citadel
> O'erlooks the surging landscape's swell.

The Indians heard no such invitation to mount the rocky cone where " dappling shadows climb." They did not dare to ascend above the line of vegetation. On the ridge and the peaks, they said, the Great Spirit dwells. The darkness of the fire tempest pursues the steps that rise above the green leaves. No footmarks are seen returning from the home of Manitou in the clouds. They had a tradition that Passaconaway, the sachem of Pennacook, was once lifted in a car of flaming fire from the summit of the ridge to a council in heaven. He was their Elijah, as the chief who, according to their tradition, was saved on Mount Washington from a general flood, was the Indian Noah. But their general belief was, that those who were guilty of the sacrilege of ascending to where the moss alone can grow, were forbidden to enter the Happy Land beyond the sunset, but must wander forever as ghosts among the wild gorges and gloomy caverns of the mountains they had dared to profane. Which is nobler, such superstitious veneration for

> these dedicated blocks,
> Which who can tell what mason laid?

or the levity, and the poverty of insight and joy, which thousands of us carry not only to the mountain valleys, but also to the sacred
43 *

observatories from which the Creator reveals the sublimity of the
heavens and the pomp of the land ?   " Whereas the mediæval never
painted a cloud, but with the purpose of placing an angel in it ; and
a Greek never entered a wood without expecting to meet a god in it ;
we should think the appearance of an angel in a cloud wholly unnatu-
ral, and should be seriously surprised by meeting a god anywhere.
. . . . . I do not know if there be game on Sinai, but I am always
expecting to hear of some one shooting over it."   It is grand to be
delivered from superstition, but not on the condition of losing the
sentiment of the sacred, the mystic, the awful in the universe, of
which superstition is either the immaturity or the disease.   We do
not necessarily gain in insight by banishing the special sacredness
which a crude imagination concentrates upon parts of nature, but by
discerning a nobler general sanctity.   A purblind vision is cured, not
when it sinks into utter darkness, but when it receives more light.

There are three paths for the ascent of Mount Washington,—one
from the Crawford House at the Notch, one from the White Mountain House, five miles beyond the Notch, and one from the Glen.
The path from the White Mountain House requires the shortest
horseback ride.   Parties are carried by wagons up the side of Mount
Washington to a point less than three miles from the summit.   The
bridle-path, however, is quite steep, and no time is gained by this
ascent.   The rival routes are those from the Notch and the Glen.
Each of these has some decided advantages over the other.   The
Glen route is the shortest.   For the first four miles the horses keep.
the wide and hard track, with a regular ascent of one foot in eight,
which was laid out for a carriage road to the summit, but never
completed.   This is a great gain over the corduroy and mud through
the forests of Mount Clinton, which belong to the ascent from the
Notch.

When we rise up into the region where the real mountain scenery
opens, the views from the two paths are entirely different in character, and it is difficult to decide which is grander.   From the Notch,
as soon as we ride out of the forest, we are on a mountain top.   We

have scaled Mount Clinton, which is 4,200 feet high.   Then the
path follows the line of the White Mountain ridge.   We descend a
little, and soon mount the beautiful dome of Mount Pleasant, which
is five hundred feet higher.   Descending this to the narrow line of
the ridge again, we come to Mount Franklin, a little more than a
hundred feet higher than Pleasant, less marked in the landscape, but
very difficult to climb.   Beyond this, five hundred feet higher still,
are the double peaks of Mount Monroe ; and then winding down to
the Lake of the Clouds, from whence the Ammonoosuc issues, we
stand before the cone of Mount Washington, which springs more than
a thousand feet above us.   The views of the ravines all along this
route, as we pass over the sharpest portions of the ridge, and see
them sweeping off each way from the path, are very exciting.   And
there is the great advantage in this approach to be noted, that if
Mount Washington is clouded, and the other summits are clear, travellers do not lose the sensations and the effects produced by standing
for the first time on a mountain peak.

Sometimes on the path from the Notch over the ridge, the cloud-
effects add unspeakable interest to the journey.   We have in mind,
as we write, an attempt which we once made with a small party to
gain the summit of Mount Washington, on a day when the ridge was
clouded, though the wind was fair.   We started in hope, and were
attended by sunshine nearly all the way through the forest.   But on
the top of Clinton there is rain and shoreless fog.   Compelled to descend, we return after reaching the lower sunshine, in the belief that
the squall has passed.   But it is raining more furiously ; yet this
time we press on, although unable to see a rod ahead, assured by the
guide that it will clear within an hour.   A slow and chilling ride for
half a mile on the rocky ridge has begun to dishearten us.   We
think of returning.   But what is this ?   How has this huge cone
leaped out of the gray, wet waste, and whence can it catch this flush
of sunlight that sweeps over it ?   It is the dome of Mount Pleasant
which our horses' feet had just begun to climb.   Hardly can we
swing our hats and scream our cheers, when it is hidden.   The frolic-

some west wind tears open the curtain at our left, and shows Faby-an's, so snug in its nest of green. But see, on the right the vapors melt under our feet, and the unbroken forests start up as if created that instant in those vast valleys. They are concealed as soon as shown ; but the dull cloud about our heads is smitten with sunshine, and we are dazzled with silver dust. Now look up,—the whole sky is unveiled, and we stand in an ocean of vapor overarched by a can-opy of blazing blue. The bright wind breaks the clouds in a hundred places, scatters them, rolls them off, rolls them up, chases them far towards the horizon, mixes them with the azure, shows us billow after billow of land, from the Green Mountains to Katahdin, and at last sweeps off the mist from the pale green dome of Washington, and invites us to climb where the eye will traverse a circuit of six hun-dred miles.

> Oh! what a joy it were in vigorous health,
> To have a body, (this our vital frame
> With shrinking sensibility endued,
> And all the nice regards of flesh and blood,)
> And to the elements surrender it
> As if it were a spirit!—How divine,
> The liberty for frail, for mortal man
> To roam at large among unpeopled glens
> And mountainous retirements, only trod
> By devious footsteps; regions consecrate
> To oldest time! and, reckless of the storm
> That keeps the raven quiet in her nest,
> Be as a presence or a motion,—one
> Among the many there; and while the mists
> Flying, and rainy vapors, call out shapes
> And phantoms from the crags and solid earth
> As fast as a musician scatters sounds
> Out of an instrument; and while the streams
> (As at a first creation and in haste
> To exercise their untried faculties)
> Descending from the region of the clouds,
> And starting from the hollows of the earth
> More multitudinous every moment, rend
> Their way before them,—what a joy to roam
> An equal among mightiest energies;
> And haply sometimes with articulate voice,
> Amid the deafening tumult, scarcely heard

By him that utters it, exclaim aloud,
" Be this continued so from day to day,
Nor let the fierce commotion have an end,
Ruinous though it be, from month to month! "

By the Glen route we cross no subordinate peaks, and do not follow a ridge line from which we see summits towering here and there,
but steadily ascend Mount Washington itself. In this way a more
adequate conception is gained of its immense mass and majestic
architecture. After we pass above the line of the carriage road to
the barren portion of the mountain, there are grand pictures at the
south and east of the Androscoggin Valley, and the long, heavily
wooded Carter range. Indeed, nothing which the day can show will
give more astonishment than the spectacle which opens after passing
through the spectral forest, made up of acres of trees, leafless, peeled,
and bleached, and riding out upon the ledge. Those who make thus
their first acquaintance with a mountain height will feel, in looking
down into the immense hollow in which the Glen House is a dot, and
off upon the vast green breastwork of Mount Carter, that language
must be stretched and intensified to answer for the new sensations
awakened. Splendid, glorious, amazing, sublime, with liberal supplies of interjections, are the words that usually gush to the lips ; but
seldom is an adjective or exclamation uttered that interprets the
scene, or coins the excitement and surge of feeling. We shall never
forget the phrase which a friend once used,—an artist in expression
as in feeling, and not given under strong stimulant to superlatives,—
as he looked, for the first time, from the ledge upon the square miles
of undulating wilderness, " See the tumultuous bombast of the landscape ! " Yet the glory of the view is, after all, the four highest
companion mountains of the range, Clay, Jefferson, Adams, Madison,
that show themselves in a bending line beyond the tremendous gorge
at the right of the path, absurdly called the " Gulf of Mexico," and
are visible from their roots to their summits. These mountains are
not seen on the ascent from the Notch, being hidden by the dome of
Mount Washington itself. On the Glen path these grand forms

tower so near us that it seems at first as though a strong arm might
throw a stone across the Gulf and hit them. There should be a resting-place near the edge of the ravine, where parties could dismount
and study these forms at leisure. Except by climbing to the ridge

through the unbroken wilderness of the northern side, there is no
such view to be had east of the Mississippi of mountain architecture
and sublimity. They do not seem to be rocky institutions. Their
lines have so much life that they appear to have just leaped from
the deeps beneath the soil. We say to ourselves, these peaks are

nature's struggle against petrifaction, the earth's cry for air. If the
day is not entirely clear, if great white clouds

> Are wandering in thick flocks among the mountains,
> Shepherded by the slow, unwilling wind,

the shadows that leisurely trail along the sides of these Titans, or
waver down their slopes, extinguishing their color, as it blots the dim
green of their peaks, then their tawny shoulders, then the purple and
gray of their bare ledges, and at last dulls the verdure of their lower
forests,—thus playing in perpetual frolic with the light,—are more fascinating than anything which can be seen from the summit of Mount
Washington itself, on the landscape below.

But let us not begin by disparaging at all what is to be seen on
the summit. Suppose that we could be lifted suddenly a mile and a
quarter above the sea level in the air, and could be sustained there
without exertion. That is the privilege we have in standing on the
summit of Mount Washington, about sixty-three hundred feet above
the ocean. Only the view is vastly more splendid than any that
could be presented to us if we could hang poised on wings at the
same elevation above a level country, or should see nothing beneath
us but " the wrinkled sea." For we are not only upheld at such a
height, but we stand in close fellowship with the noblest forms which
the substance of the world has assumed under our northern skies.
We estimate our height from the ocean level, and it is on a wave that
we are lifted,—a tremendous ground-swell fifteen miles long, which
stiffened before it could subside, or fling its boiling mass upon the
bubbling plain. We are perched on the tip of a jet in the centre of
it, tossed up five hundred feet higher than any other spout from its
tremendous surge, and which was arrested and is now fixed forever
as a witness of the passions that have heaved more furiously in the
earth's bosom than any which the sea has felt, and as a " tower
of observance " for sweeping with the eye the beauty that overlays
the globe

44

It may be that this billow of land was cooled by the sea when it
first arose, and that these highest peaks around us were the first portions of New England that saw the light.   On a clear morning or
evening the silvery gleam of the Atlantic is seen on the southeastern
horizon.   The waves, that form only a transitory flash in the landscape which the mountain shows its guests, once broke in foam over
the rocks that now are beaten only by the winds which the Atlantic
conjures, and covered by the snows that mimic the whiteness of the
Atlantic surf, out of which their substance may have been drawn.
And, since the retreat of the sea, what forces have been patiently at
work to cover the stalwart monarchs near us with the beauty which
they reveal !   We call them barren, but there is a richer display of
the creative power and art on Mount Adams yonder than on any
number of square miles in the lowlands of New England equal to the
whole surface of that mountain.   The noblest trees of New England
are around its base, and there are firs on the ledge from which its
peak springs that are not more than two inches high.   Alpine and Lapland plants grow in the crevices of its rocks, and adorn the edges of its
ravines.   Since the sea-wave washed its cone, the light and the frosts
have been gnawing the shingly schist, to give room and sustenance for
the lichens that have tinted every foot of its loosely-shingled slopes
with stains whose origin is more mysterious than any colors which a
painter combines,—as mysterious as the painter's genius itself.   The
storms of untold thousands of years have chiselled lines of expression
in the mountain, whose grace and charm no landscape gardening
on a lowland can rival ; and the bloom of the richest conservatory
would look feeble in contrast with the hues that often in morning and
evening, or in the pomp of autumn and the winter desolation, have
glowed upon it, as though the whole art of God was concentrated in
making it outblush the rose, or dim the sapphire with its flame.

The first effect of standing on the summit of Mount Washington is
a bewildering of the senses at the extent and lawlessness of the spectacle.   It is as though we were looking upon a chaos.   The land is

tossed into a tempest. But in a few moments we become accustomed to this, and begin to feel the joy of turning round and sweeping a horizon line that in parts is drawn outside of New England. Then we can begin to inquire into the particulars of the stupendous diorama. Northward, if the air is not thick with haze, we look beyond the Canada line. Southward, the "parded land" stretches across the borders of Massachusetts, before it melts into the horizon. Do you see a dim blue pyramid on the far northeast, looking scarcely more substantial than gossamer, but keeping its place stubbornly, and cutting the yellowish horizon with the hue of Damascus steel? It is Katahdin looming out of the central wilderness of Maine. Almost in the same line on the southwest, and nearly as far away, do you see another filmy angle in the base of the sky? It is Monadnoc, which would feel prouder than Mont Blanc, or the frost-sheeted Chimborazo, or the topmost spire of the Himalaya, if it could know that the genius of Mr. Emerson has made it the noblest mountain in literature. The nearer range of the Green Mountains are plainly visible; and behind them Camel's Hump and Mansfield tower in the direction of Lake Champlain. The silvery patch on the north, that looks at first like a small pond, is Umbagog; a little farther away due south a section of the mirror of Winnipiseogee glistens. Sebago flashes on the southeast, and a little nearer, the twin Lovell lakes, that lie more prominently on the map of our history than on the landscape. Next, the monotony of the scene is broken by observing the various forms of the mountains that are thick as "meadow-mole hills,"—the great wedge of Lafayette, the long, thin ridge of Carter, the broad-based and solid Pleasant Mountain, the serrated summit of Chocorua, the beautiful cone of Kiarsarge, the cream-colored Stratford peaks, as near alike in size and shape as two Dromios. Then the pathways of the rivers interest us. The line of the Connecticut we can follow from its birth near Canada to the point where it is hidden by the great Franconia wall. Its water is not visible, but often in the morning a line of fog lies for miles over the lower land, counterfeiting the serpentine path of its blue water that bounds

two states. Two large curves of the Androscoggin we can see.
Broken portions of the Saco lie like lumps of light upon the open
valley to the west of Kiarsarge. The sources of the Merrimack are
on the farther slope of a mountain that seems to be not more than the
distance of a rifle-shot. Directly under our feet lies the cold Lake
of the Clouds, whose water plunges down the wild path of the Ammonoosuc, and falls more than a mile before the ocean drinks it at
New Haven. And in the sides of the mountain every wrinkle east
or west that is searched by the sunbeams, or cooled by shadows, is
the channel of a bounty that swells one of the three great streams
of New England.

> Fast abides this constant giver,
> Pouring many a cheerful river.

And lastly, we notice the various beauty of the valleys that slope off
from the central range. No two of them are articulated with the
mountain by the same angles and curves. Stairways of charming
slope and bend lead down into their sweet and many-colored loveliness and bounty.

Next, if the day is favorable, we notice the shadows. People in
cities, who never see the extent and outline of a cloud-shadow, can
have no idea of the beauty of a range of hills, upon which the lights
and shades "march and countermarch in glorious apparition." But
this is nothing to the excitement, we may almost say the intoxica-
tion, of seeing from a mountain-top a huge cloud, miles in breadth,
spanning a valley, shedding twilight upon half a dozen villages at
once, sweeping along, chased by a broader flood of splendor, to
darken for a moment the whole ridge on whose crown you stand,
and still flying on before the west wind to pour its fleet gloom over
range after range, till it pauses in the warmer and peaceful spaces
near the eastern horizon.

And the still shadows it is in many respects an equal privilege to
see. Sydney Smith tells us that he once looked upon a small picture
by an eminent artist, in company with an enthusiastic connoisseur.

who said to him, " Immense breadth of light and shade, sir, in this picture ! " " Yes," said the wit, greatly to the critic's disgust, " about
half an inch."   In the city or level country we know what a shadow
is as cast from a large tree, or from a building, or a church-spire.
But think of a mighty mountain-trough, a mile broad and fifteen hundred feet deep, painted in a clear afternoon, half in gray and half in
gold ! Think of a pyramid, more than a thousand feet above the
ridge, flaming on one side while the shadow of the other falls off upon
miles of sloping forest ! Think, as the sun sets clear, of seeing the
outlines of half a dozen huge mountains photographed five times their
height, partly in the valleys below, and partly upon the ranges beyond ! It is thus that Nature's breadth of light and shadow, her
actual contrasts in miles which the artist must crowd into inches,
are shown on Mount Washington in clear weather by the late and
early sun.   The most impressive spectacle of this kind is the shadow
of Mount Washington itself, far and still upon the furrowed landscape.
On a clear morning of midsummer it reaches beyond the Franconia
line, and its apex rests upon the side of the broad Moosehillock.
Thence it shrinks while the sun rides higher, more sharply defined as
it contracts, till in the middle of the forenoon it subsides into a long
irregular image of the range upon the Ammonoosuc intervale near
below.   But in a cloudless evening, when there is no haze on the
west, we can see it as a dusky triangle, reaching over and beyond
the Carter range, and resting upon the Androscoggin meadows.
Thence it moves, displacing the day from hill-sides and valleys by its
lengthening sides and sombre peak, till it reaches the eastern horizon,
where it actually mounts upon the mists, and overtops the solid hills
with its phantom pyramid, exultant for a moment in the very fall of
the sun which it has conquered, before it fades in the general gloom.
Those who have once seen this spectacle, ask for no other reward for
all that it costs in labor and discomfort to pass the night on Mount
Washington.

Indeed, the most unfavorable time for visiting the summit is in the
noon of a summer day when the air is hazy.   There are no shadows

then, no wonders of color, no vague reaches of distance.   And yet, because the air is genial and the cone is not veiled by mist, such a day is generally accounted propitious by travellers.   It is better to encounter fogs, or sudden showers, especially if one has ever enjoyed before an unobstructed prospect from the peak, than to see the land-scape spiritless under a sultry noon.   Cloud-effects are the most sur-prising and fascinating pageants which the ascent of the mountain can disclose.   Let Mr. Ruskin teach us that " there is no effect of sky possible in the lowlands which may not in equal perfection be seen among the hills ; but there are effects by tens of thousands, for-ever invisible and inconceivable to the inhabitant of the plains, mani-fested among the hills in the course of one day.   The mere power of familiarity with the clouds, of walking with them and above them, alters and renders clear our whole conception of the baseless archi-tecture of the sky ; and for the beauty of it, there is more in a single wreath of early cloud, pacing its way up an avenue of pines, or paus-ing among the points of their fringes, than in all the white heaps that fill the arched sky of the plains from one horizon to the other.   And of the nobler cloud-manifestations,—the breaking of their troublous seas against the crags, their black spray sparkling with lightning; or the going forth of the morning along their pavements of moving marble, level-laid between dome and dome of snow ;—of these things there can be as little imagination or understanding in an inhabitant of the plains as of the scenery of another planet than his own."

Certainly the richest pictures that rise to us, as we write, out of the memory of more than a score of visits to Mount Washington, are combined out of clouds.   We see again the gray scud driving over the peak as we approach it, and as we ride up into its thickening mass, feel the force of the line,

From the fixed cone the cloud-rack flowed;

we remember how dispirited the visitors on the summit seem in the chilly gloom, and we see the fog filled with yellow light, then thin-ning away and knitting itself together in an instant, but soon blown

apart by the breeze to let the color of the nearer forests, and then of
the lowlands, glow through, dimly first and confused, in another second distinct and blinding, but soon orderly and glorious, as perhaps
the realities of another existence may break upon saintly eyes that
emerge from the mists of death.   We recall the strange gathering of
vapors out of a cloudless air in the early morning, and how they hang
in a circle five miles in diameter over the dome of Washington, and
a thousand feet above, while elsewhere the blue is undimmed,—a
magnificent canopy above the rocky throne of New Hampshire.   We
behold again the settling of heavy clouds over the slopes as we descend, wrapping us in blackness of darkness ; and, hastening on
through furious gusts, we come to the lower fringes of the tempest,
and look back and up to see it crouched over the ravines of Clay,
from which vast sheets of vapor are swept by the wind, their lower
edges sulphurous as they rush into the light, and now and then the
whole mass whirling apart to show the dark masses of Madison and
Adams towering in treble height through the gloom.   And then such
glimpses of the valleys !   Sinai behind and Beulah before !   We behold once more, too, with the mind's eye, the thin veil into which a
dogday shower has wasted itself, that hangs wet and still in the sun
before the three mountains which rise from the Gulf of Mexico,—a
silver sheen dimming and adorning their sinewy bulk.   We are overtaken by a rain that rages against us out of the west ; and after it is
spent, we see a rainbow arching over the long line of the Carter
range, and painting its blue-black forests at each end with variegated
flames.   We stand, also, on the summit in the morning when the sky
is clear, and view a wide plain of billowy mist

> rolling on
> Under the curdling winds, and islanding
> The peak whereon we stand.

And we look around, and see the neighboring summits jutting like-
wise above the foam, which rolls, and tosses, and plunges, and splinters into spray, as though with its milky spume it was appointed to
mimic the passion of the sea and the majesty of Niagara.   If one has

made several visits to the top of Mount Washington, he is peculiarly
fortunate, if the scenery shown to him enables him to give distinctness
to most of the pictures in the remarkable panorama which Percival
thus unrolls :—

> Ye Clouds who are the ornament of heaven;
> Who give to it its gayest shadowings,
> And its most awful glories; ye who roll
> In the dark tempest, or at dewy evening
> Hang low in tenderest beauty; ye who, ever
> Changing your Protean aspects, now are gathered
> Like fleecy piles, when the mid-sun is brightest,
> Even in the height of heaven, and there repose,
> Solemnly calm, without a visible motion,
> Hour after hour, looking upon the earth
> With a serenest smile;—or ye who, rather,
> Heaped in those sulphury masses, heavily
> Jutting above their bases, like the smoke
> Poured from a furnace or a roused volcano,
> Stand on the dun horizon, threatening
> Lightning and storm,—who, lifted from the hills,
> March onward to the zenith, ever darkening,
> And heaving into more gigantic towers
> And mountainous piles of blackness,—who then roar
> With the collected winds within your womb,
> Or the far uttered thunders,—who ascend
> Swifter and swifter, till wide overhead
> Your vanguards curl and toss upon the tempest
> Like the stirred ocean on a reef of rocks
> Just topping o'er its waves, while deep below
> The pregnant mass of vapor and of flame
> Rolls with an awful pomp, and grimly lowers,
> Seeming to the struck eye of fear, the car
> Of an offended spirit, whose swart features
> Glare through the sooty darkness, fired with vengeance
> And ready with uplifted hand to smite
> And scourge a guilty nation; ye who lie,
> After the storm is over, far away,
> Crowning the dripping forests with the arch
> Of beauty, such as lives alone in heaven,
> Bright daughter of the sun, bending around
> From mountain unto mountain like the wreath
> Of victory, or like a banner telling
> Of joy and gladness; ye who round the moon
> Assemble, when she sits in the mid-sky
> In perfect brightness, and encircle her

With a fair wreath of all aerial dyes;
Ye who, thus hovering round her, shine like mountains
Whose tops are never darkened, but remain,
Centuries and countless ages, reared for temples
Of purity and light; or ye who crowd
To hail the new-born day, and hang for him,
Above his ocean couch, a canopy
Of all inimitable hues and colors,
Such as are only pencilled by the hands
Of the unseen ministers of earth and air,
Seen only in the tinting of the clouds,
And the soft shadowing of plumes and flowers;
Or ye who, following in his funeral train,
Light up your torches at his sepulchre,
And open on us through the clefted hills
Far glances into glittering worlds beyond
The twilight of the grave, where all is light
Golden and glorious light, too full and high
For mortal eye to gaze on, stretching out
Brighter and ever brighter, till it spread,
Like one wide, radiant ocean without bounds
One infinite sea of glory:—thus, ye clouds
And in innumerable other shapes
Of greatness or of beauty, ye attend us,
To give to the wide arch above us Life
And all its changes. Thus it is to us
A volume full of wisdom, but without ye
One awful uniformity had ever
With too severe a majesty oppressed us

In order to see, within a few hours, the most impressive spectacles which the ridge displays, visitors should devote a whole afternoon to the summit, and stay all night, in the hope of seeing the sun set and rise. The first visit of this kind that we made was reported, in part, as follows, for an editorial friend :—

"I send you a greeting, this morning, from the cupola of New Hampshire. If, perchance, you are suffering from heat when this missive reaches you, let your eyes cool themselves by reading that just outside the Tip-Top House the mercury is at 34 degrees, while the wind is sweeping in rage over the peak of the burly monarch. Eastward a gale would find no such elevation this side the Alps ; westward none till it should strike the Rocky Mountains. I passed

45

last night here. This is my seventh ascent of Mount Washington ;
and yet, though I was once here so late as sunset, I never till now
slept on the summit.

"Yesterday promised so well for the excursion that I could not
resist the temptation. The temperature in the valley was a pleasant
summer heat. The ride on one of the ponies from the Glen up the
regular slope of the carriage-path, which has now turned the ledge,—
thus overcoming the most perilous part of the rocky ascent, as it had
before obviated the unpleasant mud and corduroy of the forest,—was
very easy. Gaining the ridge, after passing through the bleached
forest, in which one ought not to be surprised if he should be suddenly greeted by the witches of Macbeth, and just where the first
sublimity breaks upon the eye,—the deep green walls of the Carter
Mountain behind ; the pebbly path of the Peabody, and the tortuous
flashes of the Androscoggin below ; and the tawny spires of Adams,
Jefferson, and Madison in front, soaring precipitous out of the luxuriant forests,—we felt the keen breath of a norther, which promised
a rude reception on the summit. We rose, indeed, by climates as
well as ridges. It was July in Gorham ; late September on the
ledge ; November at the apex. The pony I rode seemed to have an
appetite for sublimity bathed in Arctic air. It was his first ascent
of the mountain ; and he clambered and snorted with evident glee,
seizing every opportunity to trot among the sharp rocks,—a process
which served more to exhilarate him than to convey exquisite pleasure
to the rider.

"But if we met a rough reception from old Boreas, we had a
warm one from the enterprising keepers of the Summit House. Hospitality at sixty-three hundred feet above the Atlantic is a virtue to
be celebrated. Suppose you do pay a dollar for the shelter, the fire,
and the excellent dinner furnished to you on the bleak crest of New
England. What do these men undergo to invite that donation from
you ? Do they not duplicate their winter ? Do they not pitch their
tents for months higher than the eagles will build their nests ? Do
they not make their home for days among blinding fogs and sweeping

sleet ? Do they not pass wild nights away from all human fellowship, when the rains that feed the Saco and swell the Connecticut
beat and divide on the roof of their cabin, and the blasts tug with
infuriate breath at the loose rock-tiles that sheathe this savage dome ?
Do they not make their home among lightnings that often spout
around them amid gusts that drown the thunder ? The benefit is
so great, and the toil of the earning so severe, that we travellers
ought to pay our dollar with no mercenary abatement of gratitude to
these spirited mountaineers, who have organized their Yankee ' St.
Bernard ' hospitality on the cold crest of our north.   In fact, one of
our hosts, with his bearded face, his careful gait, and those serious
eyes set in a head that contains more of the wild traditions of the
mountains than any other among us, looks like a monk.   There are
faithful *fry-ers*, too, in the establishment, as the copious supplies of
doughnuts attest, but they keep themselves hidden in the kitchen
department.

" Upon the summit I had the fortune to meet two cherished Boston friends.   One hurried to our mountain passes to listen to the
reverberations that are rolling around New England, since the lightning of his Fourth of July Address.   By his serene appearance he
justifies much more the title which Mr. Willis has given him,—' The
Apostle of Friendship,'—than the Boanerges character attributed to
him by the political journals hostile to his oration.   With him you
were kind enough to send us, also, one of your judges, as fitted by
the polished delicacy of his taste to pronounce on those charms of
scenery in which no region of this hill-country will ever be bankrupt,
as by his acumen to interpret and apply the slippery laws of insol-
vency.   What a privilege, after the wit-seasoned meal, to clamber
over the old cone with such companions, and look abroad upon New
England,—far off beyond the northerly borders of the Connecticut ;
far south to the mouth of the Saco ; east to where Katahdin drives
his spike into the sky, and west almost to the Catskills !

" The larger part of the afternoon was devoted to the great ravines.   The mass of Washington cannot be appreciated until we see

what enormous gullies have been cut into it, still leaving it more
bulky than any other four mountains of the range. There is ample time, we found, in two hours, to go to the edges of the three
grandest chasms which give character to the mountain when seen
from the south and east, and which can scarcely be seen at all from
either of the bridle-paths. The first of these, 'The Grand Gulf,' has
the sheerest precipices, the most savage-looking *debris*, and the
sharpest pinnacles. I felt special interest in studying its lines, on
account of the admiration I had felt for Mr. Coleman's painting of
its romantic ruins. Tuckerman's Ravine, which lies a little farther
to the west, is a far more spacious rent in the mountain. I shall
make an excursion into it the subject of a separate letter ; and therefore will pass to ' The Gulf of Mexico,' the third of the ravines, to
which we devoted the most time. We were obliged to take care, as
we stood on its perilous edge, that the wind did not sweep us from
our footing into its depths of air. This gulf is a cleft between Washington and Mount Jefferson. Its western wall, richly marked by
water-lines and ravaged by landslides, is called Mount Clay. It
balances on the north the deeply cut Tuckerman's Ravine on the
south. Seen from the bottom, the last is the grander. Looking
down from the top, the Gulf of Mexico is the more terrible. And
while the first has only even walls to rim its desolation, the last is
crowned by Mount Jefferson, and commands a grand view also of
Adams and Madison. And the afternoon is the time to see it,—when
the sun pours a sheet of light, as yesterday, up the whole southerly
wall of chippy rock, tinged with pale-green lichen, and the bottom of
the pit lies dark under the grim guard of the three peaks that bend
around it on the northeast, and have lost the sun. Those that have
not seen this view of the Gulf of Mexico, in a clear afternoon, are
unacquainted with one of the grandest spectacles which the summit
of Mount Washington affords.

" But let us return to the house, and wait patiently for sunset—for
the purple that we shall see crowning a score of ridges ; for the slow
march of the pointed shadows of our range up the opposite slopes of

Carter, and off towards Conway, dislodging the day from the hill-tops, as they move south and east; and for the calm sinking of the sun beneath a horizon a hundred miles away, twenty minutes after the valleys have seen his exit. Alas for our expectation! About seven in the evening, the north wind, which had dashed against us all day, came upon us in all 'pomp and circumstance,' with banners and streamers flying. The scud settled to our level, and drove past us with fury, to the keen fife-music of the gale. The thermometer was at about the freezing point. At first, it was a severe disappointment. But we soon found that we had been robbed of one privilege to receive perhaps a greater. The old mountain was determined to show us his teeth, and to snarl a little. What fascinating glimpses of green were given through frequent rifts in the hurrying fog! How intense, far off towards the western horizon, blazed a small lake, or fragment of river, on which the sun, hidden from us by the clouds, was shining,—a solid lump of diamond light,—the great carbuncle, perhaps, of the mountain tradition! And then what splendid colors in the furious mists! Now they would thin away, and be transfused with yellow, as they were blown southwards. Now they would coil around us lurid, as if volumes of fire-tipped smoke, surging up from a burning world. For a moment they would be dissipated by the sunshine, melting utterly away in cold silvery flickers, and then would close around us again thick, turbulent, and gray. Just as the sun was disappearing, we saw his ruddy disc, through a rift, for a minute ; and bade him farewell in the hope of greeting him in an unclouded and peaceful east, when he should return, after sinking into the Pacific, dawning on China, and kindling the sheeted walls and turrets of the Himalaya with morning gold.

"And now shall we lose the moon-rise ? No ; the propitious vapors opened in season, as they did at sunset. About nine they began to thin away, and drove southwards into the eyes of the moon, breaking in spectral battalions on its solid orb, to be steeped in amber for a moment, and then whiffed into nothingness. After a time, the heavens were swept clean, and the moon moved patiently up among the constellations, looking serenely upon the gulfs, and pits, and blasted peaks of the mountains, that are less ravaged and desolate than the continent which her own pensive halo swathes. But what are all the grandeurs of these pimple-hills to that calm, cold splendor that looks through the fresh-swept air,—that tremendous circuit of stars, from the nearest of which our globe is invisible and unsuspected, whose light, unshaken by our blustering Boreas, converges on this lonely peak,—that awful dome which floats in immensity on the pulses of impalpable force! I did not expect to get a sense of the height of Mount Washington by looking up from its roof, rather than by looking down. But so it was. I have never, in standing on the edge of the ravine near Mount Monroe, or upon the plateau that crowns the Tuckerman gulf, gained such a feeling of its loftiness and loneliness, as in looking up, last night, when the valleys were veiled, to the Dipper and the Zenith. Half a minute at a time was all my brain could bear. I can conceive how Prometheus, chained on ' the frosty Caucasus,' could endure the vulture, and the cold, and the pelting hail, but I cannot imagine how the poets strengthened him for the calm and brilliant nights, and the terrible sense of space *they* brought to him. To be fastened one night on Mount Washington alone, compelled to face the firmament, I am sure would almost crush my reason.

" In fact, I have not yet recovered from the glimpses I took. The wind swept all night over us in an unabating gale ; and as I lay under the blankets of the Summit House, that view of the sky haunted me, and drove away sleep. I seemed to have a sensation of the earth's motion,—that we were lying in that little foretop of New England, while our planet ship was scudding, twelve hundred miles a minute, over the star-islanded immensity.

" And other terrors connected with darkness and storm on Mount Washington were present also. The roaring wind recalled Shel-ley's lines,—

Listen, listen, Mary mine,
To the whisper of the Apennine;

It bursts on the roof like the thunder's roar,
Or like the sea on a northern shore,
Heard in its raging ebb and flow
By the captives pent in the cave below.
The Apennine in the light of day
Is a mighty mountain dim and gray,
.   .   .   .
But when night comes, a chaos dread
On the dim starlight then is spread,
And the Apennine walks abroad with the storm.

The wintry wrath of the gale, and the occasional gloom of the thickening scud, seemed the more dreadful when I thought,—may there not be death in it ? is it not possible that some travellers, in search of the Summit House, have lost the path since sunset, and are in danger of perishing among the wild rocks ?   You know that suffering and death are giving Mount Washington a tragical celebrity.   Then was the time to feel the meaning of that pile of stones, but a few rods below the inn, which tells where Miss Bourne, overtaken by night and fog, and exhausted by cold, breathed out her life into the bleak cloud.   She started from the Glen House, with her uncle and cousin, in the afternoon of a lovely day of mid-September, to walk on the carriage-road as far as the first opening that permits a wide easterly view.   Arrived there, although they had no guide, they were tempted on towards the summit by the inspiriting air and sky.   But fog at sunset settled over the path ; the wind became fierce and cutting ; the peak seemed to recede as they advanced ; and the young lady sank at last exhausted in the darkness, within hailing distance of the hotel, and died about ten o'clock.   I could not keep out of my mind the picture of that group,—the building of the stony wall to protect the dying girl from the fury of the tempest, the agony of the relatives as they found that her life was ebbing, their horror amid the darkness,—for there was not a ray of starlight to show them her features,—and after the spirit had fled, their awful watch until morning !   I have compared the public houses here to the inn on the St. Bernard.   And when we think of the disaster just referred to ; when we look off into the ravine, sloping towards Fabyan's, where the English-

man, Strickland, perished in October ; when we see the spot, in full
view of the Glen House, where Dr. Ball lay helpless and freezing in
the snow, after two nights' exposure, without food or fire, in an October storm ; when we recall the number of persons whom Mr. Hall,
one of the present landlords of the summit, has saved from impend-
ing death, and remember that the bones of an elderly traveller,* lost
on the ridge last summer, lie bleaching now undiscovered,—who can
say that the service which the dogs of the St. Bernard have rendered, might not be repeated on Mount Washington, if the houses
should be supplied with some of those noble animals, and should be
kept open a few weeks later in the autumn ?

" The wildness of the night affected my pleasure in seeing the sunrise, a few hours ago.   A mist lay over all the valleys.   The mountains heaved their sharp ridges out of an ocean of stagnant foam.   A
wide bank of dingy fog lay along the eastern sky.   Over this artificial horizon we saw the advent of the morning,—the wide flush of
red around a third of the vast circuit, the bubbling of rosy glory over
its fleecy rim, the peep of the burning disc, and the gradual mounting of the light, showing how

> tenderly the haughty day
> Fills his blue urn with fire.

The scene interpreted these new lines of Mr. Emerson, and also
recalled to me the passage from Browning's ' Pippa Passes ' : —

> Day!
> Faster and more fast,
> O'er night's brim, day boils at last;
> Boils, pure gold, o'er the cloud-cup's brim,
> Where spurting and supprest it lay—
> For not a froth-flake touched the rim
> Of yonder gap in the solid gray
> Of the eastern cloud, an hour away;
> But forth one wavelet, then another, curled,
> Till the whole sunrise, not to be supprest,
> Rose, reddened, and its seething breast
> Flickered in bounds, grew gold, then overflowed the world.

---

* Mr. Benjamin Chandler of Delaware, whose remains, after lying nearly a year no:
ar from the summit, were discovered a few weeks after this letter was written.

"The dawn was magnificent; but when I ascend Mount Washington again, it will be to see the night. O that the great comet would come, to be watched from such an observatory! And now let me say 'good-bye' to my pleasant companions, the eloquent ex-orator and the rapier-witted judge, who are going down by the Crawford path; to our excellent hosts; and to you, my friend, in your editorial sanctum, as I turn my face away from the billowy majesty that surrounds the summit, for the descent towards the Glen and Gorham."

And we well remember how sublime the cloud-scenery was to which that lonely downward walk, after our first acquaintance with night and sunrise from the summit, introduced us. At seven o'clock, with the exception of the fog-bank in the east, the sky was clear. But as early as ten, the air was filled, as by miracle, with piles and ranges of snowy vapor, with whose highest peaks the cone of Chimborazo could compete in color alone. "We are little apt, in watching the changes of a mountainous range of cloud, to reflect that the masses of vapor which compose it are huger and higher than any mountain range of the earth; that the distance between mass and mass are not yards of air traversed in an instant by the flying foam, but valleys of changing atmosphere leagues over; that the slow motion of ascending curves, which we can scarcely trace, is a boiling energy of exulting vapor rushing into the heaven a thousand feet in a minute; and that the toppling angle whose sharp edge almost escapes notice in the multitudinous forms around it, is a nodding precipice of storms, three thousand feet from base to summit. It is not until we have actually compared the forms of the sky with the hill ranges of the earth, and seen the soaring Alp overtopped and buried in one surge of the sky, that we begin to conceive or appreciate the colossal scale of the phenomena of the latter. But of this there can be no doubt in the mind of any one accustomed to trace the forms of clouds among hill ranges,—as it is there a demonstrable and evident fact, that the space of vapor visibly extended over an ordinarily
46

cloudy sky is not less, from the point nearest to the observer to the horizon, than twenty leagues ; that the size of every mass of separate form, if it be at all largely divided, is to be expressed in terms of *miles ;* and that every boiling heap of illuminated mist in the nearer sky is an enormous mountain, fifteen or twenty thousand feet in height, six or seven miles over in illuminated surface, furrowed by a thousand colossal ravines, torn by local tempests into peaks and prom-ontories, and changing its features with the majestic velocity of the volcano." And thus the memory of the lurid sunset and the mar-vellous cloud-diorama of the forenoon have given us a fresh appre-ciation of the passage from Bayard Taylor's " Hymn to the Air " :—

> What is the scenery of Earth to thine ?
> Here all is fixed in everlasting shapes,
> But where the realms of gorgeous Cloudland shine,
> There stretch afar thy sun-illumined capes,
> Embaying reaches of the amber seas
> Of sunset, on whose tranquil bosom lie
> The happy islands of the upper sky,
> The halcyon shores of thine Atlantides.
> Anon the airy headlands change, and drift
> Into sublimer forms, that slowly heave
> Their toppling masses up the front of eve,
> Crag heaped on crag, with many a fiery rift,
> And hoary summits, throned beyond the reach
> Of Alp or Caucasus; again they change,
> And down the vast, interminable range
> Of towers and palaces, transcending each
> The workmanship of Fable-Land, we see
> The " crystal hyaline " of Heaven's own floor—
> The radiance of the far Eternity
> Reflected on thy shore!

Everybody that visits the eastern side of the mountains hears of the snow-arch in one of the ravines of Mount Washington. It is, doubtless, to be ranked first among the curiosities which can tempt a pedestrian. Parties can descend to it with a guide from the hotel on the summit of Mount Washington—a distance of a mile and a quar-ter,—or can climb to it from the Glen—a distance of not less than five miles. It has been our good fortune to make four visits to it in successive years. Of the first of these we wrote a record for the press under the title of "A Dinner Party under the Snow-Arch of Mount Washington." It runs thus :—

"For several seasons I have wished to visit 'Tuckerman's Ravine.' The bare, thin, and curling edge of its southwestern wall, as seen from the Glen House, is one of the most striking shows of that fascinating spot. The rock-ribbed organization of the hills is grandly revealed by it; while the spirit of mountain strength, the enormous vitality that is compressed into the resisting power of a great ridge, is suggested there more intensely, perhaps, than in any other mountain line or feature of this region. The ravine is hollowed out of a spur of Washington, and the curving wall I speak of seems to be the bent and firmly braced arm of the mountain, defying the force of gravity and the gnawing frosts, with the challenge, 'Do your best, with all your tugs and beaks, against my granite muscles and persistent will!' One is continually tempted from a distance to explore a nook that wears the expression of such character.

"Moreover, there is a very striking picture in 'Oakes' White Mountain Scenery,' of the summit of Washington rising over Tuckerman's Ravine. It is the grandest sketch of the whole series, and I have often wished to verify it. Possibly, the publishers, Messrs. Crosby, Nichols & Co. will not seriously object to the liberty I shall take here, of giving *gratis* an attestation of the accuracy of that view, and a commendation of the work itself. Then again, the accounts last summer of a snow-arch in the ravine remaining so late as August, made me regret my inability to explore it, and resolve to climb into it, another year.

"At last, I have been able to do so under most favorable circumstances. Mr. Thompson, of the Glen House, has opened a horse-path from a point on the new Mount Washington carriage-road, to a lake at the foot of the ravine. A small party of gentlemen was invited by one of the prominent officers of the carriage-road company to try this path on foot, and dine with him at the snow-bank in the rocky gulf, if it still lingered in the lap of July. A more competent

or inspiring leader of such an excursion than Mr. M. it would be impossible to find.   He is the soul of the enterprise that is engineering
a wagon turnpike up Mount Washington.   With unflickering enthusiasm and unfaltering energy, he is writing his name in wide, smooth,
zigzag lines, from the base to the cone of old Agiochook, as Napoleon
engraved his upon the Simplon.   The work, it is thought, will be
finished in the course of another summer.

    ·   ·   ·   ·   ·   ·   ·   ·

    " Our party started from the Glen House about nine o'clock, in
high spirits, notwithstanding the heavy fog that hung over the mountain and filled the ravine.   We had an excellent opportunity to see
how the carriage-road is made, and what a work it is to finish it up
from the roughness of the primeval wilderness to the wide macadam-
ized track, over which we first drove a double wagon for two miles.
Leaving the carriage, we led a pony over a great ledge which the
workmen were blasting, feeling none the easier for knowing that the
fuse was burning while we crossed.   In less than a minute after, old
Washington and Carter were shouting to each other in mockery of
the discharge.   We had the privilege, also, of seeing how neatly and
comfortably Yankee workmen contrive to live in rough log-houses two
thousand feet above the level of Coös County.   Then we struck off
from the carriage-way to try Thompson's new path on foot.   O
the joy of a tramp through the aboriginal forest in such sweet air !
The smell of the fresh earth, the perfume of the plants and bark, the
spring of the moss under the feet, the sense of elasticity and freedom
diffused through the whole frame, the note of the wood-robin, the
pipe and trill of the sweet-whistler, the luscious gurgle of hidden rills,
the flash and music of merry cascades, and, when the fog is swept
away, the spots of sunshine flecking the path, the bewitching confusion of light and shadows on the trunks and boughs and among the
leaves, as the bracing breeze makes them dance and sing, and added
to all, the consciousness of nearness to the proudest summits of New
England, and the hope of catching soon their glorious crowns looking
down over savage cliffs and across grim gulfs of rock,—what pleasure

of the senses is so pure ? what medicine so kindly as the subtile elixir
with which Nature thus, taking us to her bosom again, delicately
searches every fibre of the jaded frame, strings and reanimates the
nerves, and pervades the whole being with an airy joy in mere
physical existence ?

" Our whole party were truly in mountain spirits. One of the
young engineers with us had walked from the top of Washington that
morning,—starting from an aerial island where the sun was rising
over a sea of mist, which the wind was rolling and swaying in mighty
surges and troughs of vapor, mimicking in the fleecy fog the tremendous ground-swell and turmoil of the sea. The contractor of the
road was with us, taking the excursion as pastime, for the pleasure
of conquering the ruggedness of the mountain by his iron muscles, in
addition to the satisfaction of slowly planing off the rocky knots of its
hide by his workmen. A prominent Boston gentleman graced our
company with his enthusiasm for science,—one of the modern regi-
ment of Solomons, knowing every shrub and weed, from the cedar to
the hyssop that springeth by the wall ; a man who would count it all
joy to sleep in a ravine, and have his aristocratic frame battered and
torn by rocks and trees, and his blood half sucked away by black
flies, if he could find a wild flower that had never yet been christened
with savage Greek or Latin at the altar of science. But our leader,
Mr. M., seemed most thoroughly possessed with the *poetry* of the
excursion. He climbed the steep wood-paths, declaiming in glorious
style the most stirring mountain verses from Scott's ' Rokeby.' A
cataract waked up his early reading of ' Manfred,' and brought down
an avalanche of its splendid rhythm upon our astonished and delighted
ears. The sudden sight of the dome of Mount Washington, over the
edge of the ravine, called out, as a jubilant apotheosis,—

> Mont Blanc is the monarch of mountains;
> They crown'd him long ago
> On a throne of rocks, in a robe of clouds,
> With a diadem of snow.
>
> Around his waist are forests braced;
> The avalanche in his hand;

> But ere it fall, that thundering ball
> Must wait for my command.

" Poetry poured down from the distances of his boyhood reading like the singing rills around us from the mountain top. You
remember, friend Transcript, that a judge in Georgia recently, when
there was no Bible in the court, said, ' Swear the witness on Father
Shehane's head, for he's a walking edition of Scripture.' So our
friend Mr. M. is a portly Cyclopædia of the choicest mountain poetry,
—a volume that articulates its treasures with sonorous voice and
manly emphasis.

" Thus we made the time fly in crossing the two and a half miles
of forest that lie between the carriage-road and ' Hermit Lake.' This
little sheet of water, so snugly embowered in the wilderness, would
attract more attention were it not for the frowning wall of the ravine
that looms over it, and draws the eye upward. It lies under the
southeast ridge. Emerging from the woods now, we see that the
ravine is of horse-shoe shape,—the opposite outer cliff more than a
thousand feet in height, the bottom sloping upwards towards the backward crescent wall, and the rim quite level. We climbed along the
centre of the gulf, by the bed of a stream, pausing every minute to
gaze at the grim ramparts on either hand, and to invent some new exclamation of amazement and awe. A path has been hewn out since
among the scrubby bushes, so that explorers need not go over boots
in water, as we did sometimes. Facing us, as we climbed, was the
grand curve of the precipice, symmetrical seemingly as that of the
Colosseum. It so fascinated me and made me eager to get nearer,
that I utterly forgot the snow-arch. The face of the wall was wet
with weak streams, that flash brilliantly in the sun. It bears the title,
we believe, of ' The Fall of a thousand Streams.' If Mr. M. had
been as well acquainted with Wordsworth as with Byron and Scott,
he would surely have quoted here the strangely applicable passage
from ' The Excursion,'—

> for now we stood
> Shut out from prospect of the open vale.
> And saw the water, that composed this rill,

Descending, disembodied, and diffused
O'er the smooth surface of an ample crag,
Lofty and steep, and naked as a tower.
All further progress here was barred;
. . . . . high or low appeared no trace
Of motion, save the water that descended,
Diffused adown that barrier of steep rock,
And softly creeping, like a breath of air,
Such as is sometimes seen, and hardly seen,
To brush the still breast of a crystal lake.
  'Behold a cabinet for sages built,
Which kings might envy!'—Praise to this effect
Broke from the happy old man's reverend lip;
Who to the Solitary turned, and said,
'In sooth, with love's familiar privilege,
You have decried the wealth which is your own.
Among these rocks and stones, methinks, I see
More than the heedless impress that belongs
To lonely Nature's casual work: they bear
A semblance strange of power intelligent,
And of design not wholly thrown away.
Boldest of plants that ever faced the wind,
How gracefully that slender shrub looks forth
From its fantastic birthplace! And I own,
Some shadowy intimations haunt me here,
That in these shows a chronicle survives
Of purposes akin to those of man,
But wrought with mightier arm than now prevails.
—Voiceless the stream descends into the gulf
With timid lapse;—and lo! while in this strait
I stand—the chasm of sky above my head
Is heaven's profoundest azure; no domain
For fickle, short-lived clouds to occupy,
Or to pass through;·but rather an abyss
In which the everlasting stars abide;
And whose soft gloom, and boundless depth, might tempt
The curious eye to look for them by day.
—Hail Contemplation! from the stately towers,
Reared by the industrious hand of human art
To lift thee high above the misty air
And turbulence of murmuring cities vast;
From academic groves, that have for thee
· Been planted, hither come and find a lodge
To which thou mayst resort for holier peace,—
From whose calm centre thou, through height or depth,
Mayst penetrate, wherever truth shall lead;
Measuring through all degrees, until the scale
Of time and conscious nature disappear,
Lost in unsearchable eternity!'

As we were approaching the base of this wall, I heard an exclamation that there was snow, and looking up, saw, a little way above and ahead, a patch of dirty white, which seemed to be about ten feet long. I turned again to the amphitheatre and continued climbing. Shortly the snow patch caught my eye again ; it had increased vastly in size and depth ;—a little nearer, and it seemed to open ponderous jaws ; a few feet more of climbing, and we stood at the mouth of an arching snow-cave, through which a stream was flowing lazily, increased by the water that dropped from the white and fretted roof.

" How can I hope to describe to you the rich surprise of entering this cold, crystal cabin, fashioned by a mountain stream out of the huge, shapeless quarry that is deposited and hardened there by the winter storms ? The snow sweeps into the ravine to the depth, no doubt, of a hundred feet or more ; and this bank is the last shred of the frost-mantle which the sun and fogs tear from the surface of the White Hills. If the cascade did not help them by its taste for architectural sapping and groining, they would be unable to dislodge the winter wholly from that gulf. It was some minutes before we got courage to go far into the cave. We had fears for the stability of the roof. But when we found that it was so hard as to require a hatchet to cut it, we felt reassured, trusted the span which the ice-gnome had heaved, and began to explore the cavern. It was so high that a tall man could not touch the ceiling with a five-foot staff. So many persons had laughed at Mr. M. for his accounts of the snow-arch and its size, a year ago, that we measured it with a line. It was 294 feet long, 66 feet broad, and about 15 feet deep where the snow was heaviest. The cave extended the whole breadth, and about half the length of the bank ; its roof being on an average about five or six feet thick, and very solid.

" But the most charming feature of the interior was a second and smaller arch, at right angles with the more spacious one, just about large enough for a man to pass through, at which a more diminutive stream had tried its skill. It was of exquisite gothic workmanship. The rill was responsible for the curve of the roof and the general proportions, while the meltings had caught the spirit of the work, and

laid in the finish of groovings and chasings by way of delicate orna-
ment.   Nature had put her rival ministers of grandeur and grace at
work in the two streams that channelled this snow-heap with patient
and merry chisels,—one leaving, as the witness of its fidelity, the
sombre and masculine proportions of the cave, the other flowing under
the cheerful feminine beauty of the ceiling it had wrought.   Ah, the
romantic economy, too, of that ceaseless mining and sculpture!
Where shall we find the rubbish and the chips ?   All the waste turns
to leaping and fleecy beauty, far below, on the mossy stairs of the
Crystal Cascade.   It feeds the roots of wild flowers ; it bears down
nutriment to dainty and scarlet-freckled trout ; it carries coolness to
human lips and melody to careworn hearts ;—all this before it pours
into the Ellis stream, and plunges over the Glen Ellis cataract, and
again over the Jackson falls, on its way to the Saco, that it may do
wider service in that tide, before it dies into the sea.

" The spot furnished an entirely new experience of the White
Mountains.   I had not expected to be thrilled with such surprise, so
near the summit of Mount Washington, which I had visited so often.
The stupendous amphitheatre of stone would of itself repay and over-
pay the labor of the climb.   It is fitly called the ' Mountain Colosseum.'   No other word expresses it, and that comes spontaneously to
the lips.   The eye needs some hours of gazing and comparative meas-
urement to fit itself for an appreciation of its scale and sublimity.
One can hardly believe, while standing there, that the sheer concave
sweep of the back wall of the ravine was the work of an earthquake
throe.   It seems as though Titanic geometry and trowels must have
come in to perfect a primitive volcanic sketch.   One might easily
fancy it the Stonehenge of a Preadamite race,—the unroofed ruins
of a temple reared by ancient Anaks long before the birth of man, for
which the dome of Mount Washington was piled as the western
tower.   There have been landslides and rock-avalanches as terrible
n that ravine as at Dixville Notch,—the teeth of the frosts have been
as pitiless, the desloation of the cliffs is as complete, but the spirit of
the place is not so gloomy as at Dixville,—is sublime rather than

47

awful or dispiriting. At Dixville, all is decay, wreck; the hopeless
submission of matter in the coil of its hungry foes. In Tuckerman's
Ravine there is a grand battle of granite against storm and frost, a
Roman resistance, as though it could hold out for ages yet before
the siege of winter, and all the batteries of the air.

"But I must close. Of course we dined under the snow-arch.
Between the pie and cheese there were eloquent parentheses of admiration for the crystal cave, and wonder at the proportions of the
Colosseum. We pledged our host, Mr. M., and drank to the success
of his road. Never was hospitality acknowledged in a more glorious
hall, and the pledge was drunk in pure ice-water fresh from February There is no time to tell you of our climbing the cliffs of the
ravine to the summit of Mount Washington. Just before we began
to ascend by the sheer and treacherous-looking wall, Mr. M. gave us
a noble recitation of the following passage from Scott's ' Rokeby,' and
one of our party came near verifying the experience which Bertram
would have had if his final leap had not proved successful :—

> As bursts the levin in its wrath,
> He shot him down the sounding path;
> Rock, wood, and stream rung wildly out,
> To his loud step and savage shout.
> Seems that the object of his race
> Hath scaled the cliffs; his frantic chase
> Sidelong he turns, and now 'tis bent
> Right up the rock's tall battlement:
> Straining each sinew to ascend,
> Foot, hand, and knee their aid must lend,
> Wilfrid, all dizzy with dismay,
> Views, from beneath, his dreadful way:
> Now to the oak's warp'd roots he clings,
> Now trusts his weight to ivy strings;
> Now, like the wild goat, must he dare
> An unsupported leap in air;
> Hid in the shrubby rain-course now,
> You mark him by the crashing bough,
> And by his corselet's sullen clank,
> And by the stones spurned from the bank,
> And by the hawk scared from her nest,
> And ravens croaking o'er their guest,
> Who deem his forfeit limbs shall pay
> The tribute of his bold essay.

See, he emerges!—desperate now
All further course—Yon beetling brow
In craggy nakedness sublime
What heart or foot shall dare to climb?
It bears no tendril for his clasp,
Presents no angle to his grasp:
Sole stay his foot may rest upon,
Is yon earth-bedded jetting stone.
Balanced on such precarious prop,
He strains his grasp to reach the top.
Just as the dangerous stretch he makes,
By heaven, his faithless footstool shakes!
Beneath his tottering bulk it bends,
It sways,—it loosens,—it descends!
And downward holds its headlong way,
Crashing o'er rock and copsewood spray.
Loud thunders shake the echoing dell!—
Fell it alone?—alone it fell.
Just on the very verge of fate,
The hardy Bertram's falling weight
He trusted to his sinewy hands,
And on the top unharmed he stands!

I reached the Glen House before nine, and Gorham about ten, that evening, with a strong desire to repeat the visit, and with the conviction that every lover of impressive scenery will find Tuckerman's Ravine a spot that will repay trebly the toils of a day's excursion."

Not less than five thousand persons make the ascent of Mount Washington, every summer, by the regular bridle-paths. There is year by year now, however, an increasing proportion of visitors who desire more loneliness and wildness in the track, and more adventure in the experience, than the commonly travelled routes to the summit will supply. For all such the northerly side of the ridge, as the noble scenery around its base becomes better known, will prove very attractive. The writer first became acquainted with the pictures which the northerly portion of the ridge reveals, in an excursion over Mount Adams, which was thus reported in the Boston Transcript:—

" If any of your readers have ever driven from Gorham to Jefferson, on what is called the ' Cherry Mountain road to the Notch,' they have noticed the ravine of Mount Adams, which is cut to the very heart, and up to the throat of the noble mountain. Seen from the road below, it is the most spacious and the grandest of all the gorges that have been cloven out of the White Hills. It is of an excursion up the tilted floor of this granite gulf that I sit down to write you now. How often, in riding along the road in Randolph, where its lines of lifted forest subside into the verdure of the valley, have I looked with longing up to its sheer and sharp-edged walls,—and farther up to its smooth-faced ledges blazing like mirrors with sunshine upon their moisture,—up to cascades that shook feathery silver over dwindled precipices,—up to the curving rampart that unites the two sides of the chasm, and supports the mountain's rocky spire! *There,* I have said to myself, the very spirit of the hills is concentrated. There the wildness, freshness, and majesty which ' carriage-roads ' and hurrying feet and ' Tip-Top Houses ' are driving or disenchanting from Mount Washington, are as undisturbed as when the Indians warned the daring pioneers of civilization from ascending Agiochook, on peril of the Great Spirit's wrath.

> Mark how the climbing Oreads
> Beckon thee to their arcades.

" Yet the ravine was generally believed to be unscalable. No guide or hunter could tell what attractions it concealed, or the probable character of the ground. No party, so far as we could learn, had ever been through it. But Mr. Gordon, who is as much at home in the woods as a bear, and who gets along without a compass in their thickets, by having the instinct of a bee, was ready and anxious to take charge of any person or company that would try to explore and scale it. So I endeavored to muster a small band for the attempt under his lead, knowing that we should all be safe in his charge and under his counsel. He is acquainted with the wilderness of the White Mountains as David knew the forests of Ziph, or Solomon the botany of Palestine. Last year, however, I was not successful in my efforts to collect recruits. But this month I found

enough to justify the trial.   A lawyer of Boston, who proved himself
a thoroughly furnished wood-man, a clergyman, an artist, and your
correspondent, were the quartette of novices, and with our admirable
guide formed a harmonious, and as it turned out, a competent 'quintette club ' for the excursion.

   " Tuesday, the eleventh, in the afternoon, was the time for starting.   It had rained in the morning.   The clouds were heavy and
dark after dinner, and blanketed the mountains.   But the wind was

favorable, and, according to Mr. Gordon's barometrical instinct, the
signs were auspicious for the succeeding day.   Some friends were
kind enough to escort us from the Alpine House to the base of
Adams, two miles beyond the farther side of Randolph Hill, where
we were to strike into the forest.   Just as we arrived opposite Madison, the cloak and cap of mist were thrown off, and the symmetrical
mountain saluted us in an aristocratic suit of blue-black velvet.   And
as we reached the point where we were to leave the wagon, the fog
lifted from the ravine also.   Both its sides, its upper plateau, and its

far-retreating wall looked full upon us in shadow so gloomy, as if the old mountain was making one last and crowning effort to frighten us from our enterprise, and save his savage chasm from desecration by human feet. The prospect was not very enticing, especially as the rain began to fall again when the horses stopped. But we put faith in the northwest wind for the weather of the morrow, bade good-bye to our friends in the wagon, and at four o'clock started on the ascent, along a brook that flows out of the ravine, and is one of the feeders of Moose River, which swells the Androscoggin.

" We had supposed that this brook would furnish delight enough to relieve the fatigue of the first part of the ascent, and we were not disappointed.

> Gayest pictures rose to win me,
> Leopard-colored rills.

What can be more charming and refreshing than the exploration of a mountain stream ? One minute your feet are in the deep, soft mosses—springy ottomans for the naiads—that cushion the fallen trunks along the banks. Next, you are pushing through the luxuriant growths of fern, and bush, and vine, that choke the way between the bordering birches and pines. Soon you are stopping to gaze at the rich weather-stains on the occasional smooth walls of stone ; or you pause before some scooped basin, a rod broad and five feet deep, in which the crystal water is stored to show off the dolphin hues of stones on the bottom, that have been polished by their toil of centuries at wearing out the immense granite bowl. And then the infinite caprice, and sport, and joy of the stream itself in its leaps all along the pathway from its far-up cradle, and its growth from a baby rill to a boyish brook ! Now it pours in a thin sheet of liquid glass over a broad and even rock. Now it slides in a tiny cataract along a slanting sluice-way. Now it streams in scattered fringes of pearly raggedness down a slope of rock that is striped with emerald moss. Now it strands all its silvery threads into a runnel, and pours with concentrated voice through the groove of a sharp-edged shelf, into a still pool below.

" But what folly to attempt to draw in words the curves and colors, the coyness and the hoyden frolic, the flashes and the moodiness, the laughter and the plaints of these daughters of the clouds ! What

can make the time pass quicker, or the fatigue of climbing seem so slight, as the Protean beauty and ever-changing music of a mountain rill, which nature keeps sacred to poetry before it mingles with the

more vulgar water of the valley, to begin a life of use ? Three hours
slipped away quickly, while we were mounting the stony stairs of this
unvisited rivulet that drains the sides of the ravine,—although we
had stumbled, and tested the coldness of its tide in other ways than
by drinking, and, for a great portion of the way, carried our boots
full of its liquid ice.

" It was just sunset when we reached the proper point to pitch our
camp for the night. The easterly cliff of the gorge, dimly seen
through the trees, glowed with vivid gold—the promise of a bright
day to succeed—as we stretched ourselves under the slanted birch-
bark canopy, supported on four poles, that was to guard us from
dews and rains. We could not but look with admiration at the quiet
and business-like air and movements of Mr. Gordon, as he went to
work with his axe upon a great tree, felled it, chopped the trunk into
two huge logs, stretched them out before our rude tent, and kindled
between them a noble fire. It was my first experience of ' camping
out.' I hope it will not be the last.

" It was pleasant to think, as we were drying our feet at that
cheerful blaze, whose heat drove the mosquitos also from our wigwam, that it was the first time a fire had been lighted—except, possibly, by a thunderbolt—under those solemn precipices ; the first time
that the hiss and crackle of the logs had ever chimed in there with
the buzz of human voices, and the purr of the busy brook ; the first
time that the gray cliffs had ever been looked up to, through flicker
and smoke, from a tent at twilight ; or that sparks had been scattered
aloft among the thick leaves, to mock for a moment the perennial
sparkles from the camp-fires of the night. We were at liberty to
enjoy the sensations of pioneers in the gorge, searching for a new
path to the summit of Mount Washington.

" How refreshing was the kettle of tea which was steeped and
' drawn ' for us by that beneficent blaze ! Was it because it was
made of water tapped in its granite service-pipe, half-way between
the clouds and the lower earth, that it yielded a flavor more exquisite
than the cream of the Alpine House had ever imparted before ? Some

six or eight dippers of it stimulated the memory of the lawyer of our group so that he gave us the most reviving stories, until we begged to be allowed to sleep. My little girl, five years old, was sadly disturbed, when I started, by the fear that bears would devour me. Indeed, while I was absent she became so anxious that a benevolent lady in the Alpine House comforted her with the assurance that ' all the bears in the Adams Ravine 'had mittens on their teeth.' They must also have had velvet on their paws, and cotton in their throats ; for we heard no motion or sound of any wild creature through the night-watch. The ' Great Bear ' alone, prowling all night ' around the fold of the North Star,' looked down upon our slumber. Twice I awaked, and saw the tall and faithful Gordon moving stealthily to replenish the fire, and heard the tired monotone of the brook, murmuring at its perpetual toil. But how well we rested, on our bed of spruce boughs, in the ' Gordon Hotel ; ' and how we needed all the strength which the night could inspire for the next day's task ; and how we were rewarded for all our fatigue, let me try to tell you in another letter."

" Shall we continue our conversation with your readers, Mr. Editor, about the excursion through the ravine of Adams to Mount Washington ? When I parted from you, our party were just going to sleep on our spruce couches, under our birch roof, with our feet to the fire, while the drowsy serenade of the brook served as a soporific to counteract the stimulus of Gordon's tea.

" After early ablutions in the stream, and a breakfast which a camp-appetite made sumptuous, we started for the day's toil. Our .first excitement was kindled by the gorgeousness of the morning sunlight on the sheer gray rocks of the curving wall of the ravine, far up under the pinnacle of the mountain. The glowing gold which the wet mosses intermixed with the russet and purple of the precipice. very nearly took the soul of our artist companion out of his body. (If it had succeeded in severing the balloon from its bodily basket, Gorham would have been robbed of the poet for whom it has been

48

long waiting; Boston would have lost a man of genius; and the region of unembodied and ideal beauty would have gained a true seer before the time.) He insisted that, after such an 'effect,' we must of necessity go on a descending grade of scenery the rest of the day.

"An hour's easy climbing took us to a point, above the high trees and seemingly about midway in the gorge, from which perhaps the most impressive view of the ravine is gained. Looking off and down, its sides sloped sharply to the very road in the village of Randolph. Looking back and up, its wings, fifteen hundred feet over our heads, and in places nearly perpendicular, bent and joined in a wall of bare, jagged, and threatening ledge, just under the head of the mountain, which it completely shut out from view. We were in the region of silence. There was no scream, or song, or chipper of any bird,—no buzz of any insect. We were shielded by the right-hand wall from the westerly breeze which was driving the scud over the line of the mountain peaks; and there were no leaves around us to stir and rustle at the fanning of the air. The brook had dwindled. We no longer had its path to follow. Now and then, under the large rocks, we could just hear a slight gurgle, where out of sight it was giving in baby prattle an intimation of its existence. On the steep cliffs, we could see, here and there, the motionless glass of a cascade, but it gave no sound. The only note of animal life we heard, all day, was the sharp chirrup of the chipmunk, not long after we left the camp. Our talk was, no doubt, the first sound of human voices that had ever broken that solemn stillness. The ravine lacks the great attraction of a 'snow-arch,' and does not show so symmetrical a wall as the majestic Colosseum-curve, out of which, in Tuckerman's Ravine, the 'thousand streams' seem to ooze. But it is grander than Tuckerman's in its cliffs; and far more impressive, seen midway, for what one of our party called its '*deep downity*,'—the sweep of its keen-edged walls from the very shoulders of the mountain to its feet by the Randolph road.

"From the point I have thus been speaking of, just above the line of high trees, it seemed as though we could reach the summit of the

ridge to two hours.   But here we found the greatest difficulty of the
whole excursion.   The slope was not very steep ; for a mile or more,
the bottom of the ravine was rather a gradually retreating stairway of

enormous
boulders ;
and, as an
Irishman
remarked
in ascend-
ing the
cone of
Mount
Washing-
ton, ' the
dumpers
did their
work very
badly.
The huge rocks were piled in
the most eccentric confusion ;
crevasses, sometimes twenty
and thirty feet deep and spanned with moss, lay in wait for
the feet ; thickets of scrub
spruces and junipers overgrew
these boulders, and made the
most sinewy opposition to our
passage.   Every muscle of our
bodies was called into play in
fighting these dwarfed and
knotty regiments of evergreens.
A more thorough gymnasium for training and testing the working
and enduring powers of the system, could not be arranged by art.
After six hours of steady and hard climbing,—which, added to the

48 *

three of the afternoon previous, made nine hours of toil in scaling the ridge,—we gained the plateau above which the pinnacle of Adams soars. The last part of our path out lay up the eastern wall, just where it joins the left-hand cliffs ; and here we had the excitement of grand rock scenery overhanging and threatening us as we climbed ; while the opposite rampart, covered with green, and chan

nelled by streams into very graceful lines, responded to the blasted cliffs like Gerizim to Ebal,—the hill of blessing to the mount of cursing. One could not turn the eye from side to side, without repeating mentally the passage, ' strength and beauty are in his sanctuary.'

" The last few rods of the passage out of the ravine led us up a narrow and smooth gateway, quite steep, and carpeted with grass. We sat some time in it, looking at the rocky desolation and horror just about us, balanced by the lovely lines into which the verdure of the western ramparts was broken,—not knowing what a splendid view was in reserve for us when we should step out upon the ridge. The huge cone of Mount Madison rose before us, steep, symmetrical, and sharp, with more commanding beauty of form than any other summit of the White Hills has ever shown to my eye. We were facing the southeast when we rose out of the ravine, and were so nearly under the crest of Adams that its shape was hidden from us, and also every other summit of the range. So that there was nothing to compete with the proud proportions of the pinnacle before us.

"There are very few peaked summits in the region of the White Hills. It is even said by accurate observers, that among the Alps there are not more than five that slope steeply on all sides from pointed tops. The sharpest apex is generally supported on one side by a long line with very moderate inclination. This is the case with the spires of Jefferson and Adams, seen from the upper portion of the bridleroad on Mount Washington. Nature in the mountain-lines, as in her other departments, loves to hide her strength, refrains from startling emphasis, and veils the intensity of her forces from the senses by breadth and mass in the products, which appeal to thought and imaginative insight for recognition. The sharp drawing of mountains with very narrow bases, which we often see in pictures, is due to the fact that the artist is incompetent to suggest great height by the moderate lines that inclose vast bulk, and it is weak as caricature is feeble in contrast with portraiture, or as declamation is weak compared with the eloquence of original and practical speech. But the cone of Madison, seen from the gateway of the ravine, is not only steep, regular, and pointed, but, all other mountains being shut out, it looks immensely massive. The whole mountain has seldom looked so high from below as this bare fraction of it did, which we were gazing at from an elevation of four thousand feet on its sides. And its color was even more fascinating than its form. It puzzled us to understand how the rounding lines of the summit, as seen from the road in

Randolph, could have been conjured into the lance-like sharpness here revealed to us. And how the light gray which it wears to a beholder in Jefferson, or the leathery brown it presents from the Glen, or the gray green which is its real tint when we go close to its rocks, could have transformed itself into the leaden lava hue in which it rose before us, was a stranger mystery. I feel sure that it was some trick of the light, like many of the sunset tints, and not the

color which the cone steadily presents. The effect was the more grand because it seemed as though nothing but batteries could have produced it. The peak looked like some proud fortification that had been stormed at with leaden shot by a park of artillery for years. Our artist was grieved that we had not more time to allow him in sketching the view.

"We all looked with longing eyes to the summit, which seemed to invite us to scale it ; but the sun was already past noon. and we must reach the house on Mount Washington by dark. So we resolved to make the ascent of Mount Adams, whose topmost rocks were still nearly a mile off from us. Between the spires of Adams and Madison on the ridge there is a pond of icy water, refreshing enough to weary climbers, and from this point another view peculiarly striking, and in itself worth the whole toil of the expedition, is gained. We are almost overhung by the lawless rocks of a subordinate peak of Mount Adams, which we called John Quincy Adams, and back of that was the profile line of the higher crest, bulging off and sweeping down into a ravine deep below the general level of the ridge. The rocks were very jagged, and at first sight nothing could seem more harsh and chaotic. Yet the view was strangely fascinating. I could not understand why the impression of beauty, even of unusual softness and melody, should be made by such ragged desolation. And if I had never read the seventeenth chapter of Mr. Ruskin's fourth volume of Modern Painters, I might have been ignorant of the secret. We are told there that a line drawn over a great Alpine ridge, so as to touch the principal peaks that jut from it, will usually be found to be part of an unreturning or immortal curve. The grandeur of the Alpine pinnacles is bounded by that law of symmetry. And I soon saw that the precipices of Mount Adams were in subjection to the same line of grace. The jutting rocks and the seemingly lawless notchings, like the scalloping of a lovely leaf, hinted the sweep of an infinite curve. I had often found great pleasure in detecting the recurrence of a few favorite angles and forms in the chain-like lines of hills within ten miles of Mount Washington; but the revelation of this curve by the sharp edges of the cliff of Adams was not the simple perception of a pleasant fact, but the opening of my eyes to a new page in the meaning of Nature. As soon as I returned, I sought the volume I have mentioned, and I cannot refrain from quoting in this letter the passage on the 189th page, that now lies open before me, and which I have read with new interest.

" ' A rose is rounded by its own soft ways of growth, a reed is bowed into tender curvature by the pressure of the breeze; but we could not from these have proved any resolved preference, by Na-

ture, of curved lines to others, inasmuch as it might always have
been answered that the curves were produced, not for beauty's sake,
but infallibly by the laws of vegetable existence ; and looking at
broken flints or rugged banks afterwards, we might have thought that
we only liked the curved lines because associated with life and organism, and disliked the angular ones because associated with inaction
and disorder.   But Nature gives us in these mountains a more clear
demonstration of her will.   She is here driven to make fracture the
law of being.   She cannot tuft the rock-edges with moss, or round
them by water, or hide them with leaves and roots.   She is bound to
produce a form, admirable to human beings, by continual breaking
away of substance.   And behold, so soon as she is compelled to do
this, she changes the laws of fracture itself. " Growth," she seems to
say, " is not essential to my work, nor concealment, nor softness ; but
curvature is : and if I must produce my forms by breaking them, the
fracture itself shall be in curves.   If, instead of dew and sunshine,
the only instruments I am to use are the lightning and the frost, then
their forked tongues and crystal wedges shall still work out my laws
of tender line.   Devastation instead of nurture may be the task of
all my elements, and age after age may only prolong the unrenovated
ruin ; but the appointments of typical beauty which have been made
over all creatures shall not therefore be abandoned ; and the rocks
shall be ruled, in their perpetual perishing, by the same ordinances
that direct the bending of the reed and the blush of the rose.'' '

" From the top of this pyramid of Adams, whose rocks are so huge
and lawless that it would be scarcely possible to make a horse-path
to it from the plateau, we gained glorious views of the northern country,—the beautiful Kilkenny range, the lovely farms and uplands of
Randolph and Jefferson, the long unrolled purple of the Androscoggin, making a right angle at the Lary Farm, the Pond of Safety, on
the northerly side of the Pilot Hills, and Umbagog, Richardson's
Lake, and Moosetockmaguntic, whose dreamy waters, framed by the
unbroken wilderness, are stocked with portly trout, and haunted by
droves of moose.

" The long tramp which follows next, around the bending ridge between Jefferson and Adams, is rewarded by the glorious picture of Washington, superior to any other which the range affords. The long easterly slope is shown from its base in the Pinkham forests;

the cone towers sheer out of the Gulf of Mexico, and every rod of the bridle-path is visible, from the Ledge to the Summit House. From the peak of Adams one can see as much as from the top of Washington, except the small segment of the circle which the dome

49

of Washington itself conceals. But this loss is far more than made
up by having Mount Washington thus in the picture. Gaining the
crest of the stout and square-shouldered Jefferson, our route ran next
over the dromedary humps of Mount Clay, and up the long and
tedious slope of Mount Washington to the Tip-Top House. We
reached it at seven o'clock, pretty thoroughly tired, but not so exhausted that we could not enjoy the marvellous water-views which
the setting sun kindled for us on the southeast,—Lovell's Pond, Sebago Lake, Ossipee, Winnipiseogee, and beyond them the silver sea
plainly cut by the line of the Maine shore,—the first time I had ever
clearly seen it from the summit. It was something to be truly grateful that we had been able to fulfil our plan in the excursion without
an accident, and without delay from unpleasant weather. The day
had been perfect. The mists of the morning had lifted from the
peaks when we gained the ridge, and there had been clouds enough
to shed sufficient shadows to give variety of expression to the splendid scenes with which we had made acquaintance.

"As to our satisfaction with the excursion, costing as it did no
little toil, let me say that there is no approach to Mount Washington,
and no series of mountain views, comparable with this ascent and its
surroundings on the northerly side. Your path lies among and over
the largest summits of the range. Between Madison and Adams you
have the noblest outlines of rocky crest which the whole region can
furnish. Mount Jefferson glories in the afternoon light with the most
fascinating contrast of purple and orange hues. Mount Washington
shows himself in impressive and satisfactory supremacy. You wind
around the edges of every ravine that gapes around the highest summits. You see the long and narrow gully between Madison and
Adams; the tremendous hollow of Adams itself which we climbed;
the precipitous gulf between Jefferson and Adams on the southeast;
the deep cut gorge in Jefferson on the northwest, whose westerly
bones of gray cliffs, (see sketch in the next chapter,) breaking bare
through the steep verdure, are perhaps the most picturesque of all the
rock-views we beheld; the chasm between Jefferson and Clay, divided

from the savage Gulf of Mexico by a spur of Jefferson that runs out
towards the Glen House; and the long rolling braces that prop
Mount Pleasant, and Franklin, and the tawny Munroe,—the boundaries of the ravines that you look into in riding to Mount Washington
over the Crawford path.

" The only trouble with the route is, that there is too much to see
in one day. It would be better to camp, if possible, near the summit
of Mount Adams, and thus spread the delight more equally and profitably over two days, and have a sunset and sunrise also from the
ridge to remember. This last was denied to us. We slept soundly
in the Summit House, and waked the next morning to find ourselves
wrapped in cloud and rain. But in spite of our tramp the day before, we walked from the top to the Alpine House in Gorham, through
showers and mud, a distance of fifteen miles, in less than five hours.

" P. S.—Since the excursion thus hastily described, I have been
twice over the best portion of our route. Once a small party of us
climbed the northerly slope of Mount Madison through the ' Gordon
path,' which our excellent guide ' blazed ' for us with a hatchet.
Four hours' climbing carried us to the summit. We went nearly
over to Mount Jefferson, and returned to Gorham by the same track,
down Mount Madison,—making the whole journey in fourteen hours
from the Alpine House. The second time, we rode to the Glen;
took horses to the base of the cone of Mount Washington; went
around, in the upper portion of the Gulf of Mexico, to Mount Clay;
thence to Jefferson, where we dined; thence around the edge of the
Adams ravine; up the cone of Madison, and down the Gordon path
to the foot of Randolph Hill. This excursion required fifteen hours
from the Alpine House. To all lovers of the most exciting and noble
scenery which the White Mountains furnish, I commend this northerly
route to the summit of Mount Washington, with Mr. Gordon—who
may always be found by inquiry at the Alpine House—for guide."

Thus ends the original account of our expeditions through the unbroken forests to the northerly portion of the White Mountain ridge.
49 *

We have repeated the excursion many times since the letters were written,—preferring now to take the path up Mount Madison from the foot of Randolph Hill,—and always with increased interest in the scenery, and firmer conviction that the toil is better repaid than by any other tramp in the neighborhood of Mount Washington. And here we must close our description of the scenery and emotions gained by climbing so far above the level of New England. The best way for travellers, who wish by the bridle-paths to see the most of the range to which a day can introduce them, is to ascend from the Crawford House, and go down facing the noble towers of Jefferson, Adams, and Madison, on the Glen path. If one is going up and down the same path, the Glen road, we think, is preferable. If one is to cross the ridge, the scenery will be far more impressive to ascend from the Notch, and descend to the Glen, than to reverse the process. But we will go counter to our own advice, and descend to the plains from the summit of New Hampshire by the Crawford path, for the sake of this passage by Rev. Henry Ward Beecher, that might otherwise be lost to us.

"The descent from the top of Mount Washington, towards the Gibbs House, had in it one half hour of extreme pleasure, and two hours of common pleasure. After leaving the summit hill I shot ahead of the fifteen or twenty in the party, and rode alone along the ridge that separates the eastern and western valleys. Beginning at your very feet as little crevices or petty gorges, the valleys widened, and deepened, and stretched forth, until on either side they grew dim in the distance, and the eye disputed with itself whether it was lake or cloud that spotted the horizon with silver. The valleys articulate with this ridge as ribs with a backbone. As I rode along this jagged and broken path, except of my horse's feet, there was not a single sound. There was no wind. There was nothing for it to sing through if there had been ever so much. There were no birds. There were no chirping insects. I saw no insects except spiders, which here, as everywhere, seemed well fed, and carried plump bellies. There was perfect peace, perfect stillness, universal brightness, the fulness of vision, and a wondrous glory in the heaven, and over all the earth. The earth was to me as if it were unpeopled. I saw neither towns nor cities, neither houses nor villages, neither smoke, nor motion, nor sign of life. I stopped, and imagined that I was as they were who first explored this ridgy wilderness, and knew that, as far as eye could reach, not a white man lived. And yet these thoughts were soon chased away with the certainty that under that silvery haze were thousands of toiling men, romping children, mothers and maidens, and the world was going on below just as usual. How are the birds to be envied who make airy mountains by their wings! Could I rise six thousand feet above the ground, that were substantially to be on the mountain top. Then, when the multitude wearied us, and the soul would bathe in silence, we would with a few beats lift up through the air, and seek the solitude of space, and hide in the clefts of clouds. or ride unexplored ranges of crystal white cloud-mountains, that scorn footsteps, and on whose radiant surfaces an army of feet would wear no path, leave no mark, but fade out as do steps upon the water!

"And so, for a half hour, I rode alone, without the rustle of leaves, —without hum or buzz,—without that nameless mixture of pipes, small and great, that fill the woods, or sing along the surface of the plains. There were no nuts to fall, no branches to snap, no squirrel to bark, no birds to fly out and flap away through the leaves. The matted moss was born and bred in silence. The stunted savins and cedars crouched down close to the earth from savage winds, as partridges crouch when hawks are in the air. The forests in the chasms and valleys below were like bushes, or overgrown moss. If there was any wind down there,—if they shook their leaves to its piping, and danced when it bid them, it was all the same to me,—for motion or rest were alike at this distance.

"There is above every man's head a height into which he may rise, and, whether care and trouble fret below or tear on, they become alike silent and powerless. It is only our affections that mount up, and dwell with us, where bickerings and burdens never come."

THE CONNECTICUT VALLEY.

The mountains indeed, that they may show their dignity and communicate their favors, require to be approached with great painstaking and peculiar respect. But no oriental king ever held himself in greater seclusion, or ever vouchsafed more dim and inadequate notions of his personal glory, than do they to those remote from their dwelling. The difference for the beholder of mountains, however, does not arise merely from the difficulty of receiving their forms without sight purely into the imagination, but also from the preparation of mind occasioned by the traveller's own long and laborious search after their grandeur. He pays, in his own exposure and toil and patience, the price of admission to their incomparable theatre. He gains gradually the mood to appreciate and enjoy them ; and his mind expands to their breadth, and grows up to their exaltation. A man in his easy-chair, reading a book or looking at a print, can but partially conceive their character. He treads in the edge of their imaginary shadow, instead of scaling their real height. Yet is it well worth the while to catch even hints and reflections of their wondrous substance which God made and upreared, to be seen and remembered and related among men.

The plains, all save a few barren deserts of sand, have yielded to the possession of human art. The hills, as in the old Scriptures they are called, are, indeed, everlasting. When we have left them, they cannot be forgotten or removed from our thought. As we still feel in our nerves the motion of the sea after we have planted our feet on the firm land, so the crests and hollows of the solid globe continue to make themselves felt in our mind. Away vastly they stretch in their earthy storm, their fixed fluctuation, their surge of primeval rock into the skies. Once seen, ever after remaining a new and glorious furniture of the mind, in their immense spread on the floor of the world, wondrously somehow, with no loss of size, transferred to the chambers of the imagination, they stand there, a mute, material warning against all moral narrowness and bigotry. Liberty and law, magnanimity and humility, inflexible sincerity and inexhaustible bounty, are their lessons. Purity ever descending from the heavens, in their flowing robes or frozen garb, is their perpetual example and admonition. And he that climbeth up their side, resolutely keeping the rough and devious yet ascending way, his prospect widening with every step as he goes on, till at the natural column's head, held up so mightily and so high, he trembles as between two worlds, will be reminded of his immortality.

REV. C. A. BARTOL.

PROPERLY, according to the plan we have generally followed in the book, the views of the White Mountain range from Bethlehem, and along the course of the Ammonoosuc near the White Mountain House and the ruins of the old Fabyan Hotel, belong to this chapter. They lie upon the slopes which the Connecticut drains. We wish, however, to call attention in this concluding chapter to a few prominent views of the Washington range from the Connecticut itself, and to show how the noblest of these pictures can be enjoyed in connection with the usual White Mountain tour.

There is a striking picture of the great chain from the village of Littleton, and all along the stage-route to Lancaster. Views not only of the grandest peaks, but also of the Franconia range, burst upon the traveller in connection with a breadth of open country, and rich rolls of cultivated upland that seem to be set there less for their bounty than their color, which may claim to be ranked among the rarest landscapes to which our volume has called attention. And they are a fitting introduction to the scenery around Lancaster. We have already said in the opening chapter, that if Lancaster had been made accessible, a few years ago, by the Grand Trunk Railway, it would have been the great rival of North Conway. With the attractive accommodation it now offers in its elegant and spacious Hotel, it will be sure to draw a large and increasing number of guests, every year, to submit themselves to the charm of the soothing hills that immediately encircle it; to enjoy the drives along the banks of the curving Connecticut; and, from the luxury of color and shadow spread wide over its intervale in a soft afternoon light, to mount upon the Lunenburg Hills, where the bright blue of the river and the embow-

ercd homes of the village are set in the relief and under the protection of the long White Mountain wall, tinged with the violet of de-
parting day.

There is no single meadow-view in Lancaster equal to the intervale

of North Conway. But the river is incomparably superior to the
Saco; and in the combined charm, for walks or rides, of meadow and
river—the charm not of wildness, such as the darker and more rapid
Androscoggin gives, but a cheerful brightness and beneficence—Lancaster is unrivalled.

And when the distant mountain ranges
In moonlight or blue mist are clad.
Oft memory all the landscape changes,
And pensive thoughts are blent with glad

For then as in a dream Elysian,
Val d'Arno's fair and loved domain
Seems, to my rapt, yet waking vision,
To yield familiar charms again!

Save that for dome and turret hoary
Amid the central valley lies
A white church-spire unknown to story,
And smoke-wreathes from a cottage rise.

Yet here may willing eyes discover
The art and life of every shore,
For Nature bids her patient lover
All true similitudes explore.

These firs, when cease their boughs to quiver,
Stand like pagodas Brahmins seek.
Yon isle, that parts the winding river,
Seems moulded from a light caique.

And ferns tha* in these groves are hidden,
  Are sculptured like a dainty frieze,
While choral music steals unbidden,
  As undulates the forest breeze.

  A Gothic arch and springing column,
    A floral-dyed mosaic ground,
  A twilight shade and vista solemn,
    In all these sylvan haunts are found.

Lancaster is well situated for the enjoyment of the winter effects
upon the mountains.   It was the writer's fortune once to pass a few
days in the village and its neighborhood, early in March, when the
hue of the White Mountains justified their name, and they stood up ·
in the full splendor of their snowy regalia.

It was in a week that opened a " sectional " view of winter, showing
it enthroned on the hills in the gorgeous panoply of its despotism.
The days ran over nearly the whole scale of the season's temperature, swept the gamut of its music, and displayed the resources of
its winter-palette on the landscape.   We had warm weather and
savage cold ; gray skies and cloudless blue ; the mountains were
wrapped in frosty veils, and soon stood up chiselled sharp on the
spotless sky ; still mornings dawned, when the smoke,—" the azure
pillars of the hearth,"—rose to the heights of the neighboring peaks
without bending, and were swiftly succeeded by furious gusts ; golden
evenings followed hard upon thick afternoons, and died into sparkling nights, when the valleys were lustrous with " the spears of moon-
freezing crystals."

On the first day of our visit the weather was genial, and low clouds
from the sea were scudding fast towards the mountains.   But towards night, Shawondasee and Wabun—as the south and the east
winds have been christened for us in " Hiawatha "—raised a savage
warwhoop all through the valley, and pelted the region with squalls
of snow.   On Tuesday " the fierce Kabibonokka " was on hand to
·lrive them back.   Down he came

from his lodge of snow-drifts
From his home among the icebergs,

And his hair, with snow besprinkled,
Streamed behind him like a river,
Like a black and wintry river,
As he howled and hurried southward,
Over frozen lakes and moorlands.

Only we must make exception from the poet's description in the matter of the hair. It was not black, nor gloomy. The dishevelled clouds that rushed across the hills were smitten with fitful sunshine, and fluttered in golden threads as they scattered their sparkles southward. After the furious norther had blown the sky clear, it whirled the light snow in clouds, stopped railroad trains, and brought the temperature before night to ten below zero. What plumes it fastened upon the sharpest peaks! It swept the snow over them as an off-shore, breeze loosens the spray of breaking billows, tossed it in feathery spires to flash in the sunshine, and then would whirl a cloud of the dazzling dust around the necks of the mountains, till you felt that they must gasp from suffocation. The rarest poetry of the winter scenery was painted on the eye in these antics of the hurricanes.

If one could enjoy the open air as freely, and find it as genial in the winter, as in the summer, we cannot doubt that the colors on the bleached landscapes would be found as inviting as those which blend into the summer pomp. The distant views of the great range in summer are certainly far inferior to those we enjoyed in the approach to them in March, when it swelled soft, vague, and golden,—a pigmy Monte Rosa, on the northwestern sky. Lafayette has never shown itself to such advantage in July as it did then from Lancaster at evening, when the blustering clouds parted to let its white wedge be visible, burnished to an amber blaze by the setting sun, and driven as one crystal into the chilly sky. And the Stratford peaks do not look so high and solemn in August, when the sun fevers their sheer precipices, as at such a time in their priestly drapery. On all the bald ridges and crests the silver splendor was relieved against the blue. This makes the richest charm of the Alps; and one could then drive among the White Hills as through a mimic Switzerland. Yes, and the colors must have been essentially the same. For the artist that would paint the magnificence we saw on the Pilot Hills and the White Mountain range at sunset and sunrise from Lancaster, must dip his brush into as exquisite ambers, plum tints, gold, and purple, as he would need to interpret the baptism of the evening upon Mont Blanc, or the morning glow upon the Jungfrau.

During the same visit we enjoyed a ride among the familiar hills of the Androscoggin Valley, and can recall the contrast to the gen-

eral wildness given by a drive from Gorham to the Glen. The high walls which guard that road from the northwesters had saved the snow from drifts. It lay for six miles perfectly even, to the depth of some six inches, without blemish ; and unbroken, except by a large sled-load of hay that had been driven over it, and which, over-hanging the runners, had left delicately pencilled lines all along the untrodden margins of the path. The green on Carter and Moriah, at the left, was turned into rusty bronze, and the snow which shone through the stripped trees around the roots of the forests made their sombre sides look as though they had been powdered with crystal dust. Every blackened stump along the roadside seemed an Ethiopian head crowned with a graceful and stainless turban. Each rock in the river-bed showed a fantastic nightcap. The springs were "stagnant with wrinkling frost." And at every turn, old Washington was bulging into the cold and brilliant blue with irregular whiteness; or Madison, in more feminine symmetry, displayed a fresh view of sloping shoulders clasped to the waist in ermine.

But the most impressive features of the scene were those which started out by moonlight. Then, with the thermometer at twelve below zero, and the wind cutting as you drove against it, as if determined to bite into the brain, one might easily fancy himself in an arctic latitude. The full moon turned the great hills into ghastly domes and pyramids of chalk. The air seemed weird. There was no sound of brawling brooks, or running river, or chirping insect life, as in summer. The stars flashed without sympathy in the bleak sky. Going from such a ride to the volumes of the lamented and heroic Kane, we could understand better the pictures that line the memory of the survivors of that devoted band. Those stiff, white peaks towered as gravestones over the creative forces that once filled the valley with joy, and painted it with verdure.

But what, we thought, is so mystic as the processes of Providence most familiar to us! Only a few weeks will pass before the frosty whiteness shall be chipped from those cliffs; the crystal splinters that fly from the sunbeams' chisels will melt into music, and feed the mosses of the mountain-top, and sing in the rills that dance towards the sea; and the stars will glow over the bursting promise of June.

And now we must call attention to the route by which, in the early beauty of June, or in the full splendor of summer, the traveller may be introduced to the most impressive view of the White Mountain range which the slopes towards the Connecticut command. This is

gained by passing from the Androscoggin Valley over towards the
Connecticut by what is called

THE CHERRY MOUNTAIN ROAD,

from Gorham to the Notch. The distance is thirty-four miles. At
Jefferson Hill, eighteen miles from Gorham, the distance is only seven
miles to the Connecticut in Lancaster ; but the road here intersects,
by a very acute angle, with a road across the Jefferson meadows, and
over a low spur of Cherry Mountain to the Crawford House at the
Notch, which is sixteen miles distant from Jefferson Hill. With the
exception of about two miles on Cherry Mountain—and this portion
only rough, but not in the least dangerous—the road is as good as
any in the neighborhood of the White Hills. It can easily be travelled from Gorham in seven hours.

We give these particulars because as yet there are no regular
stages on the route. Parties are sent by private stage wagons from
the Alpine House in Gorham. Comparatively few of the White
Mountain tourists have become acquainted with the scenery, or even
perhaps know of the route up to this time. But it is steadily
securing a wider attention, and is destined before long, we think,
to attract a large proportion of the travellers who now pass to
or from the Notch and the Glen by the way of Jackson and Bartlett, a distance of thirty-six miles to the Glen, and of forty-four to
Gorham.

The question of the comparative merits of the two routes, as to
scenery, is often raised. On the regular stage-road from the Glen to
the Notch, after leaving the Glen House, there is no full view of the
great White Mountain range. There is a glimpse of Mount Washington about three miles from the Glen, near the entrance to the
Crystal Cascade, and a very noble view of it on looking back after
passing Cook's, on the edge of Jackson. But after that, not only
Washington, but the range, is hidden by lower hills during the whole

distance. These hills are very lovely, and the drive is thoroughly delightful, but it does not make one acquainted, as the Cherry Mountain route does, with the whole of the Mount Washington range. And certainly if a person has once travelled the Jackson and Bartlett road, he should by all means, on the second visit, try the northerly circuit to the Notch through Jefferson.

By this Cherry Mountain route, after the first mile from the Alpine House in Gorham, we are in company with the White Mountains proper for twenty-five miles. We take them up into fellowship gradually. The range is in the shape of the body of a figure five, and we go around the bulge of it, formed by the curve in which the five largest mountains are set. First Madison and Adams come into

51

view, and we drive directly by their base and under their summits in passing over Randolph Hill.—This view we have already described in the chapter on the Androscoggin Valley.—Next, after passing the great ravine in Mount Adams,—of which we gave a drawing in the last chapter,—Mount Jefferson comes into view. Here the driver should rein up to allow something more than hasty glances at the three majestic forms that tower over the path, and especially to let passengers enjoy the castellated ridge of Mount Jefferson, whose rocks rising over a steep ravine seem to be the turrets of decaying fortifications. The artist's sketch of these romantic looking cliffs was taken, not from below, but from Mount Adams on the ridge, nearly four thousand feet above.

Riding a little farther on, we see the summits of Pleasant, Franklin, and Monroe start out above the forests on the left. Next Mouns Clay makes its appearance. And then, as we look back, the ascending line of Washington shows itself last of all, though it is the centre of the range, leaving the wilderness behind it as it mounts to a rocky crest. The point we speak of now is Martin's in Jefferson, about thirteen miles from Gorham. Have you ever seen a snake, half startled and half playful, raise its supple neck and support its wary head for a moment by a curve that is the poetry of rest? Then you know something of the vitality, blending pride and grace, of the line, seen from this point, on which the upper rocks of Mount Washington are borne to their airy majesty.

Goethe somewhere gives a picture in words of a typical Alpine landscape,—groups of deep shady trees of different species, standing out over a fresh green foreground which is fanned by soft airs that seem to put the lights in motion ; a middle ground of lively green tone growing fainter as it ascends ; wide pastures on the slopes of the higher districts, where dark solitary firs stand forth from the grassy carpet, and foaming brooks rush down from cliffs whose winding steeps are climbed by laden mules ; and above, the topmost Alpine range, where neither tree nor shrub appears, but only amid the rocky teeth and snow summits a few sunny spots clothe themselves with a soft sward on which the chamois feeds. Compared with such pictures the White Mountain scenery must seem monotonous. But there is no point in New Hampshire where its monotony is so poetic and sublime, where the wilderness, miles and miles in extent, unenlivened by a clearing or the smoke of a cabin, unravaged by the axe and unspotted by fire, flows off in such noble lines and folds from the shoulders of the bleak hills. The forms of the mountains are nobler on this side than on the side towards the old Fabyan place near the Notch. The largest members of the range are the most prominent here. The ridge is not so lank, and its braces run out with more vigor ; the ravines are more powerfully furrowed ; and Mount Washington is far better related to the chain.

Then a most striking contrast to all the preceding scenery is opened when the height of land in Jefferson is gained, and we look off towards Lancaster. At first sight there is something grander than the range behind us in the long lines crowned with forest that sweep with even slope towards the Connecticut. And what breadth of prospect ! At the left, the Cherry Mountain heaving out of a vast plain attracts us ; then at the right, the Pliny ridge, on which, far up towards the summit, the wilderness has been displaced by smiling farms ; the cultivated hills of Bethlehem glow like huge opals on the west ; and more northerly than these, and far beyond them, summits of the Vermont Mountains peer dim and blue. The view is as vast as from many a mountain-top.

But it is from Goodell's, eighteen miles from Gorham, where the road turns towards the Notch, that the scenery on a clear day is grandest. Here Lafayette, with other Franconia mountains, comes into view. From no point is a better landscape-picture of him to be gained than he offers here with that long serrated summit, and the precipices of his sides reduced to dimples. And here, too, the color of the White Hills is richest in the late afternoon light. From this point for five miles over the Jefferson meadows, in travelling towards the Notch, we ride in full view of every summit of the chain, seeing Washington in the centre dominant over all.

Such is a faint suggestion of the characteristic scenery by the Cherry Mountain road to the Crawford House. In some respects the return ride from the Notch to Gorham is more interesting, from the fact that from Goodell's we drive towards the range, seeing it darken more and more as we approach its base ; but there are some advantages in the outward ride to offset this. There is as much beauty to be enjoyed on other routes ; but for grandeur, and for

opportunities of studying the wildness and majesty of the sovereign range, the Cherry Mountain route is without a rival in New Hampshire. There is as yet no large public-house in Jefferson. If a good hotel should be erected there, the village would soon become one of the most popular resorts among the mountains, and the road we have been describing would need no further introduction of its advantages and claims.

One of the most delightful acquaintances we have made with the scenery on the Cherry Mountain road, was after a long rain, in which we had been locked up in the Franconia Notch.

" Wednesday noon, there is a patch of blue overhead, and the rain stops. Let us take wagon and be off. No sooner were we out of the Notch than the rain returned into it for two or three days further drenching. We escaped a wetting ; but not a peep of Lafayette would the black clouds permit. Does it not try the very springs of one's patience, to drive twice along the line of splendid scenery, which the breath of the west would open, and to see nothing but the proscenium curtain of ashy mist ? The whole sky was dark and wet. The world seemed ' covered with the deep as with a garment : the waters stood above the mountains.' But we soon found that there was compensation even for the angry sky and the absence of mountain views. I had never seen any mountain torrents in full power. Now, that chapter of hill-passion was to be opened. Lafayette was veiled, but he was eloquent. Every vein of the sloping fields was swollen with the recent bounty of the clouds, of which the ravines in the Franconia ridge were the almoners. Rills were promoted into brooks. Brooks were enlarged into streams. Little trout-streams were foaming rapids. The feeders of the large rivers of New England, that generally ripple along in the summer, in shrunken channels, with drowsy murmur, were roaring and frightful floods.

" Every note in the scale of fresh-water music was struck by the full baptism of those persistent clouds. You could hear the plash and babble of a new-born streamlet,—the first infant cooing of a river,— as it came soft over the bent grass ; the dash down a channelled bank of a rivulet ; the full-throated gurgle of a runnel through a rocky passage ; the singing of a rill that swept across a pasture and dived under the little corduroy bridges of the road ; the anxious baritone of a hurrying stream that seemed fearful it could not do all the business it had on hand for that day. The air was filled with the chorus of the rain. One would think that an hour or two of such rage would drain the hills of their legacy. Must not every rock of old Lafayette be pouring a tide which some magic rod has unsealed

from them ?   The great business of the hill-tops, during the drought,
seemed to be to conjure the rain for the parching fields ; now, they
had their hands full to get rid of the superfluity.   The cataracts and
cascades are tasked to their utmost.   No room for beauty now.
Duty and use are the overseers of to-day.   Next week, the feathery
spray may break over the rocks, and the thin tides break themselves
in silvery plaitings among the forest dells and chasms, over the mossy
stones ; but now, all the scuppers of the mountains must spout to
save the pastures and harvests from ruin.

   " The grandeurs of the ride towards Gorham across the prominent
streams, kept close on the limits of ravage.   The ' wild Ammonoosuc '
ran fierce and ' arrowy,' purple in his rage, just ready to burst his
bounds and desolate the fields.   At the same time, the Pemigewasset
was sweeping wood, by the thousand cords, over the tops of the corn,
in the Plymouth valley.   Large streams from districts of red-colored
earth added to the wildness of the ride by their full gutters of blood.
We saw the depredators at work that bother the stage-drivers so, and
increase the county taxes.   Rills were invading the roads, running
down and across them, gullying them, tearing the earth out, now and
then, and leaving holes large enough to upset a carriage, and almost
to hide a horse.   The large Ammonoosuc swept in right royal style
through Bethlehem, dashing a mad mass of amber and foam under
the arching bridge, which the waves leaped up to seize.   *That* was
the contribution of Mount Washington to a flood somewhere along on
the Connecticut,—his assessment on a railroad company for a bridge
swept off, in consideration of his general service as a father of fountains and a purifier of the winds.   Israel's River, in Jefferson, had
turned acres of meadow into ponds.   The Saco had dashed away
several small bridges, and interrupted for some days the travel between the Notch and the Glen.   The Peabody roared over the whole
of its broad bed.   The Moose River, that flows into the Androscoggin near the Alpine House, raced along so fiercely that a bridge was
saved only by chaining it to some trees.

"This has been the golden week of the summer. The heavy rains, of which I recently wrote you, purged the air to crystal clearness. The temperature has been cool enough to make mid-day riding comfortable. It is difficult to believe that we are living in August; by the scenery-calendar our days are transposed from the heart of September. Majestic clouds—massive fragments of the storm—have been rolling out of the west, throwing the living blue of the sky into relief with their dazzling domes, and interweaving with the cool, rich light, shadows soft as plush, as a royal vesture for the hills.

"But when their week of duty to the material world and the bodily necessities was over, they were flooded with a beauty that seemed eager to make up, by its quality, for the gray mufflers of mist that had hidden them so long from the sunshine and our eyes. And so, this week, they have been fountains of a water that refreshes the thirst of the spirit. I have visited anew all the familiar, favorite spots around Gorham, during the last few days, and have found them more fascinating in their new investitures than the first sight of entirely new landscapes would have been. All the hills stood out in court-costume.

"And now let us take a ride towards the village of Jefferson. Can anything be more fascinating than those ripples of shadow that flow down the twin peaks of Madison and Adams, chased by flushes of sunshine, which again are followed by thin waves of gloom? Let the horse walk as slowly as he will, while we feast on this thrilling unsteadiness of vesture that wanders and widens from pinnacle to base. Ride on, till summit after summit of the White Mountain chain comes out, and then return, facing their broad fortresses of forest crowned with naked rock. Notice how the shadows spot them alternately, so that Washington and Adams are kindled into light, while Madison and Jefferson are black-muzzled with darkness. Look at the flashes of sunlight on the hills, that turn acres of the clean-washed wilderness into patches of shining satin. Watch that deep shadow drop from a burly cloud to spread a velvet cloak on the mountain. Look off now, as the village of Jefferson lies at your feet, and

see the Green Mountains, the Pliny Hills, the Franconia range stand
up as exhibition figures to show off the deep furs, the silky lights, the
velvets, brown, blue, and blue-black, that are woven out of the sky
looms to-day, to invest them.

"But the most surprising beauty awaits us as we ride opposite the
great ravine of Mount Adams, and look far up to the cascades, with
which the rains have enlivened its cliffs and slides. Now for a display of mountain jewelry, such as is rarely seen. A long, narrow,
leaping stream gleams aloft,—a chain of diamonds dropped from the
neck down the bosom of the mountain. The sun looks full upon it,
while the wings of the ravine are in deep shadow, and you see a
broad wrapper adorned from the collar downwards with flashing gems.
They blaze like lumps of sunshine,—like the diamonds on the crown
of the skeleton in the pass, upon which young Arthur trod,

> and the skull
> Brake from the nape, and from the skull the crown
> Rolled into light, and turning on its rims,
> Fled like a glittering rivulet to the tarn.

The shadow falls upon the cataract, and it is quenched,—put out
more quickly than its own water would extinguish a small fire. It
does not seem possible that a shadow can so utterly cancel all traces
of the lovely sheen which lay in the gorge a moment before. But,
if we watch the passing away of the shade, we shall see the sunlight
strike the top of it again, and run down, waking diamond after diamond into glow, till the string is all alive again. Near this thread
of brilliants is a huge rock over which a stream of water is falling,
and that blazes like a mighty Koh-i-noor. The shadow ripples over
that, too, and quenches it. It flows off, and instantly the rock burns
again in the meridian light. Oh, the splendor of this picture! We
stop the wagon to watch the curious wrestle of the waters,—vapor
destroying the dazzling glory that leaps from water ; we can hardly
tear ourselves from the charming show of the sun's repeated gift of
jewels, and the clouds' continually renewing envy.

"The oldest settlers in these valleys said that carbuncles gleamed on the cliffs and in the gorges of the crystal hills. Many are the stories about the pioneers that were dazzled by their splendor, when lost among the passes, and of the parties that afterwards searched, and searched in vain, for the glittering stones. May it be that some stupid and frightened wanderer once saw, far above him in some of these chasms, some such spectacle of flaming cliff, on whose wet face the sun was shining? and that his report drew bands to explore the chambers of the hills for gems? Well, what *real* gem could have been more beautiful than that flash upon the worthless granite of the ravine and precipice? Did not the beauty we looked up to cost enough to be reckoned at the worth of diamonds. It required the whole sun, and the ocean, mother of the rain, and the volcanic force that drove the cliffs into the sky, and the laws that float and drive the clouds, to make it. It cost nature more than any real gem that belongs to a monarch's treasury. Why then should it be thought a stretch of fancy to speak of it as such? It is beauty which God counts precious in the robing of the globe, and what matters it whether he evoke it from the slow crystal chemistries of the mine, or bid it glow at once on the mountain forehead, as the sun smites its face, fresh baptized with rain? The ' great carbuncles ' of the mountains are its splendors that feed and quicken the sentiment of beauty.''

Jefferson Hill (Goodell's) may without exaggeration be called the *ultima thule* of grandeur in an artist's pilgrimage among the New Hampshire mountains, for at no other point can he see the White Hills themselves in such array and force. This view has other qualifications to justify such a claim. The distance is happily fitted, not only to display the confederated strength of the chain, but also to reveal in the essential marks of form and texture the noblest character of the separate mountains. As we have said also, the smaller Franconia group rises farther away in front, separated from them by the dark bulk of Cherry Mountain in mid-ground ; and on the right hand the savanna that stretches along the Connecticut pre

52

sents a landscape contrast of a magnitude and distinctness rarely met with.

It will not be amiss, if at this point, we summon before the mind's eye for comparison the six most attractive landscape views which the region has displayed to us, namely,—the views from Artist's Hill in North Conway; from the school-house in West Campton; from the Glen; from Shelburne about two miles below the Lead-Mine Bridge, on the east bank of the Androscoggin; from Milan; and from Jefferson Hill. In the ordinary daylight of midsummer—that is, white light, just enough tinged with color to give it warmth—these views will supply different general impressions, both of the *body* of the scenes and their color. Between Conway and Campton there will be the least, and between the former and the Glen the most difference.

As a composition, the view from Artist's Hill is very symmetrically proportioned, and is superior to any other in the variety and graduations of its forms. Mount Washington, which is always the leading object of interest, occupies the central position. The inferior hills rise from the level meadows on either hand, step by step towards his summit, which dominates over the whole scene. In this noble symmetry of multitudinous details it differs from most of the other general views of the White Hills. The Shelburne view is superior in simplicity, largeness of features, and bold picturesqueness. In graceful picturesqueness it must yield to Conway; but the mountain forms in Madison and the crest of Jefferson are more spirited and decisive. To be enjoyed by the eye, without reference to the artist's purposes, we think that the greater vigor of the mountain lines, and the marvellous beauty of the Androscoggin, flowing through the meadows from the very base of Madison, make it superior to the view from Artist's Hill. But it certainly lacks something of symmetry and agreeableness of proportions, as well as extent and harmony of gradation, to balance its greater energy and demonstrative splendor. The effect is injured, perhaps, by having an inferior figure, Mount Madison, in such a position of perspective as to overtop Mount Washington in magnitude and prominence. We have little doubt, however.

that the majority of travellers, if they could be carried swiftly from point to point, would give the preference, on the whole, to the Shelburne landscape over the others. The Milan view is superior in symmetry to Shelburne, but is not equal to Conway in variety and proportion. The arrangement gives three distinct distances almost ungraduated. First, the river and its meadow borders suddenly cut off by the dark joining of the long flattened spur of the Pilot Hills, and the abrupt and higher base of Mount Hays; beyond these nothing but a wide space of gray air; while far away in this arise the great mountains grouped in a triple-peaked pyramid, admirable in proportions, and strangely beautiful in the afternoon light, as if their surface were a conglomerate of the earth's rarest gems.

From the School-House Hill in Campton, the Franconia Mountain view shows in the composition, and especially in the nearer features, nearly as much variety and beauty as that from the hill in North Conway; but the gradations lack boldness, and two leading points of interest in the distance—the Notch and the summit of Lafayette—somewhat weaken the unity and effective simplicity of the whole. In both the Glen and the Jefferson Hill views there is not much variety of features or forms; but the grandeur of the few they have renders the deficiency of slight account, while the arrangement of them serves to emphasize individual parts, without much detriment to the symmetry or force of their associated effect.

But in these, as in nearly all other natural scenes, it is not so much the forms, and their dimensions, proportions, and arrangements which produce the effect of beauty and sublimity, as the quality, variety, and harmony of the colors which overlay and imbue them. Indeed without color there is not anything in nature capable of artistic or poetic expression. If it were possible to mould in plaster of Paris an exact duplicate of Mont Blanc, and the range of which it is the head, and to set the model in place of the removed Alps, surrounding the whole with untinted air, the necessity of color to expression would need no further argument.

When judged in respect of color, we must make a different distri
bution of the prominent White Mountain views in rank and interest.
Some points that affect the senses at first with most surprise, and
produce the most powerful effect, will have the least attractions in
a continued visit. The Notch, for instance, even if one could live
there without fear, would be found very tame as a place of residence,
on account of the grim monotony of the color upon its dismantled
walls. And of the six views, to which notice has just been called, the
Glen, where we come the nearest to the mountain monarchs, is the
least rich in color. It shows little more than a single scale of hues,
greatly prolonged and subtly graduated. The Shelburne view presents in its color-scheme a combination of two simple scales, which
together embrace the whole scene. The Milan view shows a harmony
resulting from the contrast of three different and distinct scales, which
produce a general impression of variety with very little intricacy, so
that the view has richness with simplicity. From Jefferson Hill also
we have only two or three simple scales of hues intimately blended.

We remember hearing an artist use musical analogies to hint the
character and contrasts of color-effects in these views. The Glen
theme shows the striking of complex low-toned chords in vivid
succession, as in the fortissimo passages of grand marches. The
color-music of the Shelburne landscape gives a few similar but impressive phrases run into one prolonged forte passage, enlivened by a
few points of peculiar emphasis. The hues on a scene like that which
Milan gives, suggests a pastoral strain in three or four parts, of the
character of Mendelssohn's "Midsummer Night's Dream." But in
views like that from Campton, or the Artist's Hill in North Conway,
color is displayed, not in simplicity or sombre breadth, but in variety
and splendor, and in the intermingling of several contiguous and con-
trasting scales. He spoke, too, if we remember rightly, of the difference in the subtlety, delicacy, and richness of the dominant hues in
each of these scenes, as an indication or type of the difference in the
splendor of their general effects. The gray olive hue at the Glen
expresses a sober richness, with comparatively little subtlety and deli-

cacy, making the general effect a simple and sombre grandeur. The light and rich purple-olive at Jefferson Hill, with the greater delicacy and variety displayed there, adds beauty to majesty. The blue-brown of Shelburne, the yellow-purple of Milan, and the violet-citrine of Campton, each showing an ascent of tone or hue, lead up to the orange-russet or purple, the most delicate, rich, and subtle of all, that dominates and typifies the unsurpassed magnificence of the color-harmonies of Conway.

There are very few, however, who can appreciate, or even perceive—certainly they cannot without staying several days at a time amid the various scenes just spoken of—the differences in complexity of color and richness of bloom thus indicated. But grandeur of form can be seen and felt by everybody. And the White Mountain range is so much grander when seen from Jefferson than from any other point where the whole of it is displayed, and yet is set at such a distance as to show the richest hues with which, as one feature of the landscape, it can be clothed, that we must award to this village the supremacy in the one element of mountain majesty.

And here we must turn from the hills. We have not consciously neglected or slighted any landscape in the compass of the White Mountain tour. And yet our acquaintance with the mountains cannot, at the close, be measured by our minute familiarity with their heights, contours, and hues. Unless we find them something more than ministers to outward health, unless we find them quarries of a truth more substantial than geology, and treasuries of water more vital than their cascades pour, we see them only externally, and treat them too much as toys. The senses simply stare at nature. The intellect, by means of the senses, discerns regularity and law ; artistic taste enjoys the bloom and beauty which possibly slip unnoticed from the eye of science ; but it is the faculty of spiritual insight which penetrates to the inmost meaning, the message involved in the facts and processes of the material creation.

The world was not whittled into shape, or built as an external thing by any methods of carpentry. God could not create anything other than vitally, so that it should be magnetized with His attributes, and exhale them to our faculties in proportion as they are fine enough to catch the effluence. Nature is hieroglyphic. Each prominent fact in it is like a type : its final use is to set up one letter of the infinite alphabet, and help us, by its connections, to read some statement or statute applicable to the conscious world. Mrs. Browning tells us that,

> not a natural flower can grow on earth,
> Without a flower upon the spiritual side,
> Substantial, archetypal, all aglow
> With blossoming causes.

And the ultimate service of a flower, a grain-field, a forest, or a mountain, is to authenticate some law of the social and moral world, by showing that the whole creation, material and rational, is built on one plan ; and that all reverence, all virtue, all charity, is conformity with the truth of things,—the acceptance by men of the principle that sustains the order and determines the beauty of the physical world.

The universe was created so as to serve the prophet's purposes. All the dark facts in it dissolve into ink to write the folly and doom of evil ; all the winning and cheering facts in it melt into light to commend and eulogize what is good. Whatever we see " respires with inward meaning." When we have demonstrated the law of gravitation, and have seen how its force,—hidden in the sun,— grasps thence the farthest planet, and balances a family of worlds, have we not also shown how the justice of the Infinite Mind grapples every spirit of the globe, however far they wander from him, and holds nations as well as men by the invisible tendrils of his law ? And when we untwist the rays that leap unstinted and unceasing from the vesture of the sun, and find in each wave of them light and heat, and all colors, and vitality, and find them flooding the air of every planet as easily as they visit each, and present to every eye, kindling all nature for it, with no more labor than in doing it for one; inflicting pain upon the diseased retina by the same beneficence that blesses the well one, and illumining a different world for each mind it visits, according to its culture or its purity,—have we not found a finer and vaster astronomy by our analysis and research?—found a pictured statement of the interblending of Infinite grace and truth in the rays that stream continually in upon the soul's world, and of the way they bless us and color us according to our faculty of reception, and how they visit and rule every heart and will as easily as they fall upon one?

> To win the secret of a weed's plain heart,
> Reveals the clue to spiritual things.

And all science at last "blossoms into morals." Can we suppose that a risen saint, or an angel, in looking upon the universe, sees only a countless number of enclosures to feed mortal creatures until they die? Is not every fact alive to such a spectator? Is it not a revelation of the truth and perfectness of God which he beholds glowing in the electric pulses, the force of gravity, the waves of light, the tides of life?—just as the deepest seer turned the scattered seed of spring and their various fortunes into a chapter of the world's gospel, translated the truth of a minute providence from the lily's leaf, and interpreted impartial goodness as the esoteric meaning of the broad bursts of sunshine and the uninquiring bounty of the rain? Plainly to such an eye, this globe, with all its ranks and wrappings of life, from the central fire up through its rocky bandages to its vesture of air and light, must be not so much a physical ball in space, as a translucent gospel, in which the laws of duty, purity, charity, and worship are stated in symbol.

We become truly acquainted with a mountain, therefore, when it stands to us as an exponent and buttress of principles of the spiritual order,—when in a mood of cheerful reverence we catch the truth for the soul which lies behind, and plays through its truth for the mind and its apparel of beauty. We must be able to respond to the meaning of Wordsworth's passage,—

> The immeasurable height
> Of woods decaying, never to be decayed,
> The stationary blasts of waterfalls,
> And in the narrow rent at every turn,
> Winds thwarting winds, bewildered and forlorn,
> The torrents shooting from the clear blue sky,
> The rocks that muttered close upon our ears,
> Black drizzling crags that spake by the wayside
> As if a voice were in them, the sick sight
> And giddy prospect of the raving stream,
> The unfettered clouds and region of the Heavens,
> Tumult and peace, the darkness and the light—
> Were all like workings of one mind, the features
> Of the same face, blossoms upon one tree,
> Characters of the great Apocalypse,
> The types and symbols of Eternity,
> Of first, and last, and midst, and without end.

Fancy plays with outside resemblances ; but insight perceives the
central analogies, following the lines of correspondence that tether
facts in the physical region to truths in the moral plane above.   One
who has followed a mountain rivulet to its source, and who has
also studied from a distance the shadowy furrow it has ploughed,
as the witness of its persistent toil through centuries, cannot help
feeling, after reading this passage of Mr. Ruskin, that its history is a
lesson engraved, like the earliest commandments, on tables of stone.
" A stream receives a slight impulse this way or that, at the top of
the hill, but increases in energy and sweep as it descends, gathering
into itself others from its sides, and uniting their power with its own.
A single knot of quartz occurring in a flake of slate at the crest of
the ridge may alter the entire destinies of the mountain form.   It
may turn the little rivulet of water to the right or left, and that little
turn will be to the future direction of the gathering stream what the
touch of a finger on the barrel of a rifle would be to the direction of
the bullet.   Each succeeding year increases the importance of every
determined form, and arranges in masses yet more and more harmonious, the promontories shaped by the sweeping of the eternal waterfalls.

" The importance of the results thus obtained, by the slightest change of direction in the infant streamlets, furnishes an interesting type of the formation of human characters by habit. Every one of those notable ravines and crags is the expression, not of any sudden violence done to the mountain, but of its little *habits*, persisted in continually. It was created with one ruling instinct ; but its destiny depended, nevertheless, for effective result, on the direction of the small and all but invisible tricklings of water, in which the first shower of rain found its way down its sides. The feeblest, most insensible oozings of the drops of dew among its dust were, in reality, arbiters of its eternal form ; commissioned with a touch more tender than that of a child's finger,—as silent and slight as the fall of a half-checked tear on a maiden's cheek,—to fix forever the forms of peak and precipice, and hew those leagues of lifted granite into the shapes that were to divide the earth and its kingdoms. Once the little stone evaded,—once the dim furrow traced,—and the peak was forever invested with its majesty, the ravine forever doomed to its degradation. Thenceforward, day by day, the subtle habit gained in power ; the evaded stone was left with wider basement ; the chosen furrow deepened with swifter-sliding wave ; repentance and arrest were alike impossible, and hour after hour saw written, in larger and rockier characters upon the sky, the history of the choice that had been directed by a drop of rain, and of the balance that had been turned by a grain of sand."

Or turn to this passage from Wordsworth, and see how imaginative perception reverses the commonplace of fancy.

> Rightly is it said
> That Man descends into the *Vale* of years;
> Yet have I thought that we might also speak,
> And not presumptuously, I trust, of Age,
> As of a final *Eminence ;* though bare
> In aspect and forbidding, yet a point
> On which 'tis not impossible to sit
> In awful sovereignty; a place of power,
> A throne, that may be likened unto his,
> Who, in some placid day of summer, looks
> Down from a mountain-top,—say one of those
> High peaks that bound the vale where now we are.

Faint and diminished to the gazing eye,
Forest and field, and hill and dale appear,
With all the shapes upon their surface spread.
But, while the gross and visible frame of things
Relinquishes its hold upon the sense,
You almost on the Mind herself, and seems
All unsubstantialized,—how loud the voice
Of waters, with invigorated peal
From the full river in the vale below,
Ascending! . . . .
  And may it not be hoped, that, placed by age
In like removal, tranquil though severe,
We are not so removed for utter loss;
But for some favor, suited to our need?
What more than that the severing should confer
Fresh power to commune with the invisible world,
And hear the mighty stream of tendency
Uttering, for elevation of our thought,
A clear sonorous voice, inaudible
To the vast multitude; whose doom it is
To run the giddy round of vain delight
Or fret and labor on the Plain below.

But it is when we turn from the aspects to the *science* of the mountains that the noblest symbolism appears. In them, as throughout the creation, we read the lesson of unity through fraternity. Perfect order is wrought out of interwoven service. Nothing lives isolated. All things exist by the charity of God, and the material world seems to respond to this fact by the mutual help ordained among its members. Every organization, while it is taking in what is necessary for its own subsistence and increase, must be exhaling or storing up some elements that are essential to other organizations, —perhaps belonging to other spheres of life. The sea gives to the meadow and is repaid from the hills. The forests breathe out vitality, and incorporate the poison, beneficent for them, which men and animals exhale. The equator " sends greeting " to the Arctic zone by the warm gulf-stream that flows near the polar coasts to soften their winds ; and the poles return a colder tide, and add an embassy of icebergs too, to temper the fierce tropic heats. The earth holds the moon in her orbit, and the moon makes the sea on our planet throb with life.

One of the sweetest of the Psalms is an ode on the beauty of
dwelling together in unity. And one of the illustrations in it, read
in the version of Herder, makes the mountains a more charming symbol of it than our version suggests.

> Behold how lovely and how pleasant,
> When brothers dwell in peace together!
> Thus breathed its fragrance round
> The precious ointment on the head
> That ran adown the beard of Aaron,
> And reached the border of his garment.
> So descends the dew of Hermon,
> Refreshing Zion's mountains,
> For there Jehovah gave command,
> That blessings dwell forevermore.

According to this rendering, it is the vapors first settling upon the
snowy and distant Hermon, from which rains are borne to the lower
and parched hills of Zion, that bear testimony to the moral beauty of
kindliness and interblended service among men. The law of fraternity is the moral aspect of nature,—ethics and political economy hidden in the constant order. Can we rightfully speak of society yet as
superior to nature, when it is a fact that there would be no destitu-
tion to breed despair, no cold nooks where human hearts sicken and
shrivel, away from all sympathy, no starvation in Christian lands, if
the laws of society were up to the level of the laws that rule any
square mile of rural landscape ?

And let us see how *aspiration* is commended by the emphasis of
nature. All bounty comes from the sky through heat and light,
through wind and rain, and the life of the globe pays back something
to the sky. How often we are permitted to see the mountains after
a shower, when their wooded hollows are mighty censers pouring upwards vapory incense,—tithes of the rain that had drenched their
leaves and soaked their mosses ! It goes up fragrant with the inmost quality of the shrubs and vines, the pine forests, and the soil
which the moisture had refreshed. Is not this true worship, the

return to heaven of the same grace that was given thence, with the central character of the individual expressed in it?—just as the mountains send back in aromatic thanks the soul of the rain, which came to it tasteless and scentless from the sky.

And thus every stream and river, as it flows to the ocean, yields an upward tribute, at the touch of the sun. The sea offers a great oblation. The very rocks reflect some of the heat that falls upon them, and aspire, through the lichens and mosses which they nourish, to direct communion with the air. An irreverent mind stands out of chord with nature on any level of the

> great world's altar stairs,
> That slope through darkness up to God.

And how can one that lives among the mountains, with an insight that penetrates their purposes and service, help receiving a lesson of *fortitude* into his heart? How can they but strengthen the heroic sentiments, so plainly do they tell of unselfish toil and suffering? A great deal has been written about the difference, in the effect on the poetic sensibilities, between living near the mountains and by the sea. And no more brilliant contrast of this kind has been drawn than by the Autocrat of the Breakfast-Table in the following passage :—

" I have lived by the sea-shore, and by the mountains.—No, I am not going to say which is best. The one where your place is is the best for you. But this difference there is : you can domesticate mountains, but the sea is *feræ naturæ*. You may have a hut, or know the owner of one, on the mountain-side ; you see a light halfway up its ascent in the evening, and you know there is a home, and you might share it. You have noted certain trees, perhaps ; you know the particular zone where the hemlocks look so black in October, when the maples and beeches have faded. All its reliefs and intaglios have electrotyped themselves in the medallions that hang round the walls of your memory's chamber. The sea remembers nothing ; it is feline. It licks your feet,—its huge flanks purr very pleasantly for you ; but it will crack your bones and eat you, for all

that, and wipe the crimson foam from its jaws as if nothing had happened. The mountains give their lost children berries and water ;
the sea mocks their thirst and lets them die. The mountains have a
grand, stupid, lovable tranquillity ; the sea has a fascinating, treacherous intelligence. The mountains lie about like huge ruminants,
their broad backs awful to look upon, but safe to handle ; the sea
smooths its silver scales until you cannot see their joints,—but their
shining is that of a snake's belly, after all. In deeper suggestiveness
I find as great a difference. The mountains dwarf mankind, and
foreshorten the procession of its long generations. The sea drowns
out humanity and time ; it has no sympathy with either, for it belongs to eternity, and of that it sings its monotonous song forever
and ever."

The hills and the sea are not only materially incommensurable as
to sublimity, but they represent different sentiments, and appeal to
different sympathies. A sick heart, or a weak nature, that needs
morally more iron in its blood, must find the mountains the more
medicinal companions. They are so patient ! They speak to us
from the repose of self-centred character, the ocean from the heav-
ings of unappeasable passion. All the hard conditions of our human
lot are typified by the great hills. What a tremendous experience
they undergo ! Yet they do not babble, or sob, or moan, or roar
like the discontented, melancholy sea. The powers of the air bring
all their batteries against them, lightnings blast and rive them, torrents plough them to the bone, sunshine scorches them, frosts gnaw
away their substance and tumble it down to the valleys,—and they
utter no cry. After thunder and hail and whirlwind, their peaks
look out from above the baffled clouds, and take the sunshine with
no bravado, as though it is their mission " to suffer and be strong."
Dumb patience in trouble, persistent fortitude against obstacles, the
triumphant power of a character rooted in truth over the hardships
of life and the wrath of the world,—such a lesson and the tone of
spirit that can exhibit it, they try to infuse into the soul that lives in
their society. By this effluence, even though the recipient is un-

conscious of the cause, they stimulate and soothe a flagging will or fainting heart, as the airs they purify search and reanimate an unstrung frame.

Swedenborg tells us that, in the verbal Scripture, mountains correspond to the truths of the highest plane. Certainly in the physical economy they are the eloquent types of *charity*. How impressive and cordial is the open fact that nothing in nature lives for itself,— finds its end in itself! Nothing at least that is normal and healthful does. A slimy pond and a fen are typical of selfishness, not the river and the glebe. The sun is a mighty institution, of which heat, light, and gravitation are the ever-streaming discount. The sea gives the rain, as the interest of its vast fund, for the world's good. The beauty which gratifies and soothes humanity is the perpetual dividend of the joint-stock of the universe. And charity, which is the general lesson of nature, is preached by the sovereign hills with the emphasis of heroic and vicarious suffering.

Near one of the most inspiring views of the White Mountain range we have often seen a cottage, in which a family live with scarcely any furniture, and barely supplied even with summer necessities. The walls were not tight enough to keep out the rain and the winter snows. The inmates, when we first visited them, were too poor to own a cow. The father had been continually unfortunate, though industrious and strictly temperate. The mother was in feeble health, and was plainly suffering from too low and spare a diet. The tones of her voice were saturated with misfortune. In winter, the man was afflicted with rheumatism so that he could not steadily earn his fifty cents a day by lumbering, when the snows were propitious ; in the summer, he tried to wring enough to keep off starvation out of some cold, thin land. Although this is, no doubt, an exceptional case in that district, should it be a possible case in any district of this continent ? Can we believe that there was an honest dollar of all the money hoarded in that county, so long as there was a man in it willing to work and unable to get a substantial living for his family by his work,—living on the borders of stately forests, and suffering from cold in winter,—poorly clothed, while every bear on the neighboring heights was wrapped warm by the laws of nature,—impoverished in blood, when every weed that could fasten itself into a cranny of the rocks, where an inch of soil had lodged, had its portion of food supplied forthwith by an assessment on ocean, sun, and air ?

Is it the written precept of the written Testament alone that intrudes this question ? Mount Washington soared over that hut, and what did *he* say ? What does he do with the wealth lavished upon him ? He is an almoner of divine gifts. He condenses moisture interfused in winds that blow from polar seas, and stores it up for fountains, or pours it in rills. He invigorates the breezes that sweep pestilence from our cities. He breasts the winter tempests, and holds the snows with which they would smother him, and gives them slowly in the spring, letting the torrents tear his own substance also, to enrich the intervales of the Saco and Connecticut, and to keep the mills busy that help to clothe the world. A Greek sculptor had a wild dream of carving Mount Athos into a statue of Alexander,—its left arm to enclose a city of ten thousand, its right hand grasping an urn from which a river should pour perpetually into the sea. It is a bounty no less imperial that every great mountain represents. Nay, giving its own substance, too, in its disbursement of what is poured upon it, not withholding service though the condition be pain, it is tinged and glorified with light from the cross. In respect of the symbolic meaning of the hills, far more than in relation to the depths they open to scientific and artistic scrutiny, we may quote the weighty words : " The truth of Nature is a part of the truth of God : to him who does not search it out, darkness : to him who does, infinity."

www.ingramcontent.com/pod-product-compliance
Lightning Source LLC
Chambersburg PA
CBHW020234110726

47898CB00004B/1261